I0640445

ATRAVESAR
To Break the Skin

Second Edition

C.E. Ostra

Amapolaris Press

This is a work of fiction. Names, characters, places and incidents either are products of the author's imagination or are used fictitiously. Any resemblance to actual events or locales or persons, living or dead, is entirely coincidental.

ISBN 978-0-9895477-2-7

Typeset by Amapolaris Press
Cover design by J.K. McGann

Printed in the United States of America

It does not do to leave a live dragon out of your calculations, if you live near him.

J.R.R. Tolkien

.

The Avenue is littered with wizards. Sometimes, often, they are in disguise.

Alice Hoffman, *Property Of*

⌦ Prologue ⌫

The tall man, trim and erect in his slate-blue uniform, regards the round childish faces before him, dark eyes seeming to bore right into their brains. Passing a strong hand over a neat beard and moustache, he paces the front of the room, bronzed complexion lending him the look of some looming desert god.

"What are the Five Social Precedents?" he says abruptly.

Several hands start to rise, but then lower again. Nervous eyes peer out of corners. No one is sure they want to stand out.

Perched on the big desk to his right a chipper young EdTech gives her charges an encouraging smile. But this is an ExproEd class, and most are intimidated by the presence of a Lead SocEn.

"Anyone?" she says. "Do you want Mr. Timanti to think I haven't taught you anything?" She trills a little laugh, but there's a warning in it.

i

At that, a small blonde girl raises her hand and, when acknowledged, takes a deep breath and recites in a tinny voice: "Unity, Clarity, Curiosity, Diligence, and Nonviolence."

The Lead SocEn nods. "Bueno."

The EdTech sighs her relief.

"And what is your name, child?" he says.

The girl gulps. "Lissandra."

"So can you tell me then, *Lissandra*, how you apply these precedents outside of merely reciting them in this room? How do you use them in your daily life?"

Lissandra gnaws her lower lip, unsure of what he means. She risks a quick glance at her teacher.

"Give an example," the EdTech prompts, "of when you acted at home like you do here in class, using the words of the precedents you just named."

"Well, uh," she stammers, "once I was really, like, *curious* about how the mice kept getting into our kitchen and eating stuff?" Her rising inflection makes this a question. "So I *diligently* built a trap for them and then I *nonviolently* let them go in the garden of a wayvern at the other end of Transway."

The other students look impressed. Timanti, however, just sighs.

"Gracias," he says and, with a nod to the teacher, sweeps out through the classroom door.

Down the long burnished corridor he marches, shaking his head and grimacing. Technically, the child's answer was sound – at least she used the words in a proper sentence – but she should be learning to apply these principles to loftier pursuits than rodent control.

Educational standards in ExproEd have been sliding

subtly over the last few years, but he's only recently begun to notice how much. Where once attendance was mandatory for all expro children starting at age five, lately there's been less focus on tracking down those who slip through the cracks. And also less emphasis on supplying seasoned educators for ExproEd classrooms – only the youngest and greenest now teach them.

He's positive this is somehow Ariana's doing.

Two of the three Lead SocEns must agree on any official proposal before it is adopted; she couldn't force her anti-expro agenda past him and Martinez so it seems she's gone for the soft option – incremental policy changes that don't require the formal two-thirds approval. Ingenious, really.

If only she would use her powers for good.

But even with the apparent issues brewing in Ed, many expros do learn the basics. A decent number even become Mech or SanTechs of a sort, keeping the Transway infrastructure running. But that's just it: Once they know enough to get a position say, maintaining rollers, they take it and are done; never taking the next steps, never showing any signs of real curiosity – of learning for its own sake, for the sheer joy of it. At this rate, they're never going to advance themselves, never blend seamlessly back into the population of Albakirk as was intended by the SocEns who devised the original reintegration plan. If anything, they get more foreign every year.

But it can be done. He knows it. He has his own daughter as proof.

The thought brings a smile to his face; Lana is a perfect model of successful reintegration. Child of his dalliance with a expro woman, her existence unknown to him until age eleven, she grew up cut off from all forms of tech in the ranchos – the main transer settlement on the east side of the mountains – and subject to all manner of ridiculous superstition and pseudoscience. But after her mother's unfortunate passage and a string of accompanying events, he'd discovered her among those dispossessed from rancho life (the expros of Transway), changed her name from Celan to Lana, and brought her to live with him.

A gamble. And a massive one, given her background. He had no way of knowing if it was going to pay off. But Lana has done remarkably well – academically, socially, psychologically; she's excelled in every way.

How he yearns to tell everyone the truth, to hold her up as a shining example of all that is possible. Once and for all he'll prove them wrong, the ones like Ariana who deem transers incapable of advanced learning and insist that the expros must be cut loose; no longer clinging like barnacles to the city walls, influencing upright citizens with their deviant culture.

No matter that they provide psychological and physical outlets for techs that have been (mostly) confined indoors for a century and a half. Or their inestimable value as experimental subjects so that techs are no longer required to volunteer themselves for bot testing.

He shakes his head; so shortsighted.

As far as Lana is concerned though, he has to bide his time. She's about to start her last year of regular Ed and he knows that she wants to try to continue her studies at En level. So he's not going to do anything rash that might throw her off...or influence a committee's decision. Once she's been fully accepted to an En program and it's too late to take it back then all can be revealed, with her approval of course.

Just imagine their faces when they discover that a tran-ser has ascended to the level of Engineer! That will shut Ariana down once and for all.

But Lana might be hesitant at first, might not readily agree to reveal her origins. After all, it was he who had in-sisted on secrecy when he first discovered her and brought her to live with him. He who had stressed the need to hide her background so she would be judged on her own merits and native intelligence without prejudice. So now he'll have to impress upon her the uniqueness of her position and the necessity of her role – her absolute indispensability in lead-ing her people toward a brighter future. When one has been given great advantages one has a responsibility to give back.

He's sure that in time she will agree.

Tap. Tap. Tap. Celan raps the tip of her stylus against the face of her server, lost in thought. Suddenly she freezes, snatching it up as if seized by inspiration, but ends up lowering it again with a disgruntled sigh. The big screen on the desk in front of her pulses blue-white, waiting to absorb her thoughts. But they slink away like thieves, refusing to give up the goods. She yawns, then tries to clear her mind, to focus.

Maybe she should go do something else for a while. Go to the fitness area and do a holo run. Or take a walk through the gardens. That always relaxes her. It's Saturday, she really should take a little time off. But a pang of anxiety keeps her in her seat.

Proposals. Due Ord 365, the last day of the year. Three weeks away.

She presses her lips together and tucks a lock of chin-length dark hair behind an ear. Mentally, she scrolls through the litany of options: San, Mech, Phys, Comp, Ag, Ed, Med,

Gen, and Soc. She can apply to only one. The committee for that discipline will review her proposal and decide whether or not her project idea makes the cut. If she's turned down she'll go back into the regular tech track to finish out the Ed year and be given her post accordingly.

But even if her proposal is accepted, there is no guarantee of En level placement. She'll need to present her findings to the committee by Ord 150 of the coming year. If she fails to impress they could give her a tech post in her chosen discipline or they could recommend her for En level in another. So if she wants to be a first-rate PostEd, she needs to really dazzle them.

She hunches forward, squinting at the image on the screen – a three-dimensional model of a transfer. Idly, she strokes it with a fingertip, spinning it around and around until it blurs into a whirl of colorful streaks. Then she stops it short and zooms in to the molecular level.

Transfers are the little vials that transers fill with water and use to create transferon, the substance that helps them filter out the old world's contamination without relying on tech. The techs have always been leery of the stuff, but that hasn't stopped them from trying to recreate it under laboratory conditions. Success, however, has proven elusive.

They've never been able to produce it without having their subjects "transfigure" the vials – a maddeningly inexact process involving a kind of hands-on application of electromagnetic energy. Once activated, transferon is taken either orally by dropper or transfused directly into the bloodstream through a primitive type of jet injection.

But the whole process is highly subjective, which is exactly why it frustrates and fascinates the techs so much. It obviously works or the transers would never have survived for so long outside the city, but despite recent advances exactly *how* it works remains unknown. It seems to involve the intent of the subject doing the transing and that's where things start to get really woolly.

And then there are the side effects – the unfortunate recreational aspects of transferon that tend to override the medicinal ones, at least among the expros.

Celan sighs, taps at her server, and brings up some more information.

"Transferon is separated into three classes by the use of metabolic markers: 3-BEN for Class D, 6-MAM for Class E, and 4-HYD for Class S. These are produced once transferon has been ingested by the subject and commenced its interactions with the physical system. Depending on which class is most prominent in the activation, a variety of effects ranging from excitation, to somnolence, to confusion may present in the subject. In the correct balance, however, a beneficial effect has been observed that has been shown to remediate the effects of many contaminants, including the effects of radiation."

That's it, she thinks, *the perfect project. If I can pull it off.*

Her stomach rumbles, but she ignores it.

All she has to do is get a bunch of labrecs from the Bank and collate the neural mappings of every transfigurational pathway they've ever recorded by class. Then, if she reverse-engineers the mappings back to their origins in the brain, it should be possible to create a code simulation that will tie the three classes together and balance them each time they go forward.

That would be a big step toward creating a normalized, stable form of transferon in the lab; it'll be a lot of work, but it's her only hope if she wants to make SocEn. All her other ideas are too Comp, too dull. SocEns aren't interested in programming for the sake of programming. They want next-level stuff. So transferon it is.

But who better than me? After all, I'm probably the only tech who's ever actually taken any.

This last thought makes her crack a tiny smile. But it quickly fades. SocEn is a notoriously difficult discipline to get into. She could make CompEn easily, and if she doesn't make SocEn that's probably where they'll place her. But nothing is certain. They could make her a SocTech, the ultimate consolation prize. That would be awful. And what's worse, Shariah is going for SocEn, too. Two daughters of two Lead SocEns from the same pod? There's no way both of them will make it.

The CompLab door whooshes open, intruding on her thoughts and causing her to glance up just in time to see Bryan's bright smile flash across the room. Her stomach does a quick flip and her pulse jumps unnervingly. She lowers her eyes and ducks her head; maybe he'll go talk to somebody else.

But even as she thinks this she's aware of another part of her that really doesn't want him to do that.

"Hey, Lana." Bryan slides into the empty chair next to hers, trailing a faint waft of clean, citrusy scent.

She doesn't look up. "Hey."

"Working on your proposal?"

"Trying to," she says brusquely, then immediately regrets

her tone.

"If you're too busy…"

"No, no, it's OK," she retracts, finally forcing herself to look at him. Eyes like the sky and that thatch of sandy hair; his brown skin and round, open face remind her of the sunflowers that used to grow in abundance back in the ranchos. A rush of giddiness bubbles up, but she attempts to override it with a casual tone. "What's up?"

"Well," he says, leaning in a bit. "I'm looking for a brain to pick about something, and I guess I picked yours." He grins at his own pun and her heart lurches. She has a sudden urge to kick him followed by an instantaneous flash of guilt.

"Yeah?"

"Yeah. You see, I've got this really great idea."

Celan shifts in her seat. "Is this about your proposal?"

An eager nod.

"Um, aren't we supposed to not be talking about our proposals to each other?" Bryan's brow knits and she can feel her face redden. "I mean, it's supposed to be an independent project, right?"

"Sure," he says. "Once they actually *start*. But we're still poddies for another few weeks. We're allowed to talk, bounce around ideas. That's what pods are for."

That's what pods – the primary study groups of six that they've been assigned to since age twelve – have always been for, ostensibly. But once proposals are in they'll all be split up. She may not see much of him after that.

"Well…"

He takes her hesitation as tacit agreement and dives

right in. "See, I've been thinking about the whole space question. We haven't made a whole lot of progress in cleaning up the mess down here; the whole GISH thing's had all kinds of setbacks. More and more people are starting to think that maybe we should just give up and move to Mars. But there's the fuel problem, you know? So I was thinking…why not design some kind of algabot that can create methane and then recycle itself, like on some kind of infinite loop? I think that might work better than a straight Sabatier kind of thing."

"Bioalgae or artificial?"

"Well, that's the tricky part. It's gotta be based on the real thing as much as possible but you'd want it engineered to account for the differences in gravity, radiation, etc."

"Huh."

He crosses long legs loosely, leaning back in his chair and knitting fingers together behind his head. "Of course, I don't have all the details worked out yet. But in general, what do you think? Is it good?"

It is. It's elegant and practical and could be very useful. Her father will love it.

She sighs.

Bryan frowns, taking it for disapproval. "You think it's too Ag for MechEn?"

"No, no," she says. "It's a great idea."

"That's what Shariah said!"

A sudden chill creeps over her. "You asked her too?"
And first?

"Of course. I mean, she's not interested in Mech stuff and neither are you. I figured there's no way any of us would be working on anything similar, so you'd give me your honest

6

opinions."

"Yeah, I guess so."

Cheerfully, he continues, "And I think it could really be a good thing. Help us get out where we really need to be – out there! Not only Mars, but the whole solar system – the galaxy. Maybe we're not alone. Maybe there're whole civilizations waiting for us to get off this rock and come out and meet them."

Celan tries and fails to keep the smirk off her face, lapsing into the poddies' teasing comfort zone. "Out there is right."

"What, you don't believe there's intelligent life *out there*?" He gestures vaguely at the ceiling.

"I'm a firm believer in Fermi's Paradox."

"C'mon Lana, don't be like that. Think about how many other planets there are. How many Earth-like exoplanets. I mean, we know there's life – "

"Microbes! And they probably came from us. Fell off a rover."

"Please. You know that's not true. And think about it – some of the greatest Lead SocEns have believed in at least the *possibility* of extraterrestrial civilizations. Look at us! We can't be the only intelligent life in the universe. That would just be sad."

Celan chuckles.

"Seriously. And Shariah agrees with me. You've gotta think big." He spreads his arms wide. "There's a whole universe out there!"

"And I'm sure they're just dying to meet a civilization that pretty much poisoned their whole planet and is now on the hunt for a new one to ruin," she says dryly.

But this sarcasm is lost on him. "It wasn't *us* that wrecked the old world. It was that asteroid that started the whole thing. Set off all those earthquakes – "

"Which wouldn't have been as bad if there hadn't already been contamination everywhere," she counters. "They could barely contain it as it was! Then the strike just let it all loose."

Bryan shrugs. "Well, we've made the best of what was left. And who knows? Maybe there *are* other civilizations. Maybe they've got advanced tech we can't even imagine! Maybe they can help us fix up the Earth and terraform Mars too. Then we'll have two planets. We can start a brand new civilization and really do it right this time."

He springs to his feet, giving her shoulder a playful punch before he heads for the door.

"Thanks for the feedback, though. Knew you'd have a sensible opinion."

"You're welcome," she says to his receding back. Then she draws a deep breath and turns back to the screen, but the words and images warp before her eyes until they are nothing but a terrible jumble.

"THEODORE!" TIMANTI HEARS HIS NAME called from across the loud, smoky room and looks up to spot the squat form of Frank Martinez waving him over. He cuts through the typical wayvern crowd, a self-conscious mix of soberly-clad techs and more colorful expro types, who part as one at the sight of his slate blue uniform. At the table he pulls out a chair and settles in.

Martinez sips from a glass of amber liquid and smiles, summoning a plump, yellow-haired girl in a grimy apron who gamely takes Theodore's been-a-long-day order: Whiskey.

"So what's the good word?" he prompts. "Heard from Nigel?"

"Nada. Not yet."

"But you spoke to Tsosie, right? What'd she have to say?"

Theodore grins, leaning back in his chair. "She thinks the PhysEns are going to go for it."

"And you've got the Comp and MechEns locked up?"

"They've always been in favor." He knows better than to gloat, but there's no harm in appearing confident.

Since the failure of GISH – a project using nanotech on the largest scale ever attempted in order to try to clean up old world contamination in the Earth's water cycle – resources have been freed up. That project was Martinez's baby, but its end means he now may be amenable to throwing his support behind something else – like Theodore's plan to colonize Mars. Ambitious, yes, but he's had several years in which to expand on the initial concept after Ariana and Martinez voted it down last time in favor of GISH.

He doesn't want to be outvoted again. Recent drone reports indicate that Lanzhou may be working toward a similar Martian goal. If several more years are squandered Albakirk may miss its chance at leadership on what may very well become Earth 2.0. But support must be built within the En groups first before any final vote takes place among the Leads.

"Well…well done, then." Martinez raises his glass as the girl returns with Theodore's drink.

He slips a chit into her creased palm and returns the toast, then takes a quick swig. Thus fortified, he ventures, "Any idea what La Roja's up to?" invoking their nickname for Ariana. "She's looking smugger than usual these days."

Martinez clears his throat.

Uh-oh.

"Que pas'?"

"You're not going to like this."

"Why? What is it? More 'down with Transway!' bullshit? Why anyone even pays attention to that crap – "

"No," Martinez stops him. "It's not that." A pause. "She wants to reboot GISH."

"*What?*"

"I know. But she's actually got some decent ideas. Says that we weren't aggressive enough in our approach last time. That we need faster replication."

"Too dangerous."

"And colonizing Mars is a cakewalk?"

"It's much safer than playing roulette with what little we have left! The last thing we need is a mess of grey goo."

"True, true," Martinez says, raising his hands in a placating gesture; as he lowers them he signals their server for another round. "I didn't say I agreed with her."

Theodore's gaze narrows. "But *do* you?"

"I've yet to hear all the details."

"Unbelievable." He downs the rest of his drink in one gulp and slams the glass on the scarred wood, a petulant look squinching the corners of his mouth.

Martinez grunts. "Mira, Theodore. Your Mars plan has improved immeasurably in the last few years. You've built a lot of support. But we have to consider all options. The GISH infrastructure is still in place. If it can be reused – "

"It isn't going to be your project anymore, you know. If it gets accepted," Theodore says, "it will be *hers* this time. And who knows what little extras she's planning to build into it?"

Martinez eyes him levelly. "I'm well aware of that. Believe me, I'm in no hurry to support her. But you must be aware that there is still a great longing among many people to restore the Earth. It's our home. And Ariana's going to play into that. You need to be ready for it. Don't just throw a bunch of specs at people and expect them to jump onboard. You've got to appeal to their sense of security."

"Security? What about their sense of adventure? 'To boldly go' – and all that."

"Anyone who thinks that way is already on your side."

Theodore sighs, conceding the point. Now that the initial shock is wearing off, it's fast being replaced by gratitude to his colleague for initiating this discussion. Baby or no, he must not be totally sold on the reboot yet.

"Gracias. For telling me."

A shrug. "De nada. It's not like you weren't going to find out anyway. But there's still almost twelve weeks until the resource vote. You've got time."

The yellow-haired girl reappears with their refills and trades them out for chits. Martinez eyes her ample rear appreciatively as she saunters away with the empties.

Theodore follows his line of sight. "Nice."

Martinez arches a brow. "Up for Maddy's later?"

Theodore chuckles, but shakes his head no. "Maybe some other time. Seems like I've got a lot of work to do."

CELAN'S SERVER LIES LIMP IN her hand as she curls on her bed, gazing out at the setting sun and watching the clamor of red and orange streaks fade to rose, then lavender, then finally to a deep indigo. She presses her forehead against the smooth, cool surface of the window pane and sighs. This big wall of windows has always been her favorite thing about her room. The shadows grow long but she makes no move to turn on the light.

Then her server buzzes: Shariah. Wants to go to caf.

Tossing it aside she gets up and slaps at the light switch. The sudden brightness makes her squint as she reaches to yank open a drawer from the wall module. Rummaging around, she pulls out a pair of soft jersey pants and matching top, the kind of clothes most techs wear to bed. It's been the fashion of teenage girls to wear their sleepware to dinner and Celan, ever the student, took note of this development immediately. It probably helped that it was Shariah who started it.

She shucks off her uniform and pulls on the fleecy sleepware, then stuffs feet into boots and pockets her server, bounding out of the bedroom and through the tiny kitchenette to the main door of the bunk. But it opens with a sidelong whoosh before she can press the panel, revealing a bemused-looking Theodore.

"Hi Dad," she mutters, trying to duck past him before he can start some long-winded conversation.

But he blocks her. "That's it?"

"Sorry." She backs up, chagrined.

"Headed to the bath?" he says, noting her clothes.

"Caf."

"In your sleepware?"

"It's the thing."

"It is?"

"Shariah, Bev, Kimbra, Laney..." She ticks them off on her fingers. "Everyone does it." She raises an eyebrow. "You don't want me to be *strange*, do you?"

"No," he smiles, indulgent. "Claro que no. Go have fun."

"Thanks," she says, giving him a peck on the offered cheek before heading out the door.

She hurries down the gleaming, immaculate corridor, skimming a light hand over wall panels of manicured vegetation, and into an elevator which zips swiftly down several floors. Twice it comes to a halt and more people get in – first an older couple in tan uniforms whom she doesn't recognize but still nods to, and then a gaggle of giggling four-teens, whom she ignores – before the doors open to reveal a vast atrium, where the night sky arches infinite through the transparent panes of the large pyramid rising majestically overhead.

The sight of it once thrilled her to her bones, but now she barely glances up – just takes off across the plaza, past the tinkling central fountain and its graceful horticulture, and on to the caf on the other side. When she first came to live here, she thought this was the only plaza and the only caf, but there are others – interspersed with walkways and corridors, labs and classrooms and bunks. Still, this is the main plaza, the biggest caf, and they're the ones closest to her bunk. She rarely ventures to any of the others.

A cacophony of competing conversations and aromas washes over her as she enters the big bright room. Her gaze sweeps over panoramic windows, steaming buffet tables, and seating modules, looking for –

"There you are! What took you so long?" Shariah says, coal-black eyes glittering as she links a possessive arm through Celan's.

"Seriously? It's been five minutes! What's the big deal?"

"So you haven't heard?"

"Heard what? I've been working on my proposal all day."

Her best friend tosses long, silvery-blonde hair over one sharp shoulder. "There's more to life than proposals." A dramatic pause; then she announces: "Kimbra and Ben did it!"

"What?" Celan says, eyes wide.

"Yes!" Shariah squeals, gleeful with gossip.

"How do you know?"

"She told me," Shariah says, waving an airy hand. "We went swimming earlier and got to talking. She said they were running the other day but the other people in the fitness area left. So then they were alone and they went to shower and no one else was there so they…just did it."

"But she's – "

"I know!" Shariah crows.

Kimbra's parents are SanTechs, while Ben comes from a long line of GenEns. If this becomes serious his folks probably won't be too happy.

Celan's eyes dart to the Notice board, the big screen in the back of the room that displays a constant scrolling update of all techs' social infractions. Any departure from the social precedents or excessive behavior is displayed for appropriate shaming. Do Kimbra's actions count? She shivers. In the past seven years she's never been on Notice for anything. She can't imagine someone deliberately courting it.

Shariah pulls her into the dinner line behind a pack of rowdy twelves engaged in working out the pecking order of their first year as a pod.

"Who else knows?" she whispers.

Shariah grins wickedly. "Anyone who cares to look at the views, I guess. But after all, Unity *is* the first social precedent."

"Are they on Notice now?" Celan presses.

"Probably. I doubt she cares. Besides, Ben's a step up for her."

"Maybe she'll end up a San*En*."

"Kimbra's as useless as a fuser."

"How do you know? She's not even in our pod."

"Believe me, I know," says Shariah, miffed at having her authority on the subject questioned. "I was in a playgroup with her when I was eight. And she's styled so tacky – that yellow hair. Please. She'll be SanTech for sure."

Celan gives her a dubious look. "Styling has nothing to do with it," she says.

Secretly though, she wonders how much a good style might impress a committee. Someone as highly styled as Shariah commands immediate attention. Her own brown hair and eyes have always seemed a little dull next to the more exotic looks of some of her friends. But their parents got to choose what they would look like before they were born. She already was how she was when her father found her. She doesn't think she looks bad, though – just not very striking.

"Anyway," Shariah continues as they arrange bowls and utensils on trays, "aren't you dying to know what it's like?"

Celan ladles some noodles and assorted vegetables into a bowl, an image of Bryan's sunflower face rising unbidden in her head. Would she want to do it with him? They're eighteen now and 'of age' as far as that's concerned – and it's really not that big of a deal. They teach about it in Ed and it's perfectly safe. No sicknesses or uncontrolled pregnancies like in the old world. The bots see to that. People do it all the time. But still –

There's a jostle at her elbow and she starts, sloshing some sauce on the counter.

"Are you even listening to me?" Shariah demands.

"Uh, sure."

"No you weren't! You were off in some little daydream! Don't tell me you're doing it now, too."

Celan feels her cheeks redden and she scuttles forward, suddenly very engrossed in the dessert selections. "Hardly," she mutters.

"Not even with Bryyyan?"

"No one."

"Oh, come on. Tell me."

"Just drop it," Celan says through clenched teeth. "I'm not doing it with anyone."

She turns and heads for the tables, not even bothering to stop and fill her glass at the drink station. She puts her tray down at the first open spot she sees, out of earshot of the cache of Ens occupying the other end of the table, and buries her face in her plate.

But Shariah is undaunted, taking the seat right across from her and leaning in.

"But you want to. Seriously, Lana, this is getting ridiculous. You've had a thing for him since forever. If you like Bryan, just tell him. Then you two can have some fun."

Celan swallows a mouthful of food and sighs. Then Shariah waggles a mock-ribald eyebrow and she chuckles despite herself. "Sure, I'll jump him after AgLab tomorrow and drag him back to my bunk."

"Why not?"

"It's just…" She trails off, eyes skimming over the neat rows of tables until they come to rest on the windows and the view of the Sandia Mountains etched against the sky beyond.

"What?" Shariah says, impatient. "Once our pod splits that's it, you know. He'll be off in Mech land. With a bunch of future MechEn girls."

Celan winces.

Shariah spears some broccoli and pauses en route to her mouth, pointing her fork emphatically. "So if you want him, you've got to let him know *now*."

"I know. You're right."

"So *do* it," she says. "Fortune favors the bold."

Celan swirls some noodles around her bowl, anxiety tightening her stomach.

She makes it sound so easy. She just doesn't understand…

A little knot of resentment creeps up from that tight spot and lodges in her throat.

"So what about you then?" she says, a hint of challenge in her tone. "Who do you plan to be *bold* with?"

Shariah smirks. "I haven't decided yet."

"Kirk?"

"Please. No one from our pod."

"What's wrong with our pod?"

"Nothing," Shariah says primly. "I just want to take my time. Look around a little."

"See who's lucky?" Celan says, trying to inject a little jocularity back into the conversation.

"See who's *worthy*," Shariah says, her gaze imperious.

"Oh," Celan says, and looks down at her plate again.

THEODORE LETS HIS EYES CLOSE as the door whooshes shut behind him. He takes a deep breath, nose twitching with the comforting mustiness of old books and furniture. From the heavy ancient desk and chairs to the walls lined with shelves holding centuries' worth of literary treasures his library is the place where he feels most at home. After a long day of playing Lead sometimes there's nothing more soothing to his formidable mind than the printed word on a plain white page. He smiles to himself, pressing the switch and blinking as the room fills with warm yellow light.

This room would seem strange to most of his colleagues, knowing him as they do as a stalwart supporter of technological growth. But it's the one place of relative sanctuary he has – and blessedly free from constant visual surveillance. Way back in the day his SocEn predecessors wanted to put views in every room of the bunks as well as all the public spaces, but enough people balked at having their most intimate moments recorded that they had settled for limited, entrance-only, views in living quarters.

He's thankful for this small miracle every day.

The big padded chair seems to sigh as he sinks into it, settling in for a moment before extracting some ice from a cooler under his desk. He clinks it into a tumbler and fills the remaining space with a generous pour of brown liquid from an old glass bottle. Technically, he's not supposed to have a cooler in the bunk, but he liberated this one from the lab a few years back and no one seemed to notice. He's sure it's on a view somewhere, for posterity, but it's not like anyone looks at all that footage. It's mostly just backup in case anything ever goes sideways. And a subliminal deterrent – to ensure nothing ever does.

Mentally, he shrugs. He's a busy man, with better things to do than run down to the caf for ice. He takes a long drink of the Scotch and sighs with pleasure. It's vintage old world stuff, very rare and very well-preserved.

Another sip and his neck loosens and body relaxes its erect posture. No meetings tonight, nowhere he has to be – a rarity these days. And one not likely to repeat itself anytime soon. Not after the bombshell Martinez dropped this afternoon.

Just what is she up to anyway?

He's positive Ariana must have a hidden agenda. She wasn't that big of a fan of GISH the first time around and, as memory serves, voted with Martinez out of revenge for Theodore chopping her attempts to whip up anti-Transway sentiment off at the knees. Of course, it's always possible that she's had some big epiphany; had a vision of a clean, healthy planet shining like a diamond in her mind's eye.

But that's not the Ariana he knows.

So why this retread? Why this beating (to borrow an old world phrase) of the proverbial dead horse? GISH had its shot and failed. The Earth is a hopeless mess and it's time to be looking up and out – to other planets, fresh new

19

settlements.

Why must people stand in the way of progress?

He frowns, shaking his head and wondering at the caprices of human nature. But he supposes it's always been this way. In the old world books he's read people seem to have struggled with similar problems to the ones they currently face, just on a much larger scale.

Imagine what it must have been like, with billions of people all intent upon making their little lives count for something larger! No wonder there was so much hatred and violence, so much killing. So much competition for resources (he's read his Malthus).

These days, resources are carefully meted out and, at least in Albakirk, each life is valued, precious, and allowed to blossom to its full potential. In return, people are expected to work hard, prove their mettle. No useless eaters here; not even the expros (no matter what Ariana may think). And it's his job to help shepherd all of this – marshal all this potential and direct it in a way that will prove most beneficial to humankind going forward. It's a daunting challenge.

No wonder he's tired.

He presses palms against his eyes, then reaches for the glass – which he drains, adds more ice to, and refills. Then his focus drifts to the chessboard. It's an old world board, not a holo, and it rests on the corner of his desk, where it's been since that first week after he found Lana wandering in the ruins of the old Arlo's wayvern. He taught her the game as a distraction during the period of seclusion and training when he'd prepared her to join tech society. Even at eleven she was clever and picked it up fast. They've been playing ever since.

Now where were we?

He scrolls back through the game so far – she'd opened with a King's Knight and they'd gone into a classic Philidor from there. Not many pieces lost on either side. Somewhat boring, but they've both been preoccupied with other things.

Ah yes...she came for his bishop with that rook – put him in check.

Annoyed, he slides his queen over to D8, right next to his king, and removes the offending piece. He's out of check, but now his queen is in the path of hers; she can't come for it though or she'll lose hers too.

And then, almost as if he's summoned her, the door opens and there she stands.

"Hey," she says. "Are you busy?"

"No, no. Not at all." He motions. "Ven aquí."

Lana plops down in the overstuffed chair to the right of the desk, curling one knee up under her chin and lacing fingers around her shin. He smiles at the sight of her in her favorite contemplative pose.

She nods at the glass in his hand. "Where's mine?"

Theodore chuckles. Their running joke. "And how tough has your day been?"

One word. "Proposals."

"Ah, yes. Enough to drive any future En to drink."

"I just want mine to be good," she says, craning her neck forward, eyes roaming over the chessboard. He can see the gears begin to turn as she calculates her next move.

"It will be," he says, taking a sip of his drink. "I just wish you'd tell me what you're working on."

Her posture stiffens. "I want to do this on my own."

"I know," he says quickly. "But I guarantee you – all of your podmates are asking for advice from *someone*."

"I know, it's just…"

"You want to prove you can do it yourself."

She sits back, pensive again, and gives him a quizzical look. "Well, yeah. I guess I do." A pause. "Is that bad?"

He chunks the glass down on the desktop. "Absolutely not. As a Lead, that is what you *have* to do. You must make what you want to happen happen. And never doubt yourself. You've already accomplished amazing things, Lana, and I have no doubts whatsoever that you can do anything you put your mind to." He clears his throat. "With or without my advice."

Lana beams. "Gracias."

"Anytime." He picks up his drink again and swirls it with a flourish, clinking the ice against the glass. "So what's the latest? Any great happenings in the caf?"

"Nah," she says, with a quick one-shouldered shrug. "The usual."

"Huh," he grunts. Then a thought occurs to him; he abandons the tumbler and knits his fingers together, leaning forward intently. "Do you ever hear any talk about Mars? In Ed?"

"Mars…how?"

"My relocation plan? I assume its common knowledge."

"Oh. Sure. I mean, people talk about it all the time."

"You and your podmates? Do you discuss it? In the caf maybe?"

Her eyes flick away and he thinks he detects a hint of embarrassment lurking there.

What do *they talk about at this age?*

Then she brightens. "One of them is planning a proposal.

A Mech-something. I don't want to tell what it's about before he submits it, but it definitely involves Mars."

"Excellent."

"Yeah," she says, breaking into a yawn. "Sorry. I'm not bored or anything."

"You're tired though," he says, indulgent. "You've been working hard. Go get some sleep."

"Yeah, I think I will." She gets to her feet, squints at the chessboard, and grins as she moves a knight to C7. "OK, bedtime. And check. Mate, actually."

He stares at the board. She rarely beats him. But she's right; she's boxed his king in. That other knight she'd camped out on E5 will get him if he moves it to D7 and if takes his only other move, to E7, he's technically out of harm's way. But all she has to do is slip that bishop to A3 and its over.

"Well – " he starts.

She bounds to the door, triumphant. "'Night, Dad."

Then, with a whoosh, his daughter is gone.

2

"Now, I realize that some of you will be leaving us soon to pursue your exalted paths toward En level study." The wiry old EdTech smirks. "However, that does not mean we are entirely finished with our interdisciplinary work. So please pay attention."

Shariah grimaces, poking Celan and whispering, "Just because *he* never made En..."

Celan ignores her as the EdTech continues his lecture, setting their problem for today's class: If a bee-bot's size were to be incrementally extended by two micrometers at what point would the positive effects of increased pollen-gathering surface area be cancelled out by increasing aerodynamic drag?

In the vast greenhouse their pod huddles around a workstation, to all appearances intent on being the first to find the solution.

"Bee-youtiful," Shariah whispers. "My boredom will

now be incrementally extended over the next hour while the surface area of my knowledge will barely be affected."

She nudges Bev, who says, "I can't bee-lieve you, Shariah. You're not bee-ing very interdisciplinary right now."

"It's all just bee-yond me."

They both crack up.

Lucas gives them a disgusted look before pointing his server at the screen and conjuring up a three-dimensional model of a normal-sized bee-bot. He prints and launches it as a control on a flight path into the stacks and rows of vegetation, making notations as he goes. He's the only one out of the six of them not planning an En-level proposal. He's always just wanted to be an AgTech.

Celan likes him for this, the simplicity of it. She even envies him in a way. No pressure. Happy to fly his little bee-bots around for the rest of his life. She finds the 'gardens,' as the techs all refer to this cavernous plant factory, soothing, though the meticulously-arranged crops retain little of the tangled wildness that the word garden embodied in the ranchos. The rows of crops here are stacked in rotating tiers to maximize water use, photosynthesis, compatibility, and pollination. But for all that there is something very aesthetically pleasing about them. And it's sort of fun to fly the bots around and get a bee's-eye-view of things.

She looks down at her server as Lucas' data begin to scroll out across the face of it. He's hard at work on the second model; dark hair obscuring dark eyes narrowed in concentration as he extends the abdomen and adds legs. That's another thing she likes about Lucas – he's not highly styled. He's got the same coloring she does.

But he doesn't have to worry about impressing a committee.

With a satisfied grunt, Lucas finishes up the second bot and launches it. As the new data comes in, Celan pulls it into an algorithm that will help to extrapolate the differences between the first two models to the whole series of incremental changes.

Out of the corner of her eye, she spies Bryan and Kirk whispering to each other, engrossed in something on Bryan's server. Sandy heads together, they look almost like twins, though Kirk's skin is a few shades lighter than Bryan's. She doubts they're this excited about bee-bots. Maybe it's a message from a girl. A pang of jealousy pings her middle as Bev, next to her, heaves a deep yawn, tossing glossy, red-gold curls back from rosy cheeks.

"Don't sleep now," Shariah says. "You need to bee alert."

"Stop bee-littling me." Bev pouts. "I'm getting tired of your bee-havior."

"Will you both just be *quiet!*" Lucas snaps, and they all laugh. But Shariah and Bev stop bantering and Bryan and Kirk flick off whatever it was they were looking at and get down to business.

They all crunch numbers madly, checking each other's work and comparing answers before agreeing on a solution. But the EdTech calls time before they can submit it. Another pod solved it first. None of them really cares, though, except for Lucas, who grouses about people wasting time talking. They had the right answer; they just didn't have it first.

But the last class of the day is over and there's no point in belaboring the issue. As they exit, Celan ends up right behind Bryan and Kirk, who are again conspiring over something and pay her no mind. They stride off down the corridor without a backward glance. She gazes after them, wistful.

"Hey." Shariah elbows her. "C'mon."

She tugs Celan in the opposite direction as Bev catches up to join them. The three girls walk in silence for a minute.

"So, you're doing an En proposal too, right Lana?" Bev says, drumming up conversation. "For what?"

"SocEn."

"Wow. What's it on?"

"Transferon."

Bev's eyes widen. "Wow. That's…unexpected."

"Why?" Celan snaps, annoyed.

"Just – I mean, you're usually so…*proper*, I guess," Bev stammers.

Celan grimaces.

"Does your father know about it?"

"What? Why would he need to? He doesn't have to approve everything I do."

"Uh – OK," Bev says. "I didn't mean – "

"I'm doing transers, too," Shariah cuts in. "Just not *transferon*. Mine's more of a pure sociological thing."

"On expros?" Bev says, clearly relieved to turn her attention elsewhere.

"Well, obviously. We hardly ever see the ones in the ranchos. But they're all the same."

"Well," Bev says briskly. "Makes me glad I'm going for MedEn."

"What's your topic?"

"Cell regeneration in the central nervous system after exposure to HZE radiation during insterstellar travel," she recites. "If Mr. Timanti's Mars proposal goes through I want a shot being picked for the actual mission. I mean, imagine how amazing – "

"Oh, you'll make it no problem," Shariah says. "Some of us just fall into place like *that*." She snaps her fingers for emphasis, white-blond hair rippling like a banner. Like some old world queen with everything at her feet.

"It's like my mother says," she continues, launching into a long-winded discourse on the wit and wisdom of Ariana Balor.

Celan listens mutely, a bit abashed for having been so snippy with Bev.

What must it be like, she muses, *to be so sure of yourself and your place that every knotty problem can be reduced to a simple equation? X=Y and that's that.*

It's an old feeling, this muted envy, and one that she's cycled through in regular intervals over the years. Sometimes the echo is so soft that it seems to have disappeared. But it always rears its head again – generally in an inverse relation to how seamlessly tech-like she's been feeling.

And the thing is, she *should* feel it. Her father's the same rank as Shariah's mother. She should be walking around like she owns this place. And she could have been, if her own mother hadn't been so stupid.

Theodore has told her how he begged Mair to join him in the city and raise her half-sisters here before Celan had even been conceived. If only she'd listened instead of running back to Rancho Pescados when she got pregnant because of some dumb superstitions about tech!

29

Then I would've been born here, like everyone else. I wouldn't have had to be swept up off the streets of Transway —

They've reached the plaza.

"Want to go eat?" Bev says. "I'm starving."

"Sure," Shariah says. "Lana?"

— like a piece of —

"Lana?"

— trash.

"What?"

"Caf?" Shariah says, smirking. "Or are you still busy daydreaming about you-know-who?"

Bev perks up, interested. "Who?"

"Never mind," Celan says. "Let's go."

She takes off across the plaza double time, outpacing the other two until Shariah catches up, breathless.

"Hey. Don't be so touchy. I didn't tell her who."

"Wow. Thanks."

"Oh, stop." Shariah hooks an arm through hers. "Come sleep over tonight. We can talk *privately*. Hash out this Bryan thing once and for all." She squeezes Celan's elbow with affection.

Celan softens. It's not like Shariah can help being perfect. It's just the way she is. If *she* wanted Bryan she would have him wrapped around her finger in three seconds flat.

So maybe she's got a secret formula. Something that'll help.

"Sure," she says, squeezing back. "That'd be great."

"MOM?" SHARIAH CALLS AS THEY whoosh through the front door of her bunk.

But the tiny kitchenette is empty. Shariah bounds past the

plain table and chair set and the small sink and hotplate in a few strides and enters a dim hallway, Celan at her heels.

"Mo-om?"

"In here," comes a faint reply.

Celan grits her teeth. She'd been hoping Mrs. Balor would be out somewhere.

But she trails Shariah to an open doorway pouring out soft light. In her own bunk, this extra room accommodates her father's library. In Shariah's it's a living space – squashy beige couches, modular lighting, large windows, and a slim silvery desk occupying one corner. A woman with glossy red hair is seated there, squinting at a screen.

"Dad around?" Shariah says. "I have a question about some code."

The woman looks up, crisp blue eyes crinkling in the corners. She waves an airy hand. "Out. Friday. CompEn social."

"Oh well," Shariah says. She turns to go.

Saved, Celan thinks.

"Wait," Mrs. Balor says. "Is that Lana with you?"

"Yeah."

Dutiful, Celan steps into the light. "Hi, Mrs. Balor."

The woman smiles, but there's a hint of sourness in it. "How long have we known each other now, Lana? For the millionth time, call me Ariana."

"Sorry. It's just…you're a Lead and all."

"Well so is your father," Ariana says lightly. "Do you call him Mr. Timanti?"

No, Celan thinks, *I call him Dad*. But she doesn't dare sass Ariana.

"Sorry," she says again.

31

"Lana's staying over tonight," Shariah cuts in. "Girl stuff."

Mrs. Balor's smile finally reaches her eyes. She trills an indulgent little laugh. "Well, of course. It's that age. You girls have fun."

She turns back to the screen.

They are dismissed.

ARIANA BALOR SIGHS AS THE girls' footsteps retreat down the hall and the door to Shariah's room whooshes open and closed.

Peace at last.

Though truth be told she delights in her daughter's company. Shariah is perfect: Highly intelligent and a natural leader – just look how that wishy-washy little Lana follows her around! Though she hopes that once their pod splits and they move on to En level (or not) Shariah will make some new friends.

'Yes, Mrs. Balor. No, Mrs. Balor.'

So cloying! And irritating – like a piece of food stuck in a tooth.

But she knows the situation is partially her own fault. Lana had seemed bright enough when Theodore first brought her here from Winnipeg (the surprising product of his brief affair with a local woman from that city-state); bright enough that she'd encouraged the friendship when the girls were young. They were the same age, both daughters of Leads. It seemed like a natural fit. But the intervening years have proven her first impression misguided.

The girl just lacks something.

Spirit maybe – daring. Initiative. Look at how she's styled

(or not, since Theodore never even got the chance): Beige and boring compared to Shariah, who's all striking contrasts and angularity.

If only her own mother had had as much foresight: Ariana frowns down at her curvaceous figure and again at her reflection in the screen – that garish hair and eyes, like some kind of Transway tart. No wonder she's not always taken seriously.

What was *that woman thinking?*

Someday she means to ask her, if she can tear her away from her holos long enough.

Of course, styling wasn't quite as advanced back then. The process was still new and not always exact. She could have had things altered later on, but there was a catch – once she'd grown into her adult form she was already up for SocEn. How would it have looked for her to start altering her appearance then? Vain. Silly. Not like someone to be reckoned with. So she'd vowed to rise above it. Work around it. Use it to her advantage. And mostly she has.

Ariana squints at the screen again, rubbing her eyes. She's going to need a corneal adjustment soon; she feels lucky to have made it past fifty without one but she can't put it off forever. Another thing to add to her packed schedule.

She opens up her calendar, scrolling through the next few weeks' events. Meetings, meetings…but all of them important. She's especially looking forward to Thursday; Nathan's assembled a team of crack CompTechs to work on the replicator code. It's very helpful having a spouse who's a Lead in that discipline since it was never her area of expertise. Once they get a working model together she'll be that much closer to her objective: Providing a smoke screen for the true nature of her plans for the resource vote.

Because although she does want to reboot GISH (*who wouldn't want a nice clean Earth, a nice fresh start?*) she'd like to start cleansing a little closer to home: On Transway. And that involves Pollomax – a new bot plug-in some of her like-minded MedEn associates have been working on that will help solve the problem once and for all.

All this talk of how to remove impurities…they had been well on their way to a clean bill of health, at least within their own limited environment, when those creatures came slinking back from the ranchos, setting up camp outside the walls and letting the old poisons start to work their way back into Alba-kirk. And it's not just the physical contaminants – old world chemicals, radiation – there are more subtle poisons, too. Certain practices and ideas were better off lost with the old world and should never have been allowed to be resurrected by a small minority of degenerate fools.

If only her fellow Leads understood this. But some people are so blinded by base desires that they refuse to see.

All desires have biological components, however. And so, with the proper interventions, can be controlled. Pollomax is designed to use the principle of conditioned taste aversion in order to sow the seeds of distaste for Transway throughout the tech population. The plug-in works with the nanobots the techs already use to help regulate their bodily functions by "tricking" receptors in the amygdala of the brain into asso-ciating the concept of "Transway" with the kind of aversive reaction a person gets to a certain type of food or drink after getting ill from it. The idea is that any sensory input associated with Transway – sights, smells, sounds, as well as actual tastes – will be translated into signals for the "bad taste" receptors (and only those receptors) to activate.

The main stumbling block has been in identifying the exact receptors and proteins involved in this process. They have to be very precise, because messing around with amygdalic signals can be a risky business; but they've been running simulations and it looks very promising so far. However, she's going to need to run live human tests in order to prove that the process is safe and have her findings accepted. And that, since the unfortunate demise of the bot lottery, means using expro subjects in the final analyses.

But she's going to have to wait on that part, bide her time. She doesn't want Theodore to get wind of this and try to squash it before it even gets off the ground. Let him think that the GISH reboot is her only objective. She's already got a great deal of built-in support for that – even Martinez may not be able to resist the lure of a relaunch. And there are many others who share that outlook, the Ag and MedEns especially. They're the ones with the most questions about the viability of the Martian Relocation Plan.

She'll work quietly, build support, and wait until right before the vote to unveil her entire plan. And even then she'll keep it simple – gloss over the Pollomax to make it sound like she's not so much trying to get rid of Transway as she is just trying to make it a little less appealing. And if it still seems like she might fail, well, there are always *options*.

Sometimes people just need a little of the right motivation: Perhaps if some transers managed to get out of the lab and tried to poison everyone with transferon; if they slipped it into the water supply…

That would make everyone think twice. But to organize something like that without generating recs or views in some form would be extremely difficult.

She'd tried something similar once before – banded together with two like-minded associates and took a serious risk to have a wayvern destroyed, sacrificing some tech lives in the process. It had been wrenching; and in hindsight also incredibly clumsy and stupid. But no one ever discovered the cause of the "accident" at Arlo's. Theodore had been in charge of the investigation but was preoccupied at the time by Lana's untimely arrival in his life. So he hadn't looked too deep.

At least the girl was good for something.

And in any case, it hadn't made a damn bit of difference. Didn't whip up nearly the amount of anti-Transway sentiment she'd anticipated.

But a tragic incident *within* the city is still just a pipe dream. Because she'd have to get actual transers to participate – techs in disguise would be easily identified. And how in hell would she ever manage that?

Better Pollomax. It's safer, subtler, and will accomplish the same objective – because once the techs have developed the proper aversion to Transway they will no longer have a vested interest in maintaining its infrastructure. No matter what nonsense people spout about "not bringing back the bot test lottery" and "cultural appreciation" or whatever other excuses they like to make, that is really the crux of the issue: They enjoy Transway the way it is too much to insist on reform.

Solving that problem will make things easy – once Transway is no longer desirable and no one has any use for it the expros can then finally be ordered to either: 1) turn in their transfers, accept the bots (which many have heretofore refused due to ignorant fear), and live as techs or 2) leave. Those who choose to leave will have forty-eight hours to evacuate Transway before all services are shut down and the infrastructure razed. Anyone caught in the area after that time will be banished and that will be the end of that.

And maybe, once that's out of the way, they can do something about those "ranchos." They're a little too close to Albakirk for her liking.

Ariana sighs, rubs her eyes; she really needs that corneal.

Next Friday – Ord 357. 15:00. She has an hour free then. She taps at her server, sending a request to the MedLab.

She's sure they'll find a way to fit her in.

THE TWO GIRLS HUDDLE CLOSE on Shariah's bed, their servers the only light as they scroll through the day's exchange of messages. Celan has several from Bryan. But so does Shariah. And there are others from the rest of their poddies. Nothing out of the ordinary.

"You've just got to be confident," Shariah says, slender form silhouetted against the window. Her hair shines diamond-bright in the moonlight. "I mean, we're all going to pair off eventually, have our kid, style him all nice." (Shariah's always been set on a son.) "I don't see why you two wouldn't be good together." She tsks, impatient. "Just tell him already."

Celan hugs her knees hard, picking at a cuticle. Logically, she knows Shariah's right. There's no reason on Earth not to tell Bryan how she feels; except that the thought of it makes her feel like she's about to be sick.

Because what if he didn't like her back? Or what – and this is almost worse – if he did? What if they got together and everything was going great? And then what if one day, in some unexpected way, he found out where she really came from – not from Winnipeg like her father told everyone way back when – but from Transway? And what if it totally disgusted him? Bryan's never been as anti-expro as some people but that doesn't mean he wants to kiss one.

No one's ever going to find out, she councils herself for the millionth time. *I'm as tech as any of them.*

But she's going to have to do something soon. Their pod's about to split. She needs to speak now or forever hold her peace.

"I will," she says. "Soon. Definitely."

Shariah sighs. Flicks off her server. Lies down and arranges her head on a pillow as she closes her eyes. "OK then, but it better be soon. Pods split in two more weeks."

"I know." Celan puts her server down too. "Maybe tomorrow, after stun practice. He's always in a good mood then."

"*Stuns*," Shariah says, derisive. "What a waste of time. I mean, when are we ever really going to use them?"

"We might," Celan says, "if we ever go on any of the expeditions. They need them then. Once you get away from the city there're all kinds of weird things out there. My father had to stun a bunch of them back when he used to go to Winnipeg."

"OK," her friend concedes. "But we don't need them in the city."

"We don't have them *in* the city, only practice simulations. They only need them outside, like on Transway. My father said sometimes they have to break up fights and stuff."

"Transway," Shariah sneers, putting a final nail in the conversation, "we really don't need *that* either."

Celan says nothing as she slides down between cool sheets. With Shariah breathing next to her, sleep comes quick.

She is in the plaza, walking with her pod. They pass a fountain surrounded by swaying foliage, laughing and talking in a bright happy group as a faint spray mists the air and cools their faces. The light is a peculiar diffuse, frosty lemon-yellow that fills up space like the atmosphere of a similar, but still foreign, planet.

Suddenly she halts.

"Hey!" she says, voice a curious echo. They all stop and look at her. "Can you all wait up a minute? I've got to go in there," she gestures toward the door of a MedLab, "for a minute."

"Sure," Shariah says, "we'll be right here," and turns to say something to Kirk.

Celan approaches the Lab and pushes the door panel, walking right up to the check-in counter where a white-robed man grins and points to a corridor on the left. At the end of it, another door opens and she enters a featureless room where a MedTech stands, silent in a spotless tan uniform. She prints the reader and pushes up her sleeve. The transfer glows like a soft star in the man's hand and she breathes deep as the transfusion passes through her skin.

When it hits, it's bliss. She smiles her thanks to the MedTech and rolls slowly back through the front room and outside to where her friends are waiting.

Shariah regards her, eyes skyward in friendly exasperation. "Celan, have you been fusing again?"

She nods and Shariah shrugs.

Then they all turn and continue across the plaza.

She opens her eyes and it is morning.

3

The day glides by like a stream slipping around stones. Celan floats from bunk to caf to class, more relaxed than she's been in months. She recalls the strange dream, but only in the sense of seeing it through a wall of water. It's hazy, muted, and it doesn't disturb her – even the fact that Shariah had called her by her real name, the one that no one save her father knows.

An old name from an old life, she thinks with a mental shrug.

When classes are over, she ducks the rest of her pod and heads for the CompLab – where the gruff gray walls wrap around her like an old grandfather's arms, smelling of pipe smoke and spinning stories. She points her server at the screen and it flashes on, bringing up the three-dimensional transfer model. In silence, she contemplates it, willing it to give up its secrets.

The vial itself is carved from quartz, unlike the dropper, which is made of regular glass topped with a rubber blub. Quartz is known for its crystalline structure and piezoelectric properties, so it follows that an electromagnetic pulse could be transmitted via the quartz to the water inside. But an electromagnetic pulse emanating from a human that alters the water's composition? Scientifically speaking, this phenomenon is problematic – it definitely occurs but it is difficult to measure or control. But time after time transferon is the result.

Transfusing is even more of a mystery. The pressure in the bulb of a dropper squeezed by fingers isn't anywhere near the force produced by the magnetic field and current inside a real jet injector. It shouldn't work either. But, somehow, it does.

Celan pokes a finger at the screen and starts to spin the transfer around, faster and faster, until it whirls into a bright centrifuge.

She stares at it, intent.

She blinks.

Suddenly she's standing in her ten-year-old body at the edge of a shady pond at Rancho Pescados, feeding pellets to small silver fish who murmur in a language she can't quite make out – like the ghostly music in a staticky radio signal. She leans forward to try to hear them better.

Then she's in the pool swimming – a fish herself, breathing water like air until she looks up to see her own face looming above and scattering nourishment like rain. Flourishing her tail she jumps, breaking the surface and flexing in a high arc before plunging back down with a satisfying splash, diving deeper and deeper into liquid cool until she's brought up short by a chime from her server.

Automatically, she taps it to vocal mode.

"Lana!" comes Bryan's voice. "Where'd you disappear to? Come meet us in the caf. We're hatching a plan here." He chuckles and the server goes silent.

Celan sits frozen, mind spinning. She squints at the image of the virtual vial and shivers, but whether in fear or pleasure she's not quite sure.

What just happened here?

Heart pounding, she clicks off the screen and gets to her feet. It was nothing. Just some silly daydream. Sign of a creative mind at work.

She gathers up her things and heads for the door, pausing to smooth her hair in the reflected surface of the lab window before hurrying off to the caf.

SCRATCHED BLACK BOOTS THUD IN the dust down Transway. Mingled shouts and bursts of music and laughter blast from open doorways. Two girls twirl out of an alley and move off up the street in a strange, synchronized dance, laughing deliriously.

The boy smiles; it's nice to be back in town.

He drops his pack on the sidewalk in front of a wayvern and stretches, back cracking like kindling as he takes a long pull from his water bag. Not so much a boy anymore, nineteen now – eyes already crinkling in the corners with equal parts mirth and strain. He breathes deep, taking in burnt grease and incense, stale beer, and freshly-lit smokes. Foreign and exotic once upon a time, but now they just smell like home.

Well, home away from home, he silently amends.

It's been a long year and the last time he was here it was

with the heavy charge of telling them all that Raf had passed. They'd all cried and told him he could stay if he wanted to, that he was always welcome at Alamora. He'd appreciated the offer but felt like he had to go back to the ranchos. Make the effort. He couldn't hurt his family even more by piling loss upon loss.

He's been trying hard to stay focused – keeping his head down, working in the orchards. But it just gets to be too much sometimes; the careful words, the stares and whispers. The subtle slights.

Not everyone's like that, thank Madre. He's got a couple of tios who like their cider, who'll sit down and have a few with him at the end of a long day. Laugh and relax. But lately even they've shied away, under pressure from the rest of the family no doubt. So he needs to blow off some steam, be among friends.

The ranchos can spare him; there's not much work to do this time of year. And he promised to be back by Navidad.

But first there was the leave-taking to endure: his father's stony silence, his mother's tremulous smile. One sister refusing to speak to him while the other hinted around that she might like to come with. No way was *that* going to happen. He's got enough regrets as it is.

He'd had plenty of time to brood on the hike through the old mountain pass. Not much to focus on besides crumbling ancient blacktop, spindly piñons, and the old metal sculpture of a yucca marking his almost-there point. He'll never forget the first time he saw the thing. He'd been hurried, worried, trying to make it out to Transway to talk to Rafael – to reassure him that he was still part of the family; that Dad hadn't meant everything he'd said – and there it had stood like a beacon, a sign. He'd felt a sudden thrill.

What exotic adventures awaited?

His lips twist ruefully as a man stumbles out of a wayvern, kicks a wall, and swears at the sky. Heat shimmers off the baking road, and the sun begins to swell and sink behind the mesa. He shivers.

Will they even be glad to see him? It's been so long that he's a little uneasy. Maybe they're just as well rid of him. Maybe they said all those things out of respect for Raf. Maybe they don't really like him at all.

He shakes his head to break up the pity party.

Cállate, stupid brain! It'll be fine.

Chugging the last of the water, he swings a loose arm down and shoulders his pack. Pokes his head into the wayvern for a quick minute but doesn't see anyone he knows. Maybe he should go in anyway, have a drink to calm his nerves; he's got a couple of chits floating around somewhere.

But no, he'll save it for later. Best head to Alamora and see what's happening.

SLOWLY, CELAN LADLES STEAMING SOUP into a bowl and adds some noodles, stirring it into almost a stew. It's before the main dinner hour so there's not much of a line. She prints the reader then peers around the room until she spots her pod huddled around a back table near the long wall of windows. Outside, the Sandias glow pink and orange in the reflected light of the setting sun. She inhales deeply, remembering the smell of the dusty mountains in the evening, the feeling of sun on her face. Its imagined warmth infuses her with a glow of anticipation for what the group might have planned.

"C'mon Bev, don't be like that," Kirk is saying as she sits down, "everyone does it at least once before Ed ends."

Bev is shaking her head. "It's stupid. There's no point. What's to see? A bunch of expros? Who cares?"

"Why does there have to be a point? It's *fun*."

"Lana," Bev pleads, "tell him how ridiculous this is."

Celan eyes Bryan with amusement. She raises a spoonful of soup to her lips, daintily blowing on it. "Planning an escape?" she says.

"We want to go to Transway," Kirk informs her. "To a wayvern. At night. Just for a few hours. Just to see what it's like."

"On Navidad Eve," adds Bryan. "Lots of pods go out that night…it's like a tradition. Get a little preview in so we can see what it'll be like once we're PostEd." He grins. "A light at the end of the tunnel while we're slaving away 'til Ord 150. Wes did it last year. He told me all about it."

"He told you there were naked girls dancing around," says Shariah. "That's why you want to go so bad."

She crosses arms over her chest. Bev follows suit. Bryan and Kirk exchange sheepish glances. Celan laughs. "Lucas?"

Lucas doesn't look up from his server. "Whatever. Expro girls are disgusting."

Celan spoons more soup and looks around the table. They're all staring at her.

"Don't we need a chap?"

"Wes said he'd do it," Kirk says. "Print the reader for us. Someone did it for his pod, so he's passing it on."

Shariah snorts. "Oh, Wes. Of course." She rolls her eyes so ridiculously big that Celan starts to giggle.

"What?!" Shariah says, nostrils flaring.

"You – never mind." As her chuckles die down she ventures, "It might be kind of fun."

"It might be kind of dangerous," Shariah says, recovering her dignity. "Besides, we'll all get put on Notice." She nods toward the board with solemnity.

"No we won't," Bryan insists. "If Wes chaps us it's totally legit. He's PostEd now."

"But he's not exactly going to be keeping us out of trouble."

"Of course not." Kirk grins, hazel eyes like twin candles. "That's the whole point."

"I'm in," Celan says, putting her spoon down with a clatter. "Let's do it."

"No way," Bev says.

"Oh come on, Bev," Celan coaxes. "Why not? It's totally legit and it'll be better if we all go together. Celebrate our last week as a pod. Like Bryan said, it's a tradition."

"Please," Shariah says. "It's not like we're never going to see each other again."

"No, but it's never going to be the same. We won't be working together anymore. We'll be competing," Celan points out. "Well, some of us."

This seems to bring Shariah up short. She cocks her head, considering.

"Oh no!" Bev wails. "Shariah you can't really – "

"You know," she says, looking almost wistful. "I think Lana's right. Besides, someone's got to make sure things don't get out of hand."

"I guess *we* can manage that," Bev says, giving the guys

a stern eye.

"Fine," Bryan says, ignoring her. "Lucas?"

A shrug. "Whatever."

"All right," Bryan says, rubbing his palms together glee-fully. "This is going to be *epic*."

THE SKY ARCHES AMETHYST AS the boy approaches the ramshackle house. From the back alley, he creaks open the gate and enters the dusky yard with its wide swath of neatly fenced kitchen garden – nearly empty this time of year but for some over-wintering garlic and greens. Everything else has been harvested and put up already.

"Lang!" He hears the cry and pivots right, ducking under the low porch awning where three figures pause in a game of Trains to herald his arrival.

"Que pas'?" A pixie-ish girl with flossy pink hair jumps up and nearly bowls him over in a fierce embrace. He hugs her back, lifting her off the ground and spinning her around as her legs kick futilely.

As he sets her back down she looks him over, appreciative. "You've filled out a little."

He feels his cheeks redden. "Yeah, well. I've been doing a lot of, you know..." He mimes digging and carrying. "...over there."

"We thought maybe you weren't coming back. Decided to be a good little ranchito."

He makes a face and the two others laugh, one guy with a head full of blue braids bobbling and the other's ample gut jiggling merrily as the girl takes her place back at the table, crossing her legs and smoothing her bob neat.

"So how long're you planning to stick around?" she says.

He slings his pack onto an empty chair. "Dunno. Week or two? Figured I'd take some time off for good behavior."

"You mean time for some bad behavior," she teases.

"That too."

The heavy guy looks up, flips long brown bangs off his face. "Drink, Lang?"

"Órale."

He plunges a pudgy hand into a cooler, fishes out a bottle of beer, and offers it to Lang – who flips off the cap with his knife, takes a long pull, and sighs. "This more of that chile stuff you guys made last year?"

"Yeah, and you can take a seat while you finish that," brown bangs deadpans. "Get in on this game. I'm getting my ass kicked by fusers."

"Besa mi culo!" barks the pixie, indignant. She snaps a domino into place and kicks out a chair. "Venga güey, represent the normales. My cousin needs all the help he can get."

Lang laughs and plunks down gratefully, stretching his legs and letting the exertion of the long hike fade. All of the earlier insecurity over his welcome here now seems completely ludicrous. He knew it in his head, even then, but now he feels it in his bones: These are his people. He can finally relax.

He takes another swig and crosses ankle over knee, noting a spot on the sole of his left boot that's starting to wear thin. Absently, he pokes at it. Funny, he never got into the habit of wearing sandals again, even after a year back in the ranchos. They felt too...open. But the boots are snug, enclosed. He wriggles his toes.

Safe.

A swift kick to the side of his chair brings his head up.

The pixie smirks. "What're you, aviados already? Somebody's talking to you over there."

She flutters fingers at blue braids as he digs in a pocket and extracts something small and silvery that he tosses to Lang.

"Figured you'd want that back."

Lang makes the catch and looks down at the transfer in his hand.

"Gracias," he says, lips locked somewhere between a grimace and a grin. "Few drops here and there. It'll come in useful." He pockets the thing, chugs the rest of his beer, and immediately digs in the cooler for another.

Blue braids and pink floss share a look, but say nothing.

4

Celan wakes to the wail of her alarm. Groping a hand over the nightstand she silences her server as ten- drils of vague, incoherent images swirl before her mind's eye. Slowly, fragments of the previous day begin to arrange themselves in her consciousness – the strange occurrence in the lab, the scene in the caf, agreeing to sneak out to Transway.

What was I thinking?

She rewinds further to the night before: The dream. The transfusion.

At the thought, her heart jumps and starts to pound. She curls on her side, constricted by fear and longing, trying to calm down. This needs to stop *now*. This is not rational. She didn't fuse, not in real life. They don't hand out fuses in MedLabs. It was a dream. A stupid dream. She needs to breathe.

She makes herself stretch out flat on her back and brings

shaking hands to her solar plexus. She takes several long, slow breaths and her heart rate begins to slow.

Better.

It was just some weird fluke. She couldn't really have been fusing. It was just the dream that disturbed her; stirred up no doubt by how hard she's been working on her proposal. She's got transfers on the brain.

She dredges up some reassuring knowledge: Long-term, intoxic fusers often have dreams about fusing. But you can't be a fuser at all without actual, repeated, real-life fusing. Dreams don't count. She only fused once, when she was eleven. There's no way to induce an intoxic reaction on a seven-year time delay just by dreaming about it.

That is crazy.

With a grunt she sits up and throws her legs over the side of the bed. She stands and stretches, feeling skin pull and vertebræ pop. Then she slides her feet into slippers and grabs her server, padding out of the room and through the little kitchenette to the main corridor, heading for the showers.

Walk it off. This will pass.

The shower room is silent when she enters, but a cloud of steam testifies to its recent use. She strips off her sleepware and stuffs it down the Sanichute, prints out a towel and a fresh uniform, and slips into a stall. Shucking off her slippers, she hangs her items on hooks for easy access, tucks the server in the pocket of the uniform, and thumbs the reader to release a warm gush from the spigot on the wall.

A push of a lever releases a handful of soap, and she slathers it over her body, working some into her hair and then standing under the stream and letting the water surge around her...*like that wave that ran through me, that time I....* She relaxes into it, remembering how good it felt – that sweet jump and then the spreading sea of joy.

And then their faces rise up, unbidden – her sister, Cyrinda, with her man, Taegh – the most beautiful faces in the world. Everything looked beautiful after the fuse, everything was alive. She shivers with pleasure at the thought as a strange hollow feeling creeps into the pit of her stomach; almost like she's hungry, but not for breakfast.

Legs trembling, she slides down the wall until she's sitting on the tiled floor. She hugs her legs up tight against her chest as if they could form a physical barrier to whatever entity is trying to possess her. She knows she must look strange, but there are no views inside shower stalls and there's no one else there to see.

"WELL, YOU SEEM TO HAVE thought this through very thoroughly," says Nigel Gallegos, grey eyes serious as he shifts his weight from foot to foot. "But I still have concerns about the long-term ramifications of this thing."

Theodore shrugs, letting the misty spray from the fountain refresh his face after the fusty confines of the conference room. "Not every last issue can be anticipated."

Fifteen precious minutes have elapsed since he wrapped up his Martian Relocation Plan presentation for the Lead MedEns, and, judging by Nigel's cautious praise and continued willingness to discuss it, it seems to have gone over well.

He needs to keep the pressure on though.

"True," Nigel says. "You've put a lot of work into designing infrastructure that will counteract the effects of low gravity living and radiation exposure from the lack of atmosphere. But this whole endeavor will be wasted if humans cannot procreate successfully on Mars. And even if they can, the children born there will be unable to tolerate Earth's gravity. Especially after the many generations it will take for the Earth to decontaminate. What's the point of moving there if we can never come back *here*?"

"Nanotech is advancing all the time," Theodore says smoothly. "We're currently working on adaptations to our Earth bodies to allow for better adjustment to a Martian environment. So it follows suit that eventually it will be advanced enough to allow for a little reverse engineering."

Nigel purses his lips thoughtfully.

Theodore goes on, "And if we wait until every last question is answered we may lose our chance. Martian resources are very unevenly distributed. Only certain regions are suitable for establishing the kind of colony I have in mind and we have drone intelligence that at least one other city-state may be planning a similar endeavor. If Lanzhou gets first claim, we may not be able to even do this at all. Or we'll be forced into doing it some other, inferior, way. *Their* way."

"Yes, that is certainly an issue," Nigel agrees. "But if their technology is inferior isn't their venture bound to fail? Look at the old world project – a handful of colonists survived six months during the Martian summer. But that was the best they ever managed. And those colonists ultimately perished. The more we can learn from others' failures, the more chance we'll have of a permanent success."

Theodore shakes his head. "We need to act *now*. Not wait

around watching someone else try, and possibly succeed, while we dither over details. This is too important."

"Well…" Nigel glances up at the plaza's glass-ceilinged sky and runs a hand over his close-cropped hair.

Theodore presses his advantage. "Come down to the lab with me. Take a first-hand look at what we're doing. We've built a capsule that simulates Martian conditions to a very fine-grained degree and we've been testing a new bot that shows very promising results in adapting our subjects to them."

"Now? I have a lunch meeting – "

"So push it back a half hour. This won't take long."

Nigel fishes his server out of his breast pocket and taps out a message before replacing it with a sigh. "All right, Theodore," he says. "Impress me."

THEODORE'S ALMOST BOUNCING ON HIS heels as the door of the Barsoom Room (as some of the wittier lab techs have christened the simulation capsule) closes in the wake of his quick demo. Triumphant, he escorts Nigel back down the hall and out through the waiting room of the transer lab. This impromptu tour may have just lit the crucial spark: There's a glint in Nigel's eye now that wasn't there before – one of genuine enthusiasm. Hopefully, one that will light a fire under the rest of the MedEns as well.

He thumbs the reader on the corridor door and reaches to press the panel, mind ticking off further points to make on their way up to the caf. But it whooshes open before he can touch it to reveal Ariana Balor standing on the other side.

His stomach sinks: *What can she want down here?*

Ariana loathes the transer lab. Never mind how many times he's explained that the study of transferon represents only a small portion of the experiments conducted, and that even when the subjects are under its influence they are very well-contained. They enter and exit through a special, key-coded door that leads directly onto the scrubby flats outside the city. And the reader on the main corridor door ensures that they can't just go wandering around Albakirk. Only techs can open it.

But despite all these precautions, the mere presence of transing transers in the city is enough to aggrieve her.

So now...

"Nigel," she says, with a brisk nod. Then, "Theodore, can I have a word?"

"Nigel and I are on our way to the caf," he hedges.

"And I'm sure Nigel can find his way there on his own." Her tone is tart, but her smile is a few degrees warmer than usual.

Nigel grins back. "No problem," he says. Then, to Theodore: "We'll catch up later. This really was very enlightening, I must say. Amazing work you're doing." And with that, he brushes past the two Lead SocEns and hurries off to his lunch date.

Ariana steps into the lab and Theodore swears silently. As far as Nigel's concerned, he's only just lit the spark; he needed the walk up to the caf to help fan it into a flame. But leave it to La Roja to chop off it off at the knees. With a sigh, he whooshes the door shut behind her.

"What do you want, Ariana?" he says, barely forcing a civil

tone.

She blinks big blue eyes, all innocence.

"What I would like," she says, "is a tour of the lab. I was going to ask the lab manager but seeing as you appear to be available... That is, if you're not too busy."

A stunned beat. "The lab?" he repeats. "You mean *this* lab?"

That smile again, wry now. "Do you see another?"

"No, no," he recovers. "Of course. It's just a little surprising. I mean, you must admit you've never exactly been interested in it before."

"Times change," she says, with a touch of rue. "And I believe we must change with them. From what I hear, there is quite a bit of important work going on down here these days. I'd like to see it for myself."

Theodore's eyes narrow in suspicion. This must be some kind of reconnaissance mission. She must be sniffing around his Mars simulation, trying to find flaws to exploit to bolster her own plans for the resource vote. Clever. Perhaps it's actually a bit of luck that he ran into her after all. Now he can direct her tour in an entirely different direction.

"Absolutely," he says, hearty now. "It would be my pleasure."

BEHIND THEODORE'S BACK, ARIANA ROLLS her eyes.

Idiot, she thinks. *I can't believe he doesn't see right through me.*

But if there's one thing she's learned in life, it is never to underestimate the power of some well-placed flattery. And deception, of course.

By pretending to be interested in his Mars crap, she's

guaranteed that that's the last thing he's going to show her. He probably thinks he'll bore her to tears with bot tests when that is exactly what she's come to see. She'd thank the man, if he wasn't so insufferable.

She'd actually been surprised to find him here at this hour; he'd had that presentation and she figured he'd wrangle a few poor souls into continuing the discussion over lunch. Her appointment is with Alton White, an old crony who also happens to be the transer lab manager, and who she now hopes has the presence of mind not to give any Pollomax talk away.

"...washroom on the left....completely remodeled four years ago. This room is now for pre-screening only," Theodore explains, pointing out a female tech in tan who is taking a cheek swab from a reluctant, green-haired expro. Sample taken, she plugs the stylus into her server and scrolls through results officiously.

Ariana eyes the expro with disdain. A full contingent of (his?) fellow foul specimens are sprawled on benches and chairs around the lab's bare-bones waiting room. Some of their faces are turned down or away, others stare blankly at the carefully vetted entertainments flickering on the wall screens, but a few look back boldly. One particularly scruffy one looks her up and down in a way that makes her shudder.

Nasty creature.

Then Theodore motions her forward and she turns, relieved, to trail him past a length of mirrored wall that she assumes (correctly) is some kind of one-way observation window. At its far end, he makes a sharp right into a narrow corridor punctuated by a series of nondescript numbered doors, some with red lights glowing above them.

"….special lab door that opens to the outside," his voice drones on. "Since they sometimes have transferon in their systems, they can't go through the scanners at the main gate. Subjects receive a fob when they register that transmits the key code for the outside door and the time of their appointment on the days they're scheduled in the lab. The code changes every day. Upon arrival, we screen them and decide which assignment they are best suited for. Sometimes they stay on a particular assignment for an extended period of time, such as those participating in the Mars simulations."

He pauses in front of a red-lit door. "They're a bit busy now, but if you'd like a demonstration I can arrange one for another time. Nigel was very impressed."

I'll bet.

"Well, that's a shame," she says, as the light on another door down the hall blinks off.

Theodore's eyes take on a sardonic gleam. "But we can take a look at some bot testing if you'd like."

She feigns distaste. "Fine."

He smirks, motioning her forward again. "You'll find they've become very sophisticated over the past several years. Every attempt is made to work out any bugs during the virtual stage, so very few bad reactions occur during live tests these days."

"Mmm-hmm," she says, noncommittal.

He thumbs the reader at the door and presses the panel, revealing a stark white room where a single unconscious subject reclines on a chair, attended to by one tech in blue and two more in tan. They snap to attention at the sight of the two Lead SocEns.

"Mr. Timanti, Mrs. Balor," the one in blue says, all obsequiousness.

Alton.

Ariana shoots him a warning look from behind Theodore's back and watches it register.

"Anything we can do for you today?"

Smart man.

"I'm giving Mrs. Balor a tour of the lab," Theodore informs him. "Mrs. Balor, this is Mr. Alton White, MedEn and Lab Manager."

"Call me Ariana." Smiling, she steps forward and extends her hand, keeping her eyes on his and her tone carefully flat. "So nice to meet you. I'm really looking forward to seeing some of your work."

5

Lang drags deep, filling his lungs with sweet smoke as the heat and noise of Tosh's wayvern press close around him. He leans back in the creaking chair, exhales a cloud, and takes a swig of his drink, thunking the thick glass down on the scarred wooden table with satisfaction.

Whiskey. After a week of shifts for Zeeb he can well afford it.

He taps the smoke over the ashtray, brushing his other hand over a tiny hidden pouch at his waist. The transfer is safe and sound, but he's constantly checking it to be sure. Because fifty-plus years of separation from the ranchos (and the elders' transfer-making craftsmanship) have insured that there are a lot more expros than transfers on Transway these days. There's always someone looking for someone who has one.

A poke at a separate pouch produces a satisfying rattle of chits. Not a bad day's haul, even after Zeeb's cut, especially since he's got his own transfer. Crew members without one need to rent from Zeeb and he takes an extra cut for that. So this is a pretty good deal.

There're risks though, with this kind of thing. Being on Zeeb's crew ensures that someone's got his back (they usually work in pairs) but still, he's got to be careful. Desperate people do desperate things. You have to watch the customers while they transfigure it into whatever their favorite flavor is and then watch them while they fuse it. You have to be ready to stop them if they try to run. Because it's far easier to stop someone from running off with a transfer than it is to try to track one down after.

He'd known most of this already. Back in the Rafael days he'd been a kind of junior crew member/errand boy, but now Zeeb laid out the full deal: No freebies without prior approval, barter's OK with certain clientele (he's got the short list), no fusing on the job (Lang had assured Zeeb that he wouldn't have to worry about *that*), and stay within your territory. He'd agreed to all of it, grateful to Zeeb for doing him a favor and throwing him a few shifts for the short term. Now he can afford to drink his fill, pay for his share of necessities at Alamora, and even get some nice Navidad gifts for the family. Make up for some of the agita he's caused them.

One thing Zeeb had insisted on, though, was a full makeover. Ranchos are easy targets. Lang sneaks a look at his reflection in the grimy window – plain hemp clothing replaced by a fashionably motley ensemble – and shivers. Full-on expro. No one's gonna mess with him now.

Part of him revels in it, feels like this is who he really is and good little ranchito Lang is the fake Lang. But it's scary how quickly things can change, how easy it is to slip on another skin and lose yourself.

He draws on his smoke again and exhales, contemplating.

If someone had told him four years ago that this is where he'd be now, he would've thought they'd gone crazy. Gotten a dose of some old world poison. In his mind's eye he conjures up the ghost of his fifteen-year-old self, the scrawny boy at Pranascuela solemnly receiving his first transfer. Like every student before him he'd vowed to follow the Precepts and use transferon only to enhance the natural metaphysical abilities, healing chief among them, that he'd had all his life. He'd leave the transfer at 'scuela at the end of each lesson day until his eighteenth birthday, at which point he'd be free to take it and make responsible use of transferon to keep him healthy and happy in whatever life he chose at Rancho Arqueros.

Unless they made him an elegido.

There was no way of knowing who the elders were going to tap to continue to the highest levels of sacred learning. There wasn't a test you had to take or a specific set of criteria. Obviously, healing abilities counted for a lot but they didn't always pick the most obviously gifted. Some years they didn't pick anyone. Sometimes they'd choose several. But being chosen was the highest honor anyone could receive. The elegidos glided around the ranchos in their pale blue robes radiating serenity until they became elders themselves and wore white instead.

That blue robe had once seemed like the most important thing in the world.

He takes another slug of whiskey.

63

No chance of that now.

But some fusers do get sick from CERS. So maybe he's still kind of a healer after all.

He frowns down into his glass as someone yanks out the chair across from him. He jumps, curses his nerves. Maybe not full-on expro just yet.

"Lang." A wiry guy with a shock of flame-bright hair drops into the empty seat. "Long time, güey. Que pas'?"

"Hey, Sig." Lang dips his head in greeting. "Nada. Just havin' a little drink after a hard day's work."

"How you been? I mean…"

A shrug. "Oh. You know. Doin' all right."

"Seen Jas yet?"

"Yeah. We talked."

That had been painful. He hadn't expected her to still have feelings for him after everything that had happened and their being apart for so long. He'd felt sure she would've found someone else by now. But it seemed like she was still carrying a torch.

While working at Maddy's. Lang winces.

He'd let her down easy, though, assuring her that there was no one else (there wasn't) but that he wasn't going to be sticking around long enough for anything real to happen between them.

"You two…?"

"Just friends. I mean, if you're interested." He raises a sardonic brow, knowing Sig's not big on girls. This has the desired effect. Sig chuckles.

"Playing tonight?" Lang says, changing the subject.

Sig drums in three different bands. He's always playing

somewhere.

Sig makes a face. "Eli's."

Not a very popular wayvern. It'll probably be dead.

"Need a little inspiration?" Lang says. The man across the table has the pale, clammy countenance of someone in need of a transfer.

Sig nods and starts to fumble in his pack for a chit but Lang waves him off.

"Nah. You're a friend."

"Gracias," says Sig, visibly relieved.

Lang doubts there's anything in there to fumble for anyway and he doesn't want to do the whole 'Oh shit, I lost my chit, but I'm good for it' dance. Not with someone who helped him drag the crazed wraith that Raf had become back to Rancho Arqueros that last horrible week.

"Just don't tell Zeeb I let you slide. Sabes? Can't afford to piss him off. I need a little earnings right now."

"Claro," Sig says gratefully. "I won't."

Lang downs the last of the whiskey and stands. "Vamos aviados," he says with a touch of irony.

Sig gets to his feet, shooting Lang an enquiring look. Lang shakes his head, bashful. "I mean for *you*. I'm only here for a couple of weeks. Can't be getting all CERS-ado or it'll be a bad time back home."

"Yeah, that must've been rough," Sig says and Lang gives him a you-don't-know-the-half-of-it grimace. "When're you headed back?"

"Navidad."

"And you're gonna stay back there after that? Like *forever*?"

Lang shrugs. "That's the plan."

He cuts off further questioning by stubbing the smoke out in the ashtray and pushing his way through the crowd to the door. Sig catches up to him as he opens it and they disappear into the press of people on the street in the rich blue twilight.

CELAN FLOPS ONTO HER BED face first, every limb a dead weight. This whole week has been one disaster after another. First, her screen malfunctioned in the middle of a complex coding run in Comp, holding everyone up while she was moved to a new one. The next day she somehow left her server in the caf and missed the first fifteen minutes of an exam. Then today, in GenLab, all the micropipettes looked like transfers, which unnerved her to the point that her hands shook and she dropped one, spattering its contents all over the floor.

"What's the matter with you?" Bev, her lab partner, had hissed. "You're as useless as a fuser." The epithet is so common that it usually doesn't even register. Today, though, it had felt like a punch in the gut.

"Don't feel well," she'd muttered, as they scrambled to clean up.

"Well go to a MedLab then and stop messing up our work!"

With that she'd excused herself, practically running out of the lab and tearing off her protective gear like it was strangling her. She stuffed it in a Sanichute and sat in the bathroom for the rest of the period, trying to compose herself before the next class.

But this is nothing that's going to be cured in a MedLab. *Unless it's like the one in my dream.*

A grim chuckle. That's the one thing that, try as she

might, she *hasn't* been able to forget.

Celan rolls over, tucking her server under the pillow and out of sight. No way is she going anywhere near the caf tonight. She doesn't want to see anyone.

She just wants to sleep, but the fear that another dream might come and make things worse clamps down like a vise. So she pads down the hall to the library and browses through her father's vast collection, looking for something completely unrelated to real life to take her mind off things.

She tugs down a slim volume: *Naked Lunch*. Intriguing title, but after skimming a few pages she's thoroughly soured.

More like lose your lunch, she thinks. Keeps looking.

High up on a shelf in a forgotten corner she finds the perfect thing: *Hobbits, orcs, and elves. That should do it.*

She tugs down *Fellowship of the Ring* and flips through the old, familiar pages with affection. Then she tucks it under her arm and heads for the kitchenette, carefully setting it down to make a cup of tea. She takes the little pot from its place on the shelf and thumbs the reader at the faucet, collecting a small gush. Switching on the hot plate she roots around in a drawer until she finds the tea bags and a packet of crackers.

The water is bubbling now and she pours it out. Then, mug in one hand and crackers balanced on the book in the other, she returns to her room. But a sudden thought occurs, and so she puts the book down on her bed and slips back into the library, where she pours a healthy slug of her father's best vintage Scotch into her tea.

Thus armed, she whooshes her bedroom door shut behind her and props herself up in bed, fragrant tea steaming on the nightstand. She pops a cracker into her mouth, chewing as she opens the musty cover and joins the expected party.

The tea and the novel help remove her from her recent troubles, to the point where, hours later, she barely hears Theodore come in and grumble off to bed. She's almost to Rivendell when despite her best efforts, she drowses and sleeps.

A huge moon coats the world in platinum. She's swimming toward it, up a stream that flows steadily down from the mountains. Silvery waves spill over her as gravity relaxes and she ascends, ever upwards. Finally the stream widens out into a deep pool and she rolls onto her back, bobbing weightless as the stars reel overhead. When she tires of floating, she gains purchase on the gravelly bottom and stands. Hair and limbs dripping, she emerges naked and shivering onto the shore.

Then she's clothed and dry and hiking along a twisting forest path. Up ahead, the night air is full of the beckoning sounds of music and laughter. The trunks of fir and aspen begin to thin until up on a bare rise a small stone hut is revealed, ablaze with light, a party in full swing within. She doesn't recall having been invited, but it looks welcoming so she approaches, mounting the broad steps and crossing the threshold to the inside.

Twin blasts of heat and noise hit her as she enters. However tiny the hut looks from the outside, inside it is an endless maze and she wanders from room to room before coming to rest next to a battered sofa. She stops for a moment, deliberating, as a steady buzz of conversation rises and falls around her. She has the feeling that she's looking for someone, but she can't recall who or why.

There's a happy shout to her right as two friends meet, kiss, and embrace. Her eyes dart in that direction and she's trying to make up her mind whether to try that way or not when the crowd parts like a curtain for a familiar figure. He looks good, neat and kempt, and his hair is shining blond instead of the prickly-pear shade he used to wear. He cranes his neck, spots her, and comes right over.

She stares at him, confused, until his face ignites in a grin. She's not sure whether to laugh or cry or simply hug him when Taegh takes her hands in his and looks – deep and infinitely kind – into her eyes.

She wakes with a start, mouth sour and cheek plastered against the pages of the book. The overhead light boils down from the ceiling. Squinting, she rolls over to shut it off, plunging the room into darkness. She fumbles for her server. The time reads 03:03.

The afterimage of Taegh's luminous face burns in her retinas and she blinks in trepidation. Was he haunting her? Accusing her? The awful recollection of her last moments with him in life makes her shudder. But in the dream he was kind, understanding. Was he trying to tell her something? At least she didn't dream about fusing – but as soon as the thought occurs the famished feeling tugs at her gut with renewed vigor.

Celan sits up and catches a glimpse of her reflection shadowed in the windowpane – like a ghost, insubstantial. Or an image from an old world screener.

My Life as a Tech: Act 1.

But that's ridiculous.

This *is* her real life. That other stuff doesn't count.

So why did she dream of Taegh then – why did he rise like a specter from some long gone grave of a life that until recently had been reduced to nothing but a few indistinct images and faded sensations? Sunflowers in a field. The smell of the dusty mountains. The shimmery green pools at Rancho Pescados.

That fusing dream opened the floodgates somehow and now the memories swarm like bees. Scenes from her early life – racing to 'scuela with Tanny and Max, Oso nipping at their heels; the fiesta and fireworks on Liberation Day; her mother's sad, sweet smile. And darker things – her fight with Jillyanne, the trip to Transway with Cyrinda and Taegh. Dirty feet dancing drunk around a bonfire with skirts a-swirl and head thrown back to the stars; the night air crisp as apples as Cyrinda's voice sent chills down the spine and Taegh's guitar rang like a bell.

He was a fuser. So was Cyrinda, sometimes. And so were many of their friends. It hadn't seemed like such a terrible thing back then. It was part of their whole little world, their music, their freedom and joy. But it was an illusion, a fantasy created to cover the foolish costs of a heedless existence. It was all erased years ago. It got burned away because it was bad. What Cyrinda and Taegh did was wrong and they paid for it with their lives.

But she, Celan, was saved. She's here now – safe and sound, educated – and so there is no reasonable explanation for why she should crave something so unsavory. It would be a dishonor to her father, to her pod, a disgrace to herself. Yet even as she counsels herself thus she feels desire tugging at her sleeve like a little child wheedling, 'Please? Just once, just one more time and I'll never ask for anything again.'

Maybe she wouldn't even have to fuse. Maybe she could just take a little, like from a dropper.

She shoves the thought away.

No.

Eight days until Navidad Eve. She should call it off; tell them she's not going out to Transway. But every time Bryan slips her that secret smile the words wither on her tongue.

It's just one night and it's just for a few hours and we'll all be together and we'll be perfectly fine.

And she's a tech. She'll be in uniform. What's she going to do, ask some random expro to borrow their transfer? No one in their right mind would give her any transferon even if she begged for it.

And even if she *could* somehow get some, she couldn't take it or she'd never make it back through the scanners.

So she's safe. One hundred percent.

But it's a long time before she falls back to sleep.

6

Merry and bright. Theodore whistles cheerfully as he surveys the preparations for tonight's Navidad Eve celebration. *Merry and bright indeed.*

This is shaping up to be one of the best weeks he's had in a long time.

His lucky interception of Ariana in the transer lab seems to have served its purpose – he's checked the recs and she hasn't been back to snoop around the Barsoom Room. Leave it to Alton to bore her senseless with bot tests. He'll definitely continue to keep an eye on her, but he's got plenty of other matters to occupy his attention.

Two days ago they made a huge breakthrough in low-gravity mitigation, an excellent result he's made sure to impress upon Nigel's group. Plus, he's taken Martinez's suggestion to heart and assembled a working group of Ags, Mechs, and a few interested Gens to help design a holo mock-up of a far-future, fully-terraformed Mars – one that looks and feels like home. He'll keep the interim designs of course, for reference – the bot-built colonies half-tunneled into bare Martian rock and sand that fill him with such a sense of possibility. But if others need to see more, cannot stretch their imaginations further without visual prompting, then he will stretch for them. That is what a Lead does, after all.

He grins as he gazes out across the plaza, enjoying the pleasant bustle of fir trees being hoisted upright and decked with lights and other gegaws by some junior SocTechs. Ex-pro SanTechs brought the trees in from the mountains this morning and decontaminated them. It's become traditional to share this task in common between Transway and Albakirk, and all who can pass the transferon scans at the gate will be welcomed in to view the resulting display this evening. There's usually a very good turnout.

And vice versa. There will be a flood of tech revelers out onto Transway tonight as well. Truthfully, he wouldn't mind being among them, but as a Lead SocEn his place is here for the duration of the festivities. He, Martinez, and Ariana will serve as a live demonstration of the precedent of Unity and give the Transway denizens a show of friendly faces to place with what surely must be intimidating names. The free chits they'll be handing out won't hurt either. Ariana tends to approach this task with all the enthusiasm of someone being forced to eat dirt, but seeing as how she seems to have dialed down the anti-Transway rhetoric in pursuit of loftier goals he's hoping for a better attitude from her this year.

Lana, however, will likely be among the festive throngs going out through the gate. But that's also a tradition of sorts – for the pods of eighteens to go out for a little adventure to celebrate their years together before they split. He's not going to concern himself over it. She'll be with Shariah and Bev and Bryan and the rest of them and they're not going to go too far.

And she's been so on edge lately that a night out might do her good. Proposal stress, to be sure, but she's been so jumpy he was almost relieved when he saw a little Scotch missing from his bottle the other night. He'd checked her botrecs, of course, but they didn't show more than a shot having been consumed. And it *is* the season for revelry and he's certainly not one to begrudge the occasional indulgence. Though if it reoccurs once proposals are in he'll be sure to have a talk with her. Now is not the time to be developing bad habits.

Plenty of time for that once you're PostEd.

He chuckles to himself as his server buzzes and he digs it out of his pocket, certain that whatever news it brings is going to be good.

FOR THE FIFTH TIME IN an hour, Celan peeps out her bedroom window, eyes raking the scrubby flats restlessly. The day that had dawned so crisp and sunny has clouded over until, at almost 20:00, the sky is caked in a layer of pinkish orange.

Maybe it will snow; maybe it will snow and they'll decide not to go.

But she knows it's hopeless. Nothing but a full-blown blizzard is going to stop anyone from going out to Transway tonight. And there isn't one predicted. Just flurries. Still, she shivers. The sky looks as strange as she feels.

Proposals are due a week from today. There'll be a short review period and then will come the announcements – then she'll know whether she really can cut it as a SocEn. And she needs to know, needs it to happen as fast as possible. Needs some proof that she's fine and it's all going to be OK.

Because they're getting worse – the dreams, the cravings – and the strain is starting to take a toll. She's out-of-sync, self-conscious. This is more than normal proposal stress. She must have somehow kicked off some kind of trauma from that whole horrible incident, a lifetime ago, on Transway. She should tell her father, go to a MedLab. They can do redacts on most forms of trauma these days.

But that would raise too many unanswerable questions. Because it's all there in the Bank – nothing has happened to her to account for any kind of trauma during the time she's lived here. And even if she said it was from before, from Winnipeg, that still wouldn't explain why all her scans here failed to detect anything amiss for the past seven years. She's pretty sure she knows why, though. But she can't tell anyone about *that*.

Because if anyone ever found out where she really came from it would be the end of any chance at SocEn. She'd probably end up a SanTech. An embarrassment. The crazy transer daughter.

A failure.

She cringes at the thought as her server buzzes: Shariah.

No way out now. She's just going to have to grit her teeth and deal.

THE PLAZA IS PACKED WITH revelers and the two girls skirt the outside of it as much as possible, hoping to avoid any parental entanglements. In a quiet little alcove near the main gate, Bryan and Kirk are practically dancing with excitement next to a glum-looking Bev. She purses her lips when she sees Celan and Shariah.

"About time," she says sourly. "Thought maybe you reconsidered."

I wish, Celan thinks.

"Where's Lucas?" Shariah says. "Did *he* reconsider?"

Bryan shrugs. "Who knows?" he says, just as a bored-looking Lucas emerges from the throng and lopes over to the group.

"All right." Lucas sighs like it's a MedLab appointment. "Let's get this over with."

With all now accounted for they approach the gate to find weedy, red-haired Wes and his strapping friend Victor waiting for them.

"No servers?" Wes says, double checking. He'd told them to leave their servers in their rooms instead of taking them out to Transway. Apparently there's quite a market for bootleg servers out there.

They all shake their heads no.

Satisfied, Wes prints the reader and ushers them past the throngs lined up for the scanners and out into the chilly night.

"See?" he says. "Easy."

Bev shakes her head, muttering about how they weren't even asked to declare a destination, but Bryan and Kirk give her such disgusted looks that she clamps her mouth shut and crosses arms over her chest, refraining from further criticism of the techs on duty.

"It's freezing out here," she gripes instead. "How do they stand it?"

"Walk faster," grunts Victor, pumping arms and legs with vigor. "Gets the blood moving."

"How far is it?" asks Celan.

"Kid's never been out before," Wes says pityingly.

"Of course I have," she retorts. "My father takes me to the Saturday market sometimes. I mean how far is it to the *wayvern*?"

"It's one of the closest ones, don't worry. And the most famous too. I bet even you kids've heard of Arlo's."

Her heart stops.

That can't be right.

Arlo's was destroyed the night of Cyrinda and Taegh's last show; burnt to ashes – along with both of them.

"But – " she chokes out. "Isn't that one… gone?"

Victor turns to look at her, impressed. "Girl knows her stuff."

Celan is glad for the dark so they can't see the flush on her cheeks. "My father," she stammers, "he did the investigation. He told me all about it."

"Yeah, the original one burned down years ago," Wes says. "But they built a new one right up the street. It's nice and safe. You kids'll be totally fine there, don't worry."

"They still have the original Maddy's." Victor leers.

"We are NOT going to Maddy's!" This from Shariah.

"No way," adds Bev.

Wes grins. "You have to be PostEd anyway. And you can't chap anybody in. But you *kids*'ll have fun at Arlo's. We'll be back to get you around 23:30."

ATRAVESAR – TO BREAK THE SKIN

Bryan and Kirk exchange disappointed frowns as Victor and Wes laugh and a small group of older techs approaching on the road looks up at the sound. Fervently, Celan hopes they will say something, challenge them in some way, turn them around and march them right back into the city and deliver them straight to the strictest SocEn they can find. Anything to avoid having to see Arlo's again. But the closer the group gets the more apparent it is that they've been imbibing a fair share of Transway cheer. They offer nothing aside from assorted hearty waves and slurry hellos.

She watches them go, her last escape route closing off as she curses herself for ever agreeing to this. But there's nothing to do now other than face whatever old ghosts this little adventure scares up. Hopefully, the new version of Arlo's will bear but slight resemblance to the old.

Resigned, she resumes her forward march, the lights of Transway looming ever larger and brighter. Then someone taps her on the shoulder and she jumps.

"Getting cold feet?" Shariah gibes. "You don't look too happy."

Celan shudders. "Cold everything."

"Well this *was* your idea – "

"It was Bryan and Kirk's idea."

"But you were into it."

"Whatever."

"Don't whatever me," Shariah snaps. "You were perfectly happy about it before. You were positively *glowing* that day in the caf."

"Just shut up, Shariah, OK?" She doesn't want to be reminded again of her stupidity. The after-effects of that weird dream. The way she let her crush on Bryan override her common sense. Cheerful flirting is the last thing she feels capable of right now.

"Fine," Shariah says, "I'll go talk to my *friends* then." She stomps off towards Bryan and Kirk, hooking Bev's arm and tugging her along.

Perfect, Celan thinks. *Just perfect.*

But she only has a minute more to fret before the little road they're on spills out onto the wide bright avenue of Transway, and she has to focus her full attention on staying close to her companions as they twist and turn through the maze of bodies on the sidewalk.

People of all shapes and sizes, tech and transer alike, whizz by in a blur under the white-hot glare of lit-up signs and stalls. Some of the decoration is Navidad-inspired but a good amount of it looks like business as usual. Large signs blink on and off announcing shows and bands, popular performers, games of chance. Celan's head starts to swim under the dazzle of it all. She doesn't remember Transway being this gaudy.

Suddenly, the group stops short, causing her to slam into Lucas's back. He grunts but doesn't turn around. She peers over his shoulder at the building in front of them.

Her stomach turns over.

It's Arlo's all right – an exact replica, down to the last garish mural and dirty window pane. They've even eschewed the dizzy lights in favor of the same simple wooden board outside, scrawled with the names of the bands playing that night, just like in the old days.

In her mind there's a burst of flame. Screaming. Running. Calling their names. *Cyrinda! Taegh!* Her heart starts to pound and a thin sheen of moisture breaks out on her forehead.

I can't go in there.

But Bryan struts ahead and pulls open the door as Wes and Victor take their leave with casual waves.

"Ladies," he says, chivalrous, and there's no other choice. Bev and Shariah glide past him, giggling, so she drags her mind back into the present and forces her wobbly legs to carry her inside.

CELAN SLUMPS DEEP INTO THE booth and takes a big gulp of beer, wishing she could disappear.

How much longer until 23:30?

She pats her breast pocket then remembers that her server's not there; she cranes her neck around the crowded room looking for a clock but doesn't spot one.

Having left the city at 20:15, she estimates that it took about twenty minutes to walk here. And they've only been here about twenty mintues so far. So, still over two hours to go.

She sighs and takes another swig as the music from the band onstage clangs hollowly in her head and the laughter of her podmates chitters around her. Despite a few early gripes about the cleanliness of the table and the smoke in the air (mostly from Bev and Shariah) they all seem to be settling into wayvern life nicely. Though from the sheer number of uniforms in evidence it's obvious that this is mainly a tech hangout these days.

It's a fake Arlo's – it's not even real, she tells herself again.

If only it didn't so closely resemble the original.

Across the table, Shariah turns to Bryan and raises her glass.

"Cheers!" she says brightly. "To a guy with much better taste in women than *some* people we know." She waives the back of her hand in Kirk's general direction, needling him again for his alleged ogling of their shapely server. Everyone but Celan laughs as Shariah and Bryan clink glasses and wink at each other.

Perfect, she thinks. *Now they'll get together and I'll be totally alone forever and no one will ever –*

Her throat tightens ominously and she gets to her feet, sliding out of the booth and taking off into the crowd without a word; she doesn't want to be the weird girl who cries for no reason. There's a bathroom near the entrance and so she heads in that direction, struggling to maintain her composure until she is safely alone. The women's room's outer door is propped open, but the three inside stalls are closed. She fidgets in the mirror as she waits for one to be free.

Is Shariah really going to flirt with Bryan all night?

That is just so wrong. Shariah's her best friend. She knows how Celan feels about him.

How could she?

Furious, she kicks at the trashcan and it goes skidding out into the hall.

"Hey," a voice says, "what the fuck?"

Celan ducks out of view as a stall door crashes open and a girl staggers out, completely oblivious to her presence. She hurries into the vacated stall, overhearing an angry exchange between the girl and whoever got hit with the trash can in the hall.

82

ATRAVESAR – TO BREAK THE SKIN

She slams the toilet lid down and sits, slumped sideways against the thin wall, and closes her eyes as a few stubborn tears squeeze out. Bryan had liked her that day in the caf, she's sure of it. She'd been so free that day, so relaxed and confident. But now, she can barely say two words to him.

Of course he wants Shariah, who wouldn't? She's perfect. While I'm a total fraud. The good daughter, applying for SocEn! When all I can think about is picking up a transfer and –

She jumps to her feet before she can finish the thought and bangs out of the stall, charging blindly into the hall, where she runs smack into a tall, dark-haired figure in a worn overcoat. A guy. She glances up, ready to mutter a hasty apology, but instead feels an electric shock of recognition. That face. He looks like an older version of…

"Max?" One of her best childhood friends. From Rancho Pescados.

The guy gazes down at her as if from a great height, pupils small and swimming in their own private ocean. His face is coated with a thin sheen of moisture, as if he's been running, but his breath is even. He regards her with vague, friendly curiosity – like he knows he should know her from somewhere but can't quite place her.

"Hey now, que pas'?" he drawls, scratching his chin. "Pretty girl like you shouldn't be looking so sad."

The tears threaten again and she blinks up at the ceiling to hold them in.

"Look like you lost your transfer or something. But don't worry. I can always spare a little for a sweet face like that."

In dreamtime, he reaches into his pocket and produces the vial. He unscrews the cap and draws some fluid up into the dropper. Celan parts her lips to protest but finds herself accepting a few drops under the tongue instead. She's never tasted transferon before – it's a strange sort of salty-sweet. She runs her tongue along her teeth trying to parse the flavor.

"Gracias," she says to the guy. She's positive that he's Max, but he doesn't seem to recognize her. Whatever he sees out of those flying eyes, though, it's not a tech.

"Anytime, chiqui. You have a good night."

He stuffs hands into fraying pockets and strolls to the exit at the end of the hall. There's a blast of chilly air as the door swings open and shut, and he is gone. Celan leans against the rough cinderblock wall and bangs the back of her head once, twice, against it – torn between dread and immense, intense relief.

7

Ariana's eyes tick back and forth across the plaza like a metronome, picking points of neat blue and tan out of the crowd of garish expro families with their grubby children. Too many children; every year breeds more mouths to feed. Not that they don't have the technology. It's the principle of the thing – only a small minority of them actually do any useful work. The rest are a teeming mass of ignorance and vice.

At least not all of them breed though; the sexually deviant ones can't. Plus a lot of the intoxic ones die young. There's some comfort in that.

But she'll never understand the kind of warped impulse responsible for their choosing to eschew the pursuit of genetic perfection in the first place. Why hold back progress? Some kind of sick nostalgia for suffering? A twisted lust for the special pain of martyrdom?

Transferon aside, that was truly the worst of the idiotic ideas espoused by Jane Lees and her followers – the original transers who left Albakirk rather than give up their 'miracle drug' – the idea that "genetic diversity" was some kind of righteous crusade when it was really a sad, misguided attempt to cling to an obsolete reality. Because back in the old world, centuries ago, things were very different. Procreation was a total crapshoot then and so genetic variances had to be accepted, or at least tolerated, because people couldn't choose the way they were born.

But now we can. And so there's no earthly reason for any of these defects to continue to exist.

She shakes her head, frowning. The idea that there's no genetic diversity in Albakirk is patently ludicrous anyway. Hybrid vigor is important and so they make sure they have plenty. Genes from all of the traditional human races and ethnicities are preserved in the mix, as long as they code for *positive* traits. Lees' error was in the superstitious belief that there were hidden positives in some of the negative traits – something to do with 'prana'.

Sheer mystical nonsense, no doubt a product of her own defects; though Lees' official MedRecs from her time inside the city were clean enough, legend has it that they were hacked somehow. Very difficult to know exactly what happened over a century ago, but judging by the results it is highly likely that she had the full suite of intoxic genes.

And now we're stuck with the result: Generations of her mutant descendants.

But for the moment, at least, the mutants are safely contained. All the corridors off the plaza are closed tonight and

SocTechs have been stationed at each elevator. Ariana peers down from the dais and checks for the tenth time: All are still at their posts. She sighs, reaches into a large basket, and drops a chit into an outstretched hand.

"Feliz Navidad."

The recipient scurries off down the steps with nary a gracias.

Her other hand tightens its grip on Nathan's arm and he gives it a reassuring pat. She squeezes back, grateful that her husband understands how much she hates this pointless charade. They should just put out a chit dispenser and be done with it. Handouts are the only reason any of them show up anyway.

It's even worse without Shariah here. When her daughter was younger, it had been easy to rope her into rounding out the "family" atmosphere by appearing with her parents on Navidad Eve. She shared her mother's wicked wit and the two of them always had a grand old time mocking the supplicants. But once Lana came along and Theodore allowed her to beg off it became increasingly impossible to force Shariah to do it either.

Just one of the many annoying things he's done – such as actually enjoy this inane display. As if on cue, laughter booms out as he and Martinez share a joke with an expro couple.

Probably half in the bag already.

But Theodore has proven useful lately, as well as completely clueless about her real purpose in the lab. Alton's demonstrations of the testing facilities were instrumental in helping her design a Pollomax trial. It will start in the new year and he will keep it on the quiet – give Theodore no reason to go snooping around in the Bank to see what she's been up to.

She doubts he'll be watching her that closely anyway, but it's better to be safe than sorry. And if all goes well and the trials are a success, maybe this is the last year she'll ever have to do this.

But for now she sighs, and hands over another chit.

"WHERE DID YOU DISAPPEAR TO?" Shariah demands as Celan slides back into the booth. She takes a quick swig of beer and swallows, shrugs.

"Bathroom."

"Was it disgusting?"

"Eh."

Is the room getting brighter? The lights look glowier. Maybe. Or maybe that's just the beer. Celan takes another, smaller, sip.

How long does it take to kick in?

Their table is newly laden with pitchers from which Bev and Kirk are chugging effusively and laughing, making up increasingly ridiculous toasts. Lucas looks bored but resigned. Their server zips by hoisting a heavy tray and Bryan motions to her. She gives him a quick nod that says 'Be right back.'

Shariah raises a brow. "But we just got more beer."

"Yeah, but I'm starving!" says Bryan. "Who wants food?"

Kirk and Bev cheer, but Shariah makes a face.

"What?" Bryan says, an edge of mockery in his tone. "You can't eat expro food? You're drinking their beer."

"That's different," Shariah says, shifting in her seat. "Alcohol is more…sterile. I mean, they actually touch the food. With their *hands*."

Celan chuckles, a mean sliver of her soul enjoying her friend's obvious discomfort with food not made by sanitary tech.

Well, she was *flirting with Bryan.*

"We should get the veggie quesadillas," Celan says. "With extra chile. I hear they're delicious."

Shariah's eyes narrow. "Where'd you hear *that*?"

"My father," she says primly, which is entirely untrue. That was what she and Cyrinda used to order, Taegh picking at whatever they didn't finish. He never had much of an appetite. For food, at least.

"Excellent!" Bryan says, raising a glass.

She smiles wide as he clinks it to hers, a rush of warmth flooding her chest that – whether a result of the gesture or the transferon – is entirely welcome. For the first time this evening, it seems like everything might turn out fine.

Their server reappears, cleavage heaving. "What else would you like?" she says, leaning seductively toward Bryan. He reddens. Shariah snorts derisively.

"We, uh, wanted the, uh, quesadillas – "

"What kind?"

"Uh, veggie…" Bryan starts, but seems to lose his train of thought as the server leans in closer.

"With extra chile," Celan finishes. "Two orders."

"Bueno," the girl says, and vanishes back into the crush without further ado.

Shariah's now pointedly addressing Lucas. Celan takes another sip of beer and grins.

"Thanks," Bryan says, looking sheepish.

"No problem. They can be a little distracting."

"Yeah."

"But that's how they do it. It's no big deal."

Bryan cocks his head. "You're *sure* you've never been here before?"

"Of course not. But my father tells me a lot. And he shows me screeners sometimes. Wants to me to get acquainted with Transway. SocEn stuff." The words come easy now.

"Your father. Yeah. Always seemed like he'd be a pretty heavy guy to have as a dad." He gulps. "I mean, you're always so serious."

She shrugs. "He is; it's true. Still, that doesn't mean I can't have a little fun. Once in a while…." She trails off, circling a finger around the rim of her glass, leaving Bryan to imagine what form that fun might take.

It has the desired effect. His eyes light up and suddenly he's looking at her in a way he never has before. Almost like she's something he wants to touch.

"Cheers," he says, and raises his glass again. She clinks hers to his happily.

The band picks up the pace, pounding out a jumpy rhythm that gets toes tapping. No one's brave enough to dance yet, but Bev and Kirk look like they're close. Bryan's gaze appraises them, then travels to a group of new arrivals at the next table, who are busily brushing powdery white crystals off their hair and clothes.

"Snow!" he says. "Want to go check it out?"

Celan nods. He takes her hand and tugs her out of her seat, towing her in the direction of the door. They leave a few disgruntled revelers in their wake as they snake through the crowd, but no one says much of anything about it. Then they're tumbling out onto a street wild with whipping white flakes. There must be two inches on the ground already and more is coming thick and fast. Together, they slide over the slick sidewalk and around the corner of the building to an empty lot next door.

"Look!" Bryan cries, throwing his free arm wide. "Isn't it great?"

Big fluffy flakes twinkle like falling stars in the lights from the wayvern. Celan tilts her face up, letting them shower her.

Suddenly she's one hundred percent glad she came. She wouldn't have wanted to miss this for the world. She squeezes Bryan's hand. He squeezes back. His mussed hair is haloed in a halogen glow, shining like a vision of everything she's ever wanted. Then, slowly, he pulls her close into the warmth of his body.

We really can be together. He won't hate me. He doesn't hate this.

Her heart leaps as he leans down and presses his lips to hers. They're soft and warm and taste faintly of beer and he keeps them there for what seems like an endless moment until, flushed and grinning, they finally pull apart.

"Come on, let's ditch these guys," he says in a voice like velvet. "Go back inside." He drapes an arm around her shoulders and starts to steer her toward the street, but in the opposite direction of Arlo's.

Celan balks. "You mean back into the *city*?"

He nods. Gently nudges her forward.

"But we can't get back in yet, right?" she says, panic rising. "I mean, don't we have to wait for Wes and Victor? Why don't we find somewhere else – "

"Like where? A room at Maddy's? C'mon Lana, it's Navidad Eve! No one cares about chaps. Anyone at the gate'll print the reader for us."

"But – I don't think – "

"So don't think," he says sweetly. "Don't think at all."

His arm is so warm on her shoulders, the scent of his body like a tonic. She wants nothing more in this world than to dive down so deep inside his kiss that she forgets how to breathe the air.

But she can't.

The scanners at the gate, via a halo effect in the eyes, can detect the presence of transferon up to twelve hours after ingestion. She didn't take that much, only a few drops, so in another couple hours it might wear off. But right now it would definitely show. She could feign shock at the gate; say someone slipped it in her drink…but she can't risk having them track it to Max.

Expros who slip transferon to unwitting techs (and this, while increasingly rare, occasionally does happen) are tracked down and banished. The offenders aren't killed outright – but they are blindfolded and taken far out in the desert to some unknown spot where they're left to their own devices with a little food and water. Theoretically, it's possible for them to survive and find their way back, but no one ever has. The Destierras, the expros call it.

It's possible that she and Max were unobserved by any human or mechanical surveillance and the source of her dosage would be impossible to trace. But she highly doubts it.

Bet there're views all over that place.

And if they see what really happened, see her taking the drops on purpose…

She takes a deep breath, wincing at the words she has to say. "I can't, Bryan. OK? It's not that I don't want to but – "

The warm arm slips off her shoulders and he takes a step back, looking stung. "It's not like I'm trying to force anything on you. We don't have to do anything you don't want to. I just thought you might like to spend a little time with me."

"I do, Bryan. I really, really do. But I can't right now."

He shakes his head. "Thought you'd relaxed a little."

"I have!" she says. "Really, you have no idea. I just can't go back into the city with you *right now.*"

He blinks once, uncomprehending. "I don't get you, Lana." And, turning stiffly, he marches off, veering away from Arlo's and up toward Albakirk.

Celan closes her eyes, letting feathery flakes brush her face. There's nothing she can do. She was so close to having him and now he'll never want her again. She had one chance and she blew it.

If I didn't take the transferon…

But if she hadn't, she would have been a weepy mess all night. She wouldn't have been able to flirt with him and he never would have kissed her in the first place.

It's the truth. She opens her eyes. A few bright flakes wink and go out. She heaves a sigh like a weary wind down a canyon.

Then a new voice startles her out of her thoughts.

"Hey tech girl, what's with all the drama? You couldn't

give the guy a little love?" The tip of a glowing smoke emerges from a dark corner of an alley, followed by the beak of a nose and a curled lip.

The expro's tone is mocking, but his overall air is affable.

Might as well be upfront.

"Oh I would have, believe me," she says. "But I never would have made it past the scanners."

He does a quick double take then rips into a cackle, hanks of ink-dark hair whipping around his face. She sweeps her gaze up a lanky frame covered by boots, long johns, and a frayed t-shirt under the remains of what appears to be a yellow sundress. A ratty acid-green sweater and a tatty pink scarf top off the ensemble.

"Nice dress."

He stops laughing but he's still smiling. "Nice try, tech girl."

"What?"

"Your little joke. About the scanners, I mean. No one transed you." His lips twitch from a smile to a sneer. "Ever heard of the Destierras, chiqui? Or don't they teach you about that at your 'scuela?"

"I know," she says, straightening her spine. "I know all about them. But I'm not turning anyone in."

He takes a deep drag and blows it out in her general direction.

"Oh yeah?" he says. "Why not?"

And in that measuring look is every kid she used to run around with in the ranchos when she was ten years old. Chasing each other through woods and streams and fields. Racing through the dusty old houses scavenging for anything that hadn't been picked over a hundred times already. But sitting quietly too, with the elders, and learning how to breathe, how to go deep inside and find the healing power of the Universe. She feels a sliver of light, the crack of a door where there was nothing before but a cold grey wall.

She meets his gaze. "Because I took it on purpose. I'm not really one of them."

"Well who are you then? One of their little helpers? But nah, those little shits wear grey. You're in tan. So what'd you do then, steal it? You know they'll bust your ass for that." He tips her the tilted brow of one in the know.

"I'm – Celan M – Mairs," she stammers and then picks up speed, suddenly desperate to get it all out – all the things she hasn't been able to say to anyone for what feels like an eternity. "I grew up in Rancho Pescados. Then my mom died and my sister left and when I was eleven I came out here to visit her and see her band play. But there was this big fire. At Arlo's. The old one. She and her man Taegh died, but I got away and then my dad found me. He's a tech. So now I live in the city."

The expro stares – in disbelief or wonder she can't tell.

"I came out tonight with my pod, uh, friends." The snow has stopped and she's suddenly aware of the cold. She wraps arms around herself, shivering. "I had this dream recently. That I was f – had taken some transferon. And then I woke up and felt like I really had. And then tonight I was upset and this guy Max – I think I knew him from when I was a kid – he said I must have lost my transfer so he gave me a couple of drops. So I really can't go back inside…for a while."

The expro drops his smoke and stubs it out with the toe

of his boot. Then, with stunned eyes locked on hers, he crosses the space between them in two long strides.

"Celan *Mairs*?" he says, with something close to awe.

"What?" she says. "You know me?"

"Everyone around here knows about you and your family. I mean, your mom and Arlo! Your sisters – how she tried to make them go live in the ranchos but they came back to Transway instead. It's a famous story. There's a big mural of you all on the wall behind the old Arlo's."

"*Really?*"

"Yeah. They thought you were killed that night. In the fire. No one ever found you. Cyrinda could never tell any of it. She never even remembered who she was."

Her heart clenches. "Cyrinda's alive?"

He glances away. "She was. For a little while."

Celan blinks up at scattered wisps of clouds and icy stars. "I looked for them," she chokes out. "Her and Taegh. When the fire broke out I hoped – but then people said they were gone. So I ran. I left. I was so scared."

Slowly, solicitously, he draws her rigid form close, strong hands on shaking shoulders. A fissure of sorrow cracks and begins to dissolve.

"You were a kid. You went with your dad."

"What happened to her?" she says, face wet against faded yellow cloth. He smells of juniper and campfire, laced with the faintest whiff of whiskey.

"They took her back to the ranchos. People took care of her til she passed."

"Like they did for my mom when she was walking."

"Yeah." His voice catches, and she turns her chin up in

96

time to see the shadow of some unsalved ache slide across his face.

"Who walked on you?" she ventures.

"My cousin. Rafael. We were like brothers."

They regard each solemnly other for a moment; then, suddenly awkward, drop their arms and shuffle their feet in the snowy weeds. But he catches her hand and holds it.

"Well," he says. "Since you can't go back into the city, why don't you come give me a little love instead?" He throws her a suggestive wink in a parody of lust and gives her hand a playful swing.

Celan swallows. She knows she should go back into the wayvern. Find the rest of her pod. Maybe the transferon will have worn off by midnight. But there's something so familiar about this boy, like a long-lost friend. No one will know that she took off with him; they'll all think she's with Bryan.

And she's just so sick of pretending to be someone she's not. Maybe now, for a few precious hours, she won't have to.

Decided, she prompts. "And you are?"

"Lang Shays, ma'am."

"OK, Lang Shays. But I'm not going back into fake Arlo's. Do you know somewhere else?"

"Claro. Forget Arlo's. I've got a much better place."

"Oh yeah?"

"Yeah. Just you wait, tech girl."

Celan laughs. Lang tugs gently on her hand and together they vanish down the alley.

8

They hear the party before they see it, a clamor emanating from somewhere up ahead as they round the corner of a crumbling adobe wall. A big hulk of a house dominates the end of a dark street, bodies and light spilling out into the front yard. A bonfire blazes from a pit and people cluster around it – smoking, laughing, tossing back drinks. All of them are dressed in different variations of Lang's strange attire and a few sport bizarrely-colored hair. Celan balks, squirming in her tan uniform.

"What's *that*?"

"Alamora," Lang says grandly. "It's one of ours. Not someplace techs are welcome. Present company excluded."

She gestures at her clothes. "So…this?"

A shrug. "No one'll care. I mean, you're Celan *Mairs*. People will be amazed to even meet you."

But she shakes her head. "No way. I am not telling anyone who I am. And you better not either."

"Huh," Lang says, scratching his chin. "OK. I just thought you would want – "

"Well I don't." Her shoulders slump. "I just want it to be normal for once, you know?"

"Yeah. I do."

"So don't call me 'Celan' in front of anybody. You can tell them I'm…" She pauses, considering. She doesn't want to use 'Lana' either. "Kimbra," she finally says.

"OK, *Kimbra*. No problem." He squints, looking her up and down. "Maybe we can fix this. Does that top come off?"

"Huh?"

"I mean, is it separate from the pants? Do you have something on under it?"

"Yeah," she says, reddening. "There's, like, a bra."

"So take it off then."

"What?"

"The *top*."

"Oh." Feeling more foolish by the moment, Celan unzips the top of her uniform and hands it to Lang. The chilly night air hits her instantly and she crosses arms in front of her chest. Lang removes his ratty sweater and drapes it over her shoulders like a cape. It hangs past her thighs. You can barely see the pants now. Even so, she bends down and cuffs them up to just below the knee.

"Thanks," she says, straightening as she slips her arms through the sleeves and buttons a few of the buttons.

"No problem. We'll leave this here," he says, stashing the top behind some old crates, "for later."

They skirt the crowd out in front of the house and enter through a back gate. Gallantly, Lang holds it open as a blast of tuning guitar fires up from inside, followed by a skipping staccato drum beat. He takes her hand again and dives for a wide patio, where people mob a table in front of a row of casks.

Lang waves at a handsome, broad-shouldered guy with a head full of little blue braids who seems to be in charge of drink distribution. The guy nods back and they cut through the line and draw up beside him.

He hands them each a full cup. "I was wondering where you took off to."

"Little business over at Arlo's," Lang says, taking a thirsty gulp. "Want you to meet someone."

Celan smiles nervously.

"This is Kimbra, over from Rancho Pescados."

Blue braids grins at her. "Brophy," he says, filling and proffering mugs to outstretched hands with a true economy of motion. "This your first time out on Transway?"

She nods.

"And they let you out with this guy?" He gives a low whistle.

"I didn't exactly ask permission."

Brophy guffaws. "Nice."

"Zeeb about to play?" Lang says.

"Still warming up."

"Bueno. Didn't wanna miss 'em." He tips his cup in thanks as Brophy refocuses on the thirsty masses. Mounting a few short steps, Lang yanks open a battered screen door and bounds into the house. Celan slurps the top inch off her beer and follows him.

A cloud of warm, fragrant air engulfs her as she enters a

large, cluttered kitchen, tables heaped with various bowls and platters of food. People mill around eating and talking, but the main action revolves around the far counter, where a petite girl with a flossy pink bob is perched, holding court.

"So this pinche payaso picks up the fucking pot with his bare hands and of course it's like a thousand degrees and wham – soup tsunami! Took us fucking hours to clean it all up. Well, him anyway. It's my kitchen. I run his ass."

The girl pulls a face and pokes out her smoke for emphasis. The group around her laughs as her sharp blue eyes dart up and pin Lang instantly. She gives him a sly little smirk as he hurries them past the tables and into a bustling hallway.

"Who was that?" Celan says.

"Mara. Brophy's girl. Fucking hilarious but she'll talk your ear off. I gotta go find Zeeb before they start."

He cuts through a gaggle of really young-looking girls slouched around the bottom of a shabby staircase, who all eye him hopefully, and into a cavernous main room with a low wooden riser set up against the far wall. On it, a hefty guy in a purple poncho is strumming a guitar, flanked by another guitarist and a bass player with a drummer behind them – in classic formation.

"Check, check," the big guy says into a microphone, shaggy brown bangs flopping in his eyes.

Celan plucks at Lang's sleeve. "Hey," she says into his ear. "How do you all get power in here?"

"What?"

"Off Transway? The lights? The microphones and stuff?"

"Oh." He grins. "Brophy hooked it all up. It's wired to solar panels on the roof."

"Really?"

"Yeah. He did a lot of work for the techs back in the day."

"What does he do now?"

"Mostly odd jobs around the wayverns. He can fix any-thing."

From the makeshift stage, the big guitarist is peering down at them curiously. "Lang," he intones. "Who's the new bitch?"

"Hey!" Celan says, indignant, but Lang chuckles so she smooths her hackles. Cyrinda and Taegh's friends used to talk shit like this all the time.

"Langton Shays gotta a little woman/Now I gotta get me a brand new man," the guy trills in falsetto, strumming a twelve-bar blues. Then he claps a hand over the strings and leans away from the mic. "Que pas'?" he says.

Celan cuts her eyes to her companion. "Langton?"

"No one calls me that."

"Only his most *intimate* friends," says the guitar player, waggling his brows in an exaggerated leer.

Celan turns to Lang, playing along, hands on hips like she's mad. "Is there something I should know?"

With that the big guy finally cracks, collapsing to his knees in laughter, guitar bouncing against his stomach. "He's not really my type."

"Even in this stunning dress?" Lang says.

"Especially in that ugly fucking dress." He offers Celan a damp palm and a friendly smile. "Zeeb Lavinias," he says.

"Kimbra Quinns." She switches her cup to the other hand and gives his a brief shake.

"Well aren't you just a*dor*able." But then his tone turns serious. "You take care of business?" he asks Lang.

"Claro."

"No problemas?"

"Nada."

Zeeb grunts with satisfaction and jumps to his feet, surprisingly agile for his size. "We'll talk more later. Gotta play."

"Hey boys," he drawls into the mic. "Let's go. A-two-three-four!"

The room erupts in a crashing wall of sound that sends an electric shock down Celan's spine. She twirls, suddenly ecstatic. Lang stows their drinks behind an amp as the crowd presses in and then he takes her hands, pulling her close. She feels the rhythm throb deep in her core and abandons herself to the dance.

The transferon seems to be coming on stronger now, or maybe it's the drink or Lang's touch. Or all of it together – she doesn't know. The colored lights strung around the room glitter like confetti as she bounces, spins, and dips in the crush of other bodies in motion, the experience filling her with a exuberance she hasn't known in years.

She has a fleeting moment of pity for all those suckers at the fake Arlo's.

Lang's eyes are bright, the color of pine trees on snow, and as he locks that gaze on hers the warmth of the familiar is suddenly spiked with a thrill of something more. She presses against him, released from all sense of caution, of fear. He presses right back.

After the first set they're sweating and grinning at each other like fools. Lang grabs their drinks from where they've been catching sips between songs and downs the last of his.

"Refill?"

She nods happily.

They push through the steaming throngs out to the patio, where once again Brophy fills their cups without making them wait in line.

At the edge of the mob they stand for a few moments, breathing in the frosty air and peeping at each other shyly. Then Lang nudges her toward a little nook along the east wall of the house. It's cozy and private, removed from the tumult of the party; but once they're alone and not buffered by the press of a crowd, she can't quite meet his eyes. She doesn't know what to say so she sips at her drink. It's deliciously cool after the heat of the dance.

"So do you all live here?" she finally says, groping for conversation.

"Who?"

"Brophy, Mara, Zeeb." She tastes the names on her tongue.

"Some of 'em. Brophy and Mara. Sig, the drummer. Danilo and Alex – but they're not around a whole lot. Zeeb lives at Casa del Oso but he's always over here anyway."

"Oh."

"I live here too, when I'm in town."

"Where else do you live?"

"Arqueros."

"You're a *rancho*?" This seems completely incongruous.

"Kind of."

She doesn't press further, just looks down – at the buttons of his sweater, the toes of her boots, anywhere but him.

"Hey," he says softly and she risks one quick glance up.

Lang's mouth curls into a slow smile and Celan feels a swimming sensation. She tries to shake it off, but he reaches out a hand and traces fingertips along her flushed cheek to her chin. Her legs liquefy. Tipping her face up, he moves closer, lush lips parting as they press against hers. The ground seems to tilt underfoot so she leans against the house, letting the solid wall steady her.

The kiss goes on and on. If she thought kissing Bryan was good it's nothing compared to the way she feels now – like the whole world is on fire inside her. Finally he pulls away and they gaze at each other with a kind of stunned enchantment, pulses pounding, until Lang breaks the spell.

"You're a good kisser," he says. "For a tech."

She gives him a light punch on the arm.

He laughs. "Wanna go back inside?"

"Sure," she says, torn between wanting to kiss some more and thinking that it's probably best if they take something so combustive in small doses.

They drift through the yard and up the stairs, oblivious now to anything but each other. In the kitchen Lang pauses by one of the laden tables. He puts his drink down and grabs a sopapilla, slathering it in agave syrup and biting into it with gusto. Then he turns and offers Celan a taste. She savors the sweetness on her tongue, chewing and swallowing the bite of pastry with delight.

She's positive it's the best thing she's ever eaten.

Lang wolfs down the rest and snatches up his drink again, taking her free hand in his and leading her toward the main room in anticipation of the second set. Crushed close in the crowded hall she's already dancing on the inside, heart aloft like a bird or some weightless thing. This isn't anything like how she's ever felt around Bryan. That all seems so silly now. Childish.

This is –

"Bitch!" someone screams, and shoves her hard in the back. Celan slams into Lang, both their drinks flying from their hands and spattering everywhere. There's a swipe at her hair that fails to gain a grip, then Lang spins around lightning-quick and tucks her behind him.

"What the fuck, Jaslene?" he says to a glowering girl in a short red dress.

"Fuck you, *Lang*!" The girl lunges, white hair whipping around a face that would have been pretty if wasn't so twisted with rage. People start to back up, clearing space for the fight.

"Stop it!" he says, grabbing her by the shoulders. He gives her a quick shake. "What the fuck is your problem?"

Celan can barely breathe. Does he already have a girl? Has he been messing with her this whole time? Playing some kind of game with an unsuspecting tech?

Please no. Please. Don't ruin this.

"What's *my* problem?" Jaslene slurs. "*You're* the one with the problem! Ditching me and showing up here with some stupid ranchita. Liar!"

"I didn't ditch you," Lang says. "We didn't have any plans."

"I. don't. mean. tonight," she spits out. "I mean you lying about not having a girl back in the ranchos. Lying about not ditching me for some stupid little *bitch*." She tries a knee in

107

the groin but he twists his hips and she misses.

"'Stante! I mean it."

But she's too far gone, pummeling his chest with her fists until he manages to catch hold of her wrists. Jaslene struggles, trying to break his grip, stabbing at his boots with the points of her high-heeled shoes. Celan watches, horrified, until Mara and a couple of others emerge from the kitchen and finally pull the girl off.

"Fuck you!" Jaslene yells as they drag her away.

In the main room, the music starts up again and the crowd that had gathered for the fight begins to disperse.

Lang turns to Celan, wincing. "Are you all right? I am *so* so sorry."

"What – who – was that?" she stammers.

"My ex-girl," he admits. "But I didn't know she'd be here. Or that she'd act like that."

Celan pulls his sweater tight around her. "I – I don't think I want to stay."

"It's OK. They've got her now. She won't – "

"No," she says. "I want to go back to Arlo's."

"Mira. Let's go upstairs for a minute. Take a breather."

He circles a reassuring arm around her waist and steers her toward the stairs. Dazed, Celan lets herself be led, not wanting this perfect night to end on such a sour note. On the way up to the second floor she gropes for something to say, something to restore a sense of sanity.

"So did you two just break up or something?"

"No," Lang says. "It was ages ago. Like, a year."

"Then why was she so – " A thought occurs, followed by a thrill of fear. "Is she a fuser?"

"What?" he says. "No, not Jas. She hates that shit."

"But her hair – "

"The white? A lot of people just do it for the look these days. Especially when they work at Maddy's."

"Oh."

"But she *was* really drunk. I'll talk to her later. I promise. It'll be all right next time."

Next time.

Celan's heart sinks as she realizes the impossibility of it; no one's going to chap her so she can go make out with some expro. Maybe on a Saturday, she could say she wanted to go to the market...

"I'm not even sure I can get back in this time," she says miserably.

"What? The scanners? Just hang out here until you're clear."

They've reached the landing and he maneuvers them down a dim hallway, stopping at the door to what must be his room. The music pulses below their feet, drumbeats punching up through the floor.

"How long is that though? I only took a little."

"It's always twelve hours," Lang says. "No matter how much you took."

"09:00?" She shakes her head. "I can't wait until then. There'll be no way to explain how I was out all night without a chap. I mean, we had one earlier, but now..." She trails off, biting her lower lip.

Lang furrows his brow. Then his eyes widen like he's thought of something.

"Wait here," he says, opening the door and motioning

her inside.

"What – " she starts to say.

But he cuts her off. "No time to explain. Gotta move." He turns and trots swiftly to the stairs.

"But what if Jaslene comes up here? Should I lock the door?"

"She won't," he calls back. "They've got her. And don't worry – I've got an idea. About a different door."

9

Lang winces, head split with a white-hot stab of pain. *How late was I up last night?*

Or early, actually. Dawn was definitely coming on by the time he weaved his way upstairs. He hadn't meant to stay up all night. After escorting Celan back to Albakirk he'd returned to find that the end of the concert (and the kegs) had cleared out most of the revelers. So he was going to go to bed.

But then Brophy and Mara started up a card game, and Zeeb broke out that good mead, and before he knew it...he attempts to sit up and groans, falling back onto the thin pad on the floor with a dull whump.

He'd had to hustle to get Celan to the transer lab door before the day's key code expired at midnight. There wouldn't be a new one until 7 am. Thank Madre he knew someone desperate enough to have it. One of the fringe benefits of his current line of work.

111

He chuckles weakly, wincing again. As for transferon... maybe a few drops will help the hangover situation.

The stuff he's got now is safe enough – 'scuela-grade, strictly medicinal. He always transes the fluid back to baseline at the end of his shifts. It feels somehow cleaner that way, and makes for less temptation. If he wants anything stronger he'll have to make it deliberately.

But I don't. Want it. Not anymore.

He fumbles for the vial, unscrews the cap, and draws a tiny bit of fluid up into the dropper, parting his lips and letting one, two, three drops fall into the space under his tongue. That should do it. Nothing to do now but wait for it to take effect.

He closes his eyes, breathing in the unwashed funk of the room as a soft breeze ruffles the makeshift curtains and throws a shaft of light like a lover's arm across his chest. He smiles, thinking how nice it would be if Celan was curled up next to him right now.

It's still hard to believe – some random tech girl showing up and claiming to be the long-lost Celan Mairs – and he probably wouldn't have believed it either if he hadn't been there and heard it from her himself. There was such a guilelessness to her, an engagingly lost air that could not have been fabricated; he'd bet serious chits on that.

And the way she kissed him...

His mouth goes dry.

They'd made plans to meet again on the first of January at the same place they'd parted, outside the lab. He said he'd get a roller and wait for her out on the flats. He promised there'd be no further incidents with Jaslene.

Jaslene. He groans again. *What a fucking mess!*

He hadn't thought she'd be at the party; thought she'd be working that night. Although truthfully, he hadn't really thought much about her at all. To his mind, they were long over and done.

And what the fuck does she think anyway? That he's been hiding in the ranchos solely to avoid her; too much of an asshole to be straight and say he started a new thing with some local girl?

Like any of those girls would touch me.

But that's probably exactly what she thinks. So he's got to set the record straight. Tell her – What?

I ran into Celan Mairs outside Arlo's and we really hit it off!

Maybe it's better just to let her hate him.

Sighing, he opens his eyes as the pain in his head begins to recede. His stomach gives a low rumble and he wonders how late it is. But it doesn't really matter. It's not like he has anything to do today.

Then, with a severe jolt of panic, he remembers – it's Navidad! He's supposed to be out at Arqueros for dinner. And he's supposed to *stay* out at Arqueros after that. He promised.

But now that he's met Celan that's just not going to work. He has to come back to Transway; he can't disappoint her. He'll tell them…something. A friend in need. Something.

Scrambling up, he strips off the fragrant remains of last night's party clothes and roots around in a pile on the splintery floor for his old hemp pants and shirt. He pulls them on, but twists around feeling itchy and uncomfortable, giving a long, lingering look to the leggings and dress on the floor. So much more comfortable. But he can't dress like that

113

in the ranchos. All expro'd out – they'd think there was something wrong with him.

Even more than they do already.

He grabs the ratty sweater, though. It's chilly. That they'll understand.

Jamming feet into boots he darts out the door, only to dash in again a moment later and snatch his pack up off the bed. He crouches in front of a beat-up dresser and yanks open the sticky bottom drawer, rummaging around for the little gifts he's collected for the family. Pack filled, he bounds down the stairs two at time.

The clock on the living room wall says one-thirty. They'll start the festivities around three. If he walks he won't get there until after dark – that's not going to go over well. He's got to find someone with a roller.

The kitchen and yard are deserted but maybe Zeeb is still around. He slams out the back gate and hits the alley at a pace that makes his head start to pound again. After two blocks, he slows to a walk and turns the corner. He can see it from here, though – no del Oso roller.

Shit.

His hand drifts toward his pack. Zeeb had given him a 'server' when he'd first started working for him – a clever little device that the techs use for a whole myriad of tasks. But the rogue ones like Lang's are stripped down and strictly for messaging. It's only supposed to be for business, but if he can just find out where Zeeb is...

Then he sees it.

Not the del Oso roller, but further down the street there's a different squat, four-wheeled vehicle parked. A stocky, green-haired guy is pounding on the steering wheel and shouting up at the house in front of him. Not promising, but worth a shot.

"Hey," Lang calls, and the guy turns to glare at him. He jogs over saying, "You headed out to the ranchos today? I need a ride."

The guy laughs mockingly. "Yeah, I'm headed *out*, as soon as this pinche cabron answers the motherfucking door."

Lang shoots him a questioning look.

"Fucker's got my transfer," the guy says. "Sé que lo tienes, fucker!" he yells up at the window. But the house is silent.

Lang does a quick calculation: He's not on a shift and he has no backup. If Zeeb finds out he'll be pissed.

But he needs that ride.

"I can give you all the fuses you want, but I need a ride out to Arqueros."

Interest sparks in the man's eyes. "Can you drive?"

Lang sizes him up. The guy's pretty thick; but he's taller and probably faster. He could probably take him if he tried to do a runner. Still, he hopes this means he's got a Class E on his hands. Then he'll be half asleep the whole way. Much easier to manage. Not like he has much choice at this point, though. He's got to risk it.

"Ay, ese, whatever you want. But I'm late, so let's do it. You can deal with this fucker later."

The guy slides over and tosses him the key. Lang ducks under the solar canopy and drops into the driver's seat, wedging his pack safely between his hip and the door. He taps the key to the starter and the engine whirs to life. He's never driven one of these things before but he's ridden in

Brophy's tons of times.

How hard can it be?

He presses his foot down on the right pedal and turns the wheel hard. The thick, heavy tires kick up a cloud of dust as he completes a U-turn and points the roller in the direction of the old highway. At the corner, he brakes with the left.

Simple.

"Transfer?" the guy says, sniffling a little.

Class E. Got to be.

"Wait'll we're on the road."

The guy smirks. "Think I'm gonna take it and run?"

Lang turns to him, eyes hard.

"I know you're not."

This has the desired effect: The guy's smirk turns sour and he looks away, muttering under his breath.

Mentally, Lang exhales but his relief is fleeting. Now comes the sticky part. Usually his trades are quick – the minute his customers fuse he's out of there. This time, though, he's going to have to sit through the whole thing. Watch this guy get aviados as fuck, knowing full well how good it would feel.

His grip tightens on the wheel.

There's no other choice though. He's just got to get through it. Try not to look, try not to think.

Terra Madre, I really need a drink.

CELAN HONES IN ON THE screen as her code comes to life, tracing out multi-color-coded patterns of various transferon pathways.

D, E, or S? she thinks, *D, E, or S?*

It's important that the paths branch out on their own – or-

ganically, like they would in a real person – but then coalesce
into one of the three classes or (and this is the exciting part)
reach a stable balance point between the three. Without that
element, her project would be worthless. Boring. She'd have
no chance at all. But now she's really got something.

Maybe taking those drops helped her figure it out.

She grins, then shudders a little.

That was a really close call. She still can't believe she
made it back into the city with no one the wiser about her
little adventure.

Almost: There'd been one reeling moment of terror when she'd run into Lucas at the elevator, but he'd just
smirked, and hadn't said a word. Which was good; it meant
they all thought she'd been with Bryan. She was really worried about not having gone back in with them though, because that meant that there was one rec of Wes printing her
out of the main gate at 20:15 and another of her coming
out of the transer lab at 23:50, with nothing in between.
If anyone had noticed that it would've been really hard to
explain. But it seemed like no one had. And there'd been
no one around in the lab at midnight on Navidad Eve to
question her.

So she'd breathed easier, until she saw the message on
her server notifying her of a bot anomaly detected between
20:56 on Navidad Eve and 09:56 on Navidad morning – the
time the transferon was in her system. Not that the bots
had detected *it*, though. They seemed to have shut down;
gone offline entirely during that time. She was to report to
a MedLab for a full workup.

Knees knocking, she'd gone in only to have a bored

MedTech inform her that such anomalies occasionally occurred and it was probably nothing to worry about. But she'd made sure to direct some prana into the works for insurance.

Transing the labs is an old game of hers; something she's done on every trip to the MedLab since the first, when she was eleven and terrified of her father finding something wrong with her. Because if he decided she was a defective expro and didn't want to keep her then where would she go? Back to the ranchos? To her guardian? What if Jillyanne didn't even want her back after all the terrible things she'd said? She had to make sure that didn't happen.

'Look like a normal tech's,' she used to think, squeezing her eyes shut and sending prana with intent. She used to really believe it worked.

Over the years, though, she'd begun to chide herself for being silly; telling herself that she couldn't really transfigure anything anymore even if she wanted to and that the labs were normal because *she* was normal. She kept promising herself she wouldn't do it the next time, but some habits are hard to break.

Maybe it wasn't such a silly idea after all.

Because the bizarre dreams and her intense reaction to Arlo's have proven beyond a doubt that she still has trauma from the night of the fire and it's gone undetected for seven years. Somehow, whatever she did to alter the labs to make her brain look normal had worked. It must have, because even the latest one hadn't found anything amiss. The anomaly was a deemed a bot malfunction; nothing to do with *her*. A quick replacement and she was on her way.

So maybe –

A sudden tap on the shoulder makes her jump. Shariah.

"What?" she says, annoyed.

Her best friend looms over her, glowering. "What exactly happened between you and Bryan the other night?"

Celan shrugs.

Shariah pulls up a chair, undaunted. "Seriously. Neither of you came back to that wayvern and now neither of you will say a word about it."

"You asked *him*?"

"Well, *you* seem to be avoiding me," Shariah sniffs. "And if my best friend won't tell me what happened…"

"Look, I haven't been avoiding you, OK? It's just… we've only got a few more days." She gestures at the screen.

"You're still working on your proposal? I turned mine in last week."

"Well good for you," Celan says shortly, then relents. "But if you really want to know, nothing happened with Bryan. And nothing's going to. If you're interested, be my guest."

Shariah shakes her head in wonderment. "I just don't get you, Lana. You spend all this time pining over the guy and then when he finally shows some interest – "

"We talked, OK? That's it. We aren't right for each other."

"Is he a bad kisser?"

Celan gives her a mysterious half-smile. "You'll have to find that out for yourself."

"Ugh. You are impossible!"

"I'm just busy."

"Whatever," Shariah says. "And I don't want to kiss Bryan. He's disgusting. The way he was looking at that nasty server. I'm never going out there again."

"Right," Celan says, a sharp edge creeping into her tone. "You didn't look like you were having all that bad a time."

"That's not the issue," Shariah hisses. "We all tried it and so now we know. Transway is foul. He ought to know better now. We all should."

"Yeah," Celan says, impassive.

Sharia tsks, irritated, and gets to her feet. With one last imperious look, she flips white-blonde hair over her shoulder and marches stiffly out of the CompLab.

Celan returns to the screen with a sigh, trying to pick up her train of thought from where she left it before the interruption.

Maybe she did transfigure the labs, and if that's the case then maybe she somehow transed the bots too. Shut them off on purpose. Could this an example of transferon acting 'according to the intent of the subject?'

But there was *no intent.*

She hadn't thought about her bots at all when she took that dose (or anything else, really, but she's avoided focusing on that part). But shut down they did.

So maybe that's a side effect of transferon. An inherent property. It isn't in any of the literature she's read so far, but it makes sense. Because if the bots were programmed to detect transferon then why would they need the scanners at the gate? They're not only for the expros who work in the city. *Everyone* is scanned coming back in.

That must be it.

So (for now) as long as she doesn't take any more of it when she goes outside her bots should stay online.

But that immediately creates another problem: Her geocode. All bots register their host's location at every moment of the day and all of those recs go straight into the Bank. She can't risk there being bunch of recs of her walking around Transway at all hours when there won't be any evidence of her having been chapped in and out at the gate.

So that's the first item to solve: How to alter her geocode. And there's no way to hack into the system. She can see the code just fine (the Bank is fully transparent on a read-only level), but she can't alter it. It's well known that an attempted hack is part of the CompEn final exams and that no one has ever done it successfully; they're graded on a curve based on how far they get before security shuts them down.

But that's blocking a conventional hack.

She taps her stylus against the face of her server, lost in thought: If she's really been transing the labs all these years, then she was actually hacking their code without even knowing it. So why not do the same thing with the geocode?

Maybe she just needs to think "in the city" or "inside" or something and the bots will generate the code to back it up. So as long as her intent is clear the mechanics should follow suit.

She'll have to test it though. A small trial where she's really in her bunk but puts herself in the caf – something like that. That way, even if something does go wrong she'll still be safe in the city and no harm done.

That's a good first step. And if she can get that to work, she can move on to the issue of how to get in and out of the lab unnoticed. Then she can tackle the transferon issue: Because if her proposal is accepted, she may be able to get access to a transfer.

Her proposal – no wonder it's taking so long! This is like a whole other project.

But she has to figure it out.

She can't wait to see Lang again.

"I'M SURE NONE OF YOU are wondering why I called you all here today."

Ariana Balor smiles wryly, and appreciative grins reflect back from the group assembled around the conference table.

"As former members of the GISH team, you all had integral roles in its last iteration... and I intend to make sure you're all consulted *first* about its future direction."

This makes a few of them sit up straighter. But at the far end of the room Martinez is leaning back in his chair, arms crossed over his chest.

She knew he'd be the toughest nut to crack.

Lips pursed, she plows on. "And while I'm sure we all have the utmost respect for Mr. Timanti's attempts to relocate the future of humanity to our sister world, we all know that until we can fix what is broken on our own any attempt to start over fresh carries the taint of failure. As Mr. Martinez so eloquently stated prior to the first GISH inception, 'The Earth has been our home for millennia and it will continue to be so for many more.'"

There. Let him argue his own words.

She pauses to allow for this. When Martinez says nothing, she hurriedly continues:

"But I'm not here today to debate the pros and cons of the Martian Relocation Plan. There'll be plenty of time for that in the weeks ahead. What I want to talk about today is replication."

Nine pairs of eyes blink, bright with interest. Out of the corner of hers she catches Inez Jones nudging Martinez hopefully. He ignores her.

Maybe I shouldn't have pandered so obviously. But he needs to be reminded –

She cuts off these doubts before they can derail her and refocuses. "As you know, the main challenge with the last iteration was balancing our need to replicate nanotech quickly, on a large scale, in order to identify and neutralize a wide variety of possible contaminants, while still maintaining enough control to keep things from getting out of hand if an error were to occur. No one likes grey goo."

This earns her a round of chuckles.

"To that end, I have been working with an excellent group of CompEns who have created an algorithm that both *quadruples* replication time and contains built-in failsafes that utilize quantum processing to shut down replication immediately at the first sign of any grey goo scenario."

There's a collective intake of breath. She pauses to let it sink in. Then, without another word, she raises her server and points it at the screen. A window opens, first displaying the algorithm itself (which is something only a CompEn could love) and then using animation to demonstrate its functioning with actual tech. Bots appear, replicating faster than the eye can track, and then stop and reverse, shrinking back into nothing. Each time a different pattern, each time a different path – but always responsive, always malleable.

Ten faces are now absorbed in the display, eyes tracking

each development with rapt fascination.

Jones raises a hand. "How soon will this be ready for production trials?" she asks eagerly.

"Well," Ariana says, "that depends on all of you."

Across the room, she catches Martinez leaning in for a better look. His face is still impassive, but he can't entirely hide his interest.

Gotcha, she thinks. *And you know it.*

10

Heart thumping, Celan trails the two expro girls down the stairs that lead from the lab waiting room to the door that opens to the outside, girding herself for the last leg of her final exam in Escape 101.

She'd entered the lab as a tech, pretending to look for her father; then, when all eyes were elsewhere, she'd ducked into the washroom to change her uniform out for some improvised expro gear: Fleece sleep pants, chopped indecorously short, topped by a kind of halter fashioned from half an old scarf of Cyrinda's. Not great for winter-wear, but hopefully Lang brought his sweater. The other half of the scarf she'd fixed around her head to hide her hair.

She'd made sure to wait for someone to follow out after her transformation, believing there to be safety (and anonymity) in numbers. There, she'd had great luck: the two girls in front of her had been on their way out of the building right after their pit stop in the washroom.

She hugs the folded uniform to her chest. What she will do when she comes back in she's not entirely sure. It will be late, though before midnight. She should probably change first, and come back upstairs as Lana Timanti. If anyone questions her she can say she's helping her father with something. There are certain advantages to being the daughter of a Lead SocEn, especially the one who leads the lab.

At least there won't be any recs of her having been out. The geocode test had worked beautifully, bots recording her in the caf when she was really in her bunk. And they'd kept it up for an hour, without her having to constantly think about it, until she was ready to return them to their live feed. No anomalies, no problems. Currently, they're on a timed loop showing her moving from lab, to fitness area, to bunk, and then back to the lab again around midnight.

But there were still the views to contend with. Because her egress would generate a collection of lovely views of her entering the lab, leaving by the transer door (and returning by it later) – all on record for anyone to see. A combination of luck and Navidad had kept her from being noticed last time but she can't rely on that again.

If only I could trans myself transparent, she'd thought, flashing on an old book from her father's library where the main character had a cloak that could make him invisible. *That would be perfect.*

But it had begged the question: Could something like that be possible? Not with a magic cloak, of course, but with the views themselves. They're only machinery after all – like the scans, like the bots. Maybe she could make the recorded images of herself disappear, blank the pixels somehow so they

126

didn't register her image.

That, however, had proven much more difficult; hence her current disguise. Confirmation bias should be enough to cover her for now.

She clatters down the last few steps as the expro girls exit. She marvels: no chaps, no alarms. Just fresh air, and blessed freedom. She gathers up the rest of her nerve and steps out into the night, though she can't help but flinch a little when the door slams shut behind her.

Outside she hangs back, letting the girls go on ahead. They've taken no notice of her thusfar, so when one of them turns and calls to her she freezes.

"Hey!" the girl says. She's curly-haired and pretty, very normal-looking for an expro – no crazy hair or clothes. "Better not hang around out here for long. They don't like that up there. You can get kicked out of your program."

"Oh," Celan says. "Thanks. But I'm just waiting for my man."

The girl shrugs, and she and her companion trudge on without another word.

Celan exhales, relieved. She was worried for a minute about some kind of Jaslene-type scene happening again.

Her free hand reaches instinctively for her server to double check the time – they'd said 20:00 – but hits halter top instead of uniform and she remembers that it's sitting in her dresser drawer. Squinting out over the flats, she finally spies a flash of light a little way off – a solar torch. Lang is waiting right where he said he'd be. She heads in that direction.

As she approaches, he stubs out his smoke and steps forward to embrace her. He's dressed much the same way as last time, though in a red floral number instead of the yellow sundress. She hugs him back, heart full like the rising moon. Light glints off the roller parked in the sand behind him.

She sighs happily.

"All set?" he says as they pull apart.

"Yeah, I've got it all figured out, I think. You have today's keycode, right?"

"Yep."

"So as long as I'm back before midnight I can get back in tonight," she says in a rush. "I hacked my geocode so it'll look like I'm still inside. So…" she pauses, catching her breath, "I think we should be all right."

Lang chuckles.

"What?"

"I have no idea what you're talking about."

"I transed my bots," she says. "It's not that complicated."

"Whatever," he says, hiking the hem of his skirt up to his hip. "I know jack shit about tech." A small pouch is hidden there, attached to a belt at his waist. He digs inside it, produces the vial. "But this I know. You want?"

He holds it out as Celan eyes his little setup with curiosity.

"Have to keep it hidden," he says. "Otherwise they get stolen."

She nods, but keeps her hands at her sides.

"What?" he says.

"I can't take any right now. It shuts the bots down. I haven't worked out how to keep them online yet."

"Oh."

"But I will." She grins. "Soon."

Lang shrugs. He tucks the vial away and looks her up and

down, appraising. "Nice outfit. Looks a little chilly though."

"Better this than the uniform."

"Don't worry. I raided the free box. Brought you a couple things."

"Gracias."

He lopes over to the roller and she follows, hopping in and tucking the uniform under the seat before propping her feet up on the dash. He fishes around in the back, yanking out a nubbly orange coat which he holds up semi-apologetically. It's just about the ugliest thing she's ever seen, but it looks warm so she gives him a grateful smile and pulls it on. He starts the roller and, with a spray of sand, they churn off around the city wall toward the lights of Transway.

They whir along in silence under the platinum moon until Lang clears his throat. "Well, it's a beautiful night. So I was thinking we could go for a little walk, away from everyone. Up in the hills. Just talk."

Jaslene must still be mad.

"Sounds good," Celan says.

"Yeah, well. It was kind of hectic last time with the party and everything."

"Yeah." She pauses, thoughtful. "But first, I kind of want to..." She trails off, picking at a cuticle.

"What?"

"Well, you said there was a mural by the old Arlo's – of me and my sisters and mother. I'd kind of like to see it."

Silence.

"Please?"

"Sure, I mean, of course. Didn't think you'd remember about that."

She turns her head to see his jaw set. But then he smiles, softening his features, and she relaxes. They avoid Transway's main strip, rolling through alleys instead until he halts the roller in a darkened space like a rotten tooth. The remains of the old Arlo's lie virtually untouched, the charred bones of the old building collapsed into a brooding pile. A holo shimmers above it; a memorial to the techs who died in the fire. Celan shivers like a ghost stepped across her soul.

"Didn't think you'd want to come here," Lang says.

She says nothing, just gets out of the roller. "Where is it?"

"Around back."

She follows him across the debris-strewn courtyard to where a tiny light beams like a beacon illuminating a wall of intense color – swirling shapes that coalesce into familiar faces. She stands, swallowing hard, until Lang takes her hand and approaches with her. There are bunches of drying flowers and little piles of offerings scattered along the ground. She forces herself to look up.

At the top, her mother – like she remembers her from childhood; the good times before she started walking. Soft chestnut curls, smiling eyes, hands reaching down like she wants to embrace her. Then, below and to the left, Cyrinda – bright as a star, microphone in hand, mouth open in a gorgeous roar – back-to-back with a beatific Taegh, strumming his guitar with prickly-pear-colored hair in his eyes. They look real enough to touch.

To the right of them is a sinuous Nola, the sister who ran off to Transway when Celan was only three and died in a roller accident before she ever really knew her. Nola's hair is white and wild, dark eyes fierce with the intelligence that Cyrinda always swore she possessed. Thin and solemn, her mysterious man Dex slinks like a wraith beside her.

Slightly below the two couples, in the middle of the grouping, is a little girl with brown hair and big brown eyes. She looks out at the viewer with a face radiant, reverent, like she's a witness to some exalted vision. The colors shine like summer, like joy, like everything you ever loved. Celan takes it all in before reaching out a tentative hand to touch her own painted face.

"Lang?"

"Yeah?"

"Who made this?"

"You like it?"

"It's – " And then she sees it, scrawled in the bottom corner: *R & L Shays, June 2215*

"You and your cousin?"

Lang shuffles his feet. "It was mostly Raf. He was the artist. I just did some of the colors."

She dives at him, hugging him so tight she's afraid she might break him. He knows her family, her whole secret history; he's *seen* it all…and made it beautiful.

"I love it," she says.

"I thought you might think it was weird or something. I mean, you know, since we…" He trails off, uncertain, scratching the back of his neck.

"No! Of course not."

Lang blows out a breath. "Let's go for that walk then."

THEODORE SHIFTS UNCOMFORTABLY ON THE couch next to Martinez as three-dimensional images of half-dressed girls zip across the screen on the far wall. He scoops a handful of ice from the bucket on the low, glossy table and drops it into a glass, topping it off with several fingers of Scotch. They're ensconced in a small, dimly-lit VIP room – dark red velvet walls, big squashy couches and chairs, and a screen for the selection process. Martinez points his server and stops on a promising one, zooming in for a better look at her attributes. He turns to Theodore and raises an eyebrow.

This one?

A shrug.

Whatever.

Martinez tsks, absorbed in his task. "Venga, Theodore. You must have some preference. Picking them out is half the fun. The anticipation." He pauses on the last word, drawing it out.

Theodore dredges up a weak chuckle. Back in the day, Maddy's used to be one of his favorite diversions. But it's just not the same anymore. The older Lana gets the younger these girls look. But he needs face time with his fellow Lead – news travels fast and he's already heard about Ariana's little GISH presentation. He's got to sound Martinez out as soon as possible.

"Or has La Roja finally gotten you aboard the anti-Transway crusade?" Martinez continues, a smirk tugging at the corner of his mouth. "Et tu, Theo?"

Theodore realizes he's being given an in.

"No," he says, sitting back and crossing his legs as he sips his drink. "Claro que. But I heard she may have gotten to a few of you. With the reboot."

Martinez clicks through a few more girls. "She's done

some interesting work," he says briskly. "Gave us some food for thought."

Us? It's not a good sign if he's already thinking of his old team as a unit again.

"You think it's really going to work though? This new replication technique?"

"I do."

Theodore's heart sinks but he says nothing more, leaving space for Martinez to go on. But he doesn't – just picks out a slender blonde followed by a buxom, blue-eyed brunette. Then he pauses on a girl with bouncy chestnut curls, dressed in the briefest of dresses, lips parted suggestively.

"Her?" He knows Theodore's type. Or what used to be his type; now he's not even sure. Sometimes he thinks it's almost time to settle down, find a nice woman and get comfortable. Maybe he should have done it years ago. But after Mair no tech woman really interested him – not in *that* way anyway. And with Lana, it was all too complicated.

He takes another sip of his drink and nods.

Might as well. He could use the release. But it's not like the old days – the girls back then used to be more substantial somehow, not like these silly toys. He used to be able to talk to them. Speaking of which…he glances at Martinez, who's switched to the feed of the dancers onstage, his smile wide and contented.

"Ours are on the way," he says with obvious relish.

"Órale."

A few minutes slip by in silence. Cheesy music pumps out of the speakers as two girls spin high in the air around shiny brass poles, their movements completely in sync.

Impressive, really. Very acrobatic.

"Mira," Martinez finally says, eyes still on the screen, "I know what you're thinking. And you're right. This is going to throw a wrench into your work. A lot of people were very excited about what we saw on Friday." A shrug. "But I'm still not a hundred percent convinced. After all, this is Ariana we're talking about. She may very well have a hidden agenda."

But we've got her specs now and I'm going to go through them with a fine-toothed comb. If she's up to something, *anything*, I will find out what it is."

"Something other than GISH, you mean?"

A nod.

"And if not?"

A beat passes. Then the door bursts open and, with a whoop, three girls bound into the room, bearing fizzing bottles and baring more than a little skin. Any further discussion is, of necessity, postponed for the duration.

'TERRA MADRE!' LANG'S BRAIN IS abuzz with a thousand different thoughts, all twisted up like a nest of rattlers: Celan likes the mural. She doesn't think he's some freak who's obsessed with her family. But there's no way she's really into him. With all that tech stuff she knows she probably thinks he's a total fool.

He shoulders his pack as they get out of the roller, taking the lead on a foot path that threads through tumbledown houses toward the foothills of the Sandias. The moon is fully risen now and it beams down bright as day, like a spotlight; and he's an actor on a stage who's forgotten his lines.

Say something, idiot!

But he can't think of a thing. So he pulls a bottle of Zeeb's good mead (the lone survivor of last night's New Year's Eve festivities) from his pack and uncorks it, handing it to Celan.

'A little lubrication of the situation' – as Raf used to say.

"Ladies first."

Gingerly, she sniffs the contents. Then she tips it back and takes a sip. Grins, takes another. He sighs, relieved.

"Ese!" The cry comes from somewhere behind them and startles Celan into dribbling a little liquid down her chin. She dabs it on her coat sleeve, visibly annoyed, as a thick guy with a very determined air about him approaches – the fuser Lang bartered a ride from on Navidad. His stomach sinks to his knees.

Oh shit. Not now.

"Vamos aviados," the guy says.

"I'm busy."

"You got a round trip to Arqueros," the guy says. "You only paid one way."

"Bullshit."

The guy's eyes squint into a piggy little glint. "People that don't like to share better watch out who they ask for favors."

"Later."

"Ahora."

Lang winces, then turns to Celan. "Give me a minute, OK?"

He steers the guy behind the side of a house so she can't see what they're doing, hoping against hope that she has no clue. But the guy said 'aviados'. She must know what that means. Any kid who grew up in the ranchos heard an adult say 'No aviados' plenty of times. It was a caution not to use transferon for fun, only for its healing properties.

But he didn't say 'fuse', so maybe she won't realize...

Lang taps his foot impatiently while the guy does his business and snatches the transfer back as soon as he's done, stalking off without another word, hoping he'll sit tight for a while. But no such luck. The guy struggles to his feet and manages to collect himself enough to totter back to the footpath and off in the direction of Transway. Celan watches him go, her expression unreadable.

Lang gives her a pained look. "I was late out to Arqueros for Navidad and he had a roller," he explains. "I traded him for a ride and now he thinks I'm his personal fucking medicine man or something."

But she seems to be only half-listening.

"Are they all like that?" she asks, passing the mead back to Lang as they start to walk again.

"Expros?" he says, taking a hefty swig.

"Fusers."

He sputters, coughs.

So much for clueless.

"Uh, well, it depends on the person, really," he says, trying to recover. "If they were an asshole before they'll still be an asshole after, you know?"

She glances back over her shoulder. "Do they all end up crazy?"

He considers this. There've been rumors floating around Transway for years that little Celan Mairs herself was fusing on the night of the Arlo's fire, but most people have written them off as total bullshit. And the girl next to him now is so wide-eyed and innocent that it's obvious that that's the case. He's got to tread lightly.

"Depends on what you mean by crazy," he says. "Some get totally fucked up. But some do all right, like Mara and Brophy."

"They're *fusers*?"

"Yeah. Just D and S class, though. Maybe you'd remember Brophy from when you were a kid. He was in that band Fused Up! He used to hang out with Taegh, or so they say."

Celan's brow furrows. "I remember the band. I remember Tomás – he was the singer." She shakes her head. "But that was a long time ago. Did he change his hair?"

Lang grunts, swigging more mead. "Yeah, maybe."

"Taegh never did. It was always that same purple-pink color, just like you painted it."

Her tone is soft, nostalgic almost, and Lang starts to relax. The mead's not hurting either. Maybe he hasn't scared her off. Maybe it'll all be OK.

"Do you miss them?" he ventures.

"I didn't," she says. "For a long time I didn't. I got it drummed into my head that they were bad and I was lucky to have got away when I did. But now…things've changed."

He says nothing, leaving space for her to go on.

"I had this dream about Taegh," she says finally. "He was actually a pretty nice guy, you know? I'd forgotten how sweet he was. Much sweeter than Cyrinda most of the time."

"I heard she was kind of a piece of work."

Celan frowns. "She could be a little excitable."

She reaches out a hand and he passes back the bottle.

She takes a deep draught, and then a deep breath, as if summoning up the courage to ask something else. Lang tenses.

"So have you ever done it?"

"What?" he says.

"Fused?"

And there it is – the point where the truth officially wears out its welcome.

"Well sure, I did a little back in the day," he says with forced casualness. "But a lot of people have tried it at some point. Most of 'em don't get all CERS-ado. It's not really that big of a deal. And after Raf died I wasn't gonna take any more chances."

She nods, seemingly satisfied. "Your cousin. You were really close?"

"Yeah," he says, grateful that she's honed in on Raf instead of the fusing part. "We grew up together. His folks were gone young – flash flood got 'em down in an arroyo before he was three. So my parents raised him too. We were wild together, though. Drove them crazy."

"And what are two wild cousins to do but head out for some adventures on Transway?"

"Exactly! See, we knew some people over here. Or one person anyway. Our Tio Emilio had this friend Ace. He lived on Transway and was, like, the funniest guy. Tio visited him a few times and Ace came over to Arqueros and they would tell us all these great stories. We thought it was the best, you know? As soon as Raf turned eighteen he was outta there. Wanted to see for himself."

He's knows he's babbling but he can't help it.

"And you?" she prompts, steering him back on track.

"I came for a visit. It was only supposed to be for a weekend…"

She laughs. "I know how that goes. How old were you?"

"Seventeen."

"So did you ever finish 'scuela?"

He shakes his head, bashful.

"Well, neither did I," she says and Lang grins.

They tramp along in companionable silence for a few minutes, letting this commonality sink in.

"So where'd you get the transfer?" she asks. Then guesses, "Was it…his?"

Lang sighs. This is the painful part. But she might as well know all of it. Or most of it, anyway. "Yeah. We had a real good time at first. Just having fun. But then something changed. Raf started getting real fucked up real fast; started walking. Hair all white and he just lay there, wouldn't eat. Sometimes he talked, knew what was going on, but most of the time he was…I don't know – someplace else. I freaked out, took him back to the ranchos. I hoped they could do something – "

"But they said there wasn't anything they could do," she finishes. "It was the same with my mom."

He blinks up at the moon. It blurs and then redefines itself. "After he was gone the elders came for his transfer. But he'd told me to keep it, told me to hide it. So I did."

"And they never knew you had it?"

Scratched black boots kick at a rock. "I'm a pretty good hider."

"So then you came back here?"

"I came back to tell them that Raf was gone. I gave the

transfer to Brophy. He said he'd hold it for me."

"You gave it to a fuser?"

"Brophy's as good as his word."

Celan says nothing.

"Then I went back to Arqueros. Had to be with the family. Try to be a good boy. But it's hard staying back there. Sometimes I just need a break."

She sips at the mead, meditative. "Sometimes you can't go back."

Lang halts his stride and turns to look at her. In the half-light their eyes meet and something seems to leap between them. He takes the bottle from her and sets it on the ground. Then softly, slowly, he leans down and presses his lips to hers. When they part, she's smiling, obviously pleased.

"Can we talk about something more interesting now?" he says.

"Like what?"

"Like how much I missed you all week," he whispers, sliding a hand to the small of her back and pulling her close. He breathes in a scent like sun-warmed sand and clover.

"Sure you did," she teases. "Probably hanging around Maddy's every night. I know what you expro guys are like."

"Those girls don't do anything for me."

"Really?" she says, face bright in the moonlight.

"Really," he says, and kisses her until the world splits on its axis and its molten core swallows him whole.

THEODORE STEPS OUT ALONE INTO the brisk night air through the VIP door. Normally he would have waited to leave until Martinez was ready, but his fellow Lead was deep into distraction and he'd insisted on staying long after Theodore's patience wore out. His 'release' had been perfectly adequate, but afterwards he'd felt sour. The girl had been as attractive as her image but dull as dirt.

Nothing like the old days.

He sighs, pulling the collar of his jacket up against the wind, and meanders out onto Transway. He's a little drunk, but the walk will clear his head. They'd ridden over in a roller, but he figures Martinez will be in dire need of transportation by the time he's ready to head home. One of Maddy's bouncers will drive him.

He keeps his head down, ignoring the faces rushing by. Mechanically, he sidesteps and maneuvers until the crowd on the sidewalk thins and he's passing the collapsed bones of the old Arlo's, holo hovering above it like a ghost. He stops and lets the sight send him deep into memory – of the day he found Lana here, dirty and ragged, mourning her older sister who'd perished in the fire.

He'd seen the little girl once before, at the Saturday market with Cyrinda, and immediately had his suspicions. Cyrinda called the younger girl 'sister,' though she'd had no younger sister when Theodore knew Mair. Arlo had been dead half a year at least when they met and Mair definitely hadn't been pregnant then. But this little girl would finally explain Mair's hasty departure back to the ranchos when he was away in Winnipeg all those years ago. She looked just about the right age, and there was a resemblance.

It made him livid.

He'd tried so hard to convince Mair to live in Albakirk with him and be his proper spouse, but she repeatedly de-

141

clined the offer. But just before he left for Winnipeg he felt like he'd finally worn her down; only to find her gone upon his return. He'd blamed himself, thinking he had pushed too hard.

But he hadn't gone after her. He let it go. Because he had his career to think of and a SocEn so besotted with a expro woman that he'd chase her all the way back to the ranchos was not someone who was going to be taken seriously when he came up for Lead.

And so Mair was wise to leave when she did – because if he had known she was pregnant with his child he would have tracked her to the ends of the Earth. He would have insisted that his progeny be raised as a tech and if she'd wanted contact with her child, she'd have had to agree to his terms.

Funny how life works.

Funny how, years later, that stolen child was returned; dropped into his lap like magic. Cyrinda had died in the fire and from what Lana told him, Mair was dead too. She had no one left. So she was his.

He blinks out of reminiscence as he registers a winking light somewhere beyond the old building's charred bones. There's something, or someone, back there. Intrigued, he circles the ruins by the side alley and approaches what he now sees is a mural, illuminated by a solar torch. Some kind of expro-style memorial.

As he gets closer he can make out figures – an older woman, two younger ones with men beside them, and a little girl.

Lana.

Captured at age eleven, just like he's been remembering her. And Mair, sweet and lovely as ever. And Cyrinda and the

142

other girl…

Nola.

But the Nola he remembers was younger, pudgier, mousier. This older version, with that white hair and skimpy clothes, looks disconcertingly like a Maddy's girl. He shakes his head, clearing the thought from his brain, and reaches out to trace the contours of Lana's face.

So she's a symbol to the expros. She means something to them.

This is an unexpected, but welcome, development. Because it won't be long until the verdicts are in on the proposals, and once Lana's is accepted it will be time to inform her of the need to divulge her origins. He's put it off long enough, not wanting to disturb progress on her project, but with Ariana stirring up trouble it's more imperative than ever to demonstrate the expros' potential. In only a few short months Lana will be an En level trainee and it will be time for the big reveal. She's going to need some time to prepare.

The buzz of his server jars him out of his thoughts and he fishes it out of his breast pocket. There's a message from Milton in the MechLab. They've detected a launch from Lanzhou – an unmanned craft, trajectory uncertain but it could be headed for Mars.

His stomach churns. Unmanned is good, but it could still be nanotech, some kind of bots being sent to build living quarters ahead of a manned settlement. Which is exactly what he has planned for their own endeavor.

'We will continue to monitor the situation,' the message concludes.

Theodore's head is suddenly crystal clear.

You bet we will.

He pockets the server with a grunt and turns resolutely toward the city.

Back to work: And it'll be a late one tonight.

○► 11 ◄○

"Any questions?" Ariana asks the group, sweeping an arm out to indicate the screen behind her.

They'd generously agreed to give up an early hour on a precious Sunday morning to watch a demonstration out of Alton's lab of rebooted GISH bots doing a little live-action quantum cleaning. The remains of the breakfast she'd ordered up from the caf litter the conference table. She'd wanted them relaxed, well-fed, and feeling casual, almost familial.

SocEn 101.

Setting the right tone was necessary, because there had been no way to avoid putting Pollomax in the specs. Any votable enterprise must have all action items discoverable – failing to do so guarantees an exclusion. And that's too risky. Sure, there have been occasions where people have gotten away with it. But that sort of chicanery breeds bad blood. Besides, she's positive Martinez will have examined her specs thoroughly. Her last, best, hope was in brevity. Make Pollomax seem like a formality. Make no mention of Transway at all. Her eyes dart around the table, counting. At least a third of those present share her sentiments about it anyway.

"Anyone?" she says lightly, treating them all to a smile.

A slender, dark-haired woman tilts two fingers, asking to be acknowledged. Ariana breathes easier. This MedEn is a firm part of the anti-Transway contingent.

"Yes, Karina?"

"So how soon will we be ready to present this to the public?"

Perfect.

"Well, from the looks of things not too long, though Alton does have several other obligations to attend to." She pauses, makes a wry moue. Everyone knows how busy lab managers are, especially in the run-up to a resource vote. "But we're going to wait for the big reveal until Ord 50."

There's an appreciative murmur. In some ways it's risky to wait that long – the vote is on Ord 60 and by then the MRP could seem like a fait accompli – but it could also make a new idea seem like a last-minute stroke of genius. They've been hearing about Mars forever. This will come off as fresh and exciting. Brand new and yet, because of the ubiquity of the last GISH project, familiar too.

A perfect blend.

Another tip of the hand comes from an older man, silver-sand hair cut in a strict burr – Oxendine. This one she doesn't know well. Warily, she acknowledges him.

"So do we have a name yet?" he says eagerly.

She exhales.

"I mean, we don't want to reuse 'GISH', do we? We'll

want something new, to set us apart." He cuts his eyes to Martinez. "No offense."

Ariana winces. *Don't poke the bear!* she thinks, surprising herself a little with the old world-ism.

But Martinez waves a careless hand, seemingly unperturbed.

Oxendine clears his throat. "Well then, I suggest Sanisphere," he says, and leans back – 'top that' emanating from his every pore.

The next fifteen minutes are heady; once a group gets around to naming something you can be almost a hundred percent sure that they are all on board. It's like they've just given birth and are naming the baby. Finally it's narrowed down to Sanisphere (everyone had liked that one immediately) and ReviveAll.

Ariana is beaming now. "Maybe we should take a break then? Sleep on it? After all, we have plenty of time to make a final decision."

The faces beam back in agreement and she's about to call the meeting adjourned when –

"I have a name."

Martinez. Damn him.

"Or rather a question about a name." He pauses, pointing his server at the screen to display it. "Pollomax. What can you tell me about that?"

This earns him some irritated glares. His timing's off. Can't he see they're finished? That everyone wants to go? Ariana bites her lip, hoping this means that he waited too long to bring it up.

But she has a ready answer. "Pollomax is a small but

necessary part of our new endeavor, whatever we decide to call it."

Martinez inclines his head slightly.

"Yes. Obviously it is part of this endeavor, as it appears in the specs, albeit briefly. My question is: What is the point of it? It looks like – " He palms his server and begins to scroll through the info on the screen. "Some sort of medical plug-in, am I right?"

"Yes."

"Something about the amygdala?"

"Correct."

"So I don't get it. Please explain why some sort of neural aversion conditioning is a necessary part of a clean nanotech proposition? Surely we don't need to alter our own minds in order to appreciate its glory?" He steeples his fingers, waiting. Some of the glares in his direction turn to curious stares before refocusing on Ariana.

But she keeps her poise. "Pollomax is a first, but ultimately necessary, step in this endeavor. We must be able to center ourselves and come at this in Unity and Clarity." Invoking the social precedents is always helpful.

"Yes, yes. We all know that," Martinez says, waving an airy hand. "But I question the necessity of some kind of artificial enhancement of that capacity. After all, we've all already agreed that this idea of yours is sound. How much more clarity do we need?"

Ah, the crux of it.

She takes a deep breath. "Pollomax will serve as a kind of advance guard to our cleansing endeavor," she says carefully. "It is my belief – and I know many of you here share it – that in order to do due diligence we should begin our cleanup right here in our own backyard, by removing certain pernicious influences that keep us distracted from loftier goals."

Martinez's lips twist. "I take it you mean Transway?"

She nods once, affirmative.

"So you would have us agree to alter our own brains with some kind of untested plug-in, just to get rid of Transway? Are we really that scared of it? Maximum chicken?"

A few recognize his wordplay. There are scattered titters.

Ariana stiffens. "Pollomax is being thoroughly tested and has so far proven completely safe and effective – "

"I'm sure. But my point remains. Why do we even need it?"

Ariana opens her mouth to speak but is cut off by Karina, who is eyeing Martinez with barely concealed contempt. "Because this wretched business has gone on long enough," she snaps, "and we all know it."

"All?" Martinez says, eyes wide with mock surprise. "I don't know about *all* of us, Ms. Simmons."

"Most of us then," she fires back. "The ones who actually *care*. The ones who have the sense to recognize when something isn't working and are ready to make a fresh start. The ones who haven't been unduly influenced by those creatures out there."

She pins him with her stare; his own predilections are well-known. Martinez's eyes dart furtively to the side for a moment and Ariana rushes into the fray.

"Yes," she says. "That's exactly it. For most of us, Pollomax will barely even register a difference in our behavior. Only the holdouts will notice any change at all. But it won't be anything dramatic – just a gradual loss of interest in the activities beyond our gates. And once that interest is lost, what the denizens of Transway do to maintain their livelihood is up to them. They are free to assimilate or they are free to leave. We've been dealing with this problem for over fifty years, and this is a simple, elegant, and most of all humane solution."

She pauses, shrugs. "We don't correct *them*. We correct ourselves. And once that correction is made, we move on. Toward better and brighter things – Sanisphere. ReviveAll. A clean break."

Oh, that's good.

There's a lot of nodding around the table.

Excellent.

But Martinez is on his feet now.

"Nice work," he says, sardonic. "But I for one do not like the idea of having some barely beta-level plug-in altering my brain chemistry without a full scale demonstration of how it actually works or what the side effects may be. Anyone giving their consent to this has a right to know as much. And also to know exactly what it will be used for. Some here may be so blindly obdurate that they don't care. But I'm betting a lot of people outside this room will. And I'm going to make sure they are better informed than we appear to have been."

Silence. Uneasy looks as he walks to the door.

"But if that portion were removed?" Oxendine says, with a quick glance at Ariana.

Martinez pauses. "If that portion were removed, then you could count on my full support."

He exits to a buzz of conflicting voices, everyone trying to speak at once.

Ariana sighs.

So it's going to come down to Transway after all.

DRESSED IN SHORTS AND HALTER, uniform tucked under her arm, Celan slips through the outer lab door behind a chattering bunch of expros and immediately turns left, heading out over the darkling plain. It's been ten days since she last saw Lang and she's got so much to tell him. Her proposal was accepted! She can hardly believe it, but it's true – she's on her way to SocEn. Maybe that won't mean much to him, but he'll definitely understand that something good happened and be happy for her. Of that she's positive.

And the best part is that she now has full clearance to the main observation area of the transer lab. No more vague excuses about looking for her father. She can come and go as she pleases (within reason). She still has to don a disguise to get outside, but it makes things a lot easier.

Also: she can check out a transfer! For research purposes, of course, but it'll give her the chance to experiment – see if she can keep her bots functioning normally and the geocode confined to the city even with transferon in her system. Then she'll be home free.

A fresh breeze hits her face and she basks in it, closing her eyes for a brief second before surveying the area for the roller and Lang.

Nada.

Jogging forward, she squints harder. It's dark out tonight, no moon; maybe he's hidden in a shadow somewhere. Softly, she calls his name, not wanting to shout so close to the city.

No reply.

OK, she tells herself, *so he's a little late.* She reaches for her server to double check the time but, like him, it's not there. At least she knows where *that* is though – sitting in her dresser drawer.

She shifts her weight from foot to foot and turns her head left and right, hoping for a glimpse of something moving. But the night is eerily still. And quiet – she would hear the telltale whir if a roller were approaching.

He can't have forgotten. He must have gotten stuck somewhere. Or maybe he couldn't get the roller. Maybe he's on foot.

That makes sense. He must have walked. Must have underestimated the time it would take to get here from Transway. She should sit tight and wait.

But what if someone sees her from an upper window or something? Reports an expro hanging around outside the lab? That could get ugly fast.

So that settles it; she'll head for Transway.

Meet him halfway.

FLUSHED FROM THE BRISK WALK, Celan pushes open the back gate at Alamora, nerves frayed from the last half hour's constant pogo between anger and anxiety. There'd been no sign of Lang on the road. Maybe he *did* ditch her. Or maybe they'd missed each other in the dark. Maybe he went to find her and then thought *she* ditched *him* and came back here.

Good thing she remembered where this place was.

She advances across the deserted yard to the patio, wincing at each creak as she mounts the steps up to the back door. No telling who might be around. Warily, she peeks through the tattered screen. The soft glow of an algalamp illuminates the kitchen, but no one's in there.

Stop being silly, she chides herself. *It's just a door. Just knock.*

So she raps a quick tattoo and waits with breath bated. No one appears. Maybe they're all upstairs.

She raps again, harder this time.

Nothing.

Finally frustration overcomes reticence and she yanks the door open and marches inside, calling Lang's name as she passes through the kitchen and into the hallway – where Jaslene stands, deep in conversation with a frowsy blonde. Celan freezes. Jaslene looks up and sees her. The white-haired girl narrows her eyes and takes a menacing step forward.

But in lieu of fear, a sudden fury wells up in Celan, all the adrenaline of the night thusfar surging through her like rocket fuel.

Hit me bitch. Go ahead.

This wrath must show on her face because Jaslene halts, settling for a smirk instead of a slap.

"Oh, it's little Kimbra," she coos. "Looking for Langton? He's upstairs. Mara's room. First door on the right."

Celan senses some subterfuge, but having nothing else to go on skirts Jaslene and the blonde and heads up the stairs. She checks his room first – empty. So she stows her tech uniform in a dresser drawer and returns to the first door on the right. A tentative knock produces a welcoming murmur and she turns the knob.

There are three of them: Mara and Sig, the drummer from Zeeb's band, are chatting by the window while a chubby, green-haired guy sprawls on a worn sofa – sleeve rolled up, arm braced against the armrest, transfer poised against the crook of his arm. At the sight of her they all pause. Obviously, they'd been expecting someone else.

Maybe the blonde from downstairs.

"Hey," Mara says after a moment. "You're Kimbra, right? Lang's girl? Ven aquí, if you want."

The guy on the couch returns to his fuse while Celan stares, transfixed.

"You wanna close that door behind you?" Mara says.

But she can't answer, can't move, can't breathe.

How would that feel? If I did it just once? Just one more time?

"Hey, are you deaf?"

"Aw, Mara," Sig says. "Don't scare her...probably never seen a fuse before."

Mara looks Celan over carefully. "Oh no," she says, with a tiny smile. "I don't think she's scared at all."

The words hit like a brick, snapping Celan out of her trance. She whirls, slamming the door behind her and barreling headlong down the stairs and out through the kitchen. She bounds down the steps to the yard, desperate to escape what feels like something monstrous chasing her, and runs smack into a harried-looking Lang and a visibly annoyed Zeeb.

"Ce – Kimbra!" Lang says, surprise and relief fighting for space on his face. "You're here! I am *so sorry* I wasn't there. I was running late and by the time I got there you were gone. I thought you gave up on me. I thought you were mad. Please don't be. I couldn't help it." He shoots Zeeb a reproachful look.

Zeeb sighs. "We'll finish this later," he says and stalks off

154

toward the house.

Dazed, Celan watches him go. Then she turns back to Lang, mind reeling like a cyclone.

"Que pas'?" he says, peering at her anxiously. "How did you get here? Did you walk? Did something happen?"

"It – it's nothing," she stammers, trying for composure. "Just a – just a little – just some girl who reminded me of my sister," she finishes, grasping at ghosts instead of trying to explain.

Lang's brow wrinkles, but then he pulls her in for a reassuring hug and a deliciously sweet kiss. "Well I'm glad you made it. And I know what you need," he says. "Let's go to Tosh's. Get a cider. Calm down."

"Is that a wayvern?" Even dressed like she is she doesn't want to risk bumping into any techs.

"Don't worry," Lang says, like he can read her thoughts. "It's barely on the strip."

"Are there views?"

"Hmmm. Maybe. Hold on."

He dashes into the house, emerging after a minute or two with a thin, hooded jacket. He holds it up questioningly.

"That'll work," she says.

ALL FACES SEEM FRIENDLY AS they maneuver through the crowd inside Tosh's – pretty much expro-only but Celan keeps the hood up anyway. Can't be too careful. The pleasant buzz of the room and Lang's hand on her shoulder loosen the grip of fear on her gut and she starts to relax, admiring his easy grace as he stakes out a spot at the bar and signals the hefty, red-haired bartender for drinks. She takes the cider he hands her gratefully.

"Better?" he says, circling an arm around her waist.

"Perfect."

They sip in silence, letting the comfortable clamor swirl around them, secure in their own private space. Lang pulls her closer, hand brushing her hip, and a sudden fever blooms under her skin.

Maybe we should cut this drink short. Go back to his room. Maybe tonight –

Lang nudges her, saying, "Celan, I really need to – "

"Motherfucker!"

Somewhere behind them, a table crashes over.

They break apart, necks craning to see what the fuss is about as a burly man stomps through broken glass and overturned chairs, red-faced and screaming, stalking a skinny, ragged figure.

"Pinche fuser! Gimme that chit!"

The skinny guy tries to flee but trips over a chair leg and goes sprawling to the floor. The burly man closes in with fists clenched, ready to pummel, but he's jerked back by the collar, arms pinned to his sides.

"Déjalo!"

It's Brophy. The big guy struggles against his strapping embrace.

"It's not worth it," Brophy says.

Using the momentary distraction the ragged guy gets to his feet and scurries out the side door, disappearing into the night. Roaring with rage the red-faced man finally frees himself and lunges for a broken bottle, wheeling on Brophy.

"Pinche cabron! I'm gonna fuck your ass up!"

He lashes out wildly. Brophy dodges but the guy gets him on the upswing, gouging a stripe of red across his left cheek and throwing him against the wall. He's about to come in for the kill when Lang springs forward like a cat and several bystanders follow suit, wrestling the big guy to the ground. He goes down howling as they drag him to the side door and unceremoniously hustle him out.

Celan realizes how hard she is shaking as Lang comes back inside with the others. He glances at the bartender, who nods her thanks, then hurries over to the figure slumped against the wall and crouches. Celan picks her way through the wreckage until she's standing beside him. She looks down. Her stomach turns over.

Brophy lies stunned, holding a loose flap of cheek against his face as blood seeps through his fingers and stains his white shirt scarlet. She gasps. But Lang calmly reaches out and moves Brophy's hand to his lap, letting the blood flow. Then he takes Brophy's face between his own two hands.

"Just relax," he murmurs, breathing deep.

Celan feels an odd rush in her gut, like a sudden change in altitude. The flow of blood on Brophy's face slows and then stops completely as the cut flap of cheek melds seamlessly back into the rest of his flesh. Lang keeps the hold for a few seconds more before releasing him with a sigh. Brophy shakes his head once, like throwing off a nightmare, and reaches up to touch the now-healed wound, face still stained but otherwise unblemished.

He smiles. "Gracias."

"D'nada," Lang says, "Can you stand? We should get

out of here before some tech shows up with a stun."

Brophy nods and Lang hauls him to his feet. Dumb-founded, Celan looks back and forth between them.

"Lang…" she says wonderingly.

A shrug. "Prana."

BROPHY'S GIDDY LAUGH BOUNCES OFF the walls as they tramp back through the alleys to Alamora. One arm slung around Lang's neck, he's still marveling; alternately running a hand over his face and giving Lang's shoulders a grateful shake. But with every touch, Lang's heart sinks further. Every word of praise feels like a secret critique from the Universe – 'See? You should never have left 'scuela. You could have been an elegido. Now you'll never be anything.'

It's not that special. They need to stop –

"That was amazing, güey."

He scowls. "Whatever. And you won't even need me for this kind of thing much longer. You've been doing great with the stuff I showed you."

Brophy rolls his eyes. "Transing burns is one thing." He presses a palm to his cheek. "*That* was fucking genius."

"It was," Celan pipes up behind them. "That was like elder-level healing."

Lang ignores this.

"Seriously, I mean – "

He cuts her off. "It's not that big a deal."

And that's true, in a way. Transing like he just did – the real thing like he was taught in 'scuela – isn't about will or force. It's not his own energy he was using. All he did was get out of the way and let that universal prana run through him like a current. A rush like the echo of a good fuse.

He shrugs Brophy off as they push through the gate and tromp up the kitchen stairs. Inside, Mara and Zeeb are seated with a bottle of wine between them, deep in conversation. But one look at Brophy's face and she jumps like a scalded cat.

"Terra Madre! What happened to you?"

"Little scuffle. Got cut," Brophy says as Mara grabs a cloth off the counter and runs it under the pump at the sink. "Lang fixed me up. Está bien."

She throws Lang a grateful look as she dabs at Brophy's cheek.

"Pero que *pas*?" she says.

"We were at Tosh's – " Lang starts.

"And I was working on some busted lights," says Brophy. "And Jory was there. You know how he is."

Mara nods, lips a tense line.

"Always hanging around, begging, scraping shit up off the floor…"

"So?"

"So some drunk asshole thought he stole a chit. Acted like he was gonna kill him. But he didn't touch this asshole's chit. Fucker at the next table grabbed it when his back was turned."

Mara tsks. "You can't fight everybody."

Brophy sighs as she rinses the rag, a stream of watery pink coiling down the drain. "I know, and it's not like Jory's never lifted anything in desperation. But still, it wasn't his fault."

She clucks her tongue at him again, slapping the rag

into the sink. "Let's go get you a clean shirt."

Zeeb shakes his head as they exit. "Typical," he mutters.

"What?" Celan says.

Zeeb grunts, hoisting the hefty wine bottle as Lang turns to rinse his own hands. "Drink?"

"Sure," Lang hears her chirp, followed by the scrape of a chair and the unmistakable sound of liquid emptying into a glass. His throat constricts. He could really use a drink right about now.

"Is that a dolphin?" Celan is saying, pointing to the tattoo that encircles Zeeb's wrist. "We used to see those on the astral, back in 'scuela. They helped us heal things in the ocean."

He ignores this, just finishes her pour and tells Lang to fetch another glass. Lang snatches one out of the cupboard and watches gratefully as Zeeb fills it; then grabs a chair and straddles it backwards, reaching for the wine and taking a swig. He would down the whole thing right then and there, but the sight of Celan sipping decorously shames him into putting it down half-drunk.

Zeeb's frowning into his glass now. Celan squints a query at Lang, and he shakes his head. Looks like Zeeb's in one of his serious moods. Better to wait and listen to whatever he has to say.

Finally Zeeb looks up. "None of this shit would even be like this if wasn't for *them*!" he spits out.

"Who?" Celan says, all innocence.

Lang grits his teeth, *fuck it*, and downs the rest of his wine. *Here we go…*

"The fucking techs, that's who! But I guess you don't hear much about it on your little astral plane."

Celan reddens. "We hear some." She falters, glancing at Lang again. He gives another quick shake of his head, but she doesn't seem to get it. "But I'm not sure what you mean."

"The fusers," Zeeb says. "The techs created the fusers so they could have a permanent pool of testers for all their little experiments. So they didn't have to test their own bots anymore. And now they blame *us* for it. Treat us like we're trash."

Astonishment blooms on Celan's face. "What?" she says. "From what I've heard, it was the elders who invented trans-fusing. Like it was some secret technique they had to raise their prana up fast that got out somehow to the expros. It had nothing to do with the techs."

Zeeb swallows more wine. He's dangerously flushed. Lang nudges Celan under the table with the toe of his boot, but she doesn't seem to register the gesture as a warning. He grimaces and refills his glass. Drinks deep.

"The elders," Zeeb says. "Oh yes, your sacred elders. So wise! So caring! So in tune with the Universal will!" He waves his glass around, toasting each sarcastic epithet.

"Uh…" Celan starts.

"So what about the famine then? The biggest disaster the ranchos ever had and the elders didn't do shit."

"That was right after Jane Lees died. They weren't pre-pared –"

"No more fearless leader, power vacuum; I get it," Zeeb says. "But the point is, they couldn't conjure food out of thin air so they tried to make everyone live on it – pure prana from the Sun! And these were farmers, workers. Their kids were crying and hungry and all they got to eat was a bunch of bullshit!"

"So some of them left – asked the techs for help," Celan appends. "And they got it. That's why there're expros in the first place. They probably would've died otherwise."

Zeeb narrows his eyes. "So you're defending them?"

"Who?"

"The techs!" He's almost yelling now.

"I'm not! I'm just saying – it was the elders that invented transfusing. They try to keep it secret; they don't teach it in 'scuela. But the elegidos know. That's how it got out. One of them took the expro's side; went to Transway. They showed someone. It had nothing to do with the techs."

"Yes the fuck it did! They experimented. With bots. Early on. Found out ways to make transferon less effective. People were freaking out until some old man – ex-elegido, ex-elder even, who knows? – showed them the secret. A few drops under the tongue didn't work for them anymore. They had to put it right into the bloodstream to get any effect at all."

Celan's hand is shaking as she raises her glass to her lips. She takes a quick sip, as if to steady her nerves. "But that's not true. Most of the techs hate transferon. If they found a way to stop the expros from using it wouldn't they have just – "

"Forced it on everyone? You'd think so, wouldn't you?" Zeeb says ominously. "But they needed them, you see, to test the bots. Before the expros showed up they had to test them on themselves. There was a bot lottery. People died. They didn't want to lose their new little testers, so they took out whatever was messing with transferon in those bots. But the damage was done. Now they had a permanent pool of testers. Now they had fusers."

Celan looks scandalized. "But that's – " she starts.

Zeeb plunks his glass down and leans forward eagerly, like he's waiting for her to contradict him again so he can go in for the kill.

Lang clears his throat. "Mira, Zeeb," he says. "She does have a point. I mean, was there ever any proof that that's what really happened?"

Zeeb sighs, pressing palms against his eyes. "With all due respect, Lang, you didn't grow up here. No sabes todo."

"I know," he says. "It's just…there're so many different stories that it's hard to know what to believe sometimes."

"Well, believe this," Zeeb snaps. "The elders fucked us one way and then the techs did it the other. And now they look at us like *we're* the problem. And every time we try to talk about it, to express it, they shut our asses down."

"What?" This from Celan. "How do they do that?"

Lang groans inwardly, downs the rest of his wine. *Enough already.*

He reaches for the bottle. Refills.

"Who do you think blew up the old Arlo's?" Zeeb demands. "Who killed Cyrinda Mairs and Taegh Gwens? They were speaking the truth, better than it had ever been spoken before, so they killed them!"

"The techs?" Celan says, incredulous. "That's ridiculous! It was an accident."

"And how do you know *that*, Miss Ranchita?"

"I – I told you – we hear things."

"Obviously, not enough," Zeeb says. "Everyone comes to Transway looking for a little fun, and then when they've had it back they go – to the city, to the ranchos. We're nothing to them – experiments, entertainments, *expendable!*"

Abruptly he rises.

"Hope you've enjoyed your stay," he growls at Celan and stomps out, letting the door slam shut behind him.

She stares after him, open-mouthed. Then she turns to Lang.

"What was that all about?" she says.

He eyes her accusingly. "Why'd you have to keep provoking him? You should know better than to defend techs around here."

"I couldn't help it! The techs did not blow up Arlo's! It was an accident," she says. "I know. I was there."

She looks so confused and miserable that he can't help but soften. He reaches out and touches her arm. "I know that," he says. "But Zeeb doesn't."

"I know," she says, sniffling a little. "But he's wrong. And it bothers me that he thinks we're so…evil. We're not. And the bots can't shut down transferon. Transferon shuts down the bots. That's why we have the scanners. He's got it all wrong."

"Maybe," Lang concedes.

"Definitely," she says. "I was just trying to set things straight. I mean, it's not like the techs are perfect, but the people that sign up to be testers – they're not forced into it. They volunteer. And they know it's dangerous. It's all explained to them in the waivers. They know they're taking a chance."

"Celan," he says quietly, "testing's not really a choice. It's desperation. There are a lot more expros than there are transfers these days. If you don't have one, and you don't have friends or chits in your hand, then you gotta beg, borrow, or steal it any way you can. And if you're a fuser…well, then you're really fucked."

She bows her head, rubbing at a splotch of wine on the table top.

"I'm sorry," she says in a small voice.

"Hey," he says, rising and pulling her up into an embrace. "None of it's your fault. You've had as bad a time of all this as anyone. It's just – no one knows that."

She buries her face in his chest and he nuzzles his nose into her soft hair, breathing in her sweet scent. She's hugging him so tight it hurts. Then she reaches up and pulls him in for a fierce kiss. When they finally part he's almost stupefied by desire.

"Wanna go upstairs?" he says.

She turns and downs the rest of her wine in one gulp, setting it back on the table as if it's a final resolution.

"Yes," she says. "Let's go."

⊐- 12 -⊏

Celan's heart thuds uncomfortably and her mouth goes whisper-dry as the Lead SocEn's words punch deep into her gut.

"...widespread genetic deficiencies...unstable mental and emotional functionality..."

This was supposed to have been a pleasant event, Ord 20 marking the first official meeting of this year's elite crop of SocEn candidates. It's traditional for one of the Leads to give the welcoming address. She'd thought the worst thing that could happen would be to have to endure the embarrassment of sitting through a speech by her father, but right now she'd give anything for him (or even Martinez) to be up there instead of Ariana Balor.

"...chronic predilection for depravity..."

None of her fellow candidates seem at all perturbed, though. Grouped around tables in the caf, they sip tea and munch crackers – it's off hours so they mainly have the place to themselves.

"...shockingly low IQs..."

Not that people saying terrible things about transers is anything new. Sometimes when she was younger she even joined in, determined to belie all traces of her origins. But those were stupid jokes (for the most part), not this kind of vicious rhetoric. Still, she cringes at the recollection of her own callowness – thinking of the group at Alamora, of the things Zeeb said the other night, of Lang.

Lang.

The time spent up in his room had been heady – and the feeling lingers; she can close her eyes and still feel the press of his body on hers. Being her first time, it had been a bit painful and awkward to start. But after a short pause they'd tried again, and the second time...an electric shiver runs through her, chased by an ache of longing so swift and strong that she bows her head lest anyone see it bloom on her face.

But it's followed by a stab of fear. Because she's not sure when she's going to be able to see him again.

The notice went out yesterday: There's been a recall on transer lab key fobs – some sort of error. Nothing to do with her clandestine activities or she's sure she would have been questioned. But until it's resolved there will be a tech stationed on the downstairs door, checking IDs. Bots she can trans, but to make a person not see her, or forget they saw her – well, she could probably manage it given a chance to experiment but it's not something she wants to try in real time.

He's going to think I don't want him. That I got freaked out by everything that happened. That I got what I wanted and I'm never coming back.

At least she'd been able to get him a message – Lang
had given her a bootleg server address when they parted so
she could contact him in an emergency. Any message sent
from hers would be archived in the recs somewhere though,
so she'd just said 'cancelled, key fobs: CM' and hoped he'd
get the gist. He probably would; he was smart.

But their plan to meet again this week is ruined. And
what if he doesn't get the message and thinks she's ditched
him? What if he goes back to that Jaslene girl, or finds somebody else? What if she never sees him again?

Her spine stiffens; that can't happen. It *can't*. Not after
the other night.

But there's nothing she can do about it at the moment.
And there is some small consolation: Her fingertips brush
the outline of the vial in her pocket, the product of this
morning's visit to the transer lab. She'd planned her words
carefully, striven to show professional disinterest, but in the
end it didn't matter. She had clearance. No one cared.

'How long?' the bored tech had asked and didn't even
blink when she requested two weeks. He'd scanned the code
on the vial's cap, she'd printed the reader, and that, as they
say, was that.

Research time.

A laugh nearly escapes her and she looks around, hoping no one's noticed. But all eyes are glued on Ariana. Re-
luctantly, Celan returns her attention to the Lead SocEn.

"…probably their most regrettable quality is their stubborn refusal to even attempt to evolve out of their dangerous superstitions and move forward into the light of reason.
Indeed, they seem to shrink from it, slinking back into the

169

dark corners where they can indulge in all manner of sickening vice." She says this last word with relish, biting down hard on the consonant.

Celan's stomach sinks as she thinks of what she plans to do with the vial, what she's already done with Lang. Because her fellow future SocEns are listening earnestly, nodding, agreeing with Ariana's words, even recording her on their servers to play back later for a booster shot of anti-expro sentiment, should theirs begin to wane. Not all are so captivated – some wear the neutral mask of boredom – but there are enough. Enough who believe everything they're hearing, who would look at someone like Lang with revulsion.

And that's not right.

He's a brilliant healer! He can do things you can't even imagine!

Though deep down she knows that doesn't matter either. Even if they saw what he could do, they'd still reject it. It's been the same since Jane Lees – anything to do with humans using electromagnetic energy that can't be quantified or strictly controlled is dangerous. That's why Lees had to leave, why she founded the ranchos in the first place. So what if it actually works? They don't care. Even if they saw what Lang could do they'd still hate him on principle.

And they'd hate me too, if they knew.

She shifts in her chair, eyes roaming over rapt faces until they settle on Shariah's, alight with obvious pride at her mother's oratory skills. Her best friend catches her staring and gives Celan a quick quirk of her lips and a happy little shrug, as if to say, 'Isn't she brilliant?'

Celan drops her gaze, swallows hard, and prays for this excruciating hour to end.

ATRAVESAR - TO BREAK THE SKIN

THEODORE STUDIES THE SWIRL OF amber liquid in his glass, contemplating. Then he takes a small sip, arming himself for the fight, though he's not entirely sure it will be. He's not sure what Lana will say to his 'big reveal' request, but he definitely needs to talk to her.

Ahora.

He's been so preoccupied by the whole Lanzhou launch that the delicate discussion he needs to have with her has been, of necessity, pushed to the back burner. But the mystery of the unmanned craft has been solved, thanks to some well-placed spy drones. It was headed for the Moon and not Mars – which is still a potential problem if they're trying to establish a moonbase as a precursor to a Martian venture, but it's not an immediate threat.

Funny how there's never been much of a collective will here in Albakirk to settle on the Moon. But he understands. There's just something so airless about it. Mars looks like someplace you could dig in, build things. Terraform. The Moon is just a rock.

Let Lanzhou have it.

But it still makes him nervous. Because they're not the only ones looking up and out – there are other city-states that may be planning similar endeavors. Hafar, possibly. They've got plenty of intel on the issue but the others have plenty of intel on them as well. Since the magnetosphere is still too unstable to maintain old-world-type satellites, everyone's got nano spy drones these days. Frustrating to operate but still invaluable. Keeping foreign ones out of your city while sneaking yours into theirs is a constant game the major city-states all play.

Like chess: which leads him back to Lana. They haven't started a new game in a while. That needs to be remedied soon. But for now –

He takes another sip of his drink and groans. She'll be home any minute (he left the library door open so he'd hear her come in) and he's still not sure what he's going to say.

Or how she's going to react.

Will she totally reject the idea? Pitch a fit? The thought of dealing with some kind of emotional meltdown makes him shudder. But Lana's not an overly emotional girl. She responds to logic, reason. He just has to explain it the right way and she'll see the light.

And it has to be done. Especially now that Ariana's up to her old tricks. Martinez told him all about the Pollomax. But that will only work in favor of the MRP: Too many people will balk at the idea of some half-baked plug-in. As long as she refuses to remove it, he's home free.

A sudden noise from the front of the bunk perks up his ears. He sits up straight and calls Lana's name – once, twice – but there's no response, just a whoosh as her bedroom door closes behind her.

Great.

Now he'll have to go knock and look like the supplicant, instead of having her come to him. Basic monkey-mind mechanics, but these techniques tend to work. Sighing, he puts his drink down on the polished desktop and starts to rise. Then he spots his server sitting atop the chessboard. He palms it and taps out a quick message, settling himself back in his chair to the sounds of her imminent approach.

But his daughter halts in the doorway, seemingly reluctant

to enter.

"Yes?" she says. Her voice sounds strange, sort of high and tight.

Project stress probably. No help for it.

Maybe that's his in – her project. She *is* working on transferon after all. Maybe he can start with that and segue into the other stuff from there.

"Lana. Ven aquí. We need to talk."

"Now?" she says, in that same tight tone.

"Yes. Now," he says. "It's important."

She sighs, but shuffles dutifully forward, and seats herself in the big chair as usual. Up close her face looks red and puffy, mouth a tense line. She studies her fingernails, avoiding his gaze.

"Are you OK?" he asks at once, solicitous.

She glances up, then quickly lowers her eyes; says nothing.

"What is it?" he tries again. "Project trouble? Hit a snag?"

She shakes her head no. "I – " she starts. "Well, I know it's stupid to still get upset about stuff like this but – "

"But what?"

She takes a deep breath. "We had that SocEn candidate meeting today and Mrs. Balor spoke. About expros. Transway."

"Bad?" he says.

"Awful," she spits out. "I thought you said she was over all that! That she was trying to revive GISH now; that she doesn't care about Transway anymore."

"So I thought," he says archly. "What exactly did she say?"

"Nothing I haven't heard before. But it was just so… wrong. And it went on and on and on." She presses fingertips to her temples, as if trying to ward off a headache. "And everyone was just sitting there nodding their stupid heads like they *agreed* with her. Like, 'Oh, of *course*, transers are stupid, filthy, and useless – how could it possibly be otherwise?'"

Never mind the project. *This* is the perfect in.

Theodore plunges: "You know, these kinds of attitudes only change when people have a real flesh-and-blood example to contradict them. Someone who can defy their expectations and show them how misguided their assumptions are."

Lana cracks a small, wry smile he can't quite read. "Yeah," she says. "Right."

He clears his throat. "In case you haven't already realized it, I am immensely proud of your decision to try for SocEn. You have worked incredibly hard and advanced more than I ever could have imagined. And if," and here he grins knowingly, "or *when* you are accepted to the discipline, I have an idea that I'd like you to consider."

She nods, allowing him to go on.

"As you heard today, there is still quite a bit of anti-Transway sentiment among our ranks. People are beginning to forget how important the expros are to us, both as experimental subjects and sensational outlets. But the deeper issue, as I see it, is that they are losing the concept of transers being capable of learning, of growth, when we," and here he pauses to indicate them both, "know that to be patently untrue."

"OK," she says, a sudden wariness in her tone.

"There will always be expros who aren't interested in advanced learning. And we'll always provide them with alternative ways to be useful, such as bot testing. But for those that are, I feel the time is ripe to provide them with an example. A motivation. An aspirational role model who will serve the dual role of also demonstrating to *our* people that the intellectual growth of expros is indeed possible. That they *are* capable of learning, even of ascending to the highest echelons of our society. Even," and here he regards her pointedly, "as far as SocEn."

Realization dawns in her eyes. Followed by horror.

"No."

"Yes, Lana. You."

"But," she squeaks out, pinch-faced, "no one's going to make me a SocEn once they know where I came from. There's no way they'd ever do it. I'll end up a SanTech or – "

"I realize that," Theodore cuts her off, "and I don't want anyone to deny you your hard-earned privileges on the basis of ignorant prejudice. Therefore, I propose that we wait for the announcement until after you've formally been admitted to the discipline. That way, everyone will know that you made it fair and square, on the basis of your own skills and intelligence."

He smiles indulgently, like he's granting a favor.

But Lana has the faintly green appearance of someone who is about to be sick. "Please," she says, voice shaking. "I really don't think this a good idea. What about my friends? What about the people I'll be PostEd with? They'll never treat me the same. You know they won't. I thought you wanted me to fit in, I thought I was never supposed to tell – " Her lips quiver. "Please don't make me do this."

"I am not *making* you do anything. And I know what

I am asking will be hard. I won't pretend otherwise. But you owe it – to those people out there, to the people in here, to yourself, to me – to be the best example that you can be. To prove beyond a shadow of a doubt that any expro is capable of advancement if they are willing to work hard enough. You are the best hope we have for finally erasing anti-Transway sentiment and for allowing its denizens to truly thrive. Don't you want that? To save people's lives? *Your* people?"

"I – I guess so," she chokes out.

"Bueno." Theodore grunts, satisfied. He picks up his drink and rattles it, letting the ice clink against the glass before he swallows the rest. "And remember," he continues, "you have quite a bit of time before it even has to happen. Think about what you'd like to say. I'll work with you every step of the way on your statement."

Lana doesn't seem to be listening anymore, though. Her attention is focused on the glass in his hand.

"Where's mine?" Their running joke. But something in her tone says she's serious this time.

Well, why not? She's old enough. And she looks like she could use a little fortification.

He snatches another glass off the shelf and pours her two fingers. Handing it over, he tops his off and raises it in a toast.

"To Transway," he says, with a touch of grandness.

But she doesn't toast back, just downs it and sets the glass neatly on the desk as she gets to her feet.

"Gracias," she says. "Good talk."

"How about some chess?" he says as she turns to go. "We really need to start a new game."

His daughter shrugs, her back to him.

"Maybe some other time."

She stalks out into the hall, past her room, and exits through the bunk's front door. He considers going after her, but figures she needs a chance to get over the initial shock and think things through. Maybe go for a run, or take a walk in the gardens. See one of her friends.

When she comes back, she'll have accepted it.

And she'll be ready to do her part.

⊏▪ 13 ▪⊏

It's a damp, rainy Saturday, but the kitchen is warm and dry as Lang, under Mara's watchful eye, rolls a large square of dough out on the flour-dusted counter. This homey domesticity is the perfect remedy for last night's insanity: Three fusers had made two separate hits on Zeeb's crew, making off with two of his transfers. Lang hadn't been a direct part of the action, but he'd been called in as extra muscle in the aftermath. Things are tense on the street and look like they will be for the forseeable future.

Maybe it's actually for the best that Celan can't get out right now.

"All week long I run a fucking kitchen and then these fools want me to make sopas on my day off." Mara says, bare feet resting on the table top as she leans back precipitously in her chair and sips from a mug of peppermint tea.

"You're not even making them," Lang says. "I am."

"Yeah, but I still gotta supervise your ass or you'll fuck

it up."

She glances out the window at the sodden yard and shivers, burrowing deep into her oversized sweater. "Ugh, I hate this fucking rain."

"Me too," Lang says, reaching for the bottle propped on the counter next to his sopapilla-making operation.

Mara squints hard at him.

"So what's with you lately? You been hittin' that shit," she nods at the bottle, "more than usual."

Lang shrugs. "It's just…you know."

"So where is she then? Did we scare little miss Kimbra away?" An impish smirk. "Can't imagine what we might have done."

Lang shoots her the stink eye. "She said she can't get out here – some kind of thing is going on at Pescados. It might be a while." He cocks a hip against the counter and takes a long pull, deep relief flooding his system.

Yeah, it's early, but so fucking what?

"So why don't you go see *her* then? Hop on over there and surprise her." She flutters light fingers ranchos-ward.

Lang winces. If Celan really did live in the ranchos, that would be the obvious solution. But for him to get into the city…that's much too complicated. He'd thought of astralling, trying to find her that way. But would she even be able to see his astral form? And even if she could, what if she really didn't *want* to see him? What if she'd had her fun and now she was done? Showing up in her bedroom like some ghostly stalker isn't going to win him any favors.

At least, thanks to certain members of his clientele, he knows that the key fob situation is real. She was telling the truth about that. Still, if she really wanted to get out couldn't she find another way?

He sighs. "It's not that simple. I mean, if she's really trying to blow me off it might freak her out even more if I just showed up." He takes another quick swig, wiping his mouth on his hand before turning back to the dough.

Mara snorts, derisive. "More than what? That fight? Like no one ever fights in the ranchos."

"It's not just that. Zeeb really laid into her."

"Mira, you know I love Zeeb, but between you and me? His 'poor exploited Transway' shit is ridiculous. He's making chits hand over fist – "

"I know," Lang says dryly. "But you said she saw – "

"What? A fuser? Please. She didn't look all that scared to me. More like…interested."

Lang frowns, rummaging in the cupboard for the deep frying pan. He bangs it down on the stovetop just a little harder than necessary. Mara jumps in her chair, sloshing her tea.

"Why are you being such a bitch?" she says, dabbing at her sodden sweater. "Who cares if she is? Wouldn't be the first ranchita to break bad out here."

"She's not breaking anything," Lang says. "Just because you all – "

"It's not just us," Mara hisses. "Lest you forget – you're a fuser too."

"Was," Lang corrects her. "I *was* a fuser. Now I'm not – "

"Practicing."

Lang says nothing, just grabs a knife and slashes the dough into squares, then unstoppers a jug of sunflower oil and pours a generous helping into the pan. Poking the fuel cell on under the burner, he waits for the telltale bubbles to let him know it's hot enough for the batter. He barely registers the bang of the door as Zeeb and Sig enter, hands clasped.

"Anyway, she'll be back," Mara says, trying to smooth things over. "She's got it bad for you, I can tell. First Jaslene, now this one. You must be doing something right behind closed doors 'cause it sure ain't the way you dress."

Lang grunts.

"Seriously," she says. "You're like a free-box reinona."

Zeeb and Sig cackle, then share a quick kiss.

"And as for you two – " Mara says, raising an eyebrow. "Que es esto?"

Sig smirks. "We're together now. Hope you don't mind, Mara," he says, his tone oddly challenging as he drapes an arm around Zeeb's shoulders.

"Not at all," she says. "My cousin you can have."

They all laugh as Lang hunches over the sopas with that weird lonely feeling he sometimes gets – like he's missing a joke somewhere. He *was* gone for a year though, and plenty of things happened without him. It'd feel even weirder asking them to explain.

Plus, he's got his own secrets.

Like Celan Mairs, if he ever gets to see her again.

He flicks some water into the pan to test the oil and it sizzles wildly, causing a spatter of pinpricks to leap onto his hand. Feels like – *No*. Gingerly, he drops in the first of the dough squares; taking a sidelong glance at the bottle, measuring the level. If he's not going to fuse, he needs *something*.

They just gotta understand.

ATRAVESAR - TO BREAK THE SKIN

CELAN'S BOOTS CLIP RAPIDLY ALONG the polished floor of the corridor as she rubs eyes glazed from the afterimages of eight straight hours of transfiguration neural pathways. She'd only gotten up once, to use the bathroom, and then only when the pressure in her bladder reached code red. Forget food – she had to keep going, to focus, to blot out the dread growing steadily in her heart as the safe, sturdy foundation she's spent seven years building begins to shudder, crack, and slide inexorably out from under her.

He's going to make me tell.

She still can't believe that her father is serious about exposing her as an expro. Just picturing the looks of disgust on people's faces – Shariah and Bryan for starters and then everyone else she's ever known, or ever will – fills her with such shame and fear that she's barely been able to eat, much less enjoy anything else. All she's done for the past few days is work. And although she knows that her reaction is cowardly and awful (a good person would leap at the chance to 'Save people's lives, *her* people'), she still really doesn't want to do it.

If only she could talk to Lang. Maybe she couldn't tell him *everything* (telling him that she's the daughter of a Lead SocEn probably isn't a very good idea), but she could discuss the general situation.

But there's been no reply to her message. Not that she expected one; it's too risky to send messages back and forth. The 'key fob' thing at least had plausible deniability – it was vague enough to mean anything and could have accidentally been sent to the wrong address. He was smart not to reply. But still, she wishes he'd said something.

More than that, she wishes she could see him. Talk to him in person and explain that she really does miss him. She'd even attempted to astral – flashing back on the way the elders used to have them do it at 'scuela when she was a kid. She'd breathed and hummed for an hour, but it hadn't worked. She was able to peek outside her body for a minute or two, but then vertigo took over and she'd been sucked right back in.

Anxiously, she cracks her knuckles, then lets one hand drift down to brush the small, cool vial in her pocket. It's been the only thing keeping her from completely falling apart.

It was easy once she set her mind to it – making transferon, keeping her bots working while it was in her system. All prana; all in the intent. And she's positive there's no record of her ingesting it. There've been no MedLab messages, no anomalies.

'Necessity is the mother of invention,' a wise man once said, and she's been nothing if not inventive.

But very, very careful.

She's confined herself to oral dosages – nice, safe blends of D, E, and S to give her stamina, calm, and vision in equal measure. But the desire for a real escape is building, tiptoeing around the corner of her mind. So far, she's managed to hold the line, but she can feel her resolve waning.

Because what's the point? What's the point of being a good little tech and doing everything right? What's the point of trying to get accepted to SocEn when in the end her father's going to ruin everything for her anyway? Once they know where she came from they'll probably make her a San-Tech – Lead father or no. And even if they don't, no one's ever going to take her seriously again. She'll be a freak. An oddity.

Like some kind of talking dog or –

"Lana!" It takes a moment to register the word as her name. She looks up, surprised to see she's reached the plaza, and that Shariah, Bev, and Kirk (the latter two holding hands!) are in line for the elevator, waving her over. She gives them a weak smile.

"Hey," she says. "What's up?"

Hopefully they don't want her to go do anything with them.

"Um, dinner?" Shariah says testily. "Don't you ever check your server these days?"

Crap.

They were supposed to have had some sort of pod reunion dinner tonight, which was pretty stupid considering it's only been a few weeks since they split.

But Shariah obviously doesn't think so. Arms crossed, lips pursed, she's fuming.

"Sorry," Celan says. "Got caught up in the lab."

"Whatever," Shariah snaps. "That was the whole point of dinner. So everyone doesn't get so *caught up in the lab* that we never talk to each other again."

"I said I was sorry – " she starts. But the elevator door opens and Shariah turns, shutting her out. The three of them get in, followed by several older techs who eye their little scuffle with amusement. Cursing silently, Celan stomps to the back of the line.

She is not going to apologize. *No way*. It was just dinner. One dinner in the caf out of a million they've all had together. Three hundred sixty-five dinners a year! For six years. She does the math in her head. OK, not exactly a million. But a lot.

Her hand slides to her pocket again.

She really needs to relax.

SAFE IN HER ROOM, SNUGGLED into sleepwear and huddled on her bed, Celan turns the light off and lets her eyes adjust to the dark. She takes out the vial – filled with fresh water from the kitchen faucet – and rests back against the window, legs crossed loosely in front of her. She clasps it between her palms and considers: What does she want to feel?

The thought rises – *Bliss, everything easy.*

Who'd said that? Taegh?

Bliss it is.

She drops her lids and takes a deep breath to start the process. In her mind's eye a shimmer of sparks swirls and coalesces, infusing the water with her intent. The vial starts to shine, brighter and brighter, until with a final pulse it releases. As soon as it's done, she unscrews the cap, and draws up some of the fluid.

A little less than a third: That ought to do it.

But mere drops aren't going to cut it tonight, not after the fight with Shariah. What's the point of even trying to make up when as soon as her announcement is made their friendship is over anyway? And once everyone knows she's an expro they'll probably watch her more closely in the lab and at the gate. Which means no more Lang, either.

No: tonight, just this once, she needs a *real* escape.

Celan pushes up her sleeve, wondering if she can even do this at all. She's only ever fused once, and that was years ago, in another lifetime. But she doesn't recall it having been difficult.

In truth, it had been as easy as breathing.

That's it, she thinks. *Just breathe, like it's nothing. Nothing at all.*

She touches dropper to flesh and mentally steps back, letting the forces of will and desire build the energetic momentum. Feels it zip from her brain to her hand to the vial and then back into her again as, with a squeeze of the bulb, the shot passes through her skin and into a vein. Her heart beats once, twice, and –

Holy –

Holy –

Cap and vial slip from her fingers as a wave of pleasure so intense it's almost a g-force presses her against the windowpane. She grabs a hunk of blanket in each hand and twists hard, trying to hold on.

This is different, very different, from what happened when she was a kid. Different from her nice, safe oral doses.

This is…bliss – every cell in her body ablaze with light. She wants to jump up and riot, dance in exultation. But she can barely move.

Bots, bots, bots! a tiny untouched part of her brain screams. Mentally, she reaches out, gives them a push. Then she fumbles for the transfer, tucking dropper and vial away as an odd sort of slippage begins – repeated little slips into blankness like an endless code loop, rhythmic and soothing. Every taught nerve, every fraught bundle of the particles that make up her being gathers and accumulates until some critical mass is reached and it all begins to slide as one, down and down, into a velvety wave of calm.

Celan smiles, flashing on that long gone day when she

found Taegh in the garden of a wayvern; sitting just like this, must have felt just like this. No wonder he was so –

Bzzt. Bzzt.

An odd buzzing noise, like an angry bee. She bats hands around her ears in slow motion.

Bzzt. Bzzt.

Then she realizes: Her server. Reaching and reaching, it's taking forever.

There. Got it.

She blinks at the screen. Bev. Something about dinner. How she hurt Shariah's feelings.

A warm flush of fondness envelops her then – for Bev, for Shariah, for their whole little erstwhile pod. Carefully, she taps out a message, but the blankness loop causes stutters so she reads it over twice, three times, to make sure it makes sense.

Sorry. Didn't mean it. Stressed out with project. Lunch to-morrow? Dying to know what's up with Bev and Kirk!

She sends it to Shariah then shuts the server down. No more of that tonight.

She curls around soft pillows, burrowing deep as another wave takes her, gentler than before but still glorious. Through the window, the stars shine down brighter than she has ever seen them, dazzlingly huge, pulling her up into them. The blackness and the light. The spaces in between. The world is all right. The world is right. She gazes up awed, and thoroughly absorbed.

She wishes it could go on like this forever.

LANG KICKS HIS BEDROOM SHUT behind him with a fleeting satisfaction at the sound of the slam. He fumbles in his pack, pulls out a bottle, and thunks it on the window sill.

No más, a part of him says, but he shrugs it off, tossing the empty pack on the bed and grabbing the bottle by the neck like he wants to throttle it. Yanks out the stopper and takes a swig; it burns so sweet. He tips it up for another but feels the gorge rise in his throat. Gagging, he slams it back down on the sill and sinks to the floor, head in hands.

It's no use. He's sick of the taste, tired of the smell. Sick of the fucking feeling. It's just not the same.

It doesn't have to be like before, a small voice says inside his head. *It doesn't have to be bad*.

A shudder runs through him then, so deep it's almost a sob, as he slides a hand into his pouch and draws out the transfer. It fits comfortably, reassuringly, in his palm, a bit of pearly fluid shimmering in the bottom. Class E. Leftovers from his last customer of the day.

His fingers tighten on the cap.

But Celan –

She doesn't have to know.

But his family, the ranchos –

You think they'd be any happier seeing you drink like this? It's terrible for you, worse than the fuse.

But –

Rafael's face fills his mind then – radiant, angelic. People were always drawn to him; girls always smiling, trying to catch his eye. The way he carried himself with that wry lean like anything unpleasant would slough right off.

His cousin had barely even tried in 'scuela – did just enough to get his transfer and then he was gone. Raf didn't care about being an elegido, didn't want responsibilities, and he didn't want to spend his life kowtowing to a bunch of charlatans.

Because the elders were deluded, he'd informed Lang that first night on Transway. They were never going to fix the destruction of the old world. It was too bad; the rot had gone too deep. The beautiful Terra Madre that had once been was poisoned and would be so for thousands of years. All their healing efforts were drops in a bucket. And the techs? All they could do was lock themselves away indoors. They couldn't make anything better either.

But here on Transway you could forget all that. Here there was freedom and fun. You could do whatever you wanted whenever you wanted and no one could ever tell you no.

Speaking of which…there was a special thing you could do with a transfer, something a hundred times better than the drops they got at 'scuela. Something the elders did; something they kept secret. Did Lang want to know what it was?

Of course he did.

And it was better than anything he could have imagined. All his worries, all his fears, all his insecurities all were gone; his body and mind relaxed in places he'd never even realized were tense. Nothing much mattered after that – not 'scuela, not his parents, and especially not the weird pressure that he'd felt building over the previous two years.

Because the introduction of transferon into students' systems at Pranascuela didn't affect everyone the same way. For many it merely kept their abilities from atrophying during the transition from childhood to adulthood. But for others there was a very marked enhancement in one of the three pranic modalities: Kinetics had the gift of sheer force and vitality, quixotics were possessed of a seer-like visionary quality, while empathics were capable of such close identification with another person or thing that they made excellent healing channels. And it turned out that Lang was empathic in the extreme.

Suddenly he could feel energy – almost see it, really – flowing in and around him in a way that he'd never known was possible. He could heal almost any illness or injury he touched; was almost drawn to do it. It was crazy; he'd never been more than average at 'scuela when he was younger, but now the growing expectation in the eyes of his parents and teachers and the envious whispers of his peers were starting to make him anxious.

Because as much as a part of him longed to be special, to be chosen, another part of him was scared – to be singled out, to have to be holy all the time, and, deep down, of that being the end of his closeness to Raf. They'd always talked about going to Transway together – spun a million adventures around the fire pit in the backyard with flames bright in their eyes and cider fizzing in their bellies. But that would never happen if Lang got a blue robe at eighteen. He'd be smothered in it forever.

So when Raf finally came back and offered to take him out to Transway for a weekend he'd jumped at the chance. Until Lang's father stepped in and threw Raf out of the house, shouting, 'Stay away from my son!' at the nephew he'd always insisted he loved just as much as if he'd been his own. Rafael had slunk away like a kicked dog.

Lang was so worried about him afterwards that he decided to go out to Transway himself, just for a day, to check on Raf and make sure he was all right.

But his cousin was doing just fine. When Lang tracked him down at Alamora he found Raf surrounded by a ton of good friends and pretty girls, living like a punk king on the chits he made selling transferon. He was welcomed with open arms, and the next thing Lang knew it was weeks later and even if he went home, it was all over. He'd never get a blue robe now. He'd done the choosing. And he was going to stay on Transway forever. Raf was right; they were free.

He can picture them both, like they used to be, sloping down dusty alleys under a blazing sun and a crackling blue sky. Lighting each other's smokes, talking about the mural they were painting, flirting with some girls, bringing them to see it. Showing off. And at Alamora in the evening, jamming with Zeeb and Sig. Everyone laughing, passing around bottles of beer. Going to play at a wayvern, walking in like they owned the place. Every day the same like beads on a chain, yet each bright, unique, perfect.

But then came the sickness and the pain – and Rafael walking, his face a hollowed-out calavera mask. Wresting his prone form into a roller. Desperate for a cure that last horrible week.

So now –

He twists off the cap. Tugs at his sleeve.

I can't do this.

But his throat's so tight he can barely breathe.

A little. Just a little bit.

But –

You're not Rafael!

Click. Jaw clenched, he draws up some fluid and gathers his will, hitting blindly, not looking down.

And then it's all alright.
Finally.
He's home.

HE'S BEEN DRIFTING, BUOYED ON a raft of warm waves for what feels like hours. Lang's never been to the ocean in real life, but the elders used to take them in the astral. He recalls the hypnotic surge...on and on, over and over, into infinity. He'd loved that; wished he'd been alive in the old world when the water was clean and he could spindrift weightless with the tide and have the sun and moon and stars shine down upon him. He'd dreamed about it.

But right now it feels rapturously real. So he lets it take him. On and on.

"Hey," someone's hunched over him, patting at his face. "You OK? You gotta stop doing this, güey."

It's Brophy, checking on him. They've started to worry every time he holes up in here with a bottle.

With effort, he lifts heavy lids and meets his friend's eyes shimmering in the dark. Brophy blinks once in disbelief, then sits back on his haunches, face breaking into a broad, relieved grin.

"Welcome back."

"Thanks," Lang mutters, struggling to sit up as something clatters to the floor. The transfer. Blindly, he gropes for it until Brophy snatches the pieces up, screwing them together. He returns it to Lang, who shoves it in his pouch and slumps against the wall. It hugs him like a lover.

"How long?" Brophy says.

Lang stares at him for a moment, uncomprehending.

Then he remembers: His eyes. Fusing leaves a telltale trace – a subtle shimmer like sunlight on the surface of a stream. It's only visible to others currently fusing as well but that's no problem for Brophy. His eyes are shining too. He can tell.

"Just tonight," he mutters.

Brophy reaches out and pats his shoulder.

"Better you go back to this than drink like that."

Lang says nothing.

Brophy gets to his feet. "We'll talk later, OK?"

Slowly, Lang nods and his friend retreats out into the hall, leaving him to his reverie.

14

"You win." Martinez's words bound through Theodore's brain – echoing the happy news for the millionth time today. The sense of frustration and stress that has been plaguing him since before Navidad has all just been gloriously resolved: Ariana is refusing to take the Pollomax plug-in out of the GISH reboot. Even though her own supporters are begging her to.

It's over.

And there are no other propositions out there that can compete with the MRP. If there were, he'd have heard at least a whisper of one by now.

It's happening.

We're going to Mars.

He bounces once, twice, three times on the diving board then launches himself into the pool. The water is a joyful shock and he rockets up to the surface, relishing the cleanness of it. Surfacing, he moves his arms in a powerful crawl, slicing forward like a knife.

This ought to cheer Lana up too, he thinks as he reaches the far wall and does a quick kick turn.

She's been extremely moody lately, probably due to the lingering effects of their discussion the other day. He completely understands her being unsettled by his request. It's a tall order. But she'll come around. Surely, this show of support for Transway will help improve her outlook.

He tears through the rest of his laps with fervor before switching over to ocean mode and allowing himself to float weightless. He likes to spend the last few minutes of his precious private half hour like this, bobbing with the swells and watching the stars shine through the translucent ceiling. He rolls over, enjoying the pleasant press of water against his back.

Then something brushes his leg and he looks down to see a bright green-and-yellow swish of fins – the immaculate blue tile of the pool is now a sandy undersea garden resplendent with swaying kelp and coral and dotted with the shimmering forms of a million little fish. None of it is really real, of course, just a holo programmed with the best of the old world oceans. But it's splendid all the same.

He watches the display for a bit and then flips over again, floating until the waves still and the pool returns to its prosaic form.

Time's up.

He heaves himself up the ladder and plucks his towel off a nearby chair. Tucking it around his waist, he heads for the showers, almost running right into a lithe blue-eyed woman who greets him with demure deference.

"Mr. Timanti," she says, her tone almost reverent. "Excuse

me."

"No, no," he says. "Excuse *me*. It was my fault. Got caught up in the holos."

She smiles then, quite charmingly, and meets his eyes. "An ocean holo?"

He nods.

"I like those, too."

Theodore swallows, taking in the chestnut curls peeking sweetly out from under her bathing cap.

"And you are?" he says.

"Dahlia Algren. EdEn."

"Well, very nice to meet you, Dahlia. Hope you enjoy your swim."

He grins and steps to the side, gallantly letting her pass before resuming his walk to the showers. There's an absence of a splash behind him though, so he looks back to check on her, only to find her poised on the edge of the pool, staring wistfully after him.

Maybe it's about time, he muses, *to really think about settling down*.

LANG ISN'T SURE HOW MUCH time has passed, but the initial rush of the fuse is beginning to wear off. He's still pretty aviados, but his sense of perfect peace is now riddled with the first little worms of guilt and fear. Already part of him is begging, 'Again!' but he shoves the thought away. For the moment, he can resist. But he already knows he'll do it again.

And again and again and again.

Needing more and more and more.

And then it won't be long until the real, gut-level cravings start. And the dread affliction – CERS (Class E Reaction Syndrome). It won't be long at all, not with his history. And then he'll have to fuse just to stave it off. It's not really a question of whether he's fucked or not now. It's just a matter of how fast and how deep.

Fucking Class E. I'm so fucking stupid.

But after so long away it really does feel good. Maybe even better for all he'd tried to fight it.

Rising on rubbery legs, he steadies himself against the wall before shuffling down the hall to find Brophy's door ajar. His friend's shirtless frame is sprawled across the bed in the half-light, plucking at the strings of a bass guitar. Lang stands in the doorway, hesitant, until a shift in his weight makes the floor creak.

"Hey," says Brophy, sitting up and putting the bass aside.

"Hey."

"Ven aquí."

He enters, immediately plunking down on the floor and leaning against a beat-up wooden wardrobe for support. Brophy eyes him for a long moment. Lang draws his knees up to his chest and stares at the toes of his boots.

"First things first," Brophy says. "Trans that burn."

Lang locates the spot in the crook of his arm where the fuse went in and a small red weal has formed. He covers it with his other hand and breathes once, twice, letting his prana do its work. When he removes his hand the burn is gone.

Minutes pass.

"So, you feel like shit," Brophy finally says.

Lang grimaces.

"You hate yourself. You wish it were different. You wish *you* were different."

Silence.

"Well fuck that shit. I'm glad to see you back. Took you long enough."

This last snaps Lang out of his muteness. "You think this is a good thing? You think I should celebrate? Langton is now permanently fucked. Yeah, that's a great day in history."

Brophy sighs. "It doesn't have to be like that."

"Sure." Lang sneers. "Look at Tomás, look at Taegh. Jenner. Jory. Look at Rafael. All dead, or might as well be!" He's almost shouting now. "You're an exception! And who's to say you won't end up the same?"

Brophy shrugs. "Everyone ends up dead eventually. That's life."

Lang snorts, derisive, and starts to protest but Brophy cuts him off.

"Es verdad. That's how it is. But it's not about how you die. It's how you live." He rolls off the bed, snatches his smoke pouch from the nightstand, and settles down beside Lang.

Grudgingly, Lang shifts over to make room. "And how am I supposed to live?" he says, his tone hollow.

"Like always." Brophy dips into the pouch and unrolls a wrapper. His long fingers make quick work of the smoke and he hands it to Lang, who inhales deeply as he strikes the flint. Lang exhales – shoulders slumped, defeated – then passes it back.

"Mira," Brophy says, "I went through all this same shit. Got into fusing. Then I stopped. Started drinking instead and it almost killed me. But I wised up. Went back to the fuse and I did OK. But I learned how to manage it. If you're careful and you stay behind it, you won't end up walking."

Lang shakes his head. "You're an S now, though. It's easier for you. You don't need it every day anymore."

"But I *was* an E. For a long time. You saw me – right there with you and Raf, CERS-ado like a motherfucker."

"But you weren't exactly 'staying behind it' then, were you?" Lang snipes. "You were a mess too."

"That was only at the very end. I'd been functioning, mostly, as a Class E since I was sixteen."

Lang perks up at this. For all the hours he'd spent listening to Raf and Brophy bullshit back in the day he'd never really heard Brophy's whole story. Or maybe he just hadn't been paying attention.

"So how did you stop then?" he says. "If it'd been going on so long, how did you change?"

"I don't really know. I just really, really wanted it to be over – not to be sick anymore, not to *need* it – and then I had the weirdest fuse ever. Saw all this crazy chizz and, like, my whole *life* passed in front of me. But when it stopped – boom! No más Class E. I've been an S ever since." He scratches his chin, thoughtful.

"You think I could do that?"

"Sure." Brophy passes him the smoke. "But I think you have to really, really want it."

"And you think I don't? You think I like this?" Lang says, a little testily. He draws on the smoke, tip flaring cherry red.

Brophy's eyes are shrewd. "I don't think you like it," he says softly. "I know you love it."

Lang starts to protest, but trails off as the truth in Brophy's words sinks in. His cheeks burn. He draws his knees up tighter and rests his forehead against them.

"So did I," Brophy says. "For a long time. It took me years to get to the point where it got so bad that I was finally done. You've only just started again. It's probably gonna be awhile."

Lang raises his head for another quick drag then hands the smoke back to Brophy. "So what do I do in the meantime?"

"Take care of yourself. Find something to do so you're not just laying around all fused up all the time."

"Yeah," Lang says, with mock enthusiasm. "I'm a great vendedor!"

Brophy blows twin jets from his nose and squints at him seriously. "You're a really good healer, Lang. You know that, right?"

Lang chuckles, shaking his head. "Practically an elder."

"To people around here? You might as well be. All that stuff you can do…" He waggles his fingers like he's casting a spell. "And you're good at explaining things too. I mean, I never thought I'd be able to astral until you showed me."

"But that's easy."

"Not for expros."

"But I've been doing it since I was a kid."

"Exactly. We need someone like you. Someone who knows this stuff and can show us how to do it too. Or we're all gonna end up with bots in our heads. None of those assholes in the ranchos gives a fuck."

Lang looks away, discomfited. But some small spark ignites in his solar plexus. Something like hope. He shakes his head again, but with less vigor than before.

"It's true," Brophy says. "Think about it."

Lang reaches for the smoke and takes a long, contemplative drag as the creaky floor by the door announces more visitors. He looks up to see Mara, flanked by Sig; two pairs of glittering eyes that mirror his own.

"Well, what have we here?" Mara says, lips twisted in amusement.

No use denying it. If he can see it in their eyes they can see it in his. But Lang takes his time answering, exhaling a drawn-out cloud.

"Nobody here but us fusers," he finally says.

AT LEAST THIS IS THE last place they'd ever expect her to be.

Ariana regards the smoky room sourly, skin crawling at the contact with the chair, the dirty table top (wiped down at her insistence, but with a greying rag most likely teeming with bacteria and viruses).

Mutant viruses.

She shudders at the raggedy fingernails on the hand that places the drink before her and drops a chit into its outstretched palm, making sure to avoid skin-to-skin contact and never raising her eyes from those of the man across the table.

Ironic that they're meeting at a wayvern, but it's the only place where they can be assured of even minimal privacy. This is one of the shabbier ones – only one view on the main door (she'd checked the specs beforehand) so they'd come in the side and taken a table near the kitchen, the emanations from which nearly made her gag until she got herself under control.

No chance she'll touch that drink. She nudges it aside and leans forward. "So, any progress?"

Alton White sighs, running a stubby hand through his wiry black hair. "Nada."

"There have to be some. A few at least. Even one would work. But two is better."

"It's a very delicate request."

"Making a security training screener? We make them all the time."

"Yes," Alton concedes, "but this is a rather…special one. And they're a suspicious breed. I have to find exactly the right ones to ask. Just the right amount of desperate, if you know what I mean."

He takes a sip of his own drink and Ariana makes a moue of disgust.

Alton sighs again. "I'm doing the best I can."

"Obviously not enough."

"Look, it's not the screener itself that's the problem. It's the subject matter that's spooking them. Actually simulating an attack on the city? On the water supply?"

"But didn't you promise them immunity? Tell them the Destierra would be for show? That they'd be picked up and adequately compensated – them and their families, in perpetuity? No more testing? Ever?" Her voice rises in pitch on the last word.

Of course it's all bullshit. Once they're out in the desert that's that. No one's coming to get them. But it shouldn't be hard to convince them otherwise. They're expros after all.

"Yes, of course," Alton says. "But I only got that far with two of them and they ran like the wind when they found out exactly what they'd have to do. I had to threaten to cut off their Class E to make sure they didn't tell anyone."

"So *cut* them off! *Force* them to do it."

But Alton's shaking his head. "And what if they'd rather be sick than dead? Then they can talk. And we don't want any word of this ever getting out."

"Who cares who they tell? No one's going to believe them. If they won't do it for themselves then threaten their families. Friends. Anyone they care about."

"And just how am I supposed to do all that without generating recs or views? The only place I can even discuss this is in the wayverns. Once we're back in the lab I have to be circumspect. If they're not willing to meet here there's only so much I can say. We need at least semi-willing participants or we risk exposure." He lifts his glass, downs the rest of his drink. "And that's not a risk I'm willing to take."

"But Arlo's," she says. "Seven years ago. You took the risk then."

"That was an outside job. Much simpler. This kind of inside job..." He trails off unhappily.

Ariana slumps in her seat, gnawing at her lower lip.

Stymied.

Mere weeks until the resource vote and she's at an impasse. All they need is one expro willing to pretend to try to put some transferon into the water supply and stir up some anti-Transway hysteria. Without that she won't get enough support for the GISH reboot unless she removes the Pollomax portion. And there's no way she's going to do that.

204

That was the whole point.

Her eyes roam the smoky room, raking the far wall like the answer is written there. There has to be a way to make this work. *Has* to be.

Maybe they could do a holo? But those require a whole team of CompEns to produce. She needs something genuine, but lean and untraceable. And she needs it soon.

Because as of this moment, she's fresh out of backup plans.

▭▸ 15 ◂▭

Lang's fingers thrum a jittery rhythm against the side of his glass as Celan relaxes into their booth at Tosh's and takes a long gulp of cider. Eyes alight, she grins up at him from under the hood of her jacket. He tries to smile back but fails to mirror her joy.

Her face falls. "Is something wrong? I thought you'd be happy to see me."

And he is. More than he can say. These last few weeks have felt at least a year long. He's been trying to keep his mind off worrying about when (or if) he'd see her again, but even with the fuse it hasn't been easy. So when he'd gotten her message the other day (T's Ord 55, 20:30: CM – the sweetest words he'd ever seen) he was ecstatic. But that bubble quickly burst.

Because it's inevitable: One way or another she's going to find out about the fusing.

Maybe he can keep her from the truth for a little while

if he keeps her away from anyone who might say anything, but he's already up to twice a day and, while he's not a total raging mess, too many people already know. They have eyes. And even if his are clear at the moment it doesn't matter. Word travels.

He frowns down into his glass.

You don't have to tell her.

"Lang?"

"But I do." A wince. "I mean, I am. Happy. It's just...I thought maybe you were gone for good."

She leans in, covering his hands with her own. "Well I'm not. I just couldn't get out until they fixed the fobs. I missed you so much."

"Sure."

She jerks away, stung.

Fuck. I'm such an asshole.

Celan reddens, clearly upset. "I wasn't trying to avoid you. And I'm not mad about anything that happened last time, if that's what you think."

He sighs gloomily, takes a swig of cider. "I know. I guess it's just – all this sneaking around. Is it always gonna be like this?"

"No! Of course not. I'll be PostEd soon and then I can go in and out whenever I want."

"But you're always gonna go back in."

She regards him with suspicion, like she's starting to think he's picking a fight on purpose. Which he kind of is.

Asshole.

But he can't seem to help himself; anything to avoid the real issue.

"It's not that simple," she says. "Maybe I'm a transer at

208

heart, but I'm a tech, too. At least," she adds darkly, "for the next few months."

"Huh?"

"Never mind."

"How can you be happy in there though?" he presses. "Being who you are. Isn't that's why you came out here – to be with your real people? Unless it's not. Unless I'm just a study break."

"That's not true!" Celan protests, vehement. "That's not true and you know it! What is *wrong* with you tonight?"

Nice going, asshole.

In lieu of an answer, he chugs the last of his cider as Jaslene sashays past their table, bottle in hand.

Oh, fuck *no*.

He cringes into the shadows of the booth, hoping she won't see them. But no such luck. As soon as he thinks she's passed them by, she turns on her heel and cocks her head, posing like a server.

She nods at his empty glass. "Drink, Lang?" she asks archly.

"No thanks."

"Langton Shays turns down another drink? That's one for the recs."

He stares daggers at her but she's trained her smirk on Celan.

"Either he's been a really good boy lately," she informs her, "or a *really* bad one."

As she struts away Celan demands, "What's that supposed to mean?"

Fuck.

"I dunno. She's weird."

"You've been acting weird since we got here," Celan says, tipping back the last of her own cider. "Well, weirder than normal."

"Ha ha," he intones mirthlessly.

"Seriously, Lang, what's going on with you? You know I've had trouble getting out. I still want to be with you. Nothing's changed." A pause. Her lower lip quivers. "Is there something you're not telling me? Some other girl?"

Cornered, his eyes slide around the room – a sea of faces so loud and dense it feels like it's going to crush him.

"Let's get out of here."

He slaps a couple of chits on the table and stands, diving for the side door. Celan trails him outside to the courtyard where he comes to rest leaning against a low garden wall. She hops up on it next to him and folds her hands in her lap, expectant. He takes a deep breath, girding himself.

Got to get the cards on the table.

Because if she's going to run away it's better that she does it now, before he falls any harder for her than he already has.

"There's no easy way to say this so I'm just gonna say it, OK?" He swallows hard. "I've been fusing."

"What?"

"*Fusing*," he repeats. "Every day. For weeks now."

Her jaw drops in shock, but only for a moment. Then she bursts out laughing.

"What? What are you – ?" He rakes a hand through his hair. "It's no joke, Celan. I'm a *fuser*. Seriously."

But she only laughs harder; the kind of wild, manic way you laugh when you've just managed *not* to be hit by lightning.

Baffled, he waits for her to finish.

"Celan?" he says, tentative, as her giggles die down.

She holds up a hand. "I know. I'm sorry. I just – I was so worried that you – and you were being so weird. But fusing? That's not a problem. I've been doing the same thing."

"What?"

"Every night. For weeks now."

"But – how could you – ? I mean, you're a tech. Where would you even – ?"

"I'm studying transferon for my final project – remember? They have transfers in the lab. I can borrow one whenever I want. For research. They don't care. They don't think a tech would ever actually use it."

He gapes at her, stunned.

"Lang…"

A mob of contradictory feelings fights for expression, but anger cuts to the front of the line. "And you were going to tell me this – when?" he says.

Brown eyes flick away uncomfortably.

"Well?"

"I didn't want to upset you."

"*Upset* me? Do you have any idea how hard it was for me to tell you that? I considered not telling you, too, but I thought I should be *honest.*"

"I didn't lie to you."

"But you were hiding – "

"Like I've had to hide every single thing about myself since I was eleven years old," she finishes, heel kicking hard at a loose chunk of adobe. It gives way and thunks to the ground. "Thought you said you were a pretty good hider, too."

He softens then, looking down sheepishly.

"I'm sorry, Lang, OK? I'm just used to keeping a lot of stuff to myself. And I was afraid...I didn't want you looking at me like – "

A painful pause.

"Like what?"

"Like you look at Jaslene."

"What? How do I look at Jaslene?"

"Like she's dirty or something. Tainted. I don't know."

"I don't look at her like that!"

"Yes. You do."

He sighs. "Look, I know it's stupid. But I wasn't into it when she started working at Maddy's. I know a good expro guy wouldn't care – just shrug and be like 'techs don't count' – but it bothered me. I didn't want to think about my girl being with a bunch of other guys. But I don't think she's tainted or anything. Just kind of a bitch."

This last has the desired effect: Celan chuckles.

"Besides," he adds, "being a fuser isn't the same thing."

"Really?" she says. "People look at it the same way. Like you're not really human or something."

"People can be assholes."

"Yeah," she says, eyeing him shrewdly, "but neither one is exactly ideal."

"But I don't want an ideal," he says, wrapping his arms around her and easing her down off the wall. "I want you."

And as soon as the words are out of his mouth he knows they are true. Maybe they're both flawed, but sometimes it's the imperfections – the burl in the wood, the crack in the glass – that catch you up. Catch your heart on a barb of aching fondness where the smoothness of perfection would not hold.

She hugs him tight. "Well I want you, too."

He rests his cheek against the top of her head and exhales, leaning into her. They stand like that for a long time; night air fresh on their faces, listening to the comforting hum of noise from the wayvern and breathing in rich whiffs of spring-stirred earth. Then a thought occurs and his shoulders start to shake with amusement.

"What?" Celan says, sweet face turned up.

"You really fused in there?" He lifts his chin toward the city.

"No one can tell. They only scan you at the gate, not when you're already inside. And none of them are fusing so they can't see it in your eyes."

"Huh," he says. "I guess that's true."

He drops one arm and drapes the other around her shoulders, steering her toward the alley. Dried husks of last year's vegetation crunch underfoot like discarded wrappings from a Navidad's-worth of presents. His heart, so heavy a mere half hour ago, is as buoyant as a balloon.

"Speaking of fusing – did you? Before you came out tonight?"

"No," she says crisply. "I only do it once a day. Usually at night. Before bed."

"And it doesn't keep you awake?"

"No. It's relaxing."

"And you don't see, like, visions or anything?"

"No. Not really. I just feel…calm. It depends on how

much I do though. If it's just a little I can get a lot of work done like that. It's like a calm kind of energy. But if it's more then I just kind of..."

"Drift?"

She nods.

"Really?" he says, offhand, though inside his spirit leaps. *Is she...like me?*

It seems too good to be true.

"Yeah," she says, like it's no big deal.

But if she's Class E, and she's been fusing every night for weeks...

He has to ask. "Do you ever feel, uh, sick at all? I mean, when you're not – "

Celan bristles and halts as they reach the street. "No," she says. "Of course not. I don't have *CERS*. I'm totally fine." A pause. "So, where're we headed? Back to Tosh's?" Her voice tilts wryly on this last, like Tosh's is the last place they want to be.

He wavers for another moment but then – *As long as the cards are on the table, may as well play a round.*

"Nah," he says. "I mean, who needs cider?"

Celan returns his grin and reaches up to kiss him. A few people push past them on the sidewalk but neither one notices or cares. When they finally part his heart's beating hummingbird-fast. Then her voice purrs low in his ear like a cat in a sunbeam.

"Vamos aviados," she says.

THE DOOR OF THE BUNK whooshes closed and Celan leans back against it, registering relief.

Made it.

She's still a little loopy, though. She can tell. Even though they'd tried to be careful – mixed some D in with the E to make sure they wouldn't be totally out of it – they'd still gotten pretty elevated. And it had turned out that Danilo had taken the roller, so they'd practically had to run back to Albakirk so she could make it in before midnight. But it was worth it; fusing with Lang was too good a thing to pass up.

It was nice being with him like that, all relaxed and happy, especially after all the static earlier. And his eyes! Fusing by herself for so long she'd almost forgotten that part. The way the green glittered like leaves in a sunny summer breeze was so beautiful it gave her shivers.

And the rest wasn't bad either.

And (*Thank Madre!*) once again her luck had held coming back in – she'd zipped up the stairs, through the lab, and up to her bunk unquestioned. She'd kept pinching herself though, forcing herself to stay alert just in case. But now she's safe.

Almost.

She straightens up and steals silently through the kitchenette, peering down the hallway. All doors are shut. Her father must be asleep. She draws a breath, feeling the air hit her throat like a gust of wind down a parched arroyo.

Suddenly she's dying of thirst.

Water.

Turning to the sink, she lifts a cup from the shelf and places it under the faucet. She thumbs the reader and releases a gush, immediately gulping down a few mouthfuls. Then she puts the cup under again and lets the water rush in until it's overflowing, running over her fingers like cool silk. Her eyes slip closed as she imagines herself diving deep into a verdant pool like the ones at Pescados. Swimming, floating, drifting…

"Lana?"

Her eyes fly open and her hand jerks, knocking the cup over in the sink. Panicked, she fumbles to right it.

"Are you OK?"

Her father. Behind her. He must have come in from the corridor, but she didn't hear the door.

How long has she been standing here?

And, more importantly – How long has he been standing there watching her?

She refills the spilt cup and shuts the faucet off, turning to face him as she forces her features into a neutral mask.

"Fine," she says, raising the cup and taking a quick sip. "Just getting some water."

His eyes narrow. "Have you been out?"

Her heart skips.

Out? Does he mean – ?

"It's after midnight," he notes dryly. "And you're still in uniform."

Stupidly, Celan looks down at her clothes. Of course. He means out as in 'out somewhere in the city,' not out as in 'out on Transway.' Normally she'd be in sleepware by now.

"Uh, yeah," she mutters. "I was, uh, watching a screener. At Bev's." To be safe she doesn't say Shariah's – in case he was about some Lead business involving the Balors.

"OK," he says, but he still doesn't move. He's staring at her, brow knitted in puzzlement.

Unable to think of anything else to say, she takes another sip of water, dribbling some down her chin.

Fuck.

She wipes it hastily on her sleeve, not daring to look up again.

Her father clears his throat. "OK. Well, goodnight then," he says, brushing past her and striding down the hall to his room. His door whooshes open and shut and she's alone.

Safe.

She hopes.

⊏▶ 16 ◀⊐

Black and white keys jounce joyfully as Lang's hands skim over the old piano. He's been playing for hours, loving the feel of it, thrilling at the sound – like a bird or some musical thing that sings without thought or motive, but merely because that's its nature.

But there's another motivation behind his renewed practice: Maybe some wayvern could use him, and it might turn out to be a better gig than continuing on with Zeeb. Things on the street have calmed considerably, but with he and Celan getting serious, it might behoove him to find another line of work. Being an expro is one thing, but a vendador is quite another.

Not many opportunities to play the ranchos, where the only piano he knows of resides in the casagrand at Rancho Toros. Someone's always on it. Guitars and drums are the instruments of choice there – much easier to make and maintain (and carry around). He'd learned to play both as a kid, but it wasn't until he first came out to Transway that he found his true love in eighty-eight keys.

Brophy'd restored the old world instrument for fun; one of his ubiquitous tinkering projects. The first time Lang touched it a thrill ran through him and he plunked right down on the bench and started playing along with a song on the radio, hesitant at first but then with greater confidence. It had sounded good though, so nobody minded. They'd encouraged him. Sometimes Rafael or Zeeb or someone else would come in and they'd jam. But it didn't matter if he had anyone to play with – he could create symphonies all on his own.

Music. One of the many known side effects of fusing, he thinks with a small smile.

But it quickly fades. Because he knows that he's made a choice now. There's no way he's going to be able to live in the ranchos again – not in this condition, and he doesn't see it changing anytime soon.

Not that his overall condition is that bad. He's not massively aviados all the time and mostly he feels pretty normal. But if he went back there and tried to stay he'd always be looking over his shoulder. And if anyone in his family tried to force him to do the 'right' thing and turn in Raf's old transfer, he'd be sick as a dog and doubly screwed if he had to return to Transway without it.

And the elders know he has it. That's why they wouldn't let him finish 'scuela last year. No matter how hard he'd insisted that it was not in his possession (which technically was true since he'd given it to Brophy for safekeeping) they still hadn't believed him. As deluded as they could be about some things, the elders weren't stupid.

So he'd let down his whole family and now he's about to let them down again. And the worst part is that they don't even know it yet. That's a scene still to come and he's not looking forward to it playing out.

After Navidad, he'd left Arqueros spinning his have-to-go-back-and-help-a-friend-out tale. But he'd promised to return to celebrate the birthday he shares with his sister Melia (this Friday!) and they'll expect him to stick around afterwards.

No más excuses! But he's going to have to think of some.

Maybe he can tell them he met a girl (true enough) and that he's going to stay on Transway with her. Maybe they'll be glad he at least has a girlfriend. But probably not.

It's probably gonna get ugly.

He's deep into a run, putting a nervous little trill on the high notes, when he hears the kitchen door slam in the other room. Footsteps. Mara or Brophy. They've been digging up the garden all afternoon. Spreading compost, preparing beds. Spring is coming.

Mara's been on a tear all day – cleaned the whole house this morning, with the exception of Lang's room. He was still in bed when she poked her head in and muttered a few choice words about the housekeeping habits of Class Es before resuming an intensive sweep of the hallway. The house *is* spotless though. He has to give her that.

He starts to wind down, slowing the tempo of the bars by increments until they fade out into silence. Then he rises from the bench and stretches, yawns.

"Hey." Brophy's voice, behind him. "Why'd you stop? I was liking that."

Lang turns and grins. "Thought maybe you'd wrapped up the garden stuff. Still want that astral lesson?"

"Yeah! Let me get cleaned up."

Brophy ducks back out into the hall and there's the sound of the pump being cranked at the kitchen sink. Lang plops onto the piano bench to wait, dragging the heel of his boot in half circles on the worn wooden floor and thinking about how this is kind of backwards: In the ranchos the elders would have them work in the earth *after* an astral lesson, to ground them. Plus there'd be a whole preparatory bathing period beforehand. But there's not much he can do about that; he's got to work with what he has. At least the house is clean.

Another slam of the door and he hears Brophy and Mara gabble over the rush of water. Then Mara stomps into the living room, pink hair frazzled and face frowning.

"Why are you making him do that creepy-ass shit?" she demands.

"I'm not *making* him," Lang says, stung. "And it's not creepy."

"It is. Completely. You look like you're dead or something. Or walking." She shudders.

"Well, maybe it looks like that, but it's a totally different thing. In astral travel, the soul doesn't leave the physical realm entirely," he explains. "It's more of a projection – "

"Whatever," Mara says, snatching off her gardening gloves. "It's still creepy."

"Useful sometimes, though."

An eye roll.

"You don't have to watch."

"I did last time. You need a sitter, right? To watch your bodies while you're gone?"

"Oh," Lang says. "Well, technically yeah, but as long as you're in the house at least...I mean, it's really just to make sure no one messes with us while we're not there."

In lieu of a reply, Mara stalks to the foot of the hall stairs and yells, "Sig!"

"I think he's at Zeeb's."

She ignores this and hollers again, tapping her foot impatiently, and is rewarded by the thud of feet on the upstairs landing.

"What?" Sig calls.

"Ven aquí, ese. I gotta job for you."

Sig trots downstairs obediently and follows Mara into the living room as Brophy reappears, face and hands freshly scrubbed.

"All right," Mara says to Sig. "I need you to watch these two do their creepy-ass shit."

Sig smirks, waggles an eyebrow.

"Not like *that*," Mara says, jaw clenched. "Their *astral* shit. They need, like, a bodyguard. And don't test me right now. I'm not in the mood."

Sig sobers his expression.

"Dinner's in an hour," she continues, addressing all of them. "So you better be done by then."

"Uh, are you sure – " Brophy starts.

But she's already gone, leaving the three of them in an awkward silence. Lang looks from Sig to Brophy, getting that weird feeling again like he's missing something.

"You need to change," he finally says. Two heads pivot in

his direction. "Your clothes," he lifts his chin toward Brophy. "They're dirty."

"Oh," Brophy says. "Sure." He bounds upstairs as Sig flops down on a squashy old recliner with a far-more-beleaguered-than-Lang-thinks-is-warranted sigh.

"OK." LANG CLEARS HIS THROAT. "So you remember the tones from last time?"

Brophy nods.

They're sitting side by side on couch cushions on the floor – boots removed, legs crossed loosely in front of them, backs propped against the wall. It's important for the body to be both stable and comfortable during the exercise.

"Eyes closed then," Lang says, letting his own lids drop and taking his friend's hand in his. After several minutes of deep breathing, he hums the first in a series of sacred tones meant to focus their awareness and set their consciousness free from the constraints of the physical plane. Ignoring the occasional snicker from Sig, he leads Brophy through the entire register, feeling a gradual lightness steal over him – a sense of weightlessness.

When he's sure they're not in their bodies anymore he whispers, "Eyes open."

They're side by side, floating up near the ceiling – shimmery facsimiles of the living bodies seated below. Lang sighs happily. It's usually not that easy to get the hang of this, but Brophy seems to be a natural.

A rapturous expression steals over his friend's face as he gazes down at their physical forms. Letting go of Lang he does a few quick somersaults in place, then executes a dive

224

bomb at Sig's head, causing Sig to crane his neck around, obviously unable to see either of their astral forms but dimly aware of some sort of presence in the air.

Lang chuckles, appreciative, then beckons Brophy over and takes his hand again. It's not really safe to astral solo, especially when you're new to it – it's too easy to get distracted, fly too far and fast, and get lost somewhere if you're not sure what you're doing. At 'scuela they always went out in groups. And held hands.

"Ready?"

"Órale."

"Let's circle the city."

Together they rise up through the ceiling, passing through Lang's room on the second floor (still messy, he never did clean it like he promised Mara) and emerging into the airspace above Alamora. Higher and higher they rise, until Transway is spread out below them like a living map – with the city at the far end, translucent pyramids ablaze in the sunlight.

Lang feels a rush of pure exhilaration and Brophy must feel the same, because he lets go of Lang's hand and yells, "Race you!" – taking off like a shot toward Albakirk.

"Brophy!" Lang shouts, but his friend is already out of earshot. So there's nothing to do but launch himself, quick as he can, in the direction of the city.

FOR THE TENTH TIME IN as many minutes Theodore looks down once more, in shock and awe, at Lana's botrecs on his server – and the clear spikes of 6-MAM metabolite present in her system every evening like clockwork. Every evening for the past three days, at least. But judging from her current dosages, the phenomenon dates back much further.

Incredible. But irrefutable.

She's been *fusing.*

He'd been looking for evidence of alcohol, making sure she hadn't been making a habit of it after her odd behavior in the kitchen the other night. She said she'd been at Bev's, but her georecs placed her in the lab immediately beforehand. Why lie about something so inconsequential? There was evidence of one drink having being consumed, but it was hours prior to when he ran into her. So she hadn't been drunk.

But the whole thing still seemed off somehow.

So he'd kept digging, thinking maybe there was an outside chance she'd been tempted to try a few drops of transferon during the course of her research. She's been so hyperfocused on her project that it was just within the realm of possibility that she might try something risky to help her get an edge on the investigation. After all, she did grow up around the stuff. It might not have seemed as dangerous to her as it would to a normal tech.

There weren't any bot anomalies in her recs though, not since Navidad – way before she had access to a transfer – so he'd almost given up on the idea. But transferon's rate of bot shutdown isn't always one hundred percent and something, some niggling hunch, had driven him on. Being an old Comp hand himself (and one with Lead-level clearance), he'd inserted a line or two of code into her bots – nothing fancy, just a simple flag for any of the three classes of metabolites.

He'd been careful to route the results through one of the lab subject's recs though, so they wouldn't end up under her name in the Bank. Kind of silly, actually. If someone really looked hard at it they'd be able to see the join. He'd thought he was being paranoid. Taking unnecessary precautions.

But now...how could she be using this much and still keep her bots online?

Something doesn't add up.

His hand tightens around the server, gripping until the edge of it bites into his palm.

And what the fuck is he going to do with her now? Some model expro she's going to be – she's a fuser for fuck's sake: Class E.

What the fuck was she thinking?

And where could she have learned how to do it? In the transer lab? Doubtful. She doesn't have clearance to any of the private rooms. And she definitely hasn't been going out to Transway. He ran all her georecs. Twice. Other than Navidad Eve she hasn't been out at all. True, she has an anomaly on record that night, but she was with her pod the whole time. He saw her, just after midnight, getting on the elevator with Lucas Han. There's no way anyone slipped her anything.

So how would she even know how to do it?

Unless she learned it before, as a child on Transway or in the ranchos. He can't imagine Mair fusing, but the sister? *Half-sister*, he silently amends. Maybe she showed her.

A fury rises in him then, and an urge to throw the server as hard as he can at the opposite wall. Or stomp it with the heel of his boot – again and again until it shatters into a million little pieces. But it would be a pointless gesture. He takes a deep breath and places it instead on the polished surface of the desk, raking his hands through his hair.

He's got to calm down. Think about the best way to handle this. If he confronts her in anger he won't get the truth. Maybe it's best to wait a day or two. Tomorrow's the resource vote. He needs some time to figure this out.

But all that time and effort! So many years of care. Every advantage – the best pod, the best guidance, the best encouragement. And this is how she repays him?

Class E fuser.

Is she really like the rest of them out there after all?

No. She's not. She's different. Maybe she just did it once to try to make a leap forward on her project. Maybe she liked the relaxing effect and thought it wouldn't harm her. And by the time she realized what she was doing it was too late and she couldn't stop. And now she doesn't know what to do, how to fix it.

Or maybe she doesn't even realize how much she's taking, how intoxic she is. Maybe she thinks she's fine.

That surge of anger again. And the cold fact: She *would* be fine. She'd be totally whole and healthy if it wasn't for *them* – her idiot sister and whoever else showed an innocent eleven-year-old girl how to fuse, probably for shits and giggles.

Abruptly he rises, turning to the shelf behind him, searching for his Scotch. Outside the window the lights of Transway wink in the distance.

Cheerful. Inviting.

And maybe a little too close for comfort after all.

"SERIOUSLY, IT WAS THE CUTEST thing I think I've ever seen." Sig giggles, punctuating his recount of the afternoon's astral-watch highlights to a sour Mara and a grinning Zeeb.

He helps himself to another ladle of chili from the big pot in the middle of the table. "Thanks for dinner, Mara. This is delicious," he adds sweetly.

Mara rolls her eyes. Swigs her beer. "D'nada," she mutters.

"Can I watch next time?" Zeeb says, and he and Sig crack up.

Lang and Brophy laugh too, but Lang, sensing Mara's discomfit, says, "Look, it's not really that exciting. I only made him hold hands because that's what we do at 'scuela when we're first learning."

"And really," he says to Brophy, "you shouldn't've let go like that. It was only your third time out. It's not really safe."

"Oh come on. I'm not five years old. I wasn't about to fly off into the ether. And you gotta admit – it was fun."

"Fun isn't the point, though." Lang says sternly. "This is advanced prana stuff. You need to take it seriously."

"Mis disculpas, Elder Shays." Brophy says, bowing his head and gesturing with exaggerated deference.

"I think you're going to have to spank him," Zeeb says to Lang, and then they're all roaring – even Mara.

"Sooo," she says, switching subjects as they recover their breath. "Heard from a little bird that little miss Kimbra was over here the other night."

"Yeah." Lang grins, thinking on it.

"Told you she was gonna come back."

"Yeah. You were right."

"Heard you two got aviados as well."

"Yeah. You were right about that too."

He breaks off a hunk of cornbread and shoves in a mouthful, chewing contentedly.

"So like, what's the deal with her anyway?" Mara continues. "She gonna run away from home? Come live here with us in paradise?" She spreads her arms wide, indicating the whole of Transway.

Lang swallows, winces. "I don't know what she's gonna do. I mean, she says she wants to stay where she is. With her family. But it turns out she's an E like me, so..."

Sig gives a low whistle.

"Yeah," Lang says. "I don't know how she's gonna manage that."

"But how is she even – " Sig starts.

"She's got a transfer," Lang says. "She's been fusing every day for weeks."

"Whoa."

"I know. I tried to ask her about – you know. But she says she's not sick. Still, I probably should have..." He trails off, eyes on his plate.

"'Stante," Mara says, cutting into his thoughts like she can read his mind. "Wipe that fucking 'everything's my fault' look off your face. Ahora. Do *not* start blaming yourself for this."

"But I was the one that – "

"Introduced her?" Brophy says, steepling his fingers over the neck of his beer bottle. "No you didn't. Somebody obviously did, but it wasn't you, güey."

"Exactly." This from Zeeb.

Lang shrugs, noncommittal.

"Well let me ask you this then," Zeeb continues, "if you think her fusing is your fault then who's to blame for you? Rafael?"

"No!" Lang says sharply, color rising.

Zeeb feigns puzzlement. "But he *introduced* you, didn't he? So doesn't that make it his fault?"

Lang shakes his head no. "It was my choice."

"Claro," he says, triumphant. "And it's the same with her. No one can really blame anyone else for the shit they do to themselves. We all make our choices. You made yours, she made hers – "

"And lucky for you, you made the same ones," Mara concludes, raising her bottle in a toast.

Lang shoots her a glare.

"Oh, don't be so grumpy. You fought the good fight. Held out way longer than we all thought you would."

"You all thought – " He groans, looking around the table. "Don't even tell me you made bets."

"Five weeks!" Mara marvels. "No one even came close. Zeeb gave you two weeks and we all thought he was crazy."

Brophy shrugs. "I gave it two days, tops."

"See, I definitely thought he'd make it a week at least," Mara says, addressing Brophy like this is something they've been over before. "I mean, he was all determined and shit. But then when he came back after Navidad and started drinking insanely – "

She turns to Lang, frowning admonishment. "I thought for sure it was over once *that* shit started. But you kept holding out – "

"A heroic effort," Brophy says, bottle tipped in a sardonic salute.

They all laugh.

"Chíngate," Lang says, his tone scathing.

But in truth he's trying very hard not to laugh too. Harsh

231

as these gibes may sound, they're oddly soothing. They make him feel almost normal; just another freak among freaks – not the thing with fangs he feels like back in the ranchos.

🞂 17 🞀

Voices rumble low in the library; her father, Martinez. Low, but urgent. Celan replaces the mug she was going to use for tea unfilled and slips into the hall, straining to hear. Something's definitely up.

Her father's been in a mood all morning – didn't even look at her when she smiled and congratulated him again on his success in yesterday's resource vote. He'd brushed by with barely a nod.

The other night. When I was all aviados. Maybe he suspects…

But no. He can't. There's no way for him to know what she's been up to. It must be something else, like whatever weirdness is going on right now.

"If you could just tell me *why* – " Martinez is saying, voice cracking like a spurned lover's.

Her father's voice rises in answer. "Why do you think there's a *why*? There is no why. I just gave it some careful consideration – "

233

"There's nothing careful about this, Theodore. You said it yourself; it hasn't been thoroughly tested – "

"It's fine. I ran the simulations myself. It's not going to be a problem."

"But how could you do this…make deals with *her*? You didn't need to. You had my support."

"Only if she refused to remove the Pollomax."

"Which she did refuse! That was her whole point."

"So now she has it. And I have what I want. We will clean up Transway and then we'll go to Mars. Simple."

"No, Theodore. It is *not* simple. These are *people*. People whose lives will be completely uprooted and ruined. And for what? What lofty precedent does this uphold? Most of them can't assimilate and the rest have nowhere else to go. It's nothing but murder and you know it!"

"'Stante!" Theodore barks, loud enough to make Celan jump. "It's done. There's nothing more to say."

"Oh really? What about the bot tests? You've said it all along. No one wants to go back to that. What are we going to do without – "

"We'll survive."

"And what about them?"

"They're not our problem anymore."

An angry curse chases Celan back into the kitchen, where she snatches up the mug and turns to thumb the reader just as Martinez storms past her and out the door into the corridor. As soon as he's gone she heads straight for her room. Forget the tea, she'll have water.

But her father's blocking the entrance to the hall.

"We need to talk."

"About what?" she says, far too brightly. "Did something happen between you and Mr. Martinez? I thought he'd be happy you won. But he looked pretty upset – "

"Not Martinez. Though the reason he is upset with me is related to something you recently made me realize."

"Me?"

"Yes."

A beat passes.

"I know you've been fusing, Lana."

Her chest constricts, stomach dropping straight through the floor. But she tries for nonchalance. "Fusing? What would make you think something like that?"

"Your botrecs."

"Th – that's crazy," she stammers then forces a laugh. "It must be some kind of anomaly. I had a bot replacement right after Navidad. It must have introduced some error."

"There's no error."

"There has to be."

Fear crawls up her spine. Does he know? About her going out to Transway? But how could he? Her georecs are solid. Her trick worked on that score. But the metabolites... the bots don't register them.

So how could he –

"No, Lana," he says, like he can read her mind. "The bots aren't usually programmed to register transferon metabolites since, as you must know, it tends to shut them down. But after the other night, I introduced some code to check on yours. And quite an interesting amount of Class E showed up."

"I – " she starts, but she's completely flummoxed.

235

He takes a step toward her. Instinctively, she steps back.

"I'm not angry. Not at you. Not exactly. Just please, please tell me why you did this."

"I didn't – "

He holds up a hand. "Déjalo! We can either do this the civilized way right now or the hard way later. I can take the transfer away and wait for my point to be proven when you start feeling ill…or you can admit it to me and leave us both with some dignity."

"Ill? What do you mean 'ill'? You think I have *CERS*?" Her voice strangles on the last word.

"I know you do. Or you will. Starting in…" He consults his server "…about eight more hours. Your choice: Either hand over the transfer right this minute or start telling me the truth. If you do, I will let you hold on to it for now. I have no wish to cause you any discomfort."

Celan's mind reels: He's wrong. She can't possibly have CERS. She hasn't been doing it that long. But if he takes away the transfer he might never give it back…and never let her check out another one. The thought of an innumerable string of days without the fuse to look forward to at the end makes her throat tighten.

Just because I don't need it, doesn't mean I don't really, really want it. And he said if I confess he'll let me keep it for a while.

So she's got to make this good.

"OK." She meets his eyes. "It's true. I have been experimenting a little with transferon. I got stuck on the dynamics of the Class E pathway and so I decided to try to recreate it myself. I knew it was a risk, but you've always said there are some risks worth taking."

Theodore nods. "Yes. But I don't know that I'd count transfusing among them. And however did you learn how to do it in the first place?"

Celan casts her eyes down into her mug. The surface shimmers. A flash of memory – transing water as a kid. Best not bring Transway into this. "I saw someone do it. Years ago. In the ranchos."

"And so you thought you'd just go ahead and try it yourself?"

She shrugs. "It was worth a shot."

Her father cracks a tiny smile, but then his face falls. "This is all about what I had assumed. However, there's still the matter of the CERS."

"I told you I don't have – "

"There is no way that you don't. Not with the dosages you've been taking. But don't worry; we will take care of it after the bot release."

"'Take care of it' how?"

"We'll take a little trip to Winnipeg," he says silkily. "It's your original home, right? You must surely miss it after all these years. I have a colleague there who'll be able to reset your endorphin system back to baseline without any chance of that information ending up in the Bank here in Albakirk. No one will ever be the wiser."

"Winnipeg? For how long?"

"A couple of weeks maybe."

"Can't we wait? I mean, I'm really busy right now."

"No. The sooner we fix this the better."

She grits her teeth. Every fiber of her being yearns to protest. To put her foot down and absolutely refuse to go.

But she knows it's no use. So she resorts to snark.

"Why? So I can go back to being perfect little Lana? The example for all good expros to follow?"

Theodore sighs. "I'm afraid the time is nigh when the expros won't be needing anything more from any of us. Including you. I realize now that my request for you to reveal your origins may have put a bit too much pressure on you. But don't worry; you're off the hook."

"What does *that* mean?" she says warily. "Is this about what Martinez was saying before? About 'people's lives uprooted'?"

"Ah, so you heard."

"What's going on? Are you going to do something to Transway?"

"Not immediately, no. We are going to do something to ourselves. We reached a compromise on the resource vote – Ariana and I – and there is going to be a bot release this Saturday which will contain a medical plug-in known as Pollomax that is designed to decrease our taste for certain kinds of stimulation and excitement. After a few weeks, people will stop desiring to spend time on Transway and eventually it will be disbanded."

"But what about all the people who live there? I mean, if people stop going out there what are they all going to do?"

"They have always been welcome in our city if they are willing to assimilate. If they can't or won't then they can go back to where they came from."

"Where they came from? You mean the ranchos? They won't let them back there without patrons. Where are they supposed to go if don't have one?"

He fixes her with a serious look.

"Adapt or die, Lana. That's the way evolution has always worked and it's high time this whole situation evolved. We've been far too tolerant for far too long and have allowed Transway to systematically devolve into the wretched hive it is today. It's time to clean it up. And straight prohibition won't work. People have gotten very attached to their little entertainments. Threaten to take them away and they will only grasp them more tightly, like a stubborn child does with a favorite toy. Pollomax will make the change gradually and comfortably, so they'll barely even notice. They'll just want to play with it less and less until one day they won't want it at all."

"But Transway's not a toy! Those are real people! And you're just going to cut them all off? Leave them to die?"

"What the outcome will be is entirely up to them."

His eyes are hard, black, chilling in their depths. She stares into them, unable to process the awful knowledge that this betrayal of everything her father has ever said he believed about Transway and expros is entirely her fault. Because he wouldn't be doing this if he hadn't found out about her fusing.

And now he's going to ruin everything.

LONG HOURS PASS AS CELAN paces her room like a cat in a cage; waiting for the sun to set, waiting for her father to leave. He said he had a dinner tonight and so as soon as he's gone so is she. She's not staying here. She's shutting down her bots and she's leaving. Forever.

But she was smart – after the initial shock wore off she'd stopped arguing with him, pretended to come around, said she understood that he had to do what he had to do. That maybe they'd all be better off.

Because the less upset he thinks she is the less closely he will watch her. And he still doesn't know she's been going out. If he did she's positive she'd be on lockdown. But her bedroom door still opens and so does the door to the corridor.

So she's still free.

And he doesn't know a thing about Lang. Or Alamora. He won't know to look for her there. And she has to go, to warn them, to tell them what's going to happen to Transway. She owes them that much. And then she and Lang can go... somewhere. Maybe. Hide somewhere until she's sure her father's not looking for her anymore.

Why would he even bother to search that hard? She's a disappointment – a fuser and a fuck-up and a failed experiment. He'll be glad she's gone. He can tell everyone she got homesick and went back to Winnipeg. After a while, they'll forget she was ever here.

She presses her forehead to the wall of windows, gazing out over mountains and sandy flats, trying to process the fact that this is her last time standing in this spot, her last time seeing this particular vista. She thinks of all the hours spent curled up on her bed back when her room was a refuge and the whole city was a place of learning and purpose; back when she was doing important and useful work. Bryan and Shariah and the rest of her pod – there's a pang of sadness at the thought of never seeing them again.

But they aren't like her. She isn't one of them and despite all her training and all her studies she never will be. She knows that now. Because she's not a tech, not really – she's an expro through and through.

And she just wants to be back with her own kind.

ARIANA SMILES WITH A TENDER kind of noblesse oblige at the small group seated around her table. Tonight the Balor's living space has been transformed – desk folded up and tucked away, couches pushed against the windows, and a thin silvery table and six slim chairs printed out and arranged in the center of the room. Faux candlelight lends everyone's face a rare elegance as they work their way through several choice dishes and a few bottles of wine.

It's not often that she hosts these kinds of affairs. All techs, no matter what their rank, are generally encouraged to eat in the caf. Unity and all. Too many private dinners will get you put on Notice. In this case, however, the occasion warrants it:

She won, though she still can't quite believe it.

There has to be a catch.

She sneaks a quick look at Theodore, chatting with Alton's spouse – he's very subdued this evening, picking at his food, barely touching the wine. That's not like him. Especially since he won too. He got his Martian Relocation Plan. That was the deal. In exchange for slipping the Pollomax rider into his specs at the last minute she agreed to give up the GISH reboot and throw her support behind the MRP. A compromise – always a nice touch in a resource vote. Everyone gets some of what they want and everyone's happy.

Except Martinez, that is. In all the years she's known him she's never seen him so furious.

That's probably why Theodore's off tonight.

After all, those two were thick as thieves for years (as well as partners in crime where Transway was concerned). And so as heartening as it is to see Theodore finally showing some maturity in the matter she can't help but feel for him – for what might be the loss of one of his oldest friendships.

She reaches for Nathan's hand and gives it a gentle squeeze. He squeezes back and smiles, pride shining in his soft, brown eyes. On her other side a poised Shariah sits, talking earnestly to Alton. Whatever her daughter is saying, Alton seems impressed.

Of course he is: Her daughter is perfect.

That's another thing that might be bothering Theodore; she hadn't thought to invite Lana. Truthfully, she hadn't originally planning on including Shariah either, but the girl had wheedled an invitation and by the time it was all arranged it was time to begin. She hadn't thought it would matter, but Theodore visibly winced when Shariah sat down with them.

So maybe he feels it was a deliberate snub.

Or maybe Shariah's graceful aplomb is causing him to reflect on his own daughter's shortcomings. Maybe he's upset with Lana for some reason and Shariah's flawlessness is difficult for him to watch.

Maybe Lana's been going out to Transway!

It's been happening more and more – barely PostEd chaps taking Eds out, giving them a taste of the wayverns. One of the more troubling issues from which they will soon be blessedly free.

She takes a sip of wine.

It certainly wouldn't surprise me.

She slides her knife through another delicate sliver of

lab-grown meat, face smooth and seemingly untroubled, smiling once more around the table. After they've all gone she'll check the recs, see if Lana's been racking up chaps at the gate.

That would explain a lot, and so she hopes it's true. Because as enjoyable as this victory is, the question still lingers, nibbling and nibbling at the corner of her mind like a mouse with a bit of cheese: Why? After all these years – what made him change his mind?

CELAN BLOWS THROUGH THE BACK gate at Alamora, dashing across the yard and pounding up the stairs to the kitchen. The gang's all here, circled around the table, having a late dinner, talking and laughing. But when the door bangs shut behind her they freeze.

"Ce – Kimbra!" Lang says, surprised but pleased, until he sees the look on her face. He gets up and goes to her, places hands on her shoulders, eyes wide. "What happened?"

"He's gone crazy. My father – " She tries to catch her breath.

"He caught you sneaking out?"

"Worse."

"He caught you *fusing*?"

"Yeah, kind of. But that's not the most important part. Listen!"

And so she tells them: About who she really is, about her father and the bot release, the Pollomax, the whole plan to shut down Transway. They listen, stunned.

"But my bots are offline," she finishes, swallowing hard. "So he can't trace me. And no one saw me leave the city. He doesn't know I'm here. And I'm not going back. Ever."

Silence.

Then Zeeb speaks. "So let me get this straight – you're not really Kimbra Quinns from Rancho Pescados? You're a tech spy claiming to be Celan Mairs?"

"What?" Celan bristles. "I am *not* a spy! I told you what happened. Why would I tell you anything if I was a spy?"

"No sé. But it's probably all part of the plan."

"The plan? What *plan*? I just wanted to get the fuck out of there. I told you. I *am* Celan Mairs. And I'm not a spy!"

Zeeb's gaze shifts. "Lang? Did you know about any of this?"

Lang ducks, shuffles his feet. "Well, yeah. I did know she was living as a tech."

"Lang!" This from Mara.

"But she's not really one! She's telling the truth! I mean, we've talked about a lot of things. About her childhood and about Cyrinda and Taegh and Arlo's and – I've seen her fuse. There's no way she's making this all up." But he shoots Celan a glance, as if to say – *are you?*

"Never underestimate the techs," Zeeb says grimly.

Celan pales.

"And not only," he continues, "is she one of them – sent out here no doubt to spread their propaganda and entrap the unwitting – she's also the daughter of Mr. Theodore Timanti, Lead Asshole for the entire city. Did you know about *that*, Lang?"

Lang winces. "No. Uh, I mean, I knew her father was a tech. But there are thousands of them!" He eyes Celan tensely. "Why didn't you say something?"

She tries to speak but no words come.

244

Terra Madre! This is a disaster.

Then Brophy clears his throat. Five heads swivel in his direction.

"You know," he says. "There is one way we could find out if she's telling the truth. About being Celan Mairs at least."

Zeeb narrows his eyes. "You know where to find him?"

"He was over by Jas's earlier."

"All right," Zeeb says. "Go."

Brophy bolts from his chair and disappears into the night.

"Take her in the other room," Zeeb says to Lang.

Lang nudges Celan's arm and gently steers her out of the kitchen.

IN THE LIVING ROOM, ON the old brown sofa, Celan squirms miserably.

"You know I didn't mean to – " she starts.

"I know," Lang says, staring up at the ceiling.

"You know I really am – "

His hand finds hers, gives it a squeeze. "I know. I believe you."

"Then what – "

But he just shakes his head as a flurry of footfalls and low voices in the hall herald the arrival of whoever Brophy was sent to fetch.

She can't imagine who it could be.

They all file in: Zeeb first, followed by Mara, Sig, and Brophy and Jaslene, with a stooped, white-haired man in tow between them. They release him and the old man shuffles over to the couch. Celan regards him curiously. Then he raises his head and a powerful shock of recognition jolts her to the bone. He looks thirty years older than the seven that have passed but the hawk-like face is unmistakable.

"Tomás Canelas," Zeeb announces. "Legendary lead singer of Fused Up! and one of Taegh Gwens' best friends. He knows everything that went down the night the old Arlo's burned, the night little Celan here supposedly died. He's claimed for years that he saw her alive after the fire. But everyone always thought he was full of shit."

Brophy gestures for Lang to rise and he does, allowing Tomás to sit. The stooped man lowers himself slowly, hungry eyes fixed on Celan, a spectral smile tugging at his wasted face.

"Fuser or no, though," Zeeb continues. "He *will* know if you're faking."

A beat passes.

"Ask her," Brophy prompts.

Tomás clears his throat. "What name," he says, his voice a raspy ghost of its former self, "did I call you by that night?"

Celan knits her brow, confused. He called her by her own name, as far as she recalls. What else would he have – and then it hits her:

"Aviadita," she says. "You were calling me that all night."

"Why?" Tomás says, leaning in eagerly.

"Because I was fusing," she says, face hot, not daring to look at Lang. She's never told him this story. Even when they fused together she let him believe it was something she learned in the course of her research.

Impatient, Zeeb motions for her to go on.

Sifting through memories she's fought hard to forget, she

begins haltingly. "I was – it was when I was visiting here from the ranchos. My sister and Taegh were arguing the whole week before the show about him fusing too much. She had their transfer. She didn't want him doing it around me. But I was curious, you know? He kept disappearing and she kept getting mad and I knew something was up. I wanted to find out what it was."

She risks a quick peek up at the group but their faces are closed, hostile. She continues on hurriedly.

"The day of the fire I was playing in this empty apartment. It was early. Morning. I heard Tomás and Taegh coming and they said something about fusing so I hid in the closet to watch what they did. And then I saw Taegh fuse. He didn't know I saw. Later that night, Cyrinda was getting dressed for the show and she left the transfer in the pocket of her skirt. I found it. And then I fused before they could stop me."

Tomás nods, satisfied. "It's her," he rasps. "Has to be."

If Zeeb is surprised it doesn't show. "So," he says. "Celan Mairs. Welcome back."

"Thanks," she says, uncertain of his tone.

"And if you don't mind...a little demonstration? Just so we're all a hundred percent sure you're legit."

He snaps fingers at Lang, who takes the vial from his pouch and proffers it to Celan. It's obvious what Zeeb wants to see. So, hands shaking, she pushes up her sleeve and unscrews the cap, drawing –

How much? Not too much. Don't want to be totally out of it.

– barely a quarter, much less than her normal evening dose, into the vial and positioning it against the inside of her wrist. She breathes deep, letting momentum build until she releases it and the dart of it enters her system. Her eyes close, lids fluttering as she adjusts to the altitude. When she looks up again it's into a ring of amused expressions, and several pairs of glittering eyes.

"I knew it!" Mara crows. "I knew that look the night she walked in on us. Pure anhelo!"

Jaslene snickers. Lang heaves a sigh. Celan transes away the burn, recaps the vial, and hands it back to him.

"So now…" Zeeb starts.

"What?" she says, placid now.

"OK, so it's obvious you've had a pretty fucked up time of it. And it's great that you finally get that those tech fuckers are crazy. But what's that gonna mean for us? If your father comes looking for you? Which he will."

"I – uh…"

Zeeb starts to pace, deliberation playing across his face like Comp code scrolling on a screen. "Does he know you're gone?" he says finally.

Celan shakes her head, definitive. "No. He's at a dinner. Won't be back until late."

"But he'll notice soon."

"Not until tomorrow. Maybe even tomorrow night. He has meetings all day about the bot release."

"But what about others? Your friends? Pods? Whatever you call them."

"No. Pods are split. I'm independent study right now."

In light of current circumstances, she realizes how ridiculous that sounds.

Zeeb grunts, still lost in thought.

"He can't find me," Celan says. "He can't find me without the bots. And I left my server inside."

She also made sure to short out the tracker in the transfer, though she doesn't see any real need to mention that.

"They've got drones, though," Brophy says gravely. "They could send them to every house and wayvern on Transway. Search every little nook and cranny. Find you easy."

"But those are just views," Mara counters. "Shitty ones, too. We can dye her hair and give her some crazier clothes. Another fucked-up fuser. They'll never know – "

"Yes they will," Zeeb says, "if they're serious. You think those things only do views? They have ones that can take DNA samples. They'll find her eventually; say she was kidnapped maybe if they want to save face. And then what happens? To *us*."

Everyone falls silent, processing this, eyeing Celan with increasing alarm. Desperate, she looks to Lang. "I'm sorry," she says. "I didn't mean to – "

"I know," he says, raking fingers through his hair in frustration. Then he says 'Hey!' like something's just occurred to him. He addresses the group. "What about the ranchos? I'm headed out to Arqueros tomorrow anyway. If she comes with me…they don't have any authority over there."

"The ranchos," Zeeb muses. "Some say the drones don't work so good over there."

In a flash, Celan remembers herself, age eleven, standing with her father that first day in the transer lab.

'The drones have an unfortunate tendency to malfunction in ranchos airspace.'

"They don't!" she says. "They don't work over there at

all. They malfunction!"

"Well that's good news," Zeeb says, and they all relax a fraction. "So you two can lay low out at Arqueros and in the meantime we'll be able to spread the word. Find out if they're looking for you. But no mañana. We can't take any chances. If you're going, you need to go *ahora*."

Lang eyes Brophy hopefully. "Can we take the roller?"

"Alex's got it."

"It's fine," Celan says. "We can walk."

"Sure," Lang says. "Let me grab a few things." He bounds out of the room and up the stairs.

A hush descends like sunset until Celan turns, conversationally, to Tomás.

"So," she says drolly. "Nice to see you again. Cómo estás?"

THEODORE SLOUCHES INTO HIS BUNK, palms pressed against tired eyes.

That was brutal, he thinks, heading straight for the library and the warm solace of Scotch. And not just the dinner – Ariana in full gloat mode, making sure to show off her lovely daughter and perfect family. The whole day's been a disaster: Martinez, Lana, everything going to shit.

Not bothering with ice, he pours out several fingers and downs them, grimacing.

He should be happy. He won. They're going to Mars! All his hard work, all his planning, it's all paying off. He should be fucking ecstatic.

But his chest is a dull husk.

Glumly, he refills his glass and pads down the hall, pausing in front of Lana's closed door.

Is she fusing in there? Sleeping? Working?

Maybe he should knock – see if she's still awake. Maybe they should talk a little more. Maybe he was too abrupt with her earlier. Maybe they could start another chess game.

He raises a fist, knuckles poised to rap, but a pang of uncertainty makes him lower it again.

What if she is *fusing? What if she's completely drooling intoxic in there?*

That, on top of everything else, is not something he can deal with at the moment.

He turns back towards the library; he needs to relax.

There'll be time enough to talk in the morning.

⊶ 18 ⊷

A crack of light pries Lang's eyes open like a crowbar and he squints against it, burying his face in Celan's hair. A whiff of something sweet and earthy makes him want to burrow deeper, so he nudges his nose against the nape of her neck. She shifts under the blanket and sighs, but doesn't wake up.

Better let her sleep. Gonna be a long day.

Lifting his head he takes in the crumbling adobe walls of their shelter, bits of debris scattered in the corners. They'd walked for a couple of hours last night until they felt they were safely out of tech airspace, then settled into the remains of an old casita somewhere off the broken road between Transway and the ranchos.

It had been rocky going, the night moonless and still, with only a weak solar torch to help navigate. Once, Celan had tripped and fallen, bloodying knees and palms. He'd healed them at once and she'd laughed, marveling, and kissed

253

him, and only then did the weird tension between them begin to ease.

He can't believe she never told him the whole story about Taegh. After all the stuff he'd told her.

But neither one had brought it up.

When they stopped at the casita, he'd gone in first to check for fellow travelers and unwanted critters but had found none. So they'd spread out their blanket rolls, braced the ancient door closed, and curled up tight to try to get some sleep. But it proved elusive; so they'd done the one thing guaranteed to make them feel close again, if only for as long as it lasted. After that, they were asleep in minutes.

Maybe she was just freaked out. Didn't want me thinking bad about her. But I wouldn't have. Fusing I understand.

A shudder shimmies up his spine, a twinge in the gut. Speaking of which…time for a little morning cura.

He disentangles himself from Celan and eases out from under the blanket, tucking it around her so she won't get cold. His breath puffs little clouds as he stands and hops in place a few times to get the blood moving. Then he steps outside to relieve the fullness in his bladder. From the angle of the sun he guesses it's still pretty early. They'll get out to Arqueros in plenty of time.

Ducking back inside, he scoots down against the wall, sitting with a thump on the ground. Rolls up his sleeve. Digs in his pouch for the transfer. He's just touched dropper to flesh when he feels eyes on him and looks up. Celan is sitting up and staring at him, wide-eyed, like she's never seen a fuse before.

"What?" he says tersely.

"You…do that in the morning?"

"Yes. Maybe your evening dose carries you for twenty-four hours, but mine doesn't."

She blinks for a moment, seeming not to comprehend. "Huh. Well, I feel fine."

"Good for you."

He returns his attention to the dropper, gathers the momentum, and hits. There. Just a little. Just enough. Like Brophy said – keep it as light as you can for everyday and only get super fused up when you really need to check out for a while. It'll keep you functional. Won't get so you need so much just to be well that you'll get sloppy and risk walking. Sensible Brophy.

Now he just needs to sit still for a minute and he'll be good to go. As he transes the burn and tucks the vial away, his gaze drifts back to Celan. She's lying on her side with her head propped up on one hand, tracing patterns in the dusty flagstone floor with a delicate finger, seemingly indifferent. But he catches a quick, appraising glance – probably trying to gauge his level of functionality.

"Hey, Lang?" she says, tentative.

"Que pas'?"

"Nada."

"Oh come on. Did that really freak you out so much?"

"No. It's just – you are…all right? Right? You don't have CERS?"

He shrugs. "Sure. A little bit. But that's what happens. To Class Es anyway."

"Well not to me."

"Maybe not. It depends on how much you do and how

often you do it. If you're doing it every night though…"

"I don't. have. CERS."

"OK," he says. "You don't!"

She narrows her eyes, as if to determine whether or not he's only humoring her. But then she nods, affirmative. "*You* are all right, though?"

In lieu of an answer he gets swiftly to his feet, demonstrating his steadiness. Celan stands too, shucking off the blanket and pulling the sweater he'd lent her tight around the plain blue shift she'd borrowed from Mara. She shivers, big brown eyes watching warily. So he does what he knows how to do – saunters over smiling and catches her up in his arms, spinning her around a few times before placing her back on her feet and kissing her sweetly.

"Now who's aviados?"

"Please," she says, with a Mara-esque eyeroll, swatting at him, playful.

He mock blocks, fending her off, then pulls her in for a deeper kiss. When they come up for air she's beaming a thousand watt smile.

"Hey, Lang?" she says, merry now.

"What?"

"Can we stop off somewhere on the way to Arqueros?"

"Yeah, sure. Where?"

"I want to see…there's a person I want to see. Where I used to live. She kind of raised me for a while. After my mom died. Jillyanne."

"At Pescados?"

"Yeah. By Tijeras. Up by the springs."

"Sure. But we probably should get going then," he says.

"That'll be an extra hike."

"Are there any more of those rolls left? I'm starving."

"Think so." He releases her and crouches to dig in his pack, searching for the snacks he'd brought. He hadn't brought a lot, seeing as there'd be plenty to eat at Arqueros, but he'd eaten a full dinner last night and she most likely hadn't. There are two rolls left. He tosses both to her and she crunches in eagerly. He reaches for the water bag and fills his own stomach with cool liquid. He's never that hungry anyway, right after a fuse.

"So what's going on out at Arqueros?" Celan says, chewing and swallowing a large bite. "Just a visit?"

"Actually," he says, "it's my birthday."

Her face flowers with delight. "Really?"

"Yeah, it's my sister Melia's birthday too, so they always have this big thing. We're not twins or anything, though. She's turning fifteen."

"And you?"

"Twenty."

"Wow."

"Yeah." He ducks his head, rakes a hand through his hair, a bit bashful though he can't quite say why.

"Well happy birthday then," she says, with a hug and a sweet little kiss.

His stomach dips and swoops and his soul leaps up through the ceiling to the roof, the trees, the sky. It's all good now. They're talking again – telling each other things. She was just scared before; she was so used to *not* telling.

Everything's gonna be fine.

THE DUSTY TRACK TWINES THROUGH a series of clear ponds, sparkling under boughs studded with the first tender leaves of spring. Past the last one and up a small rise, the little house comes into view – looking just as she'd left it that long-ago afternoon. Neat and tidy, flowers and herbs poking up in the front beds. Celan's stomach flutters. Abruptly, she halts.

"Is this Jillyanne's?" Lang says.

She nods.

She'd told him some more of the story on their hike over from last night's shelter. How, right after she turned eleven, Cyrinda let slip how their mother really died: Not from some 'holy sickness', but from the astral walking state brought on by excessive use of transferon, making the things Jillyanne had told her about her mother's illness lies. She'd confronted her guardian and they'd had a huge fight, which ended in her running off to Transway with Cyrinda and Taegh.

It was only supposed to be for a week though, long enough to see them play the big anniversary show at Arlo's. She was going to come back after that. Apologize. But then there was the fire, and then her father found her, and then…

She'd felt perfectly confident when she first suggested this side trip, but now that they're actually here she's starting to think that it wasn't such a great idea. Now that she's a –

I am not. *I am not like Mom was. I am* fine.

Lang clears his throat. "So where's *your* house? The one you lived in with your mom?"

"Up there." She gestures vaguely to the left.

"Oh."

Again they advance. Celan turns her head from side to side like she's about to do something bad and wants to be sure she isn't observed. She grips Lang's hand hard as they come up the front walk.

"Do you want me to wait outside?" he says.

She shakes her head no. "Stay with me."

And, taking a deep breath, she knocks.

There's a burst of barks from inside the house and a moment when the whole world seems to tip on its axis. Then the door flies open to reveal a tall, fair-haired girl jouncing a fretting baby in her arms. A big, shaggy dog stands sentry at her side, barking a few more times for good measure.

"Yes?" the girl says, eyeing them quizzically.

This has to be…

"Tanny?" Celan whispers, mouth dry.

The girl's brow furrows then springs back with a jolt of recognition. She gasps. "Terra Madre! Celan?"

"Quién es?" a gravelly voice demands from inside.

Tanny sidesteps to let them in. The dog sniffs at their heels but lets them pass unmolested.

Oso, Celan thinks. *He must be over ten years old by now.*

"Tanny, you know we don't have time to fool around. With that baby messing all those diapers, we'll be into this wash all day." The bluff form of Jillyanne stumps out of the kitchen, a long wooden paddle still steaming in her hand. Hair greyer and body softer around the edges, her presence still commands the room. But when her eyes come to rest on her guests her face goes slack with shock.

Celan squeezes Lang's hand so hard he winces. "I'm sorry," she says, finding her voice. "I am so, so sorry."

Jillyanne's slack expression mobilizes into a montage of anger and love, joy and regret. Then she sighs, putting a

259

hand on her hip.

"Where on this Earth have you been?"

"Didn't you get my letter? My father said he'd – "

"Oh, I got it all right. Living with your tech father." She wags her head disapprovingly. "That Mair. I should have known. He told me I better never tell a soul where you were. Or else."

"I'm sorry."

Jillyanne grunts.

"He didn't want me to have anything to do with being a transer," Celan says defensively. "He told everyone I was from another city-state."

"So what are you doing here now?"

"I – there was a problem. I had to leave."

Jillyanne snorts. "You ran away?"

"He went crazy – I had to – "

The older woman watches her struggle for a long moment then opens her arms and motions her in. "Well, mijita, at least this time you ran in the right direction."

Celan embraces her, alternating between laughter and sobs, in sheer relief until the distance between them feels entirely breached. Letting go, she signals Lang forward. Jillyanne eyes him critically, but seeing nothing obviously amiss nods her approval.

He sticks out a hand. "Langton Shays, ma'am."

Jillyanne bats it away and pulls him in for a bear hug. He submits meekly and Celan watches, amused, until she remembers Tanny and the baby.

"He's yours?" she says, turning to stroke a tiny pink foot.

Tanny smiles proudly. "She. Elena. After my mother. Lena

thinks it's after her, though. She just loves her. Even watches her for me sometimes."

"Wow."

"I know, right? Who'd've thought? She never was one for kids."

"But her dad?" Celan says. "Elena's?"

Tanny rolls her eyes. "Remember Joella's brother, Mick?"

"Little Mick?"

"Not so little anymore." She smirks. "But yeah. He's OK, helps out sometimes, but he's young, you know?"

"Yeah," Celan says, though she's not really sure she does. Tanny seems so much more grown up than she is. But Lang's hand on her shoulder lightens her unease.

Tanny eyes him flirtatiously. "You're a pretty one."

Lang blushes as the girls giggle, broken only by a loud harrumph from Jillyanne.

"Ándale," she says from the kitchen doorway. "We can finish catching up while you make yourselves useful."

The kitchen is warm and damp with condensation from the large wash pot bubbling on the clunky old stove. Tanny sets the baby in a cradle on the table and turns to the wringer, cranking the handle as Jillyanne dips the paddle into the boiling water and feeds clean clothes through one by one. Celan gives Lang an uncertain look.

"What can we do?" he says.

"Getting close to lunchtime," Jillyanne says, wiping her brow. "Picked some dandelion greens this morning and there's dried fish in the cupboard. Can you make tortillas?"

Celan shakes her head no but Lang nods.

"Mara's teaching me," he says.

With direction from Jillyanne, he sets about collecting the ingredients as Celan sits down at the table, feeling useless. *Useless as a fuser*, she thinks unhappily, but the thought is chased out of her head by Elena, who immediately starts to fuss. Celan half-rises and attempts to distract her with one of the little bangles dangling from the cradle. But it's no use; Elena starts to bawl.

"I don't think she likes me," Celan says as Tanny swoops in, scooping her daughter up expertly.

"Don't be silly. She's just hungry." Tanny plops into a chair and yanks her blouse down, letting Elena latch on to a nipple as Celan gawps, fascinated. Baby care is so much more private in the tech world. She hasn't seen a woman breast feed in years. Tanny raises an wry eyebrow and she turns away, embarrassed, to find Jillyanne regarding her with barely concealed amusement.

"This wringer doesn't turn itself."

"Oh right," she says and lunges for the handle, turning the cumbersome apparatus awkwardly. After a few rotations her shoulders start to ache, but she grits her teeth. No way is she going to complain.

"So how'd you two meet?" Tanny asks as she settles in with Elena, eyes clear and wide as the sky.

Celan glances over to where Lang is mixing batter in a large wooden bowl.

"At Arlo's," she says. "I was with some friends and we kind of ran into each other."

"And the techs didn't care that he was a transer?"

"Well, uh, it's kind of a long story," she hedges. "But I'm not a tech anymore so it doesn't really matter."

"So are you gonna move back here then?"

"Well…"

"We're going to see my folks up at Arqueros for a while," Lang says. "Then, I don't know. We have a place to stay on Transway."

"Do better staying here," Jillyanne says. "No good has come from that place for anyone in this family."

"We have a lot of friends there."

Jillyanne clicks her tongue in lieu of further comment.

A dark look clouds Tanny's face. "She's right, you know. Max took off there a year ago and we've hardly seen him since. Didn't even finish 'scuela." She shakes her head. "What's he gonna do without a transfer?"

So it really was *him on Navidad Eve,* Celan thinks. Sometimes it feels like she dreamed it. *Guess he got one somehow.*

"I saw him a couple months ago," she says. "I wasn't sure it was him then, but I guess it was."

Tanny frowns. "He's just not the same. Whatever he's up to over there it's no good for him."

"Transway sure didn't help your sisters any either," Jillyanne adds.

Celan feels her face flush.

"Was Cyrinda really alive?" she asks softly. "I thought she died in the fire. I didn't hear otherwise until I met Lang. He told me what happened." She swallows hard. "Did – did they bring her back here?"

"Uh huh. But we didn't keep her for long. Some elders came and took her. Said they'd look after her. A little while later, we heard she'd passed on. Not really surprising, burnt up like she was."

263

Celan shudders. Beautiful Cyrinda. As terrible as she feels for running off that night, for believing her sister was dead because people said so, she's secretly glad she never had to see her that way. She cranks the handle harder, trying to leverage the hurt in her shoulders against the hurt in her soul.

Jillyanne and Tanny say nothing.

"Batter's ready." Lang's voice cuts into the silence. "You got some room on there for me to cook 'em up?"

CELAN'S HEART LIFTS AS SHE and Lang make their way down the gravel road towards Tijeras. After the subject of Transway was mercifully dropped, the rest of their impromptu lunch had gone wonderfully well. Lang's tortillas were delicious, and it turned out he knew some good ranchos gossip about a certain Cangejos family that Jillyanne has been beefing with for years. He'd tickled her with a series of anecdotes as Tanny took Celan aside and, in sisterly fashion, explained the proper methods of contraceptive transing (which she claimed had slipped her mind after one of her encounters with Mick).

Celan, surprised but grateful for the instruction in the absence of bots, had immediately applied it to make sure that nothing would come of last night. While appealing in the abstract, a child would not be a good addition to the situation she and Lang are in right now.

But sitting in that kitchen, helping with the washing, and petting Oso had felt like being a child again herself. Like she'd run away into some kind of time warp where years went by outside, while only a few minutes passed inside of her.

And now they're going to Arqueros! She can't wait to

meet Lang's family. Celebrate his birthday! She can't believe she didn't even know it was today.

She squeezes Lang's hand, and he squeezes back as they emerge from the shadow of the pass under the old highway and circle a large cart piled high with furniture. Someone must be moving house. The men pulling the cart stop and wave. Cheerfully, she and Lang return the greeting. A few more minutes' walk and the old casagrand comes into view, flanked by the fairgrounds where they used to have fiestas.

Liberation Day. That was the best one, with all the different booths and the fireworks and –

Celan stops short, sneezes several times. Her stomach's been gurgling ever since lunch. Now it gives an uncomfortable lurch. She lets go of Lang's hand and presses both of hers against her middle as a shivery sheen of sweat breaks out on her forehead.

"You OK?" Lang says.

"I don't know. Maybe that fish…I don't think my stomach's used to that stuff anymore. How do you feel?"

"Fine."

"Well, you're more accustomed to it. I'll be fine, too. In a minute, I'm sure." She breathes evenly, in and out, attempting to direct a little prana into her stomach. The bad feeling subsides and she starts forward again.

"I'm good now."

"Bueno."

She tilts her face up to the sun – warm and bright in the green-gold spring afternoon. The earth crunches satisfyingly under her boots. Such a beautiful day! And her bots are offline forever; she's totally free. No one tracking what

265

she does, where she goes, what she eats, who she talks to – the realizations hit her in waves, each one buoying her spirits higher. Just being outside, every touch of breeze on her face is like a blessing.

"It's so funny that Lena likes Tanny's baby so much," she says, crouching down to pick some pretty purple flowers, looping the stems around her fingers like rings. "But I'm kind of glad she wasn't around today."

"Who's Lena again?"

"Jillyanne's woman. They've been together for years. But Lena never really liked any of us," she confides. "My mom and sisters and me."

"Well," Lang teases, "you *were* a pack of troublemakers."

Celan punches him lightly on the arm and bounces a few more steps, until another wave of nausea stops her in her tracks. Shaky, she tries to breathe. In. Out. Maybe her prana's not strong enough to fix food poisoning. Though even as she thinks this a cold fear creeps up her spine.

I really didn't fuse as much as usual last night. A lot less in fact. Maybe it is – NO!

She sneezes again, wiping her nose with growing agitation.

"Lang, I really think there was something in that fish. Do you think you can trans – "

"No." He sighs. "You can't trans away CERS. Believe me, people've tried. It might help a little at first but then it only comes back stronger. And the sicker you get the harder it gets to trans at all. The only thing that helps is another fuse."

"It's not CERS," she insists. "That lunch didn't agree with me. And my prana's not as strong as yours is. If you do it, it'll go away."

He shakes his head no. "It's CERS, Celan. Believe me, I've seen it. These are the symptoms."

"No they're not! It's food poisoning."

"Making your nose run?"

"That's just pollen. From all the flowers. They're *everywhere*! She shakes her hands out, scattering blossom-rings, wild-eyed. "Please just try."

"And if it comes back?"

She doesn't say anything.

"If it *does*?"

"If it does, I'll fuse. I promise."

Skeptically, he appraises her, looking like he wants to argue the point further, but finally he just places his hands on her, and breathes.

LANG KEEPS A WARY EYE on Celan as they cross a sturdy plank bridge over a plashing acequia and enter the apple orchards that mark Rancho Arqueros. She seems well enough, but how long is that going to last? They're almost home now.

For someone so smart – but a quick flash of guilt snuffs out the rest of the thought. *She's just scared. She's not doing this on purpose. Remember how freaked out you were the first time you got sick?*

And there is still the possibility, however small, that she's right. That she doesn't have CERS at all. He has no idea how much she takes on a daily basis. Maybe it's a lot less than he does.

He squints through the trees, spying a couple of female forms huddled near the base of a ladder. Hanging mason bee houses probably. He recalls a spring day like this – he and Raf drilling holes in the wood blocks for the bees to nest in, sneaking sips of last year's cider and tumbling down the rungs after they'd hung them, laughing like fools. A lump lodges in his throat and he blinks rapidly.

"Lang!" One of the forms is now hurtling toward him. Tawny limbs akimbo, the girl crashes into his chest, gazing up with bright green eyes that mirror his own.

"Melia," he says, hugging her tight and inhaling the fresh, clean scent of her honey-brown hair. "Missed you, hermanita."

"I missed you, too," she says, voice quavering. "I knew you'd come. It's been so long…Cass didn't believe me. But I just *knew* you wouldn't miss our birthday." She nuzzles against him, seemingly overcome.

Lang blinks again, sniffling.

Then Melia pulls back, lips split in a wicked grin. "Such a softie! I bet Cass I could make you cry in the first five minutes."

She turns to holler at the other figure – a dark-haired girl standing stolidly by the ladder with arms crossed over her ample chest. "Hey Cass! You're pulling my weeds for the rest of the week."

Celan laughs.

Melia whips around, eyeing her curiously. "Hey! So who are *you*? Did our Langton finally get a woman?" She plants hands on hips and shakes them suggestively as Lang takes a mock swing at her, which she deftly ducks.

"I'm Celan."

"Well mucho gusto!"

"And where are you from, Celan?" Cass asks as she approaches, arms still crossed and face sour.

"Pescados, originally," Lang says.

"Originally?" Cass snorts, ignoring him and honing in on Celan. "And when exactly was that? I've never seen you at 'scuela. Are you an expro?"

"Oh come on, Cass," Melia cuts in gaily. "Don't be like that. She's a guest!" With a wink at Lang and Celan she adds, "You can even have my room while you're here. I'll go sleep with this old caraculo."

Cass tries to give her a shove but Melia dances out of range.

"That's my room anyway," Lang says.

"Not anymo-ore," Melia sings. "That's what you get when you run away from home. Again."

"I didn't run away. I just went for a visit."

Cass grunts. "A two-month visit. To Transway."

"I came back for Navidad."

"Barely."

"'Stante," Melia says. "You two need to kiss and make up. It's our birthday! No fighting."

"Oh sure," Cass says, fixing Lang with a sneer. "Your special day. Just another excuse to get – "

"Cass," Melia warns.

"Don't 'Cass' me! *He's* the problem. I don't see why I have to – "

"She's just mad because she's up for elegida this year," Melia informs Celan. "Thinks her expro brother's gonna spoil her chances."

"I do *not*," Cass snaps so fast that it's obvious there's some truth in it.

"Hey," Lang says, placating. "No one's going to judge you on account of me. You've been perfect at 'scuela, Cass.

You're a brilliant healer."

"So were you," Cass says and turns her back, stalking off into the trees.

Lang watches her go, grimacing, until Melia says, "Well!" and hooks a jaunty arm through his. "Awkward already, I see. Might as well head on up to the house."

He's aware of Celan trailing them as his sister tugs him through the orchard and up to a small clutch of dun-colored buildings, chattering all the while. He glances over his shoulder, but she doesn't seem to be in any discomfort. Maybe it really was the fish that made her sick, and not CERS.

Then his own gut twists at the sight of a stout, well-bronzed man hunched on a bench in the sparse shade of some newly-leafed cottonwoods, intently pounding a series of holes into a set of small wooden boxes: The mason bee houses.

"Mira!" Melia shouts. "Look what I found out by the manzanas!"

Lang's father looks up, grunts, and returns to his work.

"Aw," she coaxes. "Don't be like that. It's our birthday."

As they enter the copse of trees, Melia slips her arm out of Lang's and slides it around their father's shoulders, jollying him until he looks up again.

"Feliz cumpleaños," he mutters.

"Gracias," Lang says, with a respectful nod.

"And look," Melia continues, "he even brought a friend. A *girl*friend. This is Celan," she announces, "from Rancho Pescados."

Lang's father eyes Celan hard for a moment, but he must like something he sees because his face finally cracks into a genuine grin.

"Roman Anayas," he says, putting down the hammer and extending a large paw. Lang watches as Celan gives it a firm shake, followed by a radiant smile.

But then her light dims, and she seems to pale.

Oh shit. Not now.

"Mijito!" A woman bursts through the door of the main house – Cass's dark eyes, Melia and Lang's long limbs, and a lined but lovely face alight with joy.

"Mama," Lang says, diving into her embrace.

She cups a palm under his chin and searches his face, but whatever she sees there results in a sigh of relief. "Bueno. You're looking well."

"Feeling fine," he says. "Never better. And look, here's someone I want you to meet." He waves Celan over.

"Hi," she says, lips fixed in a rictus of a grin. Beads of sweat are standing out on her brow now. "Celan Mairs. From Pescados."

She extends a careful hand, but his mother is having none of it and pulls her in for a crushing hug. Celan sways a little as she's released so Lang circles an arm around her waist to steady her. He never should have transed her. He should have insisted she fuse.

"I'm Shay," his mother says. "You look a little pale, cariño. Está bien?"

Celan sniffles.

"She was sick earlier," Lang says. "Ate something bad maybe. We had to stop a few times on the road."

The family clucks sympathetically. They've all been there.

"Well come inside and sit down," his mother says. "I'll

make you some peppermint tea."

"I think she needs to lie down," Lang says.

Silently willing Celan to hold on to her shit he scoops her up and carries her into the house, through the big, fragrant kitchen and down the hall to his old bedroom, where he lays her on the bed before closing the door firmly behind them.

"Here," he mutters. "I'll do it."

He takes out the transfer, unscrewing the cap and eyeballing the dosage. Just a little bit. Just enough. Holding the dropper between his teeth, he takes her limp hand in his and yanks up her sleeve. She doesn't protest. He hits her just before the door cracks open.

"Everything all right in here?" says Melia.

He sucks in a breath and turns, tucking the transfer away before his sister can see.

"Yeah," he says. "She'll be fine. Just give us a few minutes, OK?"

⊏► 19 ◄⊐

"Let's sit over there," says Melia, nudging Celan and Lang away from the crowded tables and toward an out-of-the-way spot under a large tree. The birthday fiesta is in full swing, thronged with an impressive array of relatives, friends, and neighbors who heap platter after platter of food on groaning tables as they laugh, talk, and chug brimming mugs of cider and beer. Celan's met so many cousins she can't even begin to try to remember all their names. But everyone's been nice and friendly – even Cass finally wished Lang a happy birthday, accompanied by a stiff little hug, before dashing into the house to bring out more cornbread.

The trio sprawls out on a carpet of wild grass, digging into their laden plates with gusto. A few musicians kick up a tune and some lively souls abandon their repast to dance.

All this needs is some hobbits and a ring, Celan thinks.

But it makes her glad to know that Lang comes from such a nice place, and such good people. Not that there's any reason why he shouldn't. It's just reassuring, is all.

She forks up another bite of potato salad spiked with chile and chews thoughtfully.

"This is really good," she tells Melia.

"Better be careful with that," Lang says. "It's spicy. Might upset your stomach."

She shoots him a quick side-eye; he's been giving her shit on and off all afternoon. But she knows she's earned it. Even though no one seems to be the wiser, that was still a close call. There's no denying it now – she's a Class E fuser, CERS and all. But so is he, apparently.

So he needs to dial it back.

"I made that," Melia gloats, seemingly oblivious to any subtext. "Well, Cass helped, but it was mostly me."

"You're a good cook," Celan says. "Like your brother."

"Lang can *cook?*"

"Our friend Mara's teaching him."

"Well," Melia informs him. "I'm gonna tell Mama. Next year, you can help prepare."

Lang grins through a forkful. "I'll deny it to the bitter end."

They eat in quiet contentment as the sun begins to slip down behind the mountains, bathing every tiny leaf and blade of grass in a shimmering radiance. An ant tickles Celan's ankle and she brushes it away absently. This light like honey, the sweetness of the spring grass, the homey smell of the cooking fires, the music and laughter burbling like a stream from across the yard – it's all so sweet and familiar. Despite the wobbly start, she feels a sense of peace and belonging. Of home.

And she's not going to make any more mistakes. She'll fuse when she needs to and no more fuss. If she's got CERS, then that's that – she's sick and the fuse is her medicine. And that's just how it's going to have to be from now on.

"Hey," Melia says, but she's not addressing Celan; she's poking Lang with a sharp elbow. "Mira. Over there."

He glances in the indicated direction.

"Fuck," he mutters, ducking his face into his plate.

"What?" Celan says. She shades her eyes with her hand and squints out over the yard. A tall, gawky guy in a pale blue robe stands beside an apple-cheeked young couple, arms around each other, chatting animatedly with Lang's mother.

Melia snickers. "The stars of Arqueros! Come to shine their wisdom upon us."

Lang turns and explains. "Carlos, Felix, and Paz," he recites, denoting each with a tip of his mug. "Carlos is an elegido, obviously. Felix is a junior mayordomo, the youngest one ever chosen. And Paz, his wife, is a seed expert who's currently expecting their first child."

"Lang went to 'scuela with them," puts in Melia.

"Were you friends?" Celan says.

"We haven't exactly kept in touch."

"Mama must have invited them," says Melia, crunching into a pile of greens. "To set a good example for you."

Lang gives her a dirty look. She grins wickedly.

"You've got chard in your teeth," he says.

Celan watches as Shay points the newcomers in their general direction.

"They're coming over here," she warns.

"Everyone smile pretty," says Melia.

They put their plates down as the trio approaches, faces

just as bogusly bright as their own must be.

"Hola, Lang!" booms Felix. "Como estás?"

"You're looking well." Paz beams, hands folded over the rounded curve of her belly. "Feliz cumpleaños. To you both."

"Gracias," chirps Melia. "From us both. Would you like to sit down?"

The couple exchange a glance and Paz nods, lowering herself onto the grass as Felix flops down next to her. Carlos looks hesitant until Melia unties her apron and tosses it to him.

"Don't want to get grass stains on your robe," she says in all apparent solicitousness, but Celan catches the glint in her eye.

There's a moment of awkward silence. Then Lang clears his throat.

"So this is my girl, Celan," he says, brushing a light hand down her arm. "Celan, this is Felix, Paz, and Carlos."

"Mucho gusto," she says.

They nod in reply.

"And where are you from?" queries Paz, eyeing her shrewdly.

"Um, Pescados originally."

"And now?"

"Now I live on Transway."

No one says anything.

"So Lang," pipes up Carlos, breaking the pause. "How long are you out here for?"

"Oh, I don't know," he says, fumbling for his pouch. "A week? Maybe longer."

Paz smiles, tossing back silky black hair. "Such a beautiful time of year. Everything blooming. The perfect time for a fresh start."

Felix nods vigorously, puppyish face eager. Despite a beard and moustache, he looks no older than Lang. "You could still go back to 'scuela…it'd only be one more year. That's not long at all."

Lang's jaw tightens a fraction as he fishes out his smoke stash and starts to roll one. "I'll certainly keep it in mind."

Paz sighs. "You had so much talent, Lang, in the healing arts."

Bitch, Celan thinks, hackles rising. "He still does."

Paz gives her a pitying look. "Which is why he should be here, nurturing it, instead of wasting it – "

"On expros?"

"I didn't say that."

"You didn't have to."

"The expros chose their own path," Paz says primly.

"Please." Celan rolls her eyes. "Most of the expros these days were born on Transway. They didn't choose anything. They have as much right to any of this as anyone else."

Paz looks to Carlos who says, "Every soul chooses the form of its incarnation."

Celan snorts and looks to Lang, but he says nothing, just finishes rolling the smoke and holds it out like a peace offering. "Anyone?"

"I don't mind a smoke occasionally," says Felix and scoots closer to him, out of Paz's airspace. She raises an eyebrow, but not at Felix.

"But how do you get by without a transfer?" she presses. "Surely you don't have those…things in your head."

"Ah, you know," Lang hedges, striking his flint and

taking a deep drag, "someone's always got one around some-where."

Carlos gives him a pointed look. "The elders can be very lenient, you know, about certain mistakes from the past. Provided you own up to them. As Precept Six says – "

Lang ignores this, passing the smoke to Felix. "Yeah, well. Like I said. I'll keep it in mind."

Melia giggles.

Paz silences her with a frown. "Turning fifteen today, aren't you Melia?"

"Uh-huh."

"Getting a transfer yourself...."

"Only at 'scuela, though."

"Not 'only'," chides Carlos. "The training period is very important. It's a big responsibility, learning to transfigure properly. You don't want to take it lightly. There can be consequences."

"I'll keep that in mind," Melia deadpans as Lang coughs to cover a laugh.

The final and most awkward silence of all descends. After a minute, Felix stubs out the smoke and gets to his feet, offering a hand to Paz who rises as gracefully as she sat. Carlos takes the cue and jumps up too, clearly relieved to have this little scene over with.

"We'd better be going," he says. "Got to get up early in the morning."

"Yes," says Paz. "I get tired so quickly now. I'm sure you all understand."

"Claro," Lang says.

"So lovely to meet you...Celan, was it? Pretty name."

Celan stares daggers into Paz's back as, with a final round of pained smiles, the interlopers glide off across the yard in the last rays of day.

As soon as they're out of earshot Melia explodes. "So lovely to meet you Celan! Was it?" she minces, feigning a haughty expression. "What a bitch!"

"Yeah," Celan laughs, relieved. "If this is how people act when they finish 'scuela, I'm glad I quit when I was eleven."

Beside her, Lang shifts uneasily.

"Really?" Melia says, interest piqued. "Was that when you became an expro?"

"It's a long story," Lang says as he rises. Then he leans down and snatches up his empty plate and mug, not looking at either of them. "Maybe another time, huh?"

He turns and heads for the tables as the girls exchange a wordless glance.

"Perfect," Melia mutters. "Just what he needed."

Celan eyes her questioningly but she says nothing more, just gathers up the remains of their meal in silence.

"Vámanos," his sister finally says, forcing some brightness back into her tone. "Might as well dance."

CELAN WHIRLS THROUGH THE THRONG, faces spinning like dizzy satellites in the light of the bonfire. As evening comes on the band is really getting into it, laying down a good groove. She bobs joyfully as a cheer goes up and a circle forms around a shimmying Melia, who pulls a red-faced cousin into the center with her. On feet too big for his body he lurches, awkward, but Lang's sister is a wonder. Light as a feather she bumps her hip into his, loosening him

279

up, making him giggle.

Celan cranes her neck, searching for Lang. He really should see this. But he's deep in a mob of tios and primos, playing some sort of dice game at one of the long tables. He tips back his mug and takes a swig, face flushed and slightly hectic. She tries a wave but he doesn't seem to see her.

Is he mad at her? Should she not have said anything to Melia about quitting 'scuela? But it's part of who she is. He knows that. And he did the same thing.

Maybe that's what the problem is.

Finally, she catches his eye. He raises his glass in a toast and grins a tilting grin as she smiles back, relieved. Then someone elbows her; Melia is watching him too, her expression unreadable.

"Enjoying our birthday, I see," she says in a tone that sets Celan's teeth on edge. But then she laughs. "Let's go get some cider before they drink it all."

Celan trails her to the kegs and there's a pleasant sort of bustle as they locate clean mugs and fill them.

"Let's sit," says Melia, slurping the top inch off her drink so it won't slosh over the rim. Celan follows suit and surveys the yard for an open spot. But every place is packed.

Melia pokes her again. "Inside," she says, and so Celan follows her into the house.

The kitchen is total chaos – every surface piled high with dirty dishes, half-eaten food wilting in soggy piles. Briskly, Lang's sister clears a spot to put her mug down and moves to the sink. "Let's get started on this," she says, plugging it up and tugging at the hand pump.

"You can scrape those into the compost bin." She points

Celan to a pile of plates and kicks a wooden bucket out from under the sink. "Then we can let them soak."

Celan complies dutifully, putting her own drink down and fumbling around for an implement. She locates a dull knife and gets to work, passing the scraped plates to Melia to rinse. They work in congenial silence for a few minutes until Melia clears her throat.

"So, how're you liking the ranchos?"

"Great." Her smile is wide and genuine. "I really missed all this."

"Did you? That's great. And it looks like you got over whatever your little problem was, too."

"Huh?"

"Your stomach problem?"

"Oh, yeah. Right. Guess it was just one of those things. Your mom's tea helped a lot."

"Uh-huh," Melia says, all traces of flightiness receding. "Look, I don't know how clueless you think we all are over here, but we do hear things. Some of us anyway. There's been talk about expros doing some weird shit with their transfers. Getting all aviados. Getting sick from it."

Celan feels a flutter of panic in her chest. She leans in, scrapes harder. "Do your parents think – "

"They don't think anything. They don't hear that kind of stuff. Papa's just mad that Lang went back to Transway at all. And Mama just worries. He hasn't really been right since Raf died."

"He's fine," Celan tries to reassure her. "People tell all kinds of crazy stories about Transway."

"Oh, really?"

"Really."

"Well then what was my brother doing with that transfer earlier? When you were 'sick'? You recovered pretty quick after that."

Her throat constricts. Lang said Melia hadn't seen, that he'd put it away in time.

"Transfer?" she chokes out. "What transfer?"

Melia ignores this, snatching up a rag and scratching at a stubborn bit of gunk on a particularly grimy plate before sliding it into the water with its fellows. "Oh come on, Celan, everyone knows he has Raf's old transfer. It disappeared right after he died. Very mysterious."

"But the elders; wouldn't they – "

"Take it away? Don't worry," she says dryly. "They're not going to take it away from him. They want him to give it back on his own. Make amends. Follow the Precepts. You know how they are."

Celan doesn't. Not anymore. But a long-ago accusation rises up, the things she'd shouted at Jillyanne after she found out the truth about her mother.

You could have stopped her! You could've taken it away!

And the answer: *They said there's nothing for it but to wait. If they're gonna come back, they do. If you take it away they're just gone.*

But her mother had been walking then; she and Lang aren't anywhere close to that. Even so, a chill runs down her spine.

"Well, what do *you* think?" she says, choosing her words with care. "I mean, if you think he has a transfer, and you think he's doing something wrong with it – "

"I don't think anything," Melia snaps. "I just know that

282

after Raf died he was really messed up for a while. He got better, a little, but then he started drinking. Just occasionally at first, but he was a major borracho by the time he left for Transway. And when he came back for Navidad he looked terrible – stank like a kicked keg and barely ate any dinner. Tio Emilio just laughed. Gave him more cider. 'Hair of the dog,' he said. Lang was drunk again by dessert." She pauses, letting this sink in.

Celan knows she should be concerned. But she's secretly grateful that at least they're off the subject of transfers. "Melia, he didn't go to Transway to drink. He's got a lot of friends there. I mean, what did you think he – "

"I told you," Melia says fiercely. "I don't *think* anything. He actually seems a lot better this time. Healthier. Happier. But I knew that that little visit from Paz and friends was gonna fuck his head up. Make him feel like shit. Get him drinking again. And now he is. Whatever he's done – whatever else he's been doing – anything's better for him than drinking like that. As far as I'm concerned he's suffered enough. They need to let it be." She motions for the plate that Celan's been holding in a death grip for the last couple of minutes.

"He's fine, really," she says, passing it over. "Aside from tonight, I've only seen him drunk like one time maybe."

"But he is doing *something*?" Melia says. "Something that's making him feel better?"

"Nothing any elder wouldn't do."

"But the expros? All the stories? There has to be some truth in it."

Celan hesitates. What can she say that's not exactly a lie

but isn't the whole truth either; something that doesn't really give anything away?

Treading lightly, she says, "Look, it's true what you've heard – about expros. That sometimes some of them get sick. But it's not from taking transferon, it's more like from *not* taking it. Things aren't as clean over there as they are here so sometimes they have to do it a little different, or take a little extra. Then when it wears off they don't always feel so good. But they're fine as long as they take some more. They're not making themselves sick. They're keeping themselves well."

The ghost of a smile traces Melia's lips. "So that's what you're doing then? Keeping yourselves well?"

"We aren't – I mean, we are – " Celan starts.

Melia's eyes narrow dangerously.

" – trying to."

"OK then," Melia says, nodding at the full sink. "I think we're done here." Scooping their mugs up off the counter she hands Celan's back to her. Then, taking her arm and patting it kindly, Lang's sister steers her back outside to rejoin the party.

"UHHHHH." A KICK TO HER calf jerks Celan awake – then another to her ankle. A shudder runs through the body in the bed next to hers.

Lang.

She'd gone to bed hours ago, not long after her chat with Melia, while he'd stayed up drinking with his uncles and cousins, barely even gracing her with a goodnight. But her irritation quickly passed: Safe behind closed doors she'd taken the lab transfer out from where it was stowed in her boot (only a day, but what feels like a lifetime ago) and gone full aviados, letting the fuse set her adrift on the waves of music and laughter floating in from the party. Curled under quilts in the soft bed she'd felt like a little girl again, sleepy and safe after having been put to bed by the adults. Back then, she'd have been tucked in with Tanny and Max, tumbled together like warm pups.

"Uhhhhh."

She hadn't heard Lang come in, but now he's writhing beside her. She touches his forehead. It's slick with sweat.

"Hey," she whispers. "What's wrong?"

"Didn't fuse," he chokes out. "Didn't fuse last night. Terra Madre!"

He bolts upright, clutching his stomach and scrambling to the window. Jerking it up he leans his head out over the sill and vomits in a gush. Celan scrambles after him, reaching to soothe. But he jerks away, slumping down against the wall, limbs twitching pitifully.

"Please," he says. "My transfer."

She fumbles for the pouch at his waist, fishes it out, and holds it up to him.

"No," he says. "Too shaky. You do it." Fingers trembling, he tugs at his sleeve.

"But I've never – "

"Doesn't matter. If you can do it to you, you can do it to me."

He lurches to his knees, leans out the window, and heaves another splatter onto the ground below.

Her own hands shaking, Celan unscrews the cap and draws up –

How much?

"Just a little," he says. "Just enough to make it stop."

Then he collapses, banging the back of his head slowly against the wall.

"Please," he says again.

Celan scoots up next to him and grabs his wrist, turning it palm up. She rests the tip of the dropper against a blue line and closes her eyes.

Pretend it's your own arm. It's exactly the same.

She draws in a breath, concentrating. The buzz begins in the back of her head and zips down to her fingertips, into the transfer, into Lang. His breath hitches for a moment and he moans anew.

Maybe she didn't do it right; maybe it didn't work!

But then a faint grin blooms on his lips. "Gracias," he whispers.

"You're all right?"

"Better by the second."

He circles an arm around her and pulls her close. She tucks the transfer back in his pouch and leans into the warmth of his body, marveling at how quickly it softens and loosens as all tension and illness evaporate. Out the window, there's a subtle brightening in the sky. Must be close to morning.

"I'm sorry," he says. "Drank way too much last night. Didn't mean to. I meant to fuse. But getting drunk and fusing for a Class E?" He shakes his head. "No bueno. You could lie down and never get up again."

"So why did you even drink then?"

"Just all my uncles, my cousins…they're used to me keeping up. Kept pouring out more and more. Birthday boy." He sighs. "I don't even remember coming back in here. I must've passed out. That's why I didn't feel the CERS coming on until it got so bad it woke me up."

He takes a deep breath. "That was really stupid."

"It's OK," Celan says quickly. "I was stupid too. I knew what CERS was. I knew all the symptoms. But I was just so sure I couldn't have it. I almost ruined everything."

She turns her head up, looks him in the eye. "But I know better now. And now *you* know better too – no más borracho. Stick to fusing, OK? You're much better at it."

Lang chuckles.

'Anything's better for him than drinking like that.' The words flash through her mind. Should she tell him about all the things Melia said? *No. Not now.* They're both tired. Better to go back to bed and talk about it later.

She rises and closes the window, then reaches out to Lang, tugging him to his feet. He rinses his mouth with water from a pitcher on the dresser then they settle back on the bed, arms around each other, her cheek resting against his chest.

"I love you, Celan," he murmurs, stroking her face with soft fingers.

She shivers. "I love you, too."

⇥ 20 ⇤

The ranchos. That's where she is. That's where she has to be. She didn't just vanish into thin air.

Theodore steps into the elevator and punches the button for the lab floor like it's personally insulted him.

Where else could she have gone?

Conversation clangs and echoes as the small coterie of Med and GenEns accompanying him chatters on about the MRP, but he's lapsed into just the occasional grunt or nod. There are much bigger things on his mind at the moment.

He's had drones quietly scouring Transway for the past twenty-four hours but they haven't turned up a thing. No trace of his daughter. And why would she be hiding there anyway? She doesn't know any expros. At least he's pretty sure she doesn't.

Mentally, he retraces his steps:

1) First thing yesterday morning he'd knocked on Lana's bedroom door to try to talk to her, but she hadn't

been there. So he figured she'd left early. Maybe (prob-ably) she was trying to avoid him.

2)   At lunch he'd messaged her several times, but there'd been no replies.

3)   Frustrated, after his 14:00 he'd pinged her server and found it sitting in her dresser drawer.

4)   So, in growing panic, he'd tried geolocating her bots, which were offline.

5)   And then, with a sickening certainty, he knew: She was gone.

But where? And *how*?

If her bots are offline, she must be using transferon to keep them that way, which means she has access to a transfer; the one she'd checked out of the lab is nowhere to be found, its tracker dead or disabled somehow. But he can't imagine her walking to the ranchos alone. So maybe she'd gotten a ride.

There were no recs of her at the gate though (and he hadn't expected to find any; she'd have needed someone to chap her out if she'd gone that way). The most likely explanation is that she left through the transer lab door. But how could she have just walked out? Surely, someone would have said something.

A search of her server's deleted messages had turned up a clue; there were two that had been sent to a rogue address, about a month apart. The first was something about key fobs, while the second gave what appeared to be a time and place to meet. There were no replies, however, and when he'd tried sending a new message to that address it came back undeliverable.

But the mention of key fobs had confirmed his growing suspicion: There had to have been expro involvement. Could she have met one in the lab and befriended them? Maybe that's where she learned to fuse as well! Though her only clearance was to the waiting area and the observation room, neither of which was private enough for that.

So maybe she'd been going out to Transway. But there he was stymied: None of her georecs put her anywhere outside the city within the last two months.

Grimly, he'd turned to the views, starting with the ones that coincided with the aforemessaged time and place: Ord 55, 20:30. Her recs put her in the lab at that time, but she wasn't showing up on any of the views. Determined, he'd rewound further – to 20:15, 20:00, 19:50...and then he saw her, walking across the waiting room and entering the ex-pro washroom. But she never came out. Or rather, Lana Timanti never did. A grubby group of expro girls, however, had emerged at 20:07, with one extra trailing behind them, looking nervously over her shoulder. Then they'd all trooped down the stairs, and out into the night.

But that was impossible! Her georecs still had her in the lab, and then in her room, and then the lab again. How could she have been able to leave and still shown up inside?

Then, with a terrible jolt, he'd remembered: Classified information – recs of experiments where transers had managed to trans *tech*; all trials of which had been understandably abandoned, their results buried so none of the expros would ever get any ideas. While there's no way she could possibly have known about any of that, there was always the outside chance that she came up with the idea on her own, out of sheer desperation.

But for now, Transway looks like a dead end – the drones have turned up nothing. The next step would be to put out a full alert, which means getting others involved, and that is something he does not want to do. Because there's no way to do it without his colleagues finding out what happened – at least the running away part – and once that's out it will have serious repercussions for both Lana and himself. Even if no one finds out about the fusing, her mental stability will come into question and he'll look completely ridiculous. A stooge. Not a good look for a man about to lead an expedition to Mars.

So he has to find her himself, without anyone the wiser, while there's still a chance to salvage this mess.

And really – why would she seek any permanent refuge on Transway? It's not like she had any close ties there, she was only visiting when he first found her. True, there was the contact she'd messaged, but after more weary view-combing, he'd turned up no evidence of her fraternizing with any expros in the lab. And it didn't look like she knew those girls she'd followed out on Ord 55.

There was a woman in the ranchos, though, some distant relative who had taken care of her after Mair passed. At Rancho Pescados, if he remembers correctly. Maybe that's where she went. Maybe she met someone she knew from childhood in the lab, someone who helped her arrange a way to get back there.

Unfortunately, the ranchos can't be searched by drone. He's going to have to go in person. It could take days or even weeks to find her.

What a royal clusterfuck!

The ding of the elevator snaps Theodore's head up to find the entire group staring at him. It appears he's been asked a question, which he has not bothered to grace with a reply. But the opening door saves him and he marches forward, trailed

292

by the nattering group, as he bites down hard on a fresh surge of anger. He takes a deep breath, telling himself that it's not her fault – she's intoxic, delusional.

But he still can't help wanting to strangle her.

He checks his server – 11:25, about thirty-five minutes until the Pollomax release. Everyone needs to be inside the city during a bot upgrade, but it only takes a few minutes. Once that's over he'll be able to begin his search. He'll need a roller, chits to trade for information (though ranchos transers don't use chits; he'll have to pick up some items to barter). But first, he'll ask around on Transway, show her image, find out if anyone's seen her. Even if she's not hiding there currently, she must have at least passed through. Someone must know something.

He'll ditch the uniform – pretend to be an expro father searching for a runaway. That should win him the necessary sympathy.

For now, though, he's got a little show to put on in the Barsoom Room. A demonstration of the latest in calcium-loss remediation in low-gravity environments. Not the flashiest topic, but at least it's a focus on something positive.

Something he can control.

WEARILY, CELAN AND LANG DRAG shovels out to a large patch of weedy ground on the far side of the orchard. There are vague outlines of old beds here but it looks like it's been a few years since they've been cultivated. They'd hoped to get in a little rest after a full morning of party cleanup, but Shay had had other plans.

Celan swats away a horsefly. "So what are we doing

again?"

Lang makes a face. "Double digging. It's like you dig a trench across the bed and then backfill it, dig another, row by row. Aerates the soil, but it takes hours. Mama says she wants to put in some extra potatoes back here, but I think she's still mad that I blew off Carlos and them yesterday."

"That and you getting drunk as fuck," Celan adds.

"Yeah," he deadpans. "That too."

"They were pains in the ass, anyway. All that white robe crap."

"It's not all crap," Lang says and she snorts but says nothing, just leans on her shovel as he bends down to mark out the dimensions of the first trench. Something glints in the sunlight, catching her eye – bits of silver in his hair near the crown of his head. Quite a few of them, too.

Fuser hair.

Does it really happen that fast?

Feeling her eyes on him he looks up sharply, running a hand over the strands in a self-conscious gesture.

"White?"

She nods.

"Fuck," he mutters. "Gotta get some more of that walnut stuff from Mara."

"You dye it black? Why not purple or something?"

"I'd look stupid like that."

She dips her head forward. "Do I have any?"

"Nope. Not yet." He brushes dirt off his hands, businesslike. "OK, so I'll start on this side, you start there. You want to go down pretty far, about a foot and a half. Pile the dirt up on the sides for the first one. We'll save it to fill in the last row."

Celan chunks her shovel into the earth, bearing down hard with the heel of her boot, feeling an unexpected rush of pleasure at the solid feel of it, the rich scent of the ground. It's invigorating. They work in silence for a while, enjoying the sun on their backs and the dulcet hum of insects.

At length she wipes her brow, and straightens. "So," she starts, tentative, "did it really bother you that much – Carlos and them?"

Lang stops shoveling and stares vaguely up at the sky, like he might find the answer written on a cloud.

"Maybe. A little. Coming back here like this and seeing everyone. They're all so happy and normal. Sometimes I wish I could be like that again."

He kicks the shovelhead with the tip of his boot, for emphasis maybe. Then his palms tighten on the wood and he turns and digs in again. Celan takes a deep breath, girding herself. There's something she needs to know.

"So do you want to stop now? Fusing, I mean?"

"I dunno." He grunts, back muscles tight with the effort of labor. "It's not that simple." Then he straightens, clearing his throat, and gives her a pained look. "The longer you fuse the harder it gets to stop. For Class Es anyway. And the CERS gets worse each time you do. You've only been at it a month. It shouldn't be too bad for you. But..." He trails off then, shamefaced.

The truth hits her suddenly, like walking into a door. "How many times," she says, "have you tried to stop?"

A sigh. "Once with Raf on Transway about three months in. That lasted like a week. Then again after he passed."

"You fused for a whole *year*?"

He grimaces, nods.

"And then you had CERS *here*? And no one knew?"

"I said I had the flu."

"Mr. Did-a-little-back-in-the-day," she says, but her tone is more amused than accusing.

"Yeah, well. You asked me all those questions about fusers. And you never told me about you."

"I know. I'm not mad."

"And I haven't been fusing this whole time. I really did quit. It's only been these last few weeks…"

She waves him off. "It's all right."

"You'd be better off, though," he says, "if you stopped now." Not entirely convincing, though, more like he feels he should at least make the effort.

Celan picks up her shovel; stabs furiously at the earth.

"I am not," she says, "going to stop."

Lang opens his mouth like he's about to say something more but shuts it again and lifts a hand to acknowledge someone approaching across the orchard.

"Melia," he says.

Celan starts, remembering their conversation. "About Melia…" she says.

But she doesn't have a chance to say more before Lang's sister is upon them, face lit up even brighter than usual. She stops in front of them and plants hands on hips like she's about to make a big announcement. Then she giggles.

"Oh shit," Lang says faintly.

"What?" Celan says.

"You guuuys," Melia drawls. "This is so amazing!"

"Today," Lang says, "is the day after her fifteenth birthday."

"Oh my," Celan says, trying to wipe a smirk off her face and failing. "Her first dose of transferon."

"It's not funny."

"But you have to admit her timing is perfect."

"You guys!" Melia says again, throwing her arms open wide. "This is so amazing!"

"You said that already," Lang notes dryly. "And shouldn't you be with your friends? Hanging out and sharing the love? Don't waste your first drops on your old expro brother."

"Oh, you," Melia says, batting eyes at him. "Don't be so modest. How better to spend them than with a couple of fusers?"

The world stops. Lang looks to Celan and then they both look at Melia, panic rising.

"Oh, don't get all uptight," she says. "It doesn't bother *me*."

"Where did you hear that word?" Lang says carefully.

"It's around." She waves a hand up toward the ether. "And don't try and deny it. *She* told me everything." The hand comes down, finger pointing at Celan.

"What?!" Lang says, rounding on her.

"I didn't!" Celan protests. "I didn't say a thing!"

"She said that you two were sick," Melia continues briskly. "And now you're just trying to stay well."

"I said *some* expros *sometimes* get sick. Because of contamination. On Transway. Sometimes they need a little extra – "

"Why'd you even say *that*?" Lang yells, all pretense gone.

"She was worried about you!" Celan yells back. "Worried about your drinking. And she knew stuff about Transway, about people getting sick. I was trying to tell her that we were fine. But she never said anything about fusing and neither did I!"

Lang glares at her, but Celan is undaunted; she glowers right back. Then the tension is broken by Melia, trilling a delighted laugh.

"Really, you two. If you're going to be fusers don't you need to be better liars than that?"

Lang winces. "Melia, there are all kinds of stories about Transway going around these days. A lot gets twisted. You can't believe everything you hear."

"I don't. Pero creo lo que veo."

"There's nothing *to* see," Celan says.

"And to think I was starting to like you."

That stings. Celan throws up her hands, as if to say 'Fine, you deal with this!' to Lang. Moments tick by, but he merely sighs, shoulders slumped, defeated.

"Mira," Melia says, in a suspiciously sober tone. "I'm not judging you, OK? And I'm not going to run and tell Mama. I just want to know that you're safe and I do *not* want to be lied to. Not by you, Langton. You're my brother and that means I've known you way too long for this kind of shit."

Lang says nothing, fumbling in his pouch for a smoke. Melia waits, implacable, as he rolls and lights one. For something to do, Celan picks up her shovel and pokes at the ground, more uncomfortable by the second. She wonders how much of Melia's earlier 'aviados' was strategic – a put-on to distract them before going in for the kill. She actually kind of admires her for that. But she's not going to say anything else; this is Lang's show now.

Finally, he clears his throat, meets Melia's eyes. "Fine," he says. "We're fusers. Class E, if that means anything to you."

298

Melia nods once, affirmative.

"That's why Celan wasn't feeling well yesterday. That's why I got so sick after Raf died. I didn't have the flu; I was trying to stop. And I did for almost a year. But that's probably why I started drinking so much. I wanted to fuse really bad but I wouldn't let myself. So I got drunk instead. But it didn't work. It was a bad idea."

He pauses, scratching his chin. Celan finds that she's holding her breath.

"But I'm, we're – trying, OK? Not to get real fucked up. Not to walk like Raf did. To just try and…live with it somehow. I don't know. But that's why we can't be here, why we're better off on Transway. We have friends there – people who've been through all this and can help."

"The elders won't," Melia says, but it's not a question, just a statement of fact.

"They didn't do anything for Raf."

"No," Melia says, "they didn't."

She reaches out and folds him into a fierce embrace; Lang grinds his smoke into the dust and hugs her back.

"I'm sorry," he says, voice muffled. "I'm really, really – "

Melia shushes him, patting him on the back, motherly.

Celan shuffles nervously, not knowing what to do. Should she go back to digging? Give them some time alone? She starts to sidle in the direction of the half-dug bed when Melia finally releases him.

"Do Mama and Papa – ?" he says, wiping his eyes.

Melia shakes her head no.

"Does Cass know?"

"About fusing?" Melia shrugs. "No. Cass is Cass. Won't

lower herself to hang out with any visiting expros. She doesn't know anything. Just that you still have Raf's transfer."

Lang grunts. Then Melia trains her gaze on Celan.

"Ven aquí," she commands. Celan approaches, hesitant until Melia pulls her in, close and warm, comforting.

"I actually do like you," Melia says as they part, giving her shoulders a quick shake. "I just don't like being lied to."

"I didn't want to get Lang in trouble."

"I know."

"And speaking of lying," Celan adds, trying to lighten the mood. "You're pretty good at it yourself."

Melia smirks. "I'd make a better fuser than you two do."

"Don't you dare," Lang says, and both girls laugh.

"Don't worry hermanito. I'm saving it for the blue robe."

"Oh, so a couple drops and you're an elegida?"

"Stranger things have happened," Melia sings, grinning. "And they need some new blood in there. People who can actually deal with this shit instead of pretending it's not happening. Maybe come clean about their own transfusing. Explain it so people don't go doing it on their own."

"Wanna spare others the fate of your fucked-up brother?"

"Maybe," Melia says.

She motions him in again, rising up on her toes and peering at him intently.

"What?" Lang says and then "Ow!" as Melia plucks a wiry white hair from his temple.

"So I'm keeping this. As a reminder."

21

Celan tugs the shift off over her head, groaning at the unfamiliar ache in her arms and back. She gives it a good sniff and frowns before draping it over the back of a chair. Getting pretty ripe. She's used to a world of printers and Sanichutes – a fresh clean uniform every day. Maybe tomorrow she'll ask Melia if she can borrow something else. Or maybe Shay said tomorrow was wash day? That might be almost relaxing compared to the last few days of digging, hauling, patching, and planting.

But it hasn't been so bad. After all the stress of their first night here, and then the next day's scene with Melia, the following two have fallen into a pleasant sort of rhythm. Work. Eat. Sleep in Lang's arms. And fuse, of course. But they haven't been taking any more than necessary.

She can almost see it: Staying here, working here, living here happy and peaceful – as long as the Carlos and Pazes of the world learn to mind their own business.

301

She sinks gratefully onto the bed and slides a hand under the pillows, groping around for the old shirt of Lang's that she's been sleeping in. She pulls it on, breathing in the mingled scents of both their bodies. Just thinking of his kiss, his touch – she wraps arms around herself and lies back on the soft ticking with a delicious shiver, the flicker of the candle on the nightstand suffusing the room with an intimate glow.

Any minute now he'll walk in here and he'll lie down next to her and he'll…Where is he anyway?

She huffs, impatient. He'd been talking to his parents in the kitchen when she told him she was going to bed. That was at least a half hour ago. Instinctively, she reaches for her server to check the time but only grabs at air.

Hope nothing's wrong. Melia wouldn't – would she?

There's a sudden tightness in her chest, a twitch in her cheek. She sits up, heart skipping, as the door creaks open and Lang enters, face dark and brow creased.

"Hey," she says.

He turns, bolting the door behind him. He's been careful to lock it since that first day when Melia walked in on them.

"Something wrong?"

Lang shakes his head no, shadows writhing in his hair.

"Did Melia…?"

"No," he says, plunking down on the edge of the bed. "She hasn't said anything." He yanks off boots and shirt and tosses them on the floor, then digs into his pouch for the transfer. Celan sees him draw up twice his maintenance dose.

"Whoa," she says.

He says nothing – just finishes his fuse and lays back, closing his eyes and resting his head against her thighs. She feels the tension drain from his shoulders as peace steals across his face. Languidly, he passes her the transfer and she draws up a large dose for herself. Might as well. If he's willing to go full aviados with his parents in the next room it must mean that they don't know anything.

It must be something else, some issue with Cass, or maybe Paz and her crew came back around.

But there's no point in worrying about any of it now, and with vial in hand she doesn't have to. She takes her fuse and blows out the candle, places the transfer next to it on the nightstand, and reaches out a hand to caress Lang's face. He stirs at the touch; then rouses himself and scoots up until they're lying side by side.

"Hey," she breathes.

"Hey," he says, rolling over and wrapping arms and legs around her. His breath puffs against her neck, sweet and deep.

Celan nuzzles into his embrace, the warm weight of him adding to the colossal calm of the fuse until she feels so safe and sound it seems like nothing could ever trouble her again. Fully entwined they're like binary stars, floating in space.

With the transfer as our center of mass.

She grins at the visual as they drift out through the ether.

LANG COLLAPSES ON HIS BACK in bliss. Morning sun streams in through the window, gilding the cozy contours of his old room. It's well past dawn. His mother must have let them sleep in. Next to him Celan shimmies and sighs. He leans over and kisses her.

"I love you," he says, cheek against her flushed chest.

She giggles. "Good."

303

"*Good?*" he says in mock outrage. "That's all you can say after that?"

"Well, it *was* good."

He rolls on top of her, straddling her hips, pinning her down. "Say you love me too."

"Mmmm…maybe," she says, still giggling.

"Oh, now you're gonna get it." He tickles her ribs. "Now what've you got to say?"

"No!" Celan shrieks, thrashing wildly.

"Say it."

"Ow!" she gasps. "OK, OK. Stop!"

He halts, but keeps his fingers poised to attack at any hint of betrayal.

"Say it."

"I love you, Lang-ton," she recites, sing-song.

"Bueno," he says, planting a kiss on her forehead before flopping back down beside her.

She smacks his chest lightly, adding, "You jackass," and they both laugh.

"I do, though, really," she adds. "And so, my love, just so you know…you have a burn," she pokes at the arm slung across her chest, "from last night."

He immediately reaches to trans it away, noting that she's doing the same thing to herself. All clear, they curl up again, sharing the knowing look of conspirators. They could have waited though, it's almost cura time. For both of them. Ever since the party, Celan has followed his lead and taken a small maintenance dose in the morning.

"I guess I have to," she'd said, solemn and reluctant like it was some kind of boon she was granting, "just to be safe." But he'd caught a dry flash of humor in her eye.

He's kind of in awe at how fast she got over the whole CERS thing. It's like once she accepted it that was that – no muss, no fuss. Impressive, but a little bit scary too, though he can't quite say how.

Her soft hair brushes his skin as she rests her head on his shoulder. "Do we have to get up? Can't we stay here forever?"

His heart sinks. Suddenly, every word of last night's painful conversation with his parents returns in a rush. The morning had started off so pleasantly that he'd forgotten all about it.

How the fuck am I going to tell her?

But putting it off will only make it worse.

"Um, Celan?"

"Hmmm?"

"We're actually not gonna be able to stay here much longer."

This rouses her. She raises herself up on one elbow. "What? Why not?"

"My parents sat me down last night, after you went to bed. They're not going to patron me again. Not until I give Raf's transfer back to the elders. We can stay a few more days, but after that…"

"But I thought you said Melia wouldn't – "

"She didn't. It's not Melia. Look, they aren't stupid. Transfers don't just vanish into thin air. They all knew I had to have it somewhere. They let it slide for a while, but – "

"Now the elders are being assholes."

"Well, uh, yeah. Kind of. Before they said I just couldn't come back to 'scuela, but now…"

305

Celan makes a face. "Hypocrites."

"Whatever. It's not like we can argue with them."

Her brow furrows for a moment, but then her face brightens. She rolls over and reaches down, fumbling for something on the floor. Lang grabs her around the waist to keep her from sliding off the bed.

"What're you – " he starts.

She pops up holding something in a closed fist.

"Those fuckers want your transfer?" she says fiercely. "Give it to them." And she opens her palm to reveal a small silvery vial.

"But that's – we can't! You have no idea how bad it's gonna be if we – "

Celan grins, jerking her chin at the nightstand. "Yours is over there. This one's mine."

"*What?*" He bolts upright, eyes traveling in wonderment from the vial in her hand to the one on the nightstand. "Where'd you get that?"

"From the lab," she says, closing her fingers over it again. "I didn't want to say anything about it when everyone was freaking out at Alamora. But I shorted out the tracker. So now we have two. Turn yours in and we'll keep this one between us. The elders get their little atonement, your parents get to be proud, and we get to stay here as long as we want – *without* having to worry about CERS. Everyone wins."

He gives a low whistle. "You are some kind of evil genius, you know that?"

"Not *evil*. Just…practical."

"Well whatever it is," he says, pecking her on the cheek, "I think I like it."

ATRAVESAR — TO BREAK THE SKIN

LANG SAILS THROUGH BREAKFAST GIDDY with relief – though he's careful not to look too cheerful under his mother's watchful eye. They'd given him a day to think things over so he's not going to tell his parents his decision about the transfer just yet. His turning it in has to look convincingly reluctant.

He and Celan had hashed out the plan as they'd prepared themselves to meet the day – how he was going to play it with his parents, whether or not they were going to let Melia in on the scheme (Celan said they'd have to – she'd know something was up if they gave back the transfer but still stayed well so it was better to have her on board from the beginning). She'd also thought it best for him to turn it in to Carlos instead of facing a whole pack of elders who might sense something amiss. Carlos, she said, will be so high on his own holiness that he won't suspect a thing.

Good ideas all. But although he respects her cleverness (and knows they have no other choice that doesn't involve serious misery), guilt still plucks at him. He's not sure he can handle seeing the pride and joy that will surely bloom on his parents' faces when he finally comes clean. But better that than anger and disgust. They've had enough of those things already.

And what's so wrong about making them happy for once?

We're really doing everyone a favor.

He brightens at the thought, chewing and swallowing the last bite of his tortilla.

"Ready?" he says to Celan. It's only the two of them at the table – his father and sisters have already eaten and gone. She nods, gathering up her breakfast things and taking them to scrape and rinse at the sink. He follows with his own, pausing beside the stove where his mother is stirring a large pot of what smells like some kind of bean stew.

"What should we do today?" he asks her, solicitous. "Do you want us to keep working on that fence?"

But she shakes her head, brown eyes soft and kind. "No, mijito. You've done enough out there, I think. Maybe you and Celan might like a little time to yourselves today though? Go up to the spring. Get yourselves washed up." She wrinkles her nose like she smells something bad, but her smile is sweet.

"Sure," he says uneasily. That twinge again.

Why does she have to be so nice – today of all days?

But that's probably the point.

A tap at his elbow. Celan motions for his dishes and he passes them over.

"But if there's anything you need later," he says, turning back to his mother, "just let us know."

"Bueno," she says, waving him off.

"OK," he says. Then to Celan, "Let's go."

THEY SET OUT ACROSS THE orchard under arching boughs, sunlight dappling their faces. Lang takes a deep draught of the soft spring air. The leaves are really starting to come in now, won't be long until the trees are in bloom. He conjures up a day – warm and drowsy, he and Celan curled up on a carpet of apple blossoms like cats in the sun. And then the harvest; the sweet snap of fruit. The autumn cider-making. Bonfires vivid in the velvet night. With her here, and the transfer, there'd be no need to live anywhere else. They could still visit Transway sometimes.

But here, we'd be home.

At the acequia they turn west, intending to follow it up to its source and find a secluded spot to bathe. He shifts the pack they'd stuffed with towels and clean clothes to his other shoulder, draping a long arm around Celan. She looks up at him and smiles and he gives her a warm little squeeze. Then a shout behind them stops them in their tracks. They spin around to see Melia darting through the trees with a funny look on her face.

"Hey!" she says. "There's some guy here for you. With blue hair. Says it's important. Something about the techs."

"Brophy," Lang says, heart sinking. "Hope nothing's wrong."

"Me too," Celan says, as Melia doubles back the way she came.

They tear off after her, pounding across the plank over the water and up a small hillock. The road comes into view with the sight of Brophy leaning louchely against a roller. With a final burst of speed, Lang passes Melia and reaches him first.

"Que pas'?" he says, panting.

Brophy shakes his head. "It's crazy," he says. Blue braids bobble. "Never seen anything like it."

"What?" Celan says, skidding up beside him. "Did my father come looking for me?"

Brophy chuckles. "Nope."

"Then what's going on? Is anyone else searching?"

"No. None of them are. They can't go anywhere. They can't *move*."

309

"*What?*"

"They're all, like, frozen."

"What do you mean?" Celan demands. "Frozen how?"

"Like literally – frozen. In place. It happened a couple days ago. People went to the lab for testing like usual, you know? The key code worked, but the techs inside were just sitting there. Like, staring at nothing. No matter what they did they wouldn't move. Didn't even blink. They didn't know what was wrong, like maybe they were all sick or something. So they got the fuck out of there. No one's been in or out since."

Celan's brow furrows, and she bites her lip in contemplation. Then Lang hears her gasp.

"The bot release," she says faintly.

"The what?" Brophy says.

"Remember what I told you? The night I escaped? There was going to be a bot release the next morning and they were putting in this new thing. To make people not want to go to Transway."

"Oh yeah," Brophy smirks. "Guess that didn't go as planned."

Celan's eyes dart side to side, panicky. "It's not funny. They all could die."

"So?"

"So they're *people*. My father. My friends – "

"But I thought you said your father was crazy."

"He hasn't always been. He used to love Transway. And he thought Pollomax was dangerous at first. He only changed his mind because of me! Because of my *fusing*. I have to fix this."

Brophy stares, disbelieving. "Are you fucking kidding me? It's not your fault, Celan. They did this to themselves. They chose this."

Her lips twist in disgust. "You sound like Paz."

"Who?"

"Never mind. And the point is they didn't choose it. Not all of them. It was my father and Ariana who forced it through. And he only agreed because of me. So I have to fix it."

"How?" Lang says.

She looks at him like she's only just realized he's there. "Transferon shuts down the bots. Remember? I transed mine to keep working even when it was in my system, but for anyone else a good dose should stop them cold."

Brophy guffaws. "So you're gonna trans 'em? Claro. They'll love that."

"Not all of them," Celan says. "Just two – Martinez and my father. Lead SocEns have ultimate clearance. Two of them can override the system. Set the bots back a version."

"And they're gonna be fine with being transed?"

"If I do it right they won't even know."

"And if they do find out?"

A shrug. "I saved their lives. What are they going to do, Destierra me? And once my father sees a real live example of the benefits of transferon, he'll have to change his mind about shutting down Transway! I mean, Martinez has been against it all along. So once my father changes his mind back it'll be him and Martinez against *her* again and everything will be fine."

Brophy just shakes his head.

"Look, my father's been an asshole lately, true. But I can't just let him *die*." Her voice breaks on the last word.

Lang's mind is reeling at the speed of events, but one

thought rises swiftly above all others. This is Celan's family. Her father. The only parent she has. No matter what the man may have done out of fear and ignorance as long as he's alive there's still a chance to change his mind. Make him understand. Put things right.

"Don't worry," he says. "We'll fix it. I'll help you."

"No," Celan says. "It's too dangerous. You stay here. I'll come back after."

"No. Your father might – "

"Lang."

"I can't let you go alone."

"I can help too," Melia pipes up.

"No," he and Celan say together.

"And I say no to all of this," cuts in Brophy, chopping a hand down like an axe. "Because right now? I'm getting back in this roller and I'm going back to Transway. And you can all just stay right here until you get some sense into your heads."

"Fine," Celan says levelly. "Go. I'll walk."

"*We'll* walk," Lang amends.

"Yeah," says Melia.

"Not you," Lang snaps, and his sister withdraws, sulking. He softens his voice. "Someone has to stay here so Mama doesn't worry. Tell her there was an emergency. We should be back before dark." He appeals to Brophy. "As long as we have a ride."

Brophy's eyes tick over their faces, like he's doing some kind of complex mental calculation. Then, finally, he sighs.

"Fine," he says, lips a tight line. "But I'm not involved in any of this. And neither is anyone else at Alamora. If you two do this – " he looks hard at Lang, "and it goes wrong – you're on your own."

Lang meets his gaze. "I know."

"All right," Brophy tells them. "Get in."

22

Lang plucks anxiously at the sleeves of the tan uniform. "It's too tight."

"They're supposed to fit like that," Celan says, thumbing the screen of her server. "This takes your exact measurements and sends them to the Bank. Then the printer prints out exactly the right size."

"It itches." His eyes cut around the room, the solid knot of dread in his gut growing larger by the minute.

The last couple of hours are a blur: hustling back to Transway, getting the keycode (which actually wasn't all that difficult; even though the techs themselves are shut down their automated systems apparently are not), and waiting outside the transer lab door while Celan went in to retrieve her server. It'd taken longer than expected, though, and he'd started to worry – until she reappeared, breathless, saying that her father must have taken it from her room, but she'd found it safe and sound in his library.

Then she'd taken his measurements and dashed back in to print him out this awful thing.

She had a plan, she said – a cover story to explain their absence from the city during the release. Her father knew the truth, of course, but they were going to wake Martinez first; he was more likely to be immediately cooperative. Then *he* could explain things to Celan's father.

While we get the last fuck out of here.

Two techs are slumped on a bench in the corner of the lab's waiting room and another is splayed at the mouth of a small hallway. They'd tried waking them by conventional means, in case Brophy was mistaken, but it had been no use. They were still breathing, and pulses beat in their wrists, but all were otherwise unresponsive.

"Anything?" he says, peering over Celan's shoulder.

"I'm looking," she says. "But there's nothing here. I pinged his server, then his bots, but they're all offline. There's nothing since right before the release, but those recs put him at Maddy's."

Lang chuckles. "So we go to Maddy's."

"But those are from three days ago, we have no idea where he is now."

"You said he thought this was all a mistake. Maybe he hedged his bets. Maybe he's out on Transway somewhere."

"I seriously doubt that. Even if he deliberately avoided the release, wouldn't he have come back in afterwards to try to wake everyone up once he saw what happened? To just disappear doesn't make any sense."

"Well, what else can we do?" Lang says. "We go to Maddy's and ask if anyone's seen him."

"That'll take forever. And we don't know how much longer everyone has! No one's eaten in three days, or had any water." She's scrolling again, feverishly. "We're going to have to wake my father. He should be somewhere right around here…" She scissors two-fingered at the screen, like she's honing in on something.

"Shit!"

"What?"

Her shoulders slump. "He's in the Barsoom Room."

"The what?"

"The Mars – fuck!" she yells in lieu of explanation.

"What's the matter?"

"It's right there. Right down the hall!" she gestures angrily at the aperture where the one tech lies sprawled. "But you have to thumb the reader to get in there and I don't have clearance."

"Oh," Lang says. But then he brightens. "What about one of these guys?" He tilts his head toward the passed out techs. "Maybe they do. And they're not exactly gonna mind if we borrow their thumbs for a minute."

"Yes!" she cries, throwing her arms around his neck. "Brilliant!"

But her joy is short-lived. After dragging three separate bodies over to the Mars Room reader, and mashing three disturbingly slack thumbs against it with no result, they're no closer the their objective and Celan is swiping at her server ever more desperately.

"Can't we just wake one of them up?" Lang says, indicating the bodies at their feet. "Maybe they know where to find the guy who can open the door."

317

"No. That gets too complicated. We don't know how many we'd end up having to wake and the more there are the more chance someone might ask too many questions, or notice the transfer. And if there are more of them than there are of us – "

"Well what, then?" he snaps.

She looks up, takes a deep breath, exhales. "There's one other thing we can try."

"What?"

"We can wake Ariana."

Lang balks. "But isn't she the one who hates Transway? That doesn't sound like such a good – "

"We'll have to wake her now anyway if we can't find Martinez. Maybe it's even better to do her first."

"But if she finds out we transed her – "

"She won't," Celan says firmly. "We'll only give her a little. A balanced dose. If she's a little disoriented, well, she's been unconscious for three days. We'll say we shook her awake or something. Once she sees what the bot release did, she'll be so freaked out that she won't even question it. If we can get her down here to wake my father up before she's had too much time to recover it'll be easy to distract her while we slip him some too."

"That's a pretty big if, Celan."

"Well, what other choice do we have?" she spits back. She's resumed her frantic flicking at the little screen. "I mean, maybe you were right. Maybe Martinez said 'fuck it' and he's halfway to Winnipeg by now."

Lang opens his mouth to reply but the barely controlled panic in her voice stops him cold. At this point, she's only just holding her shit together.

"Look!" she says, holding her server up triumphantly. "Ariana's in the caf. We can walk right in there."

"OK," he relents. "Let's try it."

ARIANA BALOR BLINKS RAPIDLY, EYES shifting side to side until finally her vision begins to clear and focus – on the face of Lana Timanti. The girl is saying something, holding out a cup of water. Ariana's mouth is pasty and dry, horribly so, and there's a funny taste in it like –

What in the world...

She'd just been sitting here in the caf, having lunch with Nathan and some of his CompEn colleagues. How could she have passed out? Weakly, she turns her head, bringing on a wave of vertigo. She's been turned around in her chair, with her back to the table. Nathan is next to her, slumped against Begay. She glances over her shoulder. Everyone is like that. The whole table. The whole caf. They all look like they're –

What *happened*?

She opens her mouth to speak but only a dry rasp comes out.

"Mrs. Balor – Ariana?" Lana says, proffering the cup again. "Drink some water."

"Ech – "

"It's OK," Lana says. "You were out cold."

"What?" she coughs out.

"The bot release. It did something bad to everyone."

Ariana reaches a hand out for the water, but it trembles in midair until Lana says, "I can hold it for you if you want."

The girl's ingratiating tone snaps her back into some

319

form of coherence. She wills her hand still and snatches up the cup, pouring the fluid down her throat; cool tendrils expand downward, through her esophagus, into her stomach.

"You might just want to sip it," Lana says faintly, but Ariana ignores this, running tongue over furred teeth, testing out her stiff jaw.

"Mrs. Balor? Are you OK?"

"Of course. Yes. What's going on here, Lana? Tell me exactly what happened." She starts to rise, but Lana puts a hand on her shoulder, keeping her in her seat.

"Just rest for a minute. You haven't moved in three days. You might get dizzy if you stand up too fast."

"What are you talking about – three days? I just sat down here a few minutes ago."

Lana shakes her head. "No. It's been three days. There was something wrong with the bot release. It shut everyone down. Here, look." She holds up her server so Ariana can see the date.

Tuesday. Ord 66.

Ariana stares, jaw slack with shock. Then she fumbles in her breast pocket for her own server. She swipes at the screen, bringing up the relevant information.

Three days – that's impossible!

But there it is, incontrovertible: Ord 66. And here they are, her own georecs: Location unchanged, not even by the smallest decimal. For three days.

"But you – how are *you* awake then?" she says, groping for a thread of sense in all this.

"I – I've been away," Lana says.

She said it was the bot release, Ariana thinks furiously. *The Pollomax! But that couldn't have caused this. There must be some other explanation.*

She scrolls through the georecs: Her current location stasis began at 12:12:28 on Ord 63. Not even fifteen minutes into the release. Her throat tightens again, not with dryness but with fear. This is very, very bad.

" – to Winnipeg," Lana is saying. "My father let me visit there for a few days, now that regular Ed is over. I was going to get the upgrade when I got back."

Ariana's brow knits. Travelling by herself? Without an escort? In one of the long-haul rollers? Shouldn't the Leads have been informed of this? It sounds highly irregular. But Theodore's always been indulgent with the girl. And here she is – obviously unaffected somehow.

She blinks, mind still spinning, as a shuffle of feet brings her eyes up to register a tall, black-haired man in tan standing beside Lana.

"Who is this with you?"

"John Sanchez," Lana says. "SocTech. He accompanied me to Winnipeg."

The tall man nods. "Good afternoon, ma'am."

"And you just returned?"

"Yes," Lana says. "About an hour ago. The gate was closed out front and we didn't know what to do. No one was at the scanners. So we went to ask around on Transway and they said no one had been in or out of the city since Saturday afternoon. So we figured it must have been the bot release that caused whatever happened. They gave us the key code for the transer lab so we could get in and find the Lead SocEns and try to wake them up somehow to do an override."

But Ariana's only half-listening. Her mind is ticking, ticking. What could have gone wrong with the bots? She swipes at her server. It had to be the Pollomax, that was the only change other than routine upgrades. Pollomax was supposed to cause aversion, but only to a very specific stimulus: Transway.

Could it have been a case of too much, too soon? Could the aversion have spread somehow to include *everything*, to the point where no one was motivated to do *anything*? Was there some factor not accounted for in the simulations?

But we did live tests!

On expros, though – their brains are wired differently.

But we compensated for that, didn't we?

A chill runs down her spine.

Maybe not enough.

"My father's in the Mars Room," Lana continues, two bright spots of color burning high in her cheeks, "but we can't get in there. As soon as you can walk we need to go and wake him up – as soon as possible!"

Yes, they will have to wake Theodore. And she will have to tell him that her miraculous Transway cure caused everyone to go comatose for three days. And when he finds out that the Pollomax wasn't safe after all that'll be the end of their whole Transway deal. And it may only have been a tiny error. A misplaced decimal. Something easily fixed. But once the Lead Ens find out about this fiasco they'll never agree to do anything like it again.

Unless none of them ever realize how long they were out. Or why.

Her gaze drifts upwards. Lana's practically wringing her hands. Of course she's worried about her father. But a few minutes more won't matter.

Ariana clears her throat. "I'd like to wake my spouse first, if you don't mind."

"Uh – "

"No problem, ma'am," Sanchez says crisply. "Where is he?"

Ariana points to Nathan and Sanchez inserts himself between them – shaking the man vigorously then stopping and shaking him again.

"It was really hard to wake you up," Lana offers. "We had to shake you for a while."

Ariana frowns. Shaking someone out of a coma shouldn't be –

There's a jolt to her elbow as Sanchez rises, still ministering to Nathan, who's now murmuring groggily.

– but it obviously works.

"Get him some water," she orders Lana.

The girl hurries over to the drinks station as Sanchez steps aside, allowing her full access to her spouse. She pats Nathan's cheeks gently; his eyes are still closed but they are moving beneath his lids. She bites her lip.

Restore the Bank. That's all he has to do. Restore it back to fifteen minutes before the bot release on Ord 63. Wipe the last three days out of existence. Nathan's a Lead CompEn. He'll know what to do. All they need from Theodore is clearance – but that's a thumbprint on a server; they can do it while he's still out. Say the release was halted due to a system-wide anomaly. No one will ever be the wiser.

Except for Lana and this Sanchez fellow.

She'll have to think of a way to ensure their silence.

But that shouldn't be too hard. Lana does want that SocEn placement after all. It would pain her to approve it (mediocrity should never be rewarded) but if it's for the greater good…

"Nathan," she says, soft but urgent. "Nathan, wake up."

FINGERS TREMBLING, CELAN HOLDS THE cup under the spigot, mind racing fast enough to cause motion sickness.

It had taken at least ten minutes after the oral dose of transferon for Ariana to really begin to come around. They hadn't wanted to fuse her – thinking it too risky between the burn and the chance that she might wake before they could erase it – but now she wishes they had. They hadn't wanted to leave evidence, but a nice hit of Class E in the back of the neck probably wouldn't have been noticed and would've kept her docile enough to maneuver down to the lab before her faculties began to return.

Thank Madre for Lang's quick thinking on the request to wake Nathan; he must have slipped him some transferon during that little 'shake and wake' charade. But as she trots back across the caf with the water she can see that the man still hasn't regained full consciousness.

How much did Lang give him? How long before he wakes up?

Mr. Balor. What bad luck! If they'd noticed him, they could have moved him before they woke Ariana, hidden him where she wouldn't have seen him until she'd done what they needed her to do. Stupid uniforms – everyone looks alike.

She draws up alongside Lang and holds the cup out to Ariana. But the Lead SocEn ignores her, frowning down at Nathan, slapping his face harder. Celan and Lang exchange a quick glance: How long before she figures out something's off?

"It took a while for you to come around ma'am," Lang says, as if to forestall any suspicion.

"Did you time it?" Ariana says, not looking up. "How many minutes?"

Celan opens her mouth to answer as Nathan's eyes fly open.

"Wha – " he splutters, thrashing around and nearly sliding to the floor before Lang catches him under the armpits and sets him upright.

Ariana motions for the water and then waves them both off, imperiously demanding a few minutes alone with her spouse. Celan and Lang retreat to the wall of windows to regroup.

"Do you think she knows?" Celan whispers, shuffling nervously.

"I think she was just worried about her man."

"But my father," she says. "Once we wake him up who knows what he might say? The last thing he probably remembers is that I ran away before he could send me off to be de-fused somewhere. And now there'll be two of them watching and listening. Both totally awake."

Lang shrugs. "There's nothing we can do. We started this. We're just gonna have to go with it."

"We're going to have to wake him and *run*," Celan says. "Dose him and get the fuck out of there."

"Sounds good to me."

They both turn and look longingly out the window to the mountains. Then: "Lana! Sanchez!" Ariana's voice summons them again.

Dutifully, they approach.

"Yes?" Celan says.

"Nathan and I have talked it over and we've decided. We will go and wake your father. You two stay here."

Her heart drops to her knees. "What? Why?"

"There's some sensitive information – " Ariana starts, but Celan cuts her off.

"No!" she says. "I have to go. I have to see him."

"And you will, of course. Once he's been fully briefed on the situation."

"No," Celan insists. "I have to see him *now*."

"Lana," Ariana says, with uncharacteristic solicitousness, "I know you must be terribly worried about him and that speaks so well of you. You've done such a fine job here. Really. A job worthy of a future SocEn. I can't imagine how frightened you must have been, coming in here to find us all like this." She gestures around at the still-slumped forms. "But now you know that we can be woken and that your father will be fine. There are some serious issues at stake here, however. More than you can imagine. And I, as his colleague, need to discuss them with him *alone*."

Celan gnaws the inside of her cheek anxiously.

Then Lang speaks up. "Ma'am, I understand you have these, uh, security concerns. But the waking process can be kind of involved. Why don't we come down to the lab with you and wait outside the door. That way we'll be right there if you need any help, but you can still have your privacy."

He says this flatly, like it's an offhand suggestion and doesn't matter one way or the other. But Celan almost collapses with relief. And Ariana only considers it for a few seconds before nodding and rising.

"Yes, fine. Thank you, Sanchez. That will work." She turns back to Nathan, who's now tapping feverishly at his server, and motions him to his feet.

Celan risks a quick glance at Lang; he gives her a reassuring wink.

"Gracias," she mouths, as they trail the two adults out of the caf.

☞ 23 ☜

It's not going to work, Ariana thinks, panicky, as the elevator plummets towards the transer lab. *Nathan's right, even if we set the date back to Ord 63 right before the release, how do we account for the anomaly?*

Because people are going to wake up on the floor, weak and bleary-eyed, in all sorts of positions. They'll know something happened – but what? There needs to be some explanation. And what of the views? At 11:45 on Ord 63 the views will show everyone going about their business as usual. They'd have to splice in the moment when everyone passed out, and then show them waking up a few minutes later, *before* noon. But from the sound of her spouse's hectic server-tapping, he's definitely trying to work that out.

And even if he can, what to do about these two...

She eyes Lana and Sanchez sourly. Ensuring Sanchez's silence about the restore shouldn't be hard. SocTechs are simple creatures. Throw him a bone and he'll do what he's told. Lana, however...

Even if she can come up with a plausible explanation (other than covering her own ass) and promises the girl the highest SocEn candidate recommendation in exchange for her discretion, there's still a possibility that she will say something incriminating to someone at some point.

Someone like Theodore.

But this Sanchez might be the key to her silence. Because Ariana thinks she detects the filaments of some fond feeling between them. The little looks. The body language.

Maybe he's the solution: Theodore *had* trusted him with Lana – wherever she went, surely not all the way to Winnipeg. Maybe he still had doubts about the Pollomax and sent them out of the city as a precaution. And maybe the choice of this particular young man to accompany her was at Lana's specific request. Maybe there's some sort of romance going on between them. If there is, and if the girl wants to keep him close, a threat to his position might be all it takes keep her mouth shut.

Ariana takes out her server, scrolling through PersRecs.

Sanchez. Here he is – Or rather, here *they* are: There are two techs with the name John Sanchez. One is a runty little GenTech and the other actually is a SocTech, albeit one with a shock of flame-bright hair. Neither looks anything like the man to her right.

She sucks in a breath. Could she have heard wrong? Could it be Don Sanchez? Or Ron? Or is something else going on? She opens her mouth to ask for clarification but immediately shuts it again. If something *is* going on it might be better not to alert them that she's wise to it just yet.

330

She taps at her server again. No Don Sanchez. Or Ron.

And now that she has a chance to observe him more closely, there seems to be an odd touch of scruffiness about the man. That lank hair, a shadow of stubble on his jaw. Dirt under the fingernails. She shudders. Maybe he isn't a tech at all. But that would mean –

The elevator doors part and the party advances into the corridor, Ariana leading the way to the lab at the far end, Lana's words from earlier running through her brain, 'The gate was closed up front and we didn't know what to do. So we went to ask around on Transway'.

Maybe it wasn't a 'we'; maybe it was a 'she'. And maybe she met this man there. Or maybe...she already knew him. Ariana's pulse quickens; she'd completely forgotten about her plan to check into Lana's chaps at the gate. To see whether or not she'd been making a habit of going out Transway. Because if she has or even if she hasn't –

Maybe there's a simple way to shut her up forever.

Ariana whooshes open the lab door and steps inside, motioning the others past her.

"Just a minute," she says, before turning a sharp right and printing the reader to the observation room. "I want to see if White's in here."

She ducks inside, shutting the door behind her, confident in the knowledge that the large window facing the waiting room is one-way only. None of them can see her bend down and rifle through the pockets of the slumped tech at the control panel. None of them can see her pull his stun out and slide it into her own pocket.

She emerges to find a fretful Lana, a po-faced whoever-he-is, and a smiling Nathan who nods, affirmative. He can splice the views. Perfect. Just a quick review of the last half hour in the caf and lab to see what Lana and this man have been up to, and then all they need is Theodore's thumb.

Because she's just found a reason for the anomaly.

CELAN TAPS HER FEET IN an anxious dance, pooching out her lips and sighing. Lang gives her shoulder a reassuring squeeze. It can't be much longer until Ariana gives up and has them to try to wake her father. It must be twenty minutes at least since she and Nathan went in there.

She reaches for her server again to check the time.

11:57, Ord 63.

What the – ?

Celan freezes. Lang nudges her and she meets his questioning look with the server, which she holds up to display the wrong time and date. He shrugs; uncomprehending.

Then the whoosh of the door makes her jump.

"Your father is waking now," Ariana says coolly, stepping forward and allowing it to close behind her. "Along with everyone else."

"But how did you – ?"

"We did a full system restore back to Ord 63. It was the only way to bring everyone back around quickly. But the real question here is: How did you wake up Nathan and I? The kind of comatose state we were in can't be broken by mere shaking and slapping."

Celan says nothing, just gapes at her, mind blank.

Then Lang steps in. "With all due respect ma'am, it most definitely can. At least, it worked for us."

Ariana's eyes narrow. "Such words of wisdom from Mr. *Sanchez*. Expro scum. Now tell me who you really are."

"What – ?" Celan starts, but before she can finish the thought she's being spun around and yanked down the corridor. Without saying a word Lang's message is clear: *Run*.

And they do – back through the waiting room, jumping over groggy forms on the floor, heading for the door to the outside and freedom – until an electric jolt hits her square in the back and everything goes black.

THEODORE LOOMS OVER THE PRONE form on the floor. The black-haired man curls fetal-like, snuffling and muttering. He aches to kick him again, to feel the satisfying crunch of another broken rib against the toe of his boot. But he doesn't want to kill him. Not yet. Not like this. He wants him to *suffer*.

Because this is the end. The end of every hope and dream he ever had for his daughter. And this boy will suffer beyond measure for what he did – corrupted her, confused her; took something pure and beautiful and defiled it in the worst way possible. Turned her into a fuser; made her do his bidding. *This* was the problem all along. Not simple curiosity, not a desire to get ahead in her research, but a desire for this stinking piece of shit.

He hadn't wanted to believe it when Ariana first told him what had happened: How, with Lana's help, this parasite had entered the city and attempted to destroy the entire population by dosing the water supply with transferon, then letting the expros in to do what they would. It was only due to the Balors' natural resistance and quick thinking that

Albakirk had been saved. But the proof was irrefutable – everyone had been knocked out, there were incriminating views of Lana and this man in the lab, and Ariana and Nathan both had traces of transferon in their systems. No other possible way that *that* could have happened.

Somehow (again, Lana) the expros got wind of the plan to dismantle Transway and this had been a desperate attempt to stop it. And they'd used his daughter – *his* daughter – to do it.

How she'd begged and pleaded and tried to *explain*. If he would only listen to how they'd tried to help! Some almighty bullshit about how the whole city had been rendered unconscious for three days by the Pollomax in a bot release which never actually took place. And how she and this little shit were actually the ones who'd saved them all. Ariana was lying, Lana insisted. She'd altered time! All complete garbage, of course. The ravings of a mind destroyed. By this vermin.

"He's a good man," his daughter had sobbed.

She *loved* him.

Theodore draws his foot back and – crack – another rib snaps. The boy writhes, gasping, gagging, whimpering in pain.

We'll have to run a scan. Don't want him bleeding out internally before the Destierra.

And it must hurt even worse than it normally would – the fucking fuser is already showing signs of CERS. But he'll make sure the boy is fixed up a bit before they send him out in the desert. Don't want a mess in the roller. And it'll give him a little time to take in his fate with all his faculties intact, knowing what's coming and fully dreading it.

It will be all the better to watch him die that way.

↶ 24 ↷

As the small phalanx of rollers fades into tiny dots in the distance, Celan turns a slow circle, taking in the vast expanse of desert under the blue dome of sky. Rock and sand and scrub as far as the eye can see. A wasteland. But it doesn't matter. Her father had whispered 'wait' as he'd handed her a suspiciously heavy bag containing more, no doubt, than the traditional portion of food and water.

Destierra my ass.

She crouches and throws open the top flap of the pack, peering in. Sure enough – aside from a large thermos and extra packets of rations there's her server, a stun, and, rattling around in the bottom, a small silvery vial. He was never going to let her die.

Asshole.

Not that she's angry about the extra equipment, just the fact that she's sure there's been no such charity for Lang. Her father thinks it was all *his* fault – that either he turned her into a fuser or that he exploited her condition somehow; lured her into going along with some ludicrous anti-tech plot. She never should have told him about hacking her geocodes and going out to Transway. But she was just trying to explain. To show him how it was all her doing, how Lang never *made* her do anything; that he'd only been trying to help.

But her father wouldn't listen. He'd looked on her with pity. Pity and disgust.

Her cheeks redden, but with anger not shame.

Fucking Ariana. Fucking liar! *If I ever see that bitch again I'll –*

Her fingers clench into a fist with the itch to hit at the same time as a sick, scared feeling seeps into her gut, constricting her throat, making her wince. The thought of Lang – Madre knows where, stuck out someplace like this, sick as a dog. He never should have come. She shouldn't have let him.

So she has to find him.

Because there's no way that she is just going to sit here and wait for her father to show. What's he going to do with her anyway – take her to Winnipeg? Change her name (again!) and leave her there to live out her life among strangers? A nobody nowhere? With Lang dead and gone?

No way. I'm going to find him.

The time for tears is over. The time for understanding is done. They will never understand. She and Lang and the people like them will always be the villains because Ariana and the people like her will just lie and lie and lie forever and they're the ones who will always be believed. It will never be right and there's no way she can fix it. But there is one thing she can do:

Find him.

Celan stands, then reaches into the pack and pulls out her server.

Won't be needing this, she thinks, positioning it on top of a large boulder. Let her father ping it here. By the time he arrives she'll be long gone. Speaking of which…they'd given her some kind of inoculation before she left. She's positive it contained some kind of tracker.

She shrugs the pack onto her back and closes her eyes, letting her awareness sink deep into her own system. Sure enough, she can see a little light blinking, drifting through her veins like a ship on a river. She hones in and concentrates until it goes dark.

Her eyes flutter open and she blinks against the sun-scorched glare. They'd blindfolded her before putting her in the roller and six hours dark still has her dazzled. But it doesn't matter. They could blindfold her all they wanted; all she'd had to do was let her astral form rise out of her body, just a few centimeters, and she could see everything. She's been marking time and position by the sun, as she was taught as a child in the ranchos. They took her due west, following the old road out over the mesas, veering slightly north after a few hours.

She's also been tracking distance. Rollers can go up to forty miles an hour on level terrain. It feels like they were doing close to that – say thirty-five average to account for rough patches where they slowed to a crawl.

So she's maybe a hundred and eighty miles from Albakirk, NNW.

From what she could see when they left, it looked like

Lang was taken south. If they followed the old road that way too, and went about a hundred eighty miles…

She wishes she could astral – see him, speak to him, find out exactly where he is and how he's doing; tell him to wait for her. But her prana's not strong enough for that. And even if it were, to leave her body out here unprotected would be suicide.

And I am not *going to die.*

She turns and positions herself along a direct diagonal. Hopefully, he isn't too sick yet. Hopefully, he'd thought of doing some of the same things she had. Hopefully, he's headed her way even now and they can meet in the middle.

Ninety miles. SSE.

She squares her shoulders, takes a deep, fortifying breath, and launches herself in that direction.

THE SUN STABS DOWN – POISONOUS, unrelenting. Sweat boils off his brow and into his eyes as Lang staggers forward another step, shivering, not even bothering to wipe it away. It's not going to stop. It's started now and it's not going to stop until he's dead. Or wishes he were.

And he's wished that about a million times in the last forty-eight hours.

He shudders again, retching as he recalls Celan's father – terrifying in his anger, looking like he wanted to beat him dead. His ribs are still tender, despite his having taken full advantage of the small dose of transferon they'd given him before the Destierra to heal the worst of the damage. But that's long worn off now and the final dive begun.

The CERS itself won't kill him; he's been through it before. But that time he was in his own bedroom, in his own house, with his mother bringing him soup and everyone fussing over his terrible flu. Out here with the exposure and dehydration he's screwed.

He shakes his water bottle. Almost empty. If he could just find some water somewhere, no matter how noxious, he might be able to transfigure it into something potable.

But there's only sand and scrub and rock.

At least they won't get to see it, won't get to watch his demise and gloat. The first thing he did was disable the tracker. Because he's positive that's what the second shot was – a bot; some way that they could find him, maybe send a drone out to watch him die. But he did what Celan would have done, still his breath and turn his gaze inward until he could see the thing inside him and send prana to it, short it out. He's sure it worked. There's nothing out here, nothing following him. He's alone.

His throat constricts – part thirst, part sorrow.

Celan.

He wishes he could blame her for dragging him into this, but she hadn't forced him, hadn't manipulate him in any way. She hadn't even wanted him to come. He'd made the choice all on his own. And she couldn't have fathomed that it would all turn out like this. She's probably suffering as much as he is right now.

Maybe even worse.

Because she did what she did thinking she would save them – her family, her friends. Thinking she would save them and that they'd know she loved them. And that she wasn't *bad*. It would change their minds, make them realize that even as a Class E fuser, she was still worth something.

And, if the situation were reversed, wouldn't he have done the same?

This last tears a sob from his chest. His family, his mother, Melia. Do they know what happened? Do they know that he's never coming home? Maybe not yet, but they will. They'll hear somehow. People will be leaving Transway and some of them will go to the ranchos. They'll tell them. And then –

His gut spasms and he heaves into the dust. Drags the edge of his sleeve across his mouth. Another step and his legs give way. He falls to his knees.

Terra Madre. Just let this be over. Let me go.

UP ONE RIDGE THEN DOWN, Celan pads lightly over the ground, running at an even pace, barely winded. The land is cooler, greener here. The foothills of some sort of mountains.

This is easy.

As easy as a mix of Class D & E can be.

She'd started to flag a couple hours into her initial sprint and had to stop and figure out something to help her along. But she got the mix right; she's got energy to burn and is feeling no pain.

She jogs up a short rise and into a copse of trees – the perfect place for a pit stop and a little food and water. As good as she feels she's aware that it's at least partially an illusion. She still has to tend to the basics every once in a while.

She seats herself on a boulder-sheltered log and digs in her pack for the thermos.

Her main concern now is the approach of evening. They'd dropped her off at what looked like noon and from the angle of the sun it appears to be close to 15:00 now. On Ord 68

340

that's not a whole lot of daylight left to work with. Once the sun goes down she's not sure what she's going to do. Find shelter of some kind? She'll have to. Too dangerous to keep running at night, unless there's a full moon.

She tries to recall its most recent phase as her mind drifts to an image from her recent re-read: The moon after Lothlórien, all out of sync. They'd travelled just like this – that little fellowship. Sometimes they had to run all day and night through dangerous territory, with terrible things after them: Orcs. Wolves.

And Ariana Balor, the Balrog herself.

But they made it through, and so will she.

Celan raises the thermos to her lips, closing her eyes and drinking deep, until a scream-like cry shatters the air and her arm jerks involuntarily, sending the thermos flying to the ground. She scrambles up, scrabbling in her pack for the stun as the life-giving fluid dribbles away down a little rill and stains the dirt dark.

The unearthly cry comes again and then she sees it – a mountain lion, a giant nasty one with an extra set of crooked yellow teeth sticking up at odd angles from its massive maw, poised to strike on the rocks above her. It leaps and she fires, heart racing as the big cat collapses in a heap at her feet. Carefully, she pokes it with the toe of her boot. It's totally out.

Good to know these things really work, she thinks, pocketing the weapon.

Though after recently being on the receiving end of one, she knows that firsthand. At least she can be reasonably sure that any more encounters like this one won't be a problem.

341

But this, she thinks, reaching to retrieve the empty thermos, *most definitely will.*

HE DOESN'T KNOW HOW MUCH time has passed; it's all just pain. Clothes a stinking mess, writhing in the sand, sun burning, each breeze a dagger. No relief. And now there's a sound like a mosquito in his ear. A horrible grinding whine. Lang grits his teeth, covers his ears, and tries to burrow into the ground. Anything to escape it.

Then suddenly, mercifully, it stops.

He gulps deep draughts of air with a prayer of thanks that something, just one source of agony, has ceased. But it seems he's exchanged a new terror for the old – there's someone standing over him, saying his name.

"Lang? Lang! It's him!"

A strong hand grasps his arm. He pulls back, wincing at the touch.

Is this real?

"Lang. Hold still. Shit. Mara! Ayúdame!"

Mara?

"Pinche Class E."

Mara!

Another hand grabs him and he goes limp. Looks up, incredulous.

"Brophy?" he croaks at the figures holding him. "Mara?"

Wisps of pink bangs against blue sky. "Fuck those assholes. You really think we'd leave you out here to die?"

His sleeve's jerked up, there's a quick flash of silver and then...

Ahhhhhh.

The pain falls away and he's lifted up, up – into the massive beating heart of the sun.

"SO HOW'D YOU FIND ME? Astral?" Lang guesses, sprawling out across the back seat of the roller. It would normally be an uncomfortable position, but after the dose Brophy gave him he might as well be laid out on a featherbed.

From the driver's seat, Brophy nods. "I followed the tech rollers. Saw where they dropped you off."

Lang raises his head a fraction to peer down at his body, newly arrayed in his regular expro clothes. Mara and Brophy had brought them; had helped him out of the soiled tech uniform. They'd left the wretched thing in the desert.

Good riddance.

"Thought you said I was on my own."

Brophy shrugs.

Mara turns and eyes Lang with one brow raised puckishly. "Transway's done, ese. No más. We're all gonna have to go. A hundred miles they said, at least."

"The techs?"

"Yeah. We're headed north, gonna try to find a way to live without them. We're gonna need people with skills."

"Like healing."

"Like lots of things. But yeah, your fused-up ass is kind of a necessity."

"A necessary evil," Brophy says, and they all laugh.

Lang lies back again, watching the silver-white canopy of the roller shudder against the sky like a mobile above a crib. Then, all of a sudden, it hits him – *Celan!*

He struggles to sit up, saying her name and 'Wait!'

Up front, Mara and Brophy share a look.

"We have to find Celan!"

Brophy clears his throat. "OK, this is gonna sound really fucked up and I'm not exactly sure how to tell you. But Zeeb has this theory and it's not like we have a hundred percent proof or anything but it actually makes a lot of sense when you think about it – "

"She was in on it," Mara says, cutting off this exposition. "Either that or they used her too. But I seriously doubt it. She was the bait in a trap and you were the one they caught. Used this whole thing as an excuse to shut down Transway."

"No!" Lang says, as a jolt from the roller lays him out flat. He grabs Brophy's head rest to pull himself upright. "She would never do that. The bots. The shutdown. It was all real. She wasn't faking any of it. They Destierra'd her too! She's probably as sick as I was. We have to find her!"

Mara rolls her eyes. "You really think her daddy's gonna let her die? He's probably on his way to get her right now."

"No he's not!" Lang protests. "He hates us."

"Hates *you*," Mara corrects. "Trust me. He won't let anything happen to *her*."

But the memory of the black rage in the man's eyes is unforgettable. Even if her father were to go looking for her, it wouldn't necessarily be to save her.

"No. I have to try and find her. Maybe I can astral…"

At this, Brophy hits the brakes, halting the roller in a cloud of dust.

Both of them turn. "No."

"Yes," Lang says, defiant. Then, "You can't stop me."

"You can barely sit up straight," Mara says, throwing her

hands up in disgust.

"Doesn't matter."

"Yes it does," Brophy says. "You're too weak right now. You can't go by yourself. You'll get confused. Lost."

Lang gives him the most entreating look he can muster. "Please," he begs. "You know her. You knew her sisters, her whole family back in the day. You know she wouldn't have done this on purpose.

"You *know*."

Brophy sighs; Mara starts to speak again but he holds up a hand for silence, gold-brown gaze flicking thoughtfully over Lang's face.

"All right," he says. "But one hour only. That's all the time we can spare. If we don't find her by then we let it go. Agreed?"

Lang nods, swallowing. "Agreed. But we'll find her. We'll find her and you'll see. It wasn't a trap. She would never do that."

Then softer, under his breath. "She loves me."

☛ 25 ☚

Celan swallows hard against the dryness in her throat, pawing at gritty eyes as she churns through scrub to the top of a mesa. She needs to get to higher ground, survey the lay of the land. See if she can spot a river or lake. Several hours have passed since her path into the mountains (and the hope of mountain streams) was blocked by a deep ravine. Impassable, so she'd had to range along its edge, hoping that it would thin out or disappear altogether. And it had, finally, at the foot of this plateau.

She pauses, panting, taking in the desert lands spread out around her in the amber light of sunset. A beautiful scene – if she wasn't about to die there.

I am not *going to die.*

But she needs to find water soon. So, with a final burst, she hurtles over the top and stops for a moment, letting her heart rate slow. Then she looks around and blinks, disbelieving, at the sight before her eyes: The bare top of the mesa broken by the sight of several tall figures moving around the shimmering outline of some sort of vehicle.

But it's not a roller. It's something else; an odd, star-shaped craft. Maybe it's from some other city-state. But that doesn't matter. There are *people* with it, three of them – all tall and pale and dressed in fluid yet neat white garments. She's too desperate to care who they are; if they're out here in these dry lands they must have water.

But for safety's sake…

She pats the stun, still jammed in her pocket within easy reach since the incident with the mountain lion, then skitters over rock as fast as possible in their direction. At fifty meters she starts to yell.

"Hey! Help! Hello!"

The trio turns as one to look at her as she stumbles towards them. At twenty meters she skids to a stop, breathing hard, swaying with fatigue and dehydration. Her hand slides into her pocket, but she doesn't take out the stun, just keeps it ready.

They are all very tall, over two meters at least, with smooth marble-like skin that looks almost like some manmade substance, and they have very large, slightly slanted, blue or green eyes – so bright they could almost be fusing.

Elves, she thinks wildly, suppressing a laugh.

They regard her with undisguised curiosity.

"Hey," she says. "I'm Celan Mairs and I'm kind of – lost. And thirsty. Do you have any water?"

One of the two blue-eyed ones leans in and peers down at her, obviously surprised by something.

"Chan," he says simply.

348

"OK, Chan. Is that your name? Nice to meet you. But please, do you have any water? Agua? H_2O?"

A beat passes. Then the man says, "Yes. Of course."

"Well can you spare some?" she says, teeth gritted in frustration, fingers tightening on the stun. She doesn't want to use it unless she absolutely has to.

But Chan says nothing, just holds out a hand, palm up, and lets the shape of a thermos slowly materialize in it.

Celan's jaw drops in shock; they must have some kind of printer somewhere. But she doesn't see any in evidence. Maybe it's in their vehicle. A remote of some kind.

"How did you – ?" she says to Chan, as he hands her the solid and real and (as a peek inside reveals) full cup. She releases her grip on the stun and drinks gratefully.

Chan grins, impish, and flicks his wrist so his palm faces outward. There's a glint of metal at the base of his index finger.

"A ring?" Celan says, taking another gulp of water.

"Quantum band," Chan corrects.

She stares at it for a moment, stunned, then bursts out laughing, twin jets of water shooting from her nose. She hollers on, stamping the ground until she can barely stay upright.

Of all the things.

And if another city-state has tech like this her father might as well give up on Mars. They're definitely going to beat Albakirk there; and from the looks of them, maybe they already have.

The trio watches her with polite bemusement until she gets herself under control.

"So," she says, watching as the cup slowly refills itself, "tell me, where are you all from?"

Chan says nothing.

"I mean, which city-state? You're definitely not from Albakirk." She gropes for the farthest-flung one she's ever heard of. "Canberra?"

Chan smiles. "Oh, we're not from any of your 'city-states.' We're Plejarans," he says, as if that explains everything.

Celan gulps more water, wipes her mouth on the back of her hand. "Plejarans?" she says.

"From the Pleiades."

"The – what? Wait. Isn't that a star or something?" she stammers, suddenly dizzy again. Confusion merges with dehydration and recent hysteria and she plunks unceremoniously down on the ground.

"Well, it's a cluster of stars. The Seven Sisters you call them. Or used to, anyway. Poetic. I always liked that." Chan smiles wistfully.

"So you're not from Earth," she says. Chan shakes his head no, still smiling. "And so you're here…why?"

"A quick check-in. Gathering some data."

That she understands.

"About us? Earth?"

A nod.

"So you're…monitoring us?"

"Yes." He looks vaguely offended, like she's suggesting they might be up to something more nefarious.

"Uh – " she starts, but she's utterly stumped.

Finally, one of the other Plejarans speaks; the other blue-eyed one. "Don't worry," he says. "We haven't meddled in anything. Leave no trace." He nods, virtuous.

"And you are?"

"Ness," he says. "Nice to meet you."

"Uh, nice to meet you too."

"And I'm Ree," says the last one, the one with the green eyes. Even though their bodies all look pretty much the same Celan has the distinct impression that this one is female.

"Uh, hi," she says, "I'm Celan."

"Yes, we know."

A thought occurs: "How did you learn to speak our language? I mean, since you're not from Earth. Do you have some kind of universal translator or something?"

Ree's eyes twinkle like she's inviting Celan in on a fabulous joke. "We don't really 'speak' it at all."

"Huh?"

"Thought and intent are universal. I speak in my language and you speak in yours, but our minds can understand the meaning behind the words all the same. It's called transentience, and it is the marker of a, shall we say, *civilized* species."

Celan considers this, reaching for a pretty pebble from the mesa top, feeling its warm smoothness in the palm of her hand. She turns the rock over and over, rivulets of sweat trickling down her back. She takes another swig of water. Finally she looks up at them again.

"So how many civilized species are there in the – galaxy? Universe? Whatever."

"Many hundreds," says Chan, "in the K'Shiran Convention. Outside of that – " He spreads his arms wide, indicating untold possibilities.

"The K'Shiran Convention?"

All three Plejarans share what appear to be indulgent looks.

"The galactic assembly," Ree explains. "Of which we are a part."

"So how come no one here has ever heard of it? Or," she adds hastily, "have they? How many city-states have you talked to?"

"None," says Ree. "We haven't directly communicated with any of you. But we have had a few run-ins, over the years, with certain individuals. Nothing like this, though. You actually approached us, with full transentience! You came over and talked to us, just like you would with people from your own world. And then, when we told you where we were from, you didn't cower in fear or run away or try to attack us or fall down and worship us or any of the other kinds of reactions typical of subsentience."

"But I needed water," Celan says, a little guiltily, thinking on the stun.

"And so you asked."

Her eyes travel to the themos in her hand, then back up to Ree.

"Until you did that," Ree continues, "we couldn't have helped you. At least not directly. We were bound by the tenets of the Convention."

"Which are – ?"

"Article 19," Ness cuts in, a bit prim, "stipulates no direct communication with subsentient lifeforms. We could do experiments – "

"You experimented on us?!" Celan shrieks, springing to

her feet, hand brushing the stun again. If they think they're going to try anything funny –

"Not us," he says, soothingly. "But we *have* been keeping tabs. I mean, we were the ones who discovered your world originally, so we kind of have a vested interest."

"Oh," is all she can say to that.

"It's very lucky we ran into you when we did. We don't really come around here all that often anymore. Ever since..." He trails off discreetly.

"The destruction of the old world?" Celan finishes, taking a well-aimed stab in the dark.

"Well, yes," Ree says, not unkindly. "It seemed likely that yours was a subsentient species headed for extinction, so there really wasn't much reason to return. But we do still check in occasionally."

"And now," Chan says, beaming, "we finally have some progress to report! A new transentient species joining the Convention is always a cause for celebration."

Celan's lips twist. If one fucked-up, thirsty fuser constitutes progress in their book she's almost afraid to see what the rest of the galactic denizens are like. But they're all so enthused.

May as well play along.

"So how exactly do we do that? Join, I mean."

"For that," Chan informs her, "you'll have to come with us."

⇒ 26 ⇐

"What a nightmare," Ariana says, false concern ooz-ing from her every pore. "I am *so sorry* it all turned out like this. I could never have fathomed that Lana would ever get mixed up in anything of this magnitude. I mean, she was always such a *simple* girl, wasn't she?"

Theodore steps out from behind his desk, circling around to the front and leaning back against it, arms crossed over his chest. His palm itches for the tumbler of Scotch he'd hastily tucked away when they came calling – Ariana and her daughter, come to pay their condolences. He marks Shariah's sallow face and downcast look with distaste.

Your daughter. Of course. Had to twist the knife.

"I'm sorry, too," the girl says, voice an earnest rasp. "But I still can't believe Lana would ever have done something like this. Try to hurt us all. And now she's – "The girl chokes on this last, eyes cutting up and out the window, blinking rap-idly to fight back tears.

Shit.

"But even if she *did* do it," Shariah continues, "she was obviously mixed up. I don't see how you could – "

Ariana wraps a comforting arm around the girl's shoulders. "Now, now. We talked about this. You know the rules – giving people transferon without their consent results in an immediate Destierra. And that applies to everybody. Even the children of Lead SocEns. After all, Unity is the first social precedent."

"Who cares about stupid precedents?" Shariah says, suddenly fierce. "She was my *friend.*"

Ariana's face hardens. This little show of sympathy is clearly not going as planned. Despite everything, Theodore almost smiles. But he catches himself in time. That would be bad.

Can't give the game away.

He clears his throat.

"Shariah," he says, soft as a sigh. "I know how you're feeling, and I – I feel the same way. I will never get over the loss of my daughter, whom I loved dearly. But from my point of view, now that we know the whole story, it seems that Lana actually, albeit unwittingly, made a huge sacrifice – for the greater good."

Shariah opens her mouth to protest, but he holds up a hand so she closes it and lets him go on. "My daughter sacrificed herself to show us the error of our ways in letting Transway remain intact for as long as we did. None of us could have known just what that error would entail, how deep it would go, and how hard it would hit once the truth was laid bare. But now we do." He shifts his weight, letting his gaze drift out the library window. "And so now, we must not mourn her, but instead respect the sacrifice she made. For all of us."

Shariah's crying openly now; Ariana pulls her daughter close.

"Yes," she breathes, brushing a sodden strand of hair from the girl's eyes. "You see? Lana *was* your friend – even if she was so addled with transferon that for a time she couldn't see it. She made a mistake, and she paid the ultimate price. But her sacrifice…that will live forever."

The girl takes a deep, shuddering breath and wipes her wet eyes on the sleeve of her uniform. Her snuffles begin to recede. She nods once, miserably.

"And because of that sacrifice, nothing like this will ever have to happen again."

Ariana looks to Theodore for confirmation and he dips his head in acknowledgment. But inside his gut twists.

All right, you've had your fun. Now get the fuck out of my face.

The woman must somehow register a hint of the ire lurking behind the impassive mask, because she shakes off her obsequious mien and snaps into business mode.

"I think we should give Mr. Timanti some space now, Shariah, don't you? We'll need to talk, of course, later," she says to Theodore, "about Martinez."

"Yes," is his short reply.

Martinez seems to have vanished from the city entirely. There's no record of him since right before the attack, and it looks like he was at Maddy's when he disappeared. Did the expros kidnap him, kill him? Was taking one of the Lead SocEns out of commission part of their plan? No one knows. If he doesn't return within another five days he'll be declared dead, which will mean the inopportune selection of

357

a new Lead SocEn.

"Just give me some time," Theodore adds, for good measure.

Ariana's lips purse into a contrite little pout and she gently but firmly steers her daughter toward the door. At the threshold, she pauses. "If you need anything – " she starts.

But he waves her away.

The door whooshes shut and he exhales.

Finally.

Theodore dives back behind the desk and roots around for the tumbler, draining it in one long gulp. Then he yanks out a drawer and rummages around until his hand connects with a cool rectangular square. A server. Not his real one, but a special one. A rogue. He's been checking it all day, increasingly frantic.

Where in the fucking hell is *she?*

He stabs a finger at the screen. No change. Nada. He'd told her to wait. He told her he'd be there. But her tracker's disabled and it seems like she'd abandoned her server where they dropped her before taking off somewhere else.

It's only been six hours though. And Lana has food and water. And a stun. And a motherfucking transfer.

And he has drones.

He'll find her. He's not going to lose her. So what if she has to spend a few years in Winnipeg? They'll be able to fix her, release the hold of transferon on her body and mind and give him back the daughter he knows and loves. He's already got a plan to explain the need for his taking an emergency trip up there: A relative of hers (uncle? brother? half-brother, maybe?) whom Theodore urgently needs to talk to and explain what happened to Lana in person.

And maybe, just maybe, when all the dust settles – once she's safely ensconced and his term as Lead SocEn is up – he'll do something unprecedented: Leave Albakirk and live out his life in another city-state. With his daughter.

Give her the father she deserves.

Because she can't be gone; she can't be lost.

He just has to *find* her.

▭➤ 27 ◀▭

Celan's breath comes shallow; mind on fire – *Come with us. Come with us.*

Apparently, the main body of the K'Shiran Convention is presently housed in a massive station powered by a Dyson swarm not far from Alpha Centurai ('Not far at all!' Chan had added bracingly). It's standard protocol, he'd said, to bring at least one representative from a newly-transentient civilization there as soon as possible in order to be formally acknowledged.

But they have to leave *now.* Like, within the next fifteen minutes. 'The wormholes are cyclical,' he'd explained, 'and this cycle is almost over. We were cutting it close in coming here, but we only needed a short time to gather data. We'll return you in the next cycle: eighteen Earth months from now.'

After being assured that eighteen months was really eighteen months and not a thousand years in the future ('Of course,' he'd replied, 'or how would anything ever get done?') she'd requested, quite reasonably, a few minutes to decide.

So now she stares out over the sunset lands – torn.

She could wait. Keep looking for Lang. She could ask them to come back and take her next time. Chan had let her keep the miraculous refilling thermos so she'll be fine, water-wise. They definitely said they could do that.

But what if (and this is almost too terrible to consider) Lang is already dead and there's nothing she can do? What if the Plejarans leave and she's left all alone out here – with no way back to the city and nowhere else to go? She can't survive for eighteen months on her own.

And this is the chance of a lifetime. A chance to prove herself worthy. Useful.

Frantic, Celan searches the rim of the mesa as if at any moment a familiar face might pop up over the edge.

I can't just leave him to die!

Maybe she can ask the Plejarans to help her find him first. Make sure he's safe. But a look back at the trio of pale figures and the thought shrivels in her head. Fifteen minutes. Even with all their tech, there won't be time.

She gnaws at her bottom lip, her options revolving faster and faster in her brain until she thinks she's going to be sick. Maybe they can drop her off in the ranchos. Maybe she can get a search party together. Maybe she can –

Then, out of the corner of her eye, she sees a faint shimmer, a disturbance in the air off to the right. At first it seems like some trick of the fading light, but it grows brighter, more defined, until it takes on the form of –

"Lang!"

He must be on the astral, but then who's watching his body? Or is he –

"Are you OK?" she demands. "How did you find me?"

"Hey Celan," his avatar says, grinning as it coalesces more fully. "I'm fine. Brophy and Mara saved me. They found me and then Brophy helped me find you. I was a little, uh…"

Fused up, she finishes in her head. *Of course.* If Brophy went looking for Lang he would've taken a transfer with him; he would've known what condition he'd find him in.

"But I'm good now," he adds.

"So where's – " she starts, but is cut off by another shimmer in the air as Brophy materializes next to Lang.

"Just thought I'd give you two a little privacy."

"Gracias," she says wryly.

Not like anything can happen with him on the astral.

"So where are you?" she says. "I mean, physically. Are you close?"

"Not really." Lang shrugs. "But now that we know where you are…just sit tight. We can probably find you by morning. Will you be all right until then?"

"Yeah. My father put a transfer in my pack." Brophy and Lang exchange a glance at this. "He was going to come get me, I guess. But I shorted out the tracker and left the server where they dropped me. I don't want anything from him. Ever again."

Lang looks relieved to hear this, but Brophy's squinting quizzically off to the left, in the direction the Plejarans.

"Who's that?" he says, with a hint of suspicion.

"I – well, uh – " Celan stammers. In her joy and relief

at seeing Lang she'd almost forgotten about them. But she's suddenly glad she's not the only one who can see them. It hadn't occurred to her before that maybe she'd been imagining things.

How to explain…but there's no simple way. So in lieu of further talk she merely turns and marches back to the waiting figures, motioning for Lang and Brophy to follow and hoping that the Plejarans can see astral bodies. And that she's not the only one who's transentient. Or this is about to get a whole order of magnitude weirder.

Chan, Ness, and Ree, however, appear unruffled. They eye Lang and Brophy pleasantly.

"Good evening," Chan says.

The two boys nod their greetings.

"Are you coming with us too?"

Lang asks, "Who are you?" at the same time Brophy says, "Are you Plejarans?"

"Yes, we are," Chan says, tickled. "However did you know that?"

Brophy shrugs. "You see a lot of strange stuff as a Class S."

"But this is no dream," Chan tells him.

"So you're, like, *here* here? Materially?"

Chan nods.

Brophy whistles low. "Wow."

Celan finds her tongue again. "This is Chan. Ness. Ree." She waves a hand toward each of them in turn. "I met them out here while they were collecting data. There's like a… council. Of galactic elders. It's called the K'Shiran Convention and apparently we're transentient now so we can go there and meet them in person. Maybe they can help us fix up the

Earth. They want me to go with them. Get us acknowl-edged."

"Órale," says Brophy, pumping a flickering fist in the air. "Do it!"

"For how long?" Lang says immediately.

Her face falls. "They say it'll be eighteen months before I can come back. The wormholes are cyclical, and the current cycle is just about to end. So if I'm going to go I have to leave now."

"Five more minutes," Chan adds. "That's as far as we can delay. You don't want to get stuck in a collapsing wormhole. Very nasty."

"Holy fuck." This from Brophy. "Can I – ?" He's eyeing the trio with deep awe. "Can I go look at your ship? Can I – can I touch it?"

Chan and Ness share amused looks. "Go right ahead," Ness says.

Brophy's shimmering form glides over to the sleek, star-shaped vessel. He runs insubstantial hands along its smooth flanks, marveling.

Lang and Celan are left facing each other.

"I don't want to leave," she says, stepping forward as if to embrace him. But her hands pass through nothingness. A sob escapes her. "But if I don't go now…"

She leaves the thought unfinished. They both know a lot can happen in eighteen months. A lot can happen in eighteen minutes.

Lang bolsters his expression into something stalwart. "But you have to," he says. "Don't worry about me. I'll be all right."

"Really?"

"I don't want you to go. But I understand. If this is real, if this is what they say it is, then you *need* to go. With Transway destroyed who knows what's going to happen? This could be our last best chance."

"I know," she says, cheeks wet with grief.

"So know this too. I love you, Celan. And you're my girl. Forever."

She sniffles once, but then an odd sort of calm steals over her. "You promise?" she says.

"I do."

"And you'll be fine here?"

"I will. I'm going north with Mara and Brophy."

"I love you, too, you know. And I'm sorry. About everything."

"It wasn't your fault."

"But it was – "

"No," he says. Then: "I wish I could kiss you."

"Me too," she says, "I wish we could – "

But the moment is broken by Brophy gliding back from his examination of the Plejaran ship. He zips up to them, starry-eyed with wonder.

"You won't *believe* – " he starts.

But Chan is calling, "We have to go! Now."

And then there's nothing left to say and no more time to say it. Celan rakes her gaze over Lang like she's memorizing every pore, like she's savoring what might well be her last view of another human being –

For a while, she tells herself, *not forever. I'll be back in eighteen months.*

366

Lang winks bravely, once. And then there's nothing else to do: She turns away from his flickering form and walks on wobbly legs to where the Plejaran ship stands. Chan lifts his hand and uses the quantum band to coat her in the same biofilm the Plejarans use to keep their systems intact in foreign environments.

When he's done, she shrugs her pack up on her shoulders and meets three pairs of glittering eyes.

"Vamos aviados," she says.

Author's Note

This is for Jill, and Hal, and Paul from Farmington, and all those others who (to paraphrase Philip K. Dick) suffer entirely too much for what they do.

Many thanks to early readers Marshall and Jason, and to James for his excellent notes on the first installment, *To Get Across*.

Also thanks to Mike – for one perfect day in Seattle.